W9-BXG-624

Praise for *Blood Acre*

"*Blood Acre* is as compelling as it is, finally, astonishing. Convincing apocalypses come our way very seldom, and this is one. I read it straight through, helpless to quit."
—Reynolds Price, author of *Roxanna Slade*

"Peter Landesman brings to radiant life a dark, disorienting, and violent vision, rendered in gorgeous prose. Severed from trust, love, connection, faith, and the promise of his youthful self, his protagonist pulls us through a world that is beautiful."
—Andrea Barrett, National Book Award-winning author
of *The Voyage of the Narwhal*

"Like Peyton Loftis, Nathan Stein and his doomed career through New York are thoroughly haunting. Peter Landesman couples the ripeness of Styron with the grit of George V. Higgins and comes up with a dizzying new genre: New York Gothic Noir. *Blood Acre* is that rarity: the soft-boiled thriller, where every wound weeps, every memory stings, and every dream festers."
—Stewart O'Nan, author of *A World Away*

"*Blood Acre* is like forked lightning over Manhatttan at 3:00 A.M. Peter Landesman will electrify you, he'll illuminate a world. It's not anything you've seen before."
—Paul Cody, author of *The Stolen Child* and *So Far Gone*

"The more remarkable or original a creative accomplishment, the more one searches for earlier works with which it has something in common. In its vivid and marvelously rendered account of a flawed and disoriented human being moving inexorably toward his destruction, *Blood Acre* is reminiscent of Malcolm Lowry's brilliant *Under the Volcano*. In its depiction of that human being searching for redemption while lost in a violent storm that is both emotional—within him—and meteorological, Landesman's novel brings to mind the drama of a maddened king on a blasted health: but in giving an ever-deepening definition to his central character during the last two days of his life. Landesman is describing not a Lear but a fully American protagonist, a vestigial Gatsby for the end of the millenium."
—James McConkey, author of *Court of Memory*

PENGUIN BOOKS

BLOOD ACRE

Peter Landesman is the author of *The Raven*, which won the Sue Kaufman Prize for best first novel from the American Academy of Arts and Letters. His journalism has appeared in *New York*, *The New Yorker*, and *The New York Times Magazine*. In addition to his writing, Landesman is a painter whose work has been shown at galleries in New York City and Long Island. He lives in New York City.

# BLOOD ACRE

Peter Landesman

PENGUIN BOOKS

PENGUIN BOOKS
Published by the Penguin Group
Penguin Putnam Inc., 375 Hudson Street,
New York, New York 10014, U.S.A.
Penguin Books Ltd, 27 Wrights Lane, London W8 5TZ, England
Penguin Books Australia Ltd, Ringwood, Victoria, Australia
Penguin Books Canada Ltd, 10 Alcorn Avenue,
Toronto, Ontario, Canada M4V 3B2
Penguin Books (N.Z.) Ltd, 182–190 Wairau Road,
Auckland 10, New Zealand

Penguin Books Ltd, Registered Offices:
Harmondsworth, Middlesex, England

First published in the United States of America by
Viking Penguin, a member of Penguin Putnam Inc. 1999
Published in Penguin Books 2000

1   3   5   7   9   10   8   6   4   2

Copyright © Peter Landesman, 1999
All rights reserved

PUBLISHER'S NOTE
This is a work of fiction. Names, characters, places, and incidents are
either the product of the author's imagination or are used fictitiously, and
any resemblance to actual persons, living or dead, business establishments,
events, or locales is entirely coincidental.

THE LIBRARY OF CONGRESS HAS CATALOGED THE HARDCOVER EDITION AS FOLLOWS:
Landesman, Peter.
Blood acre/Peter Landesman.
p.   cm.
ISBN 0-670-88207-0 (hc.)
ISBN 0 14 02.8236 X (pbk.)
I. Title.
PS3562.A4762B58   1999        98–21330
813'.54—dc21

Printed in the United States of America
Set in Sabon
Designed by Betty Lew

Except in the United States of America, this book is sold subject to the
condition that it shall not, by way of trade or otherwise, be lent, re-sold, hired out,
or otherwise circulated without the publisher's prior consent in any form of binding
or cover other than that in which it is published and without a similar condition
including this condition being imposed on the subsequent purchaser.

Then Judas, which had betrayed him, when he saw that he was condemned, repented himself, and brought again the thirty pieces of silver to the chief priests and elders, Saying, I have sinned in that I have betrayed the innocent blood. And they said, What is that to us? see thou to that. And he cast down the pieces of silver in the temple, and departed, and went and hanged himself. And the chief priests took the silver pieces, and said, It is not lawful for to put them into the treasury, because it is the price of blood. And they took counsel, and bought with them the potter's field, to bury strangers in. Wherefore that field was called, The field of blood, unto this day.

Matthew 27: 3–8

# CONTENTS

# THE NIGHT BEFORE

A night dark beyond emergency. The waves, rising skyward, have begun to tear at the beach, carrying away trash cans and blankets and here and there a door. Wood skids float off, riderless life rafts wheeling in the boil. The checkerboard of houselights in the Luna Park projects dims, flickers off, then back on. Sparks rain from the elevated tracks where the F train has stopped, stranded between stations. On the boardwalk lies a lone figure, limbs outflung. Her dress is split in two, some floral print, once red, once pretty, twine—or is it seaweed—wraps her neck. The gun-metal staring eyes. A frozen gasp. She is dragged from the boardwalk across the sand to the water's slushy edge, dragged past the lips of frozen foam, and, bobbing in the lee of a wave-break, shoved off, like a rowboat or a canoe, riding the swells up then down, flexing to the form of the water. Behind the boardwalk an engine coughs to life. A car pulls away, the long rip of tires on the wet pavement carried another direction by the wind. In the lightless slur of ocean and air a hundred feet from shore there is no one to see two waves collide and collapse, shooting under the body, heaving, pulling it in, spinning it, and spinning it, and spinning it—

# SUNDAY

**2 P.M.** Can it be—the sun and moon occupying the same piece of sky?

Above Coney Island the momentary overcast has pulled apart like cotton batting, but it has only confused matters. Dry snow whirlpools on the boardwalk into narrow cyclones, weaving between the rails. Below, strung along the frozen beach, a high-tide mark of harbor refuse, clothes, bottles, the skeletons of household appliances thrown from the piers, unnameable mounds shrouded in frozen seaweed and foam snaking out of sight past Brighton Beach. Past the blackened ruins of the wood rollercoaster banking and rolling above an empty lot, the tarred lattice threatening collapse. Past the Wonderwheel and its love seats rocking out of sync, squealing in the wind. Past other rides, the giant octopus, the skeet shoots, the basketball throw, seven blocks of tarpaulined cotton-candy stands, the Sea Land clam bar, a large brick building bearing the legend ORIENTAL HOT BATHS barricaded by plywood sheets and wrapped in ribbons of graffiti. A pair of sneakers dangling from a telephone line kicking like amputated feet toward the backside dumpsters of Famous's where red paint spells FUCK WHITIE.

At the boardwalk rail, Nathan Stein sips at his cold coffee. He peers nervously across the peeled lip of plastic lid at the motionless harbor but doesn't see a thing. The oily slush is much higher now, these few hours later, hovering like ground fog rather than sitting on actual land. His cashmere coat billows around the middle; signs of heavier times. His eyes, luminous, green and clear, follow a white bloom of gulls attending a garbage barge right to left, out to sea. He contemplates a storm front moving in from open water, a solid line of the high purple thunderheads that usually mean summer, now covering the breadth of the horizon, billowing toward land.

His eyes are bad. That might explain things. They are worse now without his glasses. She'd knocked them away last night, he doesn't know where. He lifts his head up the beach, as though to see again the little scene, but finds only a galloping posse of stray dogs, adjusting their direction in small increments en masse across the ice, like a flock of birds.

But here, this cold offering no hope of thaw, these days in early December. A forty days and forty nights arrested in perpetual winter, as if someone had opened the door to the true outdoors. The papers say the face of weather everywhere seems to have been radically altered. In New York this past summer damp, sooty days were followed by sweeps of ovenheat. Since then there has been, amid other confusions, disarray amongst the trees. Two months ago, while the leaves of some had been singed at the edges, others were at the height of their promiscuity, continuing to flower and bud and discharge lurid fragrances that had a somnolent, hypnotizing effect. The old and new piers in Brooklyn and the Seaport and up and down the Hudson have been taking water.

Mercifully, the wind has dropped. At the bleating of his watch alarm Nathan's hand motions over his right coat pocket, then roots to the bottom there for the plastic vials. His fingers ache, the tips are raw. His wrist stings against the lining, the blood clotted by the cold. Other scratches have surfaced. Here and there the impressions of teeth.

But some kind of bird is rustling in the trash under the boardwalk, chirping away. Nervously rolling the vials in his fingers, Nathan looks not down but up, for the sun, and finds instead sun and moon like dim bulbs hanging vague and cold in opposite corners. The sky smolders with winter light, a football sky, once a blank scoreboard waiting to chronicle an afternoon of mud and scraped knees, of Nathan uncoiling like a human spring, running for the cheap seats beyond a fortress school and its squinty windows. Soon, though, the air will take him in. And he'll be gone, backing out of the gate, lifting slowly away from JFK, the craggy Manhattan skyline grabbing up at him and the surrounding stews of filth and monotony that are the outer boroughs twirling below him down and down and down, the cobalt swimming pools of Forest Hills and Great Neck scattering like gems. Then one last flush, and nothing but the drone of jet engines, that lush cottony sea of cloud and the hushed subservience of a stewardess. The plane south to Tegucigalpa, a jittery puddle-jumper over the straits to that island Roatán. The sliver of white beach, water the color of lapis stone, the thick trees murmur behind him—

But for now this strange bird and its ceaseless chirping. And the sun, like everything else, has snuck up on him. He raises his hand, inadvertently saluting the Statue of Liberty where she stands on the water from this distance like a curlicue of smoke. Wherever he looks these days he shields his eyes, as though from an eclipse. All week he's had this feeling of calamity. Somewhere Christmas is lurking, sometime soon. And Hanukkah. The commercials on the TV are growing urgent. It all seems to mean something, but he can't bring himself to care. Like the legions of shoppers he no longer lives in weeks or even days. He is down to hours. Sometimes it feels like minutes.

The bird, he finally realizes, is inside his blazer, his Twenty-first-Century Message Center/Beeper. He clutches his side, as if shot, and peers in: *Doctor E—urgent—call immediately*. And he'd managed to forget. Though of course now Nathan replays that time he sat in the doctor's office with Maria holding his hand so tightly she was cutting off the blood. "I'm sorry, Nathan," the doctor was saying, looking out his picture window with its view of Park Avenue. "I can't tell you how sorry I am."

Nathan had merely nodded, peeling Maria's fingers away, a small smile creeping across his face. It isn't me.

It wasn't him. It was Maria, sobbing, hysterical, "I didn't

know. How could I have known? It's not my fault my god please forgive me hailmaryfullofgrace."

Nathan had looked casually over the doctor's shoulder, at the assemblage of framed family faces that lined his sill. He looked past the windblown hair and the smiles and boat decks and through the window down Park Avenue, wanting to bring himself to some sort of conclusion, to achieve, even, some state of grace; knowing he should; that he would, he believed, his gaze plunging into a yellow river of taxicabs, if given time, he would actually *feel* something.

A violent burst of shivering rips through, and Nathan, reaching for the railing to steady himself, tips back his head and blinks. Though still he feels no cold. It stays vague and somewhere far outside him, weather beyond the window, something he can go out in if he wants. Doctor E had forgotten to warn him about that, this numb impenetrability, so easily mistaken for perfection, for immortality. He tries and fails to laugh at himself, at the cruel swindle, opening his mouth to release the laughter but releasing instead dry breath, staccato pants. So tasting the sea air on his tongue he puts there a pill or two, he doesn't know which ones, he didn't see the colors, or the time—is it even time? And another for good luck. Why not still another? Why not, feeling little, stretch out in a rented room, turn on the oven, open his lips, pour in the whole vial, and truly feel—finally—nothing at all?

His eyes swim. Pinching them shut, his throat—as always these days—raw, the pills click inside his mouth like subway tokens.

Upwind, blue smoke and sparks flush through the boardwalk slats. Squinting unhappily without his glasses, Nathan spots movement below. Quickly he looks left and right up the beach and walks on, his shoes squeaking on the frost. But something alarming on the water has caught his eye. Unhappy, he tosses his coffee cup over the rail, clutching wood, and peers out.

Below him, a half-naked figure paces the shadows of a flaming oil drum, back and forth across the daylight. A nasal honk beneath the boardwalk, a whoop, a bellowed, "Hurry fools! Prepare thyselves!"

The pacing stops. Out in the light appears a head of thick red hair, a chin held aloft, then a pair of white tennis shorts fluttering at his hips, more loincloth than garment. The rest of him a flaccid patchwork of pinks and blues, his areolae puckered and browned like two gunshot wounds to the chest. He staggers on his heels, knees locked, bearing a blue-and-orange plastic horn with the logo of the New York Mets, a silhouette of the midtown skyline and the motto CATCH THE RISING STARS, the crackerjack prize from that fan remembrance day years ago when the Mets were contenders and the roster was filled with young talent. Ballasting himself in the wind, he aims the trumpet behind him. Out leaks a gurgling bleat.

"Clowns!" he cries. "Fools, come on!"

One by one they emerge. From the open doorway of a tin cabana recessed beneath the boardwalk, short and fat, short and thin, old and withered, tall and stooped. At a windchill of minus ten Fahrenheit they are barefoot and equipped to swim. Racing suits, satin running shorts, a T-shirt and thong. Their bodies smoke. They wander the ice and cross ridges of frozen seafoam, obscured in shrouds of vapor.

Nathan would have laughed, but the sight haunts him instead. From behind, it seems an insurrection by inmates from a mental institution, their enactment of some joker's hypothesis about their primordial origins.

A fainter, garbled cry downwind.

The drunk has drifted, blowing his trumpet at the clouds gathering at the horizon, as though summoning the gods in New Jersey. He points threateningly. "Prepare ye, wimps!"

In the lee of a wave-break, a pair of hookers has stopped to watch. The bathers stamp the ice and pound their arms, but the hookers stand still, warding off the cold with routine refusal.

So it is a false alarm, Nathan sees. The water is clear. He palms down his thinning hair then leans his elbows on the rail like a man with nothing on his hands but time, hoping this, actually believing it to be, his very last time here—that plane south awaiting him on the tarmac, its engines whining—and looks more closely at the scene as though these few extra inches, if nothing else, will clarify it all.

Two men are probing through the cord grass of Jamaica Bay, high-stepping at a jog. Across the tops of the grass, the control tower at JFK; the tails of taxiing jets crossing like the fins of prowling sharks. Beyond, a mountainous landfill where clouds of birds are ripping off in the wind; beyond that, a tourist's diorama of Manhattan laid out end to end, red warning lights slowly blinking among the high-rises.

Two figures await them a hundred yards on. Unable to see down past his knees, Errol Santos stops to snap the collar of his coat around his chin, his eyes skittering about, taking the sparse clouds of gulls hovering overhead for signs of what lurks within.

A big man in his mid-thirties, just now giving up the battle against his tendency to turn to fat, Santos rustles through his coat pocket and produces a pack of cigarettes. He offers one to his own mouth and puts another to his companion's lips. Unshaven Barbados, the lines on his face saying drugs or the years of weather; he could be thirty-five, he could be fifty.

Santos draws deep and his chest tightens at once, his reedy exhale already a thin sigh, pulling air as if through a coffee stirrer. It's happening faster and faster; he pats his coat pockets, pats them again, then rummages through the old tissues and paper clips and pencil stubs for his inhaler, finally finding the little blue thing in his pants pocket. He pumps it into his mouth, pinching twice, his plumber's gas. The relief is instant, and even grants him a bonus shot of adrenaline to the heart, momentarily lightening his mood, clearing his eyes. By now he's forgotten which comes first, the cigarettes or the asthmatic strangle. He has inhalers planted everywhere, a little pump for every occasion, in the glove box of the car beside his lighter, on his bed stand, in his coat pocket with his cigarettes, one with the other, one always following the other.

"You should cut that." Barbados peers at him from under his cap.

Santos turns his head to offer his usual reply but Barbados has trudged on.

The body rests broken on a bed of grass, arms and legs akimbo. The cheek has been pulled back, the meat picked at. Prints of muddy claws cross the bridge of the nose.

One of the cops looks up. "You Brooklyn?"

"Why not," Barbados says.

"No blood," the other cop says.

Santos gestures downward. "You look underneath?"

The first cop shakes his head. "Hell of a place to leave a body."

"Who is this?" Barbados asks the partner.

The partner shrugs. "It's not his fault. He's new on the job."

Santos looks over one shoulder then the other. "Is this even Brooklyn?"

The four men, faces averted against the wind, scrutinize the empty marsh as though for a signpost. Snowy egrets return their stares.

"It doesn't matter," Barbados says. "This isn't a homicide."

"You still have to make the call," the partner says.

Barbados points his chin. "You make it."

"Suicide?" the neophyte asks.

A gull glides down and hangs overhead to investigate.

"In a manner of speaking," Santos says.

Above, an approaching growl, then the whine of jet engines reversing themselves. They all lift their heads. A massive plane passes at a thousand feet, skidding sideways in the crosswinds; the belly opens and the landing gear unfolds and locks into place. Santos waits, and nothing falls.

He used to consider the age of the deceased and compare it with his own. He'd think two more years and he's dead, three years left, eleven to go. This boy in the grass is no more than twenty, maybe twenty-five. Santos reads the obituaries of his cases. He still makes bargains about natural causes. Heart disease.

MS. Something exotic and cruel. Would he be happy enough to die at fifty, at fifty-three?

He says, "They hide in the landing gear and hang on for the ride. Every now and then they fall asleep, or they're not ready. And then the doors open."

The neophyte looks up, then down at the body, the surprise on his face telling a story of human flight, of falling like a stone through long seconds to the promised land.

Barbados sniffs. "Third bird this week."

The neophyte's partner is swinging his head, looking over both shoulders. "I don't know, this just feels like Brooklyn."

Barbados toes at the corpse's arm and lifts it off the ground and delicately places it over the head. Backstroking swimmer. "Now it's Queens."


In the car, Barbados takes them between empty lots and roller-coaster ruins. They pass a patchwork of trailers and tin sheds, plots of weedy flourishes clicking with ice, dead space compressed by the shapes of more dead space around. They pass a dark street of eyeless brick, a receding forest of I-beams bearing the elevated F train above, high square vaultings where the hollow snapping of pigeons' wings echo like gunfire. Shafts of murky half-light hang from the tracks in an infinity of gauzy curtains. The few cars and pedestrians pass through and pass through, vanishing and reemerging closer as through the slowmotion camera wink of old memory.

They drift to the curb. This street where no one lives crawls with life. In the alleys, a maze of coops, constructions of plastic sheeting and boxes slumped with snow. Tracks in the snow-dust begin nowhere, wander like goat paths and converge at a phone booth down the block where a man in thin leather jacket and baseball cap stamps his feet and leans out of the booth into a shaft of light. A small boy appears in a doorway and heaves a plastic bag of garbage out into the street and goes in again. Barbados falls asleep.

His jaw cradled in the crook of his arm, Santos eyes the fallen eaves across the street, the buckled doorways, thinking law school then the academy, then five years on the street, then five out of uniform, coming up on six now, and still he wanders like an alien through streets on which he was a child. He passes his hand over his face, closing his eyes, as though to erase what he has seen, his legs twitching, his lips moving against the tacky cold of the car seat, in his feet somewhere far below he can feel the subway, distant like surf, breaking upon him, and Santos wakes—has he fallen asleep?—his eyes searching the ceiling of the car. Following the train's guts sweeping by overhead. The shower of sparks like birthday flares burn piss-holes in the snow. Barbados, awake now, brings the lighter to his face. Up the street a man has stopped at the phone booth as before a confessional. Pusher and his buy shuffle hands in a kind of two-fisted shake. Santos watches Barbados watch the business, his deep black, even innocent, eyes like the eyes of a young girl; like himself, once a child of promise.

The radio under the dashboard emits a fart of murmured static. The buy at the booth straightens and cocks his head, as an animal will at a sign of danger. From above, a whistle, as for a dog. The silence around them all, suddenly, sinister. Dark faces fill the doorways. The buy skids away, running the way he came. A bottle whistles overhead and powders against a wall to the car's left. A child's shriek fills the canyon. "Fuck," Barbados mutters, and takes them quickly around a corner and down a street ending at the boardwalk and sky. Santos reaches for his inhaler.

The thousand marquee bulbs above Famous's blink off, on.

"Look," Santos says, rubbing a porthole in the glass.

Barbados leans over. Inside Famous's, at the window bar, stands a man, short, pear-shaped, his breaths hanging before him in yarnlike balls of vapor, pushed rapidly forward like a smoker's trick by the next, and the next. He dabs his glistening forehead and neck with a handkerchief. Looking down at his watch, his chins multiply. Krivit.

"You call him?" Barbados asks.

Santos shakes his head. "Wait here a minute."

Outside on his feet he inhales the briny cold, drops his cigarette in the snow, and walks a long diagonal to the door. The plexiglass flaps behind him. A family stands at the counter, joylessly chewing. In the rear a black man labors over a clatter of steaming fry-o-matics while a well-groomed Pakistani gazes at a mute TV. An out-of-town game, 49ers and Seahawks, Santos thinks, the away team in their white uniforms veiled as ghosts, the home jerseys tackling bodiless helmets and a floating leather oval.

"My guess, you weren't expecting me today."

Krivit sets down his cup of coffee with a click. "Am I expecting anyone?"

"You come all this way for the hot dogs?"

"Everybody does." Smiling a gummy smile, Krivit dabs at his forehead with the back of his hand.

Outside, in the street, Barbados has pulled the car alongside a baby blue police cruiser.

"A little early for you, isn't it?" Santos says. "You're making office hours in the daylight now?"

"I like to keep my nights free for other business."

"I remember."

Barbados is leaning on the horn. The cruiser's passenger window drops. Bleary-eyed, a teenage cop pats his cheeks while his partner sleeps openmouthed behind the wheel. Barbados makes a gun with his hand, fires.

"So," Santos says, "what do you have?"

"Nothing for you."

"Something for someone."

Krivit shifts his coffee cup forward then back. "Having a slow day, Detective?"

"Slow, fast, it's a day. You've never been at a loss."

"I'm generous. There's plenty to go around without repeating myself. Doubling back is bad for business. But maybe later. Yes, later, probably." Krivit lifts his hand, limp-wristed, and wriggles his fingers. "For now, hasta la vista, Tino."

Santos blinks at this bottom-feeder, swallowing the metallic taste of contempt. Though who it's for he can't say. Fat rat, yes—but who's asking what from whom?

He shoves at the door with his shoulder, hands in his pockets. A stop sign shivers in the wind. A ship brays offshore, a foghorn if there were fog, calling to—what?

He starts for the car but a figure, his chin in the collar of his cashmere coat, brushes past him toward the door. The face is instantly known to him.

"Cold enough for you?" Santos says.

"What—? No, not interested."

"Nathan, it's Errol. Errol Santos."

Nathan Stein looks back at him, his eyes blinking, focusing with recognition. "You haven't changed."

Stein looks to Santos made up for an older part, a better one, hair thinner and streaked with chalk, but his face taut and his body slim. "We've both changed. But you look good, Nathan. Isabel told me you looked good."

"She's your sister. She has to tell you that."

"Well, terrific for you anyway."

Nathan lifts a hand. "Not really." He points vaguely to his watch.

"Look, I don't want to keep you."

"Maybe a beer sometime," Nathan says, taking a step away. "We'll catch some tunes downtown."

"Maybe Bradley's. Like the old days."

Nathan cocks his head. "Bradley's is gone, Errol."

"Since when?"

"They sold the piano. Since? It doesn't matter. Years— Well, Errol." Nathan looks about him, as though for a trap door in the air. "So how are you?"

"Like you see. How are you?"

"Fine. Real good. So—" Nathan is grinning. "So how *is* Claire?"

"Fine, Nathan. She's fine."

"Good. Good."

"I'm sure she'd send her regards. If she knew."

"I'm sure."

Santos pulls at his cigarettes and holds out the pack.

"No thanks," Nathan says.

"Go ahead."

"I don't smoke."

"You used to."

"That was a long time ago."

Santos lights up and blows a thin breath toward the sky. "Not so long," he says. "It was good of you to give Isabel a job."

"Errol, it's been, what, four years, five?"

"Well, I never thanked you."

"Your mother had more to do with it than I did. It was an easy handoff, a pass of the baton, mother to daughter—"

"Still, I hope she's no trouble. And how's—" Santos peers into the air, searching. The smoke coils and fades in the low winter light.

"We live uptown," Nathan says. "Maria. Her and her boy, Benny. What, Errol, have you been keeping tabs?"

Santos shrugs a shoulder. "We go back in a hundred different directions. It's just information, Nathan. My mother works for your father practically before I was born. Now my sister works for you. I used to know everything about you all by myself. Now what I know they tell me, but just dribs and drabs. It's sad."

A funny smile crosses Nathan's face.

"But Benny, right," Santos says. "I remember now. Maria and Benny. Wow, she was something. And she was a keeper. And her kid, he was just a baby." Santos grins. "Daddy," he says. "I never would have guessed."

"Daddy," Nathan repeats dryly. "I don't think I'd go so far as to say that."

"I have to say I can't see it."

"I wouldn't." Nathan steps back, clutching at his belt. "Sorry," he says. "She beeps me ten times a day." He peers down at the readout. "It's the only number she has."

Santos sucks deeply on the cigarette, reflecting. "They need attention, Nathan."

"We all need attention, but she's got her daughters."

"Daughters? I thought it was a son."

Nathan looks up. "Son?"

"Yeah, Benny."

"Oh, Maria."

"Maria," Santos repeats. "Who are we talking about?" But he holds up his hand, his face darkening. "It's none of my business."

Santos searches the street. The junk shops on Surf Avenue are opening. He motions toward the door. "Let me buy you a cup of coffee."

"I'd like to Errol, but—" Nathan thumbs back through the doors, "I have a meeting."

Santos stares through the murky plexiglass at Krivit, who spots them and smiles the same gummy smile. Santos returns the gaze.

"He'll always play both ways," he warns Nathan. "You never know what he's saying in the other guy's huddle."

"He's just playing the game, Errol, keeping the clock moving, nudging things along when the rules get things stuck."

"That's what worries me. He's not interested in outcomes. Milton never trusted him."

"Milton? My father doesn't trust anybody—" Nathan begins, then stops. Some clock tolls the hour. An illuminated dial inset within the Wonderwheel, suspended above the barren carnival, hanging like another early moon, making the light shift. Santos blinks a stray snowflake out of his eye, thinking of Nathan's money, Nathan's clothes, Nathan's side businesses, his little ventures, his stable of Latina mistresses with whom he famously argued—Santos could have had all that. He was always smarter than Nathan, always a step ahead; already in law school Nathan was leaning on him, pawning favors for homework and crib notes.

Nathan shifts from foot to foot. "Anyway."

Barbados pulls up to the curb and knocks on the window, motioning to Santos, aiming his finger onward.

"Okay. I'll tell Claire I saw you."

"Do that."

"You ought to come down to Brooklyn some night."

"I'm in Brooklyn all the time." He looks about him. "Like now."

"You know what I mean, Nathan."

"Same apartment?"

Santos kicks at the old snow. "That's right. She'd be thrilled. You'd be surprised."

"I guess I would."

The plexiglass doors of Famous's flap closed. Santos spins in the snow and, squinting upward, heads for the car. Up and down Surf Avenue Russians are smoothing blankets over the sidewalks, laying out pairs of old boots and rusty pliers, lampshades, authentic jackets from the Red Army. There is something threatening about the open day, the light a diversion, the sun not quite what it seems, not high enough, even for winter; a shadow washing over the city.

"Wasn't that Milton Stein's son?"

Santos nods.

"That apple didn't fall far."

"It's a big tree."

"You were friends," Barbados says. "More. Compadres, no?"

Santos waves a hand, as if to say, Where would I begin?

As the Ferris wheel sinks from sight he slumps against the car door, his eyes locked on ten years ago. On a yellow room one summer night kneeling over his father. Reek of iodine and urine. Santos saw the skull through the old man's skin, the caved and wasted face. Everything phony slips off the dying and his father arched his neck to tell him the last thing. The dead will take the living with them if they can, and he wheezed his son's name to draw him closer in, but Santos pulled back against the wall and listened to his father suck at the cold air between words. His father said that in the courts and the billable hours is the carnival of the powerful and the insane while your people walk blind and helpless. His father said that the life Errol would one day feel he was missing was occurring in the streets. And since that day, on this planet, what has he done? By that autumn Santos stepped out of his suits and his law-firm offers and into dank bars full of sweaty cops. Knights of old, wielding their stubby little guns. Into the streets, his father had said. Into the streets. After his first collar, downtown to central booking and a meet with an A.D.A., he stepped into the sour spice of a hall strewn with men, men sleeping along the walls, propped up on elbows to stare stonily into the dingy middle distance. It looked at first like a railway station in the dead of night in a far part of the world, the bums, the unwashed drunks, the reek of refugee dishevelment and sleep and malnutrition. But here and there they wore parts of patrolmen's uniforms, the pants or the shirt, or the blue cap pulled low over the eyes, their street shoes. Pretenders, kids, those beat cops, twenty, twenty-two, buzz cuts and puffy cheeks and semiautomatics and off days in front of the tube. Stepping quickly over their legs, like a halfback running through the tire drill, Santos turned for the main waiting chamber where a fuzzy TV in the corner played soaps to blank-faced and slack-jawed cops. An emergency room at a public hospital but without the urgency.

What Santos has done, he has done it there. He has done it in elevator shafts and dumpsters. He has done it in fields of rubble where sheets of newspaper roll in the wind.

All that school gone to waste. All that law and the money to come. His sister Isabel thought he'd gone mad. He hardly understood it then himself; today, he's forgotten his reasons for almost everything.

Warily, Santos eyes the horizon. There are clouds, he sees, over open water, black as thunder. Like a herd, or cavalry, body parts and animal shapes charge toward shore, fists, the fleeting contour of faces, vanishing as soon as they appear, dark horses rearing up.

Inside Famous's, Nathan's footsteps turn no heads. He slaps his arms and breathes in the tepid air, wanting to be glad to be here. After all those Sunday excursions from Queens and then Manhattan in the Silver Shadow with Milton, the pastrami, the foot-longs.

The friends he's brought, the women, Claire a dozen times, for this taste of old New York. Errol Santos—when *weren't* they here together, riding the train all the way out, kids leaving behind a wake of minor mayhem. Now Errol is thicker around the middle than Nathan remembers and shorter, with his hair slicked across the front of his scalp.

The fact is none of it is much to remember. Lately Nathan has been robbed of his ability to sentimentalize. Like a camera his shutter opens and closes, recording, not thinking, not feeling, while what sticks to mind is the opening scene of *La Bohème* when Marcello, staring out his attic window at an infinity of Paris rooftops, mourns the consuming appetite of love, while Rodolfo, hungry and cold, burns the manuscript of his five-act tragedy for fuel. Nostalgia, what is that? A settling of scores, small acts of vengeance and indiscretion between the now and then, the past and present.

"Buddy," Nathan says with false bravado.

"Mister Stein."

"It's cold."

"It's cold, yessir."

Behind the counter the old black man stands on wooden skids laid over pools of brine and sandy mud.

"Staying out of trouble?"

"Am, sir."

Nathan wags his finger. "You're bad for business."

Buddy smiles and his toothless face presses in like a rotten fruit. "How many?"

Nathan looks over his shoulder at the stand-up bar lining the window. At one end, a pair of men eating: businessman, junkman. At the other stands Krivit.

"Three. With everything. And coffee."

"Four fifty."

Nathan peels off a twenty, holds up his hand. "Keep it," he says, and goes to the window bar with the tray. He passes a hot dog to his right.

"I don't like to be kept waiting, Stein." Krivit taps his watch. "One hour. How could you be late today?"

He grabs at the hot dog and the right side of his face balloons, his eye almost disappears. As Nathan lifts his coffee, his sleeve falls away. A patch of skin on the wrist has purpled.

"That's a nice little scratch there."

"Damn cat," Nathan says, spilling coffee, snatching at a used tissue on the counter. He dabs nervously at the brown puddle but feels Krivit's eyes on his wrist again and slides his hand deep in his coat pocket.

"You don't have a cat," Krivit says.

Nathan feels first surprise, then indignation, having believed for the moment his own lie.

"The cunt bit you too, you know," Krivit says. "You got to watch that these days."

Nathan grins, gathering his wits, and spreads out his hands dramatically. It is something he's good at, something he knows to do, screw up his mouth and arch his eyebrows in an attitude of profound disbelief: Can you believe it?—as he might do at Yankee Stadium when someone all of New York reveres and counts on does something incomprehensibly witless, drops a pop fly, boots a routine grounder; things thirty thousand rabid fans would not ever have done themselves—not for eight million a year. His profound disbelief in the face of dramatic but ultimately trivial things. Can you believe what the judge said? Can you believe she actually bit me?

"You shouldn't let them get away from you," Krivit warns.

Nathan knows there is a question he should ask but he side-steps it, slides around, finds something else. "Just tell me what you have."

"A little deep-sea fishing."

"The fishing," Nathan says, "is still better up north. Washington Heights—"

"Minnows, Stein. Greedy minnows. Bullshit. Boring."

"Boring," Nathan echoes.

"Today I'm offering ambition. Russian kikes."

Nathan sips at his coffee then sucks in, his tongue burnt. "I don't do ambition." He fingers his tongue. "Ambition is complicated."

A pleased smile plays on Krivit's lips. "I got you this because you fucked up, and you need to make new friends."

Nathan passes him a second hot dog. Krivit shrugs his left shoulder. Nathan glances over at the family standing by the counter. The father wears heavy black clothes, the mother a peasant dress and wool shawl. An older girl in her twenties, slim, tight jeans and sweater. An anonymous boy levels at Nathan an expression darkened either by adolescence or plain wrath or some combination of both. They all have the parboiled features of Slavs, people with thick fingers and pillowy palms. No makeup, no flash. No one is talking, no one is having fun. It could be a regular family outing.

Krivit takes a swipe at his forehead, panting. "They look like peasants, but they're into smack, whores, rackets. Not big time. Not yet. But just wait. The Russians will own Brooklyn. They'll own everyone."

The parents and the girl nibble at their food, their eyes roaming over the plastic menu displays overhead. The boy glares on, unrelenting, as though waging some dumb high-school war.

"It's the kid?"

"His brother. Bail denied. That's all we're talking about. A simple writ."

"That's what I'm doing here?"

"It's due tomorrow."

Nathan looks at him. "Tomorrow."

"If we have to maybe we can have the case sent Rodriguez's way." Krivit wipes the corners of his mouth. "You can still arrange for that?"

Nathan considers his coffee, as though the cup itself holds the consequences of bribing a judge. "Tomorrow," he says again. He has taken liberties with Judge Rodriguez only once, and even he would be hard-pressed to call it an actual buy: he'd given

Rodriguez tickets to *Madama Butterfly*, his own coveted seats—eighth-row-center orchestra—in return for the small accommodation of rescheduling a hearing past the statute of limitations for a speedy trial, that magic date after which you fly as free as a bird. But the business with Rodriguez was harmless, really, if not just. The defendant, a thief of petty sums in a neighborhood of crack dealers and junkies, an irritant to everyone, was set free on the condition of skipping town. Goodbye and good luck.

Nathan's hands settle before him in an attitude of prayer. Down the window bar it is just the junkman now, moved on to a paper cup of beer. "I had this friend who once mentioned that he knew somebody who once mentioned he might be able to do something."

"You still have these friends?"

"My friends can become their friends, but what are the terms?"

"Two-fifty."

Nathan darts another look back at the family.

"Don't look at them again. They don't eat on Mulberry Street and thumb their noses at the cops. They're in they're out, they'll slit your throat in broad daylight, bim-bam."

"Two hundred fifty thousand," Nathan murmurs.

"A rush job. They're anxious people, family people. Regular Waltons."

"What's mine?" Nathan asks.

"Fifty."

"Fif—"

"Fuck you, Stein. You keep fucking up all over the place, you're stealing bail bonds, you have some real estate thing going on, this phone scam, your stock goes down not up, know what I mean?"

"How do you know—"

"Think of it as a temporary readjustment in your share price."

Nathan swallows. "Pricing yourself out of a future, Krivit."

Krivit's glasses have steamed over. "Look, you fuck. Don't you threaten me. I can get anybody. I'll get your bonehead partner.

That schmuck. He'd sell his goddamn mother. He'd suck his own cock for twenty bucks. What's his name?"

Nathan shakes his head. "He's not a partner. He works with Milton."

"That's your problem."

"Schreck. Oliver."

"That's him. That fuck."

Nathan does not often look at Krivit. He doesn't, for instance, even know the color of his eyes. Now he sees that they are light blue, almost pretty. Nathan smiles to himself. A song comes to his head, the climactic aria from last night's *Figaro*, the sweet soprano in the lead opening her mouth to the cavernous Met and setting free the birds. And Isabel, sitting beside him in a lovely red dress, a flowery print, and black hair swept back in a bun. Her hand in his, her fingers long now and talented. Nathan begins to hum, falsetto.

"So why me?" he says between phrases. "Why not Milton?"

Krivit scowls. "He's got bigger fish to fry." He lifts his shapeless arm and waves it through the air to the muddy floor, the barren streets, the abandoned Wonderwheel. The sneakers kicking at the wind. Fuck Whitie.

"You're what I could get on short notice. You need— Will you just cut out that serenade?"

Nathan stops. His eyes follow a squad car rushing up Surf Avenue, its headlamps blinking and emergency lights spinning. It takes a corner fast and heads for the boardwalk. Twenty years ago, Coney Island children came to the windows of Milton's Silver Shadow and offered pocket change for a ride. Milton took the pennies and nickels and came out of Famous's with a box of hot dogs for all of them. He lifted them and put them behind the wheel, laughing; they stretched over the leather and touched the true wood paneling, black kids all of them, good kids, kids with half a chance until tomorrow. Then he drove away complaining to Nathan with sweeps of his fat hand, Nigger this, Nigger that. Spic whores.

Now in this neighborhood there are no phones. No one is calling. Across the street the carcasses of lesser cars sit charred and glazed with ice. Milton hasn't come down here in years. You sow too many seeds you end up with a jungle that swallows you whole.

A second squad car emerges under the subway trestles and follows the first. Sirens wail in the distance, bending on the wind. Krivit cranes his neck, trying to see the boardwalk.

Though standing still, at the sound of the sirens Nathan feels he is almost running, almost lurching. A trickle of sweat crosses the back of his neck. But there on the TV it's now the Eagles in white and the Packers in green. Though the game quickly dissolves into a local news update, a shot of a stormy Caribbean sea, the underside of a capsized boat. Bodies riding out the swells facedown, their hair and clothes puffing up and back, up and back. A wave breaks and they're gone.

Noting his calm, laying claim to it, Nathan takes out his best gold pen and unfolds a matchbook from Gambone's Ristorante. He clears his throat. Dully now, with studied disinterest: "What's the charge?"

But Krivit has seen something on the boardwalk and is on the balls of his feet.

Nathan prods his arm.

"Drive-by." Krivit brings his attention back. "When you come down to it Jews aren't any different from wops, just better at it. Who would have thought?"

"Why are they keeping him?"

"Fly risk."

"Would he fly?"

They both look outside. Across Surf Avenue, the El train screeches slowly through the Luna Park Houses at third-floor level, the third rail lighting up the towers with high strobe flares. By the time the tail-lights of the last car have pulled out of sight the platform's windblown vacancy feels permanent, as though the trains haven't come for years.

"Wouldn't you?" Krivit says.

Nathan puts down the pen. "Then he's gone."

"It's not your problem."

"What do they have?"

"A kid in the car who says our boy pulled the trigger."

"Did he?"

Krivit wipes his forehead. "Sure. Why not. What's it to you?"

Nathan coughs lightly into his fist, but he's stirred up the dirt in his chest. The cough screws deep, excruciating, and fighting it an immense weariness descends. If he didn't know better, he'd be thinking heart attack. Krivit has been going on about something or other, a litany of Nathan's indiscretions, his faults, like the plagues, blood, locusts, darkness, slaying of the first born . . .

But his heart, he's been told, is drum tight; a vault with plumbing, as the doctor said, obviously grateful to be able to pass that little tidbit along.

By the time Nathan is coughed out he feels kicked in the ribs. "And where's said witness?"

"Building snowmen upstate."

"And his last attorney?"

Krivit, saying nothing, probes a molar with his pinky. Answer enough. Nathan nods once, slowly. The father puts down a half-finished hot dog and leads the family toward them. Nathan yanks off a leather glove and turns, extending his hand. The father reaches into his coat and tosses a brown paper package the size of two hardcover books onto the window bar and brushes by; the family follows and pushes one by one through the swing doors and out.

Nathan watches them walk down the street. The boy—an argument, a planned escape—has bolted down an alley.

Krivit slides the package out from under Nathan's hand, opens the end and peers in. A pink tip of tongue breaks through the seam of his mouth. He reaches in and prowls around with his fingers.

"Hey, I got a good joke," he says. "You'll like this. There's this old wop and this old Jew sitting on this park bench. And this real babe walks by. I mean the real thing. Young, blonde, stacked."

Krivit pulls his hand out of the package, for a moment forgetting the bricks of cash inside, as though remembering something of superior interest and proven benefit.

"And the wop turns to the Jew and he points at her and he says, 'I screwed her. I mean, I really screwed that broad.' And the Jew nods and his eyes narrow and his mouth starts watering and he turns to the wop and says, 'Yeah, outta what?' "

Laughing, Krivit bobs his head like a bird. It is a lesson, practically a proverb. Nathan feels a brief, surprising surge of affection for this fat middleman. It is unearned, he knows, but there it is all the same, as fleeting as a light breeze that comes from nowhere and just as quickly leads nowhere, a mistake; and there it goes, going—after all these years Krivit is practically family—gone.

He watches Krivit feel around in the paper package and pull out a smaller one the dimensions of a single brick. Krivit leaves it on the metal bar between them. He shoves the larger package between the flaps of his coat, then raises a finger, as though testing the wind. "Don't let the cunts get in the way of business." His high strained voice reminds Nathan of his rabbi from Ozone Park: Stay the course, stay focused, you're slipping, Nathan, slipping—

"Don't fuck this one up, Stein. They're not forgiving. And I know."

"What do you know?"

Outside, the Russians are abandoning their blankets and running for the beach. The Pakistani manager of Famous's pushes through the door to the street, his hands on his hips.

Again, Krivit cranes his neck. "I hear things," he says. "Weird things." He taps his ear. Not bothering to turn to Nathan he produces a fat manila envelope and leaves it on the counter. "Here's the history, docket number, the rest. Don't forget, Stein. Tomorrow."

Tomorrow, fifty thousand, tomorrow, fifty thousand. Nathan weighs the options. Options but no choices. And no questions. It's fifty G's and tomorrow's tomorrow's tomorrow—

He slides over the last hot dog to Krivit. "You should think about losing some weight," he says.

Krivit shoots him an angry glance. "Fuck you."

"Look at me."

The corners of the fat man's lips lift in a gradual smirk: "Yeah, look at you."

The drunk, led back into the fold, has not stopped at the water-line. Instead, extending the plastic trumpet in a kind of fascist salute, he goosesteps calmly into the slush. The other swimmers hop on the beach, prancing back and forth at the water's edge. Some, closing their eyes, throw out their arms martyr-like to take the full force of the sub-zero wind. As though redemption lurks somewhere between agony and humiliation. One young girl, hugging herself, cries ohgodohgodohgodohgod. Then someone declares, "Time," and the members of this club, many looking as though they're hoping for second thoughts but are too dazed to find them, kick their way in. The water, a pebbly slush only a few degrees and a couple minutes from solid ice, barely budges at their waists. Undeterred, they lock hands in a circle, firing up and down in their places like pistons. The drunk has not stopped. His shoulders go under.

He cries, "Come on, losers!" His bluish hand breaks the surface and groggily waves them on.

"One! Two! Three!" they bellow, and go down, vanishing without a ripple. They emerge seconds later, blue-faced, eyes pinched, unable to scream, like tardy babies funneled through the womb and fired out, misshapen, slimed.

"Stupid fucks," says someone safely on the beach. A Korean in a cheap parka hammers his palms together. A photographer kneels and snaps away, catching the bathers in attitudes of stoicism and madness.

All that can be seen of the drunk: a patch of red hair, a flap of his shorts, his heels, a lip of orange plastic trumpet.

"Goddamn it, he's done it again," a bather complains. Two wade out to retrieve him while the others leap and pirouette and scream in the refrigerated air, searching up and down the beach and across toward Jersey as though for the purpose for what they've done. Others strike a pose for the photo-journalist.

Then a true scream, a woman's ringing shriek.

No one knows what is happening. Someone yells, "Shark?" People are running in place, knees high in the harbor. Someone points toward the floating drunk. A sluggish swell passes through him. He hangs in a dead man's float and looks to have been decapitated. No, not him, but past him a second pair of heels breaks the surface. Someone grabs the drunk and shoves him like a piece of driftwood toward the beach. Two hookers waiting there cross their arms with sudden interest as someone goes back waist-high, reaches in and tows back the corpse and leaves it face up, half in half out of the water. Hands clawed, mouth open, it lies between two flaps of ripped red cloth like a food offering; part torment, part repose.

The hookers approach the corpse like cops, without issues. One toes the ribs. "She's pretty."

"She was."

"Know her?"

They consider her.

"Black," the first says. "Or Chicano."

"How can you tell? She's all fucked up."

# 5 P.M.

A motionless string of red brake lights humps all the way to Queens over the Kosciuszko, traversing the dark below. The dashboard, blinking 5 P.M., sets an underglow off Claire Proffitt's chin as the bridge jounces disconcertingly beneath. Opposing headlights are massing for miles. An ambulance behind surges forward a few inches at a time. No one is moving, there is no place to go; the ambulance's siren falls silent, its emergency lights go dark. Ahead, a haze of yellow construction lights; Rikers Island, just a few miles away, will be an adventure.

At a full stop, Claire glances at the newspaper on the dashboard, folded back at a two-inch filler column on page seventeen:

### REFUGEE BOAT SINKS; 40 DIE

A boat crammed with Dominicans trying to slip into the United States capsized and sank in icy, heavy seas, killing at least 40 people. Many more are missing and feared dead.

One survivor said 107 people were crammed aboard the *Saint John*, a refitted 30-foot fishing trawler, which sank five miles off Cape Engaño, the easternmost point of the Dominican Republic . . .

Exhausted already, Claire leans over the wheel, myopic in the snow flurries, watching the blinking lights of planes gathering in their landing patterns. Planes dropping out of the darkness, gliding low overhead into LaGuardia. She is mere days from her week's vacation to—she's already forgotten the name; perhaps she never knew it, doesn't *need* to know it. She'd simply given her travel agent her orders: heat, loneliness, blind stupor. Picking her plane out of the sky, she again has her vision of her equatorial sea infinite and pure, the long waves marching on a white beach, crashing in clear sheets over the sand, the spent breakers racing back to do it again, while behind her, the exhilarating piles of mountain heaped on mountain—

Easing down the bridge, the four lanes of traffic pour grain by grain into a half-width of shoulder swept clear of rubble. Police cruisers and highway crews. A circle of flood-lit pavement: strewn shards of metal, a door, a wheel, bolts and screws. Cops with orange slickers and neon batons.

She reaches for the tape player. Still that old tape of Nathan's, Herbie Hancock's first album that he liked so much. The two of them together always had a soft spot for first albums, first books, first movies, the first blush, the courage and safety in anonymity, nothing but possibility and raw hope.

> . . . Thousands of Dominicans try to enter the United States each year by crossing the turbulent 90-mile Mona Passage between the Dominican Republic and Puerto Rico in rickety wooden boats. The Border Patrol has captured over 8,182 this year alone.

Through and gone, the cars cavort like liberated animals over the four empty lanes. Streets and row-houses give way to long unlit slopes peaking and rolling toward other streets, more highway, then more water. An endless clutter of headstones back to back and wing to wing, obelisks, virgin marys boxed in by competing apostles and multiple replications of the savior Jesus Christ himself. Airborne haloes tossing in the night like legions of Frisbees. More row-houses, more foundries, more cemeteries, Jewish this time, the stones lower, roomier, less of a crowd, ironically enough less of a push. In death, she thinks, they change their tune: composed, patient, they grant everyone around them a wide berth.

An off-ramp into a street of two-family duplexes with windows flickering blue with TV light. A neighborhood of cops and firemen; of plastic-sheathed sofas bearing cats; young sons spending their lives leaning over engines and hiring themselves out to the parents' friends.

Stopped at a zebra-striped gate, a guard box beyond which a narrow causeway humps over the water to Rikers Island, Claire is recognized. The guard, a woman, looks disappointed. "You," she says, and puts her finger to her watch. "What," she asks, "is your problem?"

Claire offers her the grin of the guilty but ever-loved child, then a look of commiseration, then disbelief. "I'm backed up. I'm bored. I have no life."

Anybody with style and grace this night will get what she wants. The guard lifts her eyes toward a passing plane and summons for Claire a look of motherly aggravation. "Don't be long. Don't be outside. Something's coming. I heard it on the radio."

In the waiting room of the Rose M. Singer ward for women, a guard in blue sits investigating her long clawed fingernails painted alternately pink and indigo. Her holster is empty. Outside this cubicle, two more women armed and large peer down from an elevated watch desk behind a slab of bulletproof plexiglass. No one has moved since Claire was last here. And no man in sight. When she first left law school she thought that a plus. Women in the cells, women holding the guns, sweeping the floors, calling the shots. All around Claire nothing but women. But today she smiles stiffly, taps her toes, very nervous: the place is vibrating, teetering on the edge. The women's ward at Rikers Island looks like anyplace else—dirty and bare and hard, a laboratory of unhappiness.

In the cubicle window, Claire focuses on her own reflection, touching her cheek, her face fine and ruddy, as though permanently lashed by wind and sun, suddenly afraid, as though the voyage already has been made—

A girl enters in prison grays, blurry-eyed and groggy; coppery skin and the flat, sloped face of the interior tribes, wrapped in a shy quiet that seems to have ancient origins. Her coal black eyes never rise above knee level. And she is pregnant, well into it, and seventeen, if that.

She lifts her cigarette, inhales deeply, closing her eyes in ecstasy.

Claire lowers herself into a chair across from her. "Regina Núñez," she reads off the docket folder. "You know any English?"

The girl shrugs.

"Well I don't know Spanish. Let's see. Possession. Resisting arrest. You have court tomorrow—but no one's been filing motions. Why hasn't anyone been filing motions?"

Regina says nothing.

"Haven't you had a lawyer?"

"He don't come."

Claire sniffs. "You drunk, too?"

The girl looks at her slippers and takes a breath. "I spilled something."

"You smell like you've been dipped in whiskey." Claire's eyes linger on the girl's swollen belly. "Maybe you shouldn't drink."

"I didn't ask for you," the girl says, and her eyes, slippery, their hold on things tentative at best, lose their grip, tracking some far-off place, not home, Claire thinks, but some place she dreams of going. Hollywood. Disneyland. Niagara Falls. The girl's eyes pool. Teary nuggets fall to her lap. Behind all this, a child.

Claire leans forward but feels no desire or need to touch her, or offer comfort. "You've been here three months. Let's at least get you to make bail."

"I don't have money," the girl says.

"It's just five hundred dollars."

"Too much."

"It's not that much." Claire points at her folder. "There's an address here. There's family?" Claire instructs herself to breathe. "Okay. Who is it—was it? Your lawyer."

The girl holds out her palm, as though, there in her hand, the lawyer will appear.

"I need the name. I need to know where to start."

"Nathan Stein."

Claire looks up abruptly. "What did you say?"

"Nathan Stein?"

"That's what I thought you said. And how long have you known Mr. Stein?"

"Know him?"

"How many months, how many years?"

The girl shrugs. "I never—"

"Have you actually met him?" Claire demands. "Have you seen him? Has he ever been here?"

The girl gives a look of defeat. "Mr. Stein will come."

Before Claire's eyes opens an encyclopedia of heroes and villains and combats won and lost, and poisonings and bloodshed. White knights. Fair maidens. Ancient history disinterred from the mud.

"You want your child born and raised in a prison? Because that's what will happen if you wait." She shuts the folder. "You are going to give birth in a hospital like a human being."

The girl is sobbing into her hands.

"I'm taking your case. You're mine."

Nathan's watch, or is it his beeper, chirps like that captive bird somewhere beneath his coat. But the commotion on the boardwalk is spreading. People are lining the rail. A body in red has been dragged up the sand. "Oh, God," he says, and begins to run, wincing at the tug of his suit against a wound he doesn't remember, this one across his left rib cage. Everywhere dogs are barking. He feels the pull of the boardwalk and heads there, then finds his body veering off, taking him another way. He jogs back across Stillwell, under the El, and, looking over his shoulder, slows to a gimpy walk, clutching his chest. "Shit," he breathes. It's all gone, his stamina, his air.

The tide of cold shade has risen high on the brownstone and brick. On the rooftops a forest of naked antennas grabs at the porous light. In a plexiglass door between a doughnut shop and a shoe repair, a girl leans, examining her nails. When Nathan stops she lifts her face. She was one of the girls he'd seen earlier on the beach. Eyes set deep in blue caves.

"Where's your friend?" he says.

The girl cocks a hip. "What's wrong with me?"

"There's nothing wrong with you."

"I'm better than her. White meat's better." She laughs at her own joke. The glass door fogs.

Nathan looks up and down the street, wanting in some place, though not necessarily this place; just some shelter, to solve some need as unutterable and instinctive as a baby's, like air but not as good.

A stairwell narrow and corkscrewed as a steeple's. Nathan's eyes climb the bowed steps, the shaved banister, the girl's thin legs into her skirt, following the gradual warmth of the building that ends at the second floor. The hallway, cold and gray with dirty light, disappears at both ends. There is a strip of yellow under one door and then other closed doors. Doorways clotted by shadow. The girl enters the lighted room without knocking, and Nathan follows.

A thickly walled space, a perfect cube, a high closed window ticking with blown sand and snow. A bulb hangs from the ceiling. Someone has made gestures of cleaning up, a sagging bed unconvincingly made. Beside it a pressboard nightstand painted brown in imitation of wood grain. A half-full glass of stale, bubbled water, illuminated under the dim lamp like a fetish. In the summer the street below is sandy, and salt-dust floats in the room and collects in the lee of upright things, but now the room is clammy and cold, the dust has fallen, and everything is coated in a thin, gritty paste.

"You want dope? Crack, smack, meth? We could do it now." She drops atop the ragged bedspread with her back against the wall. "Or whatever."

Nathan's eyes have settled on a calendar Scotch-taped over the bed, wrong month and old year. He sees there a shot of distant beach: Roatán, or some place just as good. Under an unseen brilliant moon a ribbon of radiant sand meets a white blameless sea. The breathy voice fades in, and Nathan works the private rhythm in his head, *The Girl from Ipanema*, a young woman rising from the water, passing up the beach—

The saxophone slides in, charming all the señoritas out of the water with thin sighs—

Wearily, the girl unbuttons her thin jacket and the blouse underneath and slips both together off her shoulders. She is narrow, more frail than her clothing has described. Her breasts are adolescent, her skin pale, blue, translucent; her ribs like notched acknowledgments of misdeeds, of bad memories unforgotten.

Nathan meets the girl in the middle of the floor. She is no more than sixteen or seventeen, he sees, her makeup a mask. Her tongue appears in the corner of her lip. Everything she is doing is young and tutored. And he, he knows, is here because he has been, because he can, because he will. Not because he wants to, but because he could. It feels, like everything lately, as needless as it does inevitable. And always what follows is a little dream, a shallow, furtive thing. Usually what comes to mind is someone from his long ago or his day-to-day, someone he's already left, someone safely behind him. Atop one woman he'd imagine another, and another, until, exponentially removed from his life, he'd be as good as dead, beyond harm, dreaming his little dream, until he twitch twitch twitches and opens his eyes, waking from the glorious twilight of his midday nap, and it all comes crashing down around him: the hard strip of lamplight, the touch of her clammy skin, her foreign smell, the crater in the middle of the cheap mattress beneath them like a foxhole—

A soft chirp at his belt. With immense relief, Nathan reaches inside, peering down at the darkened beeper display. Frowning, he reads the message again, losing himself for a moment, then looks up to find the girl naked and blue before him. She has left her socks on. He steps back, shrugging, Can you believe it, at a time like this? Smiling, he presses his business card into the girl's palm

NATHANIEL STEIN, ESQ. ATTORNEY AT LAW

and leaves her standing.

Then gone, safely behind his car's salted windows, switch-backing through traffic across the Belt Parkway to the strains of Leontyne Price's *Aïda*. His eyes are everywhere but the road, set-tling for a moment on a sheaf of papers on the floor, a brief due in court last Thursday, finished Friday morning early, forgotten Friday morning late, disregarded until now. Cars honk from every direction. He straightens the wheel—he has been drifting between lanes—then reaches for the volume control and calibrates six speakers the size of quarters embedded in the doors and ceiling, a woofer in the glove box, tweeters hidden in the dash, the console as bright and elaborate as a pilot's cockpit—all of it compliments of Julio, who, thanks to Nathan and a brief miraculously unearthed in time, is back on the street in time served instead of inside for fifteen-to-life.

The phone in his breast pocket buzzes. He holds up his watch to the light in the rear-view mirror; not yet four.

"Hello? Hi . . . No, I wasn't— . . . a new client . . . no, not a lot of money, only a couple grand, that's it, look— . . . What music. That's just traffic. Some accident, ambulances everywhere . . . Around eight. I'll come by . . . what? I'm losing you. An under-pass. A tunnel. Hold on, I'm losing you—"

Placing the phone face-down on his thigh, he lifts his thermal mug and sips at old, cold coffee. He sips again, holding the liquid in his mouth, and lifts the phone, uncapping the unceasing chatter. "Wait, what? . . . Serena, how could I? I haven't been near a tele-vision all day. What about what boat, can't we talk about it later I have to make a few calls, some bad boys at Rikers Island . . . Serena? I'm going to lose you. Yes, eight o'clock. Yes, I promise. Another tunnel . . . I'm losing you—"

Nathan taps the mute button, flicks the mouthpiece into place and slides the phone in his pocket. The barge-like car bears him along, shooting him through a bottleneck of orange work trucks and zebra-striped barriers into wide-open sky. Leaning forward on the wheel, his eyes lift, his own voice simpering a few famous bars.

Now his beeper vibrates, a cricket caught under a plate. He fumbles with dials and buttons small enough to be bumps or imperfections of design. He presses them individually and in various combinations, accomplishing nothing. The sound of a blaring horn makes him raise his head, and one hand on the wheel, eyes everywhere—road, lap, pocket, speedometer, road—his thighs close around his thermal mug as something jerks his head to the right. A red sedan has pulled alongside and is keeping his own pace exactly. The passenger leans forward, as though the driver has said something admirable about Nathan's car. As though Nathan's car were noteworthy, especially elegant, a vintage model, which it isn't: it is a badly beaten 4×4 with running boards and caged lights and a smoked plastic windbreak, everything a TV voice-over narrating the journey of a 4×4 across a butte somewhere—it looked like Hell—told him he had to have, and Nathan, sucker for a hitch to a dream, believed.

He squints over at the men. Both are wearing suits. Their car drops back, and looking at their silhouettes in the rear-view mirror, Nathan understands that the car has been tailing him all along; for the last few weeks, it seems. He had never had any doubt he was being followed, though until now they had acted with discretion. Today, a change has taken place; they want him to know.

"There," Nathan murmurs, pressing down. He shakes his head. A miracle. How is it done—it almost doesn't matter what the message says—how words transmit through air—who needs actual talk—we have answering machines for when we're not at home and Twenty-first Century Message Center/Beepers for when we are.

A little proud, a little smug, he doesn't understand: how had he ever gotten along without it? Pressing thumb and forefinger in rapid succession, he squints at the tiny screen:

Cabrón. Fuck you and your tunnel. Turn on your phone.

Refugees have been straggling into the Spindrift all afternoon, emerging from the snow singly and steadily and already a little tight. Everyone a conspiracy of one, a statue of something. Opposite the bar three big windows bordered by tinsel and Christmas lights face the street and the Red Hook piers and the harbor beyond—alternating pictures of the dingy radiance inside the bar and the length of barren lamplit waterfront across the street, so that if you turn your head with either each coming or each going of the lights' blink you have opposing views of the world, in and out, you and them. You and some other you, Claire thinks, watching through her own reflection the snow devils rising off the street and jigging out of control, collapsing like drunks in the doorways.

Down the street the hulking converted warehouses of the Jehovah's Witnesses are recast as castles in the sky. The artificial turrets looming over the entrance ramp to the Brooklyn Bridge trumpet the veiled threat: now passing up God's Kingdom. The young men and women in their heels and trench coats are filing past the bar to mealtime or to their homes, a good day's work done. They've turned out their *Watchtower* in the tens of thousands in fifty languages, convincing the world that the Big Bang is a hoax, that Christ's crucifixion wasn't enough to purge us of original sin, that we must go door to door for deliverance. Brooklyn, Claire knows, is home base, their safe haven, one of seven spots on earth prophesied by someoneorother to survive the apocalypse. She thinks that sweet and hopeful. Fixing on her face an economical smile, she returns their cheerful nods.

Someone in the bar has actually brought a baby. The cries grate on her; she feels them like radio signals in her fillings, setting her on edge. And underneath the murmurings from the perky blonde anchoring the local TV news, the outside sweeps in through the windows. In comes the clanging of the distant buoys. In comes the constant hiss of traffic along the Brooklyn-Queens Expressway.

Claire returns to the bar. The baby is wailing. The bartender, a small Greek with corkscrew hair, has turned his face up to the TV. There, footage of a sinking boat and the hunched backs of drowned bodies—the Dominicans, she assumes—dropping one by one beneath the waves as the unseen news helicopter hovers overhead, its rotors spreading the choppy water while one of the bodies—can it be?—actually seems to be waving.

"Martini," Claire says, eyeing the little Greek pouring her gin. She worries about him. Last week, the Arab who owned the bodega a few blocks away was shotgunned in cold blood, blasted into the racks of Snickers and M&M's. It's the Old West out there once again, these city store owners pioneers in their way, risking everything to nickel-and-dime their way to some low-fat version of prosperity. Bartenders are no different; any old nut can wind up at the end of their bar, running a tab, waiting for closing time to reach inside his jacket. Her own clients, for instance; thanks to her they are walking around free on bail, or just plain free. Claire resolves to call the *Times* when she returns from her holiday, have her paper chucked at her door from a passing car. She will phone an organic produce company and have delivered to her live and virginal things. She will shop for clothes exclusively by phone. She will buy a new phone by phone. She will call friends when she knows they will be out, preferring tape to an actual human being. More and more a life by proxy.

"This is no place for children," she proposes, to no one, as the baby wails on. Pouring and straining Claire's martini, the Greek brings the glass forward by the stem, as if offering his grandmother a rose.

Santos has appeared beside her. She is plucking macadamia nuts out of a bowl of bar mix, shoving aside the pretzels and the little orange fish. "Where have you been?" she asks, and busies herself by pulling his jacket down at the bottom; it seems, this minute, too short. She presses the back of her hand to his cheek. "Don't get too comfortable. If I have to keep looking at that baby we'll have to leave. I'm sorry—you were saying?"

"I wasn't. We had an extra call. Another illegal fell out of a plane. Or he jumped."

"They're just dying to get into this country. I don't understand it." Outside, a sudden volley of thunder. "And this weather," she says.

His porcelain neck and hands, she sees, his black suit, damp, clinging, revealing every mystery, mysteries she once thought she had solved. But he has, lately, become strange again. He is growing puffy and obscure, an emblem of contrast and contradiction.

"Unfortunately," she says, "I can't get *too* drunk. At some point tonight I need to go to the office." She picks at his lapel. "You won't guess who I ran into today. Well, not into *him*, exactly. It was one of his little messes."

A blank expression crosses Santos's face. "I saw Nathan, Claire."

She cocks her head in confusion. "Extraordinary. That's just what I was going to say."

"After all these years, it's incredible, he actually looks better."

"It was typical of him, some pregnant kid in Rikers he just over-looked, just left her there. He never would have done that ten years ago, maybe five years ago. I never could understand his method. Not that he ever had one, just shooting from the hip, no strategy at all. One day, Robin Hood, the next day—whatever he is."

She sees he has, in fact, if not looking directly at her, been taking her in.

"You're not breathing, Errol," she says. "Breathe—"

Her hand, long and slender, rests between them. Santos sets his over hers. She makes a half-hearted attempt to pull away but he holds her down, looking directly into her face.

"It was strange seeing Nathan today," he says. "It's been years. Everything comes back in a flood."

She responds with an ironic smile, impenetrable, she knows.

He releases her, waving down the bartender. "I'll get us some coffee."

When it comes neither of them touches it. Claire stares ahead blankly, as if unconscious of her surroundings. Though she feels the air alive around her, feels every little thing, every grain of dirt under her shoe, every floating dust mote, the electric fields around the lamps, the breezes of microwave, the ultrasound, the invisible, sourceless currents. The Herbie Hancock still playing in her empty car down the street, the endless loop of tape going around and around and around. Nathan's tape.

The thunder comes steady now, close, then echoing far.

"It sounds like target practice," Santos says.

"No," Claire replies, "it's war."

This bar, for example, had finally felt purged, swept clean of the past. But now with Errol here alone, in the flesh, seeking, it seems, her help—

"Claire, you said we could talk about it. About a child," he begins.

She clears her throat. "So that's what's on your mind. Sort of strange timing. This wouldn't have to do with seeing Nathan, would it?"

"Time is what I'm talking about. I want to be a father, I want to send something out there, pieces of us—"

"Out *there*—?" Claire points. "*Pieces?*"

"We aren't getting any younger."

"Well," she says, "usually one gets married first."

Again she feels him taking her in, overturning every particle, every thought, in that thorough detective manner of his.

"Don't look at me so hard," she says.

"I've considered marriage, too," he replies.

Claire grips the lip of the bar tightly, light-headed. "Tell me," she says, "did Nathan remember about us?"

Santos finally sips at his coffee.

"Did he ask about me?"

He begins to answer but she turns from him. She has changed her mind; she doesn't, after all, want to hear the answer.

A silver Chevrolet pulls up outside the window, in the mirror. Claire hears honking. She points a finger. "Isn't that your little friend?"

Santos turns around. "Excuse me," he says, with his over-bearing politeness, and heads for the door.

"Errol—" When he turns around, she says, "I don't want to see him again. Nathan," she says, to clarify. "I don't want it to start all over."

She watches him run into the street, ankle-deep in snow, leaning into the driver's window, his breath rising and twisting away in the wind. She remembers the first time she met him. Nathan had arranged it, of course, an evening with law school chums, to begin at Jackie's Topless. Ruth was there, and Oliver Schreck. The whole gang, of sorts. And next to the footlights sat Nathan and Errol, best of friends, so like adopted brothers, war-riors in jeans and penny loafers without socks. Two chuckling cousins, she liked to imagine, who had pledged to run off to the strip club together at the height of the tedium of a family dinner but had never actually done so, until years had passed and their navels had grown to long gashes, and slapping high fives like middleschoolers at the varsity game they geared up the courage to flee after dessert. But they were in over their heads. It wasn't what they thought. The light was dingy and the men's room reeked and the unairbrushed girls were spotty with patches of cellulite and other minor glitches of construction. And later, they would slink into bed and with closed eyes and lax tongue wordlessly make love to their groggy women—Nathan to her, Errol to his young wife—kneading thigh and breast and puffing the right name, "Am I big enough, Am I big enough," but in their minds fucking against the men's room stall the sixteen-year-old stripper with pubescent tits and pristine mons who had leered at them repeatedly from the stage, shaking at them her cottoncandy promise until each dropped a twenty at her feet, after which she looked over not again, not ever, not even a mistaken glance—

"I have to go," Santos says. He has returned out of breath.

But Claire is unable to move. The roar of surf has returned to her ears. A little white road climbing and dropping, the tropical villages steadily passing. Their tin churches, signs in a language she never heard of—a kind of paradise.

She blinks it away. "But you just got here."

"I'm sorry."

"They can't do it. You're off duty."

He is fumbling with his coat, nervously squeezing his pockets. "I don't know what's going on. I'll meet you later, back at your place."

She stills his hand. "Errol, are you okay?"

He looks up. "They called me."

"Why would they do that?"

"They didn't say. That almost always means something, when you ask and they won't say."

Claire, worried, arranges on her face a smile of certainty. "You worry too much. It's nothing." She searches up and down the bar. All signs of the crying baby have gone. "Check for me here when you get back."

Santos slips out; the tail-lights of the car taking him away fade then turn a corner.

"It's nothing," Claire says again, this time to no one, not even herself.

Back again at the middle window facing the harbor, she slides her free hand into the pocket of her jeans while in the competing reflections the wedding invitations she still remembers hover, blurred around the edges like a late-night commercial for romance, the same homemade paper with pressed flowers, the same florid print:

> *Nathan Stein and Claire Proffitt*
> *request the pleasure of your company . . .*

That was six years ago. Nine years ago, Nathan's big victory for his father was an actual innocent man, a petty thief who had been manhandled by police who quarried up and inside him in search of cocaine-packed condoms. They had found nothing. They had the wrong apartment, the wrong man. An anonymous Dominican, an easy patsy. But Nathan, through the nights writing his opening and closing, drawing up lists and lists of questions for cross, questions for redirect, stirred the indignation of the court and the newspapers, until, like his father, he was more conductor than lawyer, inspiring articles and talk shows, making a martyr of his client, stumbling upon this image of himself as a desired man—a man actually desired for the right reasons. In Washington Heights, he was a hero.

The attention eventually faded, Nathan had more work than he could handle, and he and Claire took the opportunity to run. He had had his heart set on Honduras, for reasons unclear to Claire at the time. That interminable ride to Tegucigalpa, a drive far outside that city to the home village of a client of Milton's, where in the mornings they were handed a glass container with the milk still warm. New York vanished. Milton's reach withdrew. Their walks were slow and endless and lovely. Outside the village, the grass chewed low made winding shapes between the goat tracks burned into hillsides. Straight young pine trees bisected the tops of the hills, a boundary separating some grass from other grass. By late afternoon a wind began, and the criss-crossing clouds piled up behind the hills. Days and days and days and all those young pines leaning into the wind, all that grass sighing at once.

Their last afternoon, atop a hill, the clouds descended nearly to them. It was a Sunday, and they could hear church instruments calling and answering each other from four or five different corners of the village at once. Goats tore at the ground, children's shrieks and a dog's barking flew upward, circled, evaporated. Brown squares of garden and disks of small homes and circles, circles of women's heads and circles of swollen bellies of children wandering in circles, collecting wood, scrubbing, picking, always with something in their hands, a hoe, arcing high overhead in a half-circle and cutting into the corn. Older children with more circular baskets. Half-sober half-dressed shoeless men weaving along the banks of the brooks toward their semicircle of thatch roof in compounds swept and groomed by other hands and goats. Everything had geometry, everything in its place, in its order.

The curtain of rain in the distance was already pounding some other place; it looked to be falling in surges, and Claire knew that the darker streaks must really have been something when they hit the mud.

A drum beat had started up somewhere behind them, steadily, vaguely threatening. The air was unfocused, tenuous with a fragile peace bargained for by grand compromises. In the distance the rain crashed against the trees.

Nathan pulled one of Claire's hands up to his mouth and bit on a knuckle, an opening, the sort of affection from him she'd dreamed of. She thought she'd lost it without having won it in the first place. Her forehead settled against his spine.

The first spit of spray passed over them. The thunder was underfoot.

"Claire," Nathan said, "we're going to get creamed." They were both twenty-six.

By the hand she led Nathan to the line of pine trees that divided the grass and sat them down adamantly, as if she had prepared something particular to say. Nathan sat behind with her between his knees and braced them together.

The grass on the hillside ripped, the trees knelt. Claire stiffened in Nathan's arms. Then it came in cold sheets, firmer than she expected, like soft wood. Nathan bent to her, but the press of his lips was lost in the weight of the rain. She reached up and pulled his head down to her, and against her ear his chest rose and fell, rose and fell, that side of his face, she felt, the only part of him that kept warm and dry.

When the rain stopped the air was peculiar, empty of sound. Slowly the grass rearranged itself.

She looked to him, his hair a wide dark curtain, face streaked and dripping. A thin veil seemed to drop between them, the feeling of a shared, rural peace, blurring for a moment her suspicions. Nathan hummed. She felt her heart melting.

They skirted down the hill. It was dark then, with dusk this time, the spaces between the trees and the tops of the village roofs more and more blue. Their little shabby house loomed before them.

Nathan tried to light a match for the cigarette he had somehow forgotten to put to his lips, but both were wet, and when he failed to light either he dropped them in the grass, and for a time they confronted each other like two enemy forts, mute, waiting—

The hospital's lobby staff gives Nathan the impression not of paid workers but retirees on social security. The old black guard sitting half-on, half-off a high stool beside the turnstile, his fixed-smile demeanor, his uniform the formal-informal combination of chauffeur's cap and old gray cardigan. Up the elevator, in Nathan's hand always the same scrap of paper with the hospital's address and a room number. On the sixth floor a pail of water and a mop bar entrance to the nurses' station. The long green hallway is silent, two opposing rows of green doors as quiet as linen closets.

Nathan stares wearily at the label outside 614. The name was there last night. It is there now. It might not be next time. That was what he thought yesterday. He thinks it again now: she's still there. Gone, a small harbored hope.

He knocks lightly. No answer. He pauses, then begins to push. But hearing footsteps down the hall he turns his head sharply, catching a glimpse of the heel of a shoe, a dark trouser cuff, pulling into a doorway.

Nathan watches, then walks through, "Jesus Christ," blinking, his nostrils flare against the reek: urine, ammonia, something else, something harder to take. A trash can blooms, soiled paper towels, latex gloves, a crusty syringe. A half-filled bedpan in the sink, the remains of her dirt, listing in a greenish muddy puddle. He is intimate with her shit by now.

But Nathan stands a moment in confusion. He looks at the bedpan, again at the bed. Emaciated, her hair thin and greasy, unwashed for weeks it seems, this woman is not who he expected, no Washington Heights beauty queen stopping traffic on the dance floor of Limelight, but a kind of dishwater blonde, moneyed Upper West Side material. Admiring the chiseled bone structure of the face—yes, Columbus Avenue, linen pants, Museum Café—now betrayed and plunged into an old woman's crusty death. She stares ahead at the air but does not see it, as though she is asleep or fixed in a trance, perhaps already dead, though her eyes have not gone to stones.

He yanks aside the edge of the bisecting curtain and faces a bank of windows purpling with the twilight. In the office across the street many of the windows are actually alight, whole offices of little desks and drafting tables at which little people sit beneath banker's lamps, flanked by cartons of Chinese food. He steps to the foot of the other gurney where, superimposed on all the deadlines and ambition in the window, stands a transclucent replica of himself haloed by the bright gauze of the curtain behind him.

Once, Nathan was beautiful. He can still remember when he was approached at parties or on the street by someone claiming to work for a modeling agency. Have you ever thought about becoming a model, you'd be great, couple you with some yuppie mom on one of those sun-splashed solarium porches, full page in the *New York Times Magazine,* a killer wife on your arm, smoking Kools. Or no, a lanky blonde piggybacking, you're laughing so hard having that dreamily great time plastered across bus stop billboards, catching them all over Broadway with those baby blues of yours or are they green? Or Land's End, at the edge of a pier, that dimpled chin of yours, khakis yes, sandals, the water, you like the beach? You ever go to the beach?

The beach. Yes, he likes the beach.

Once he'd actually called the number on the card. He'd had a feeling about her. He'd mentioned he liked opera so she'd suggested Sfuzzi's, across from Lincoln Center. She was waiting at the end of the bar. Long dark hair and a tight black skirt an inch beyond mere allusion and into the region of out-and-out promise. She moved fluidly between subjects. His subjects, what he did, when he did it. Depositions. Trials. She was most curious—fascinated really—about those conjugal visits at Rikers Island she read about in *The New Yorker.* How does a murderer fuck, do you think? Is he sensitive and generous, does he wait for her, or possibly remorseful? Or does he do it like he wants to kill her? She led him back to her apartment through the snow. There had been no talk of cigarettes or Land's End. She didn't bring up her agency, the subject of his modeling never arose, and before she asked him up to her place it crossed his mind that the feeling he'd had about her was correct. It amused him. He said yes, coffee, fine, a drink, a drink better yet. Why not? he thought. It was a benign sort of trick, the sort he might have played himself.

Within fifteen minutes she'd flung down the Murphy bed with one hand while undressing with the other in a minimal and practiced show of effort. She was all fun, paper-thin, loud, an exhibitionist. He half thought she'd ask him to show her how they did it in jail. As if you'd know, she'd say. And he did. And he kept thinking she wouldn't like it. And thinking, too, about her neighbors on the other side of the wall. How many of her climaxes had they heard over the years, scorecards on the table, that one, that one, no way, faked that one for sure. He'd call again, he said, later, smiling at the door, buttoning his coat with one hand, waving with the other in his own show of minimal and practiced effort. She was expert at saying hello. Nathan the good-bye artist. Even before the doorman let him out he'd forgotten her.

"Nathan"—said with neither surprise nor pleasure.

Maria has been watching him. Maybe watching this, this very thing about the good looks with which he knows he has swindled even her. And maybe she is thinking the same thing he is: What a shame. What a waste.

She waves her scabby lips, shriveled fruit. Her cheeks, Nathan sees, are no longer sunken. There is nothing left to sink, or give. She is picked clean: her eye sockets, protruding through the skin as though they lie atop it, make with the bridge of her nose the figure of a cross. Beneath the covers the body is dissolved, without contours, hardly a ripple across the surface of the blanket. They've cut her hair since yesterday. It is shorn unevenly, mere tufts in places, the scalp bared in others, like a sheep's. It gives Nathan the impression that she has been hurried along an assembly line into some sort of institution, prison, concentration camp during an epidemic of lice; that there are many more just like her on the other side of the walls, others up and down the long corridors, in the wards above and below, shorn and freshly disinfected; and that these people are not ill but mad, the criminally insane. Maria's hair gives Nathan the impression that she has gone bad.

"Nathan." She speaks a full octave below her former voice, as though someone else is speaking for her, a heavy smoker, a whiskey-voiced transvestite, someone who is really expecting him. Maybe—it does actually cross his mind—someone he deserves.

A skeletal arm drops out of her blanket and motions toward the chair at the foot of her bed.

"Who have you told that I'm here?"

Nathan hangs his head.

"You are no good, Nathan. Though your friends love you. Ruth was here today. Somehow she knew."

Nathan, alarmed, checks his watch. "Today?"

Maria's cracked lips part, in a smile, Nathan supposes, but the effect is monstrous, a demonic sneer.

"And *I* love you. But you are no good now. I'll tell you what has happened. You've become just like your father. When you were fat I couldn't tell you apart. I used to think that you'd crawled inside his body. You laugh. Look at you, laughing. You made fun of him your whole life, the things you said about him, but now look. You waited your whole life to be something else but you never were anything but him. Did you tell anyone, Nathan? Does *anyone* know I'm here?"

Nathan shuts his eyes. He has been going around without her for more than a year, bringing along with his bottles of wine his new excuses: Maria has to stay late at work; Benny is sick; Maria's mother is not well. When is it that he thinks up these lies? Even he doesn't know. Does he conceive of them over time, making certain they are enough unlike the ones preceding; or do they come to him while he stands at the front door, ringing the bell, spontaneously, randomly coming to him, and he is merely lucky the lie is different enough, for it is, all the lies are *different* enough. Or is he so practiced at producing excuses that they merely fly out of his mouth via a direct conduit between his lips and the lying part of his brain?

Maria doesn't come, can't, won't, won't ever again. And by the way, didn't I tell you? She is dying.

The world is not that gullible. It is merely too afraid to insist.

"I am dying."

"Yes," he says.

"Yes."

Yes. Nathan traces the sweaty creep diagonally across the base of his neck. As though he has said not *yes* but *guilty,* as though he is giving it again, in case she didn't believe it the first time, her verdict: guilty.

Maria lets her head drop toward the window and the office building across the way. "They're always watching," she says dreamily. "You don't know. They send signals."

Nathan sighs, then leans forward, solicitous. "What do the signals say?"

"That they're going to kill me."

"They look too busy."

"There is an aerobics class on one of those floors."

"Tuesday and Thursday nights."

"And don't you *love* that," Maria scolds.

"I was only kid—"

"Young girls shaking their tits at me in the window. They *want* me to die."

I'm sorry.

We'll be happy.

Nathan says neither of these things.

A light comes to her face, a union between stillness and sweat-sheen and the dingy blue light. Her lips harden and curl. Eyelids flutter, pupils capsize, as blank now as a marble statue's. Beneath the blanket she brings her feet together and lifts the jagged knobs of her knees. Her arms lift, her head turns, and her eyes, rolling and rolling, now return, staring with electric certainty at the drab gray wall. Stilling, breathing quietly, she doesn't move until her position hardens over the long seconds into a Christ-like pose. Nathan half stands, seeing not Maria but something using her, inhabiting her body, again that thing that awaits him, too. Dementia. Sign of last days.

Up Nathan goes, looking away, taking a wide berth around Maria's outstretched arm, reaching for the phone. He dials, lifts his wristwatch and counts to fifteen. This is a nifty thing he's learned. His own 900-number charging $99.99 a call for nothing. He wanders the city, using phones at offices, at friends', calling himself, holding on for the required fifteen seconds, and hanging up. Most offices will miss the calls, not enough digits to stop the eye. A hundred bucks a pop, he can make what, twenty grand, forty, before someone catches on, before he's long, long gone. It is horrible, he knows. Horrible, especially, here.

Nathan puts down the phone and goes to stand by the window. Outside, the streets have darkened, the sky has paled, weighing down with the dull fog of a hundred million pricks of light. Television, reading lamp, billboard, tail-light, streetlight. Wires pass across the window, offensive, closing him in. The snow swirling around out there doesn't yet amount to anything, merely a manifestation of the cold.

Wringing his hands, looking back, briefly, at Maria's demonic grin, he turns toward the snow and remembers. A second date. She came armed with a chaperone. "This is Benny," she'd said. "Today he is four. And I am twenty." It was a prepared speech. And she paused to permit time for the math, as a stage actress will leave a space for laughter. Ultimately, it was this indifference toward all that, her nonchalance about her unwed motherhood, that won him over. She was different, and insistent on him seeing her as different. It wasn't beyond her to know full well that she, her *tribe*, was merely his taste, that she was merely the momentary head of Nathan's barrio queue. Standing firm, with her hand like a hat on her boy Benny's head, her eyes flashed defiantly. She'd given birth at sixteen. There it was. It was all clear now: she intended to resist. Interesting, she shall resist. Nathan asked her what she did. She merely laughed, she waved her hand. It does not matter, she said. What I do, it has nothing to do with me.

The sheets shift. Maria's arms lower, her legs slide beneath the covers. Her eyes slide and focus on the first thing that comes into her view: Nathan's empty chair. Craning her neck: "He has gone already?"

"Here."

Her eyes, locating him at the window, stalk him as he returns to his chair..

"Come sit by me," she says.

"Me?"

She cannot have meant him. Nathan's chair is Nathan's chair, distant, the doghouse. But Nathan sits beside her, and she takes his hand. Between her bones he feels swollen.

"I have been in this bed for a week," she says. "The people in this bed always die. I don't know how many corpses I am lying on top of." She wipes her face with the back of her hand. "I want you to know that I come from a wealthy family. My father bought for nothing that property on Roatán before I was born, before the resorts, before the airstrip. Trees and beach and water—who knew the world would want it?"

Maria pauses, out of breath, and Nathan, hearing a whisper in his ears, scans the room, suspiciously eyeing the bedstand, the gurney, the intercom wired to the nurses' station outside. You are a liar, says the bouquet of near-dead flowers tossing in front of the heat vent. You are a traitor, hum the fluorescent bars.

"We would be rich, if we sold it," Maria is saying. "We would be happy, if we built on it. I once thought we would together, Nathan, build a house, both of us, on the water. Be happy. I gave it to you in case something happened to me so that you could— still be happy. I wrote it down. We did that together. Your father was a witness."

You are a coward, Nathan hears. But he throws a sweeping glance around the room. The flowers, it turns out, are saying nothing at all.

"But I can't depend on you, Nathan. I have taken back my piece of Roatán. All of it. There is nothing you can do. The will is done. It's with my things. You get nothing. I want you to know I have seen to it. You will get nothing."

Nathan swallows, takes back his hand, his plane ticket, his vision of white sand, and clutching it all moves back to the chair at Maria's feet. She opens a Bible to a particular spot, most of the lines scored under, the margins darkened with notes. "For the wrath of God, Nathan, is revealed from heaven against all ungodliness and unrighteousness of men, who hold the truth—" She clears her throat. "The invisible things of the world are clearly seen"—looking up to train her gaze on Nathan, now closely examining his fingernails—"and who changed the truth of God into a lie, and worshiped and served the creature more than the creator who is blessed forever amen. For this cause God gave them up until vile affections, fornication, wickedness, covetousness, maliciousness, envy, murder, debate, deceit, malignity, whisperers, backbiters, *haters* of God, Nathan! spiteful, proud, boasters, inventors of evil things." Whispering now: "Disobedient, Nathan." She levels at him a disdainful stare, and continues by heart: "Who knowing the judgment of God, that they which commit such things are worthy of death, not only do the same, but have pleasure in them that do them, Nathan, *fornication*, Nathan! Do not. Do not—"

Nathan is sweating viciously. His eyes have shut.

Maria closes the Bible, her withered pinky finger marking the place. "Genesis. Your book, Nathan. The race of men whom I have created, I will wipe them off the face of the earth—man and beast and reptile and birds. I am sorry I ever made them." She nods. "Amen."

Maria leaves the Bible on her chest like an offering. "We are all God's children," she says.

"We could well be," Nathan replies hoarsely.

"Father Cleary helped me to see."

"He's not even Catholic."

"What does it matter what he is," Maria snaps. She calms, smiles. "I did want you to see, too. But you are too late. Praise God, I want Father Cleary to bury me. I want him to put me in the ground. And I want people to know who I was and what I did. I want Benny to know who I was. There is so much to be learned from my life." She covers her eyes. "But I won't be able to tell anyone what it is."

Maria trembles with comprehension. Glimpses of inconceivable dark, outer space, the misunderstood distances beyond the sun—a better and better view. Then a bitter expression crosses her eyes. She has seen something at the end of the bed. Her lips purse: it is Nathan. She opens her mouth to say something, deliver a final blow, then stops herself—

They both have heard it, and they stiffen at the same time, as dogs will at the first detection of danger: mad singing, hooting, sputtering laughter. The silhouette in the gauzy curtain rises out of the shadowbed and stands atop it and begins to sway, tubes and tape waving about the face, emitting a tra-la-la medley of childhood ditties.

Nathan focuses on a point in space over Maria, his face drained of all embarrassment and contempt. Maria, though, sits upright in bed, facing the curtain, enraptured. She watches the silhouetted contortions with courteous, even studious, attention.

Two residents and two male nurses, big men with broad backs and thick arms, come, and wielding a long syringe subdue Maria's neighbor, holding her until she goes limp and falls silent. They tie her down and reattach her tubes and tape them, then leave. Their footsteps fade down the corridor.

A last-minute bleat—Nathan grabs for his beeper but finds it with nothing to add. Then silence. The silence that comes after a loud noise; a strange, bad quiet that has the feel of permanence, as though the woman has not been put down but murdered.

The shadowbed is flat and still. Maria looks with weary suspicion toward the stillness, searching the translucent curtain for signs of life. Nathan watches the curtain himself, but as a child will keep an eye on the kitchen door while raiding a jar of honey, he stands, lifts the phone again, dials. He listens for a ring, then his own voice, "You have fifteen seconds to terminate this call—" Wincing, he brings the receiver to his hip, where his voice murmurs softly against the wool tweed. He is hating this. He counts out the fifteen seconds, lightly replaces the receiver, "Hey," he says to her gently. He bends near, remembering her in the morning before she washed. She was savage, full of rage, rampant with grace. Now she won't answer him. For a moment he believes she isn't alive. She lies weightless and silent and her body hidden. "Hey," he says again. She blinks. He tucks the top hem of the blanket under her shoulder, though he doesn't know why, except that it feels right. He touches her cheek with his fingertips. "I have to go," he says.

Still, the body under the covers and the tufts of hair on her head don't move. Though her eyes see. They have lost the glaze, and they are huge, outsized in her new head. She takes everything in through there, sight, sound, touch. Nathan knows he should stay but he can't repel the urge to leave, as though something is pulling him, something from out of the ground.

"Maria. I have to, I must, go."


Paper cups full of steam in both hands, Santos steps off the boardwalk onto the beach. A crowd has gathered at the waterline around a pen of yellow caution tape. The uniform cops there wander the perimeter, their flashlights dragging circles of light in the sand. Streaks of snow, as if the air is filled with hay. Beyond, the harbor's backwash bares pink lips of foam. Noise of boiling water, the frenzied clang of buoys. Thunder has begun to blast away far offshore.

Barbados, who had raced ahead, emerges out of the crowd and strides forward. But he is not picking his nails, blowing his nose, looking up, away, into the sky for his multitude of distractions.

"Why us—?" Santos begins.

"We have a situation here," Barbados says. The look on his face is new. There is none of the usual calm or active disinterest when they find their corpses. In the beginning there was horror and morbid fascination and numb voyeurism. Once there was pity. Now, at the scene, they give their cadaver as much attention as a shoe that needs tying. But Barbados is agitated. The two of them stand shapeless in their overcoats, their backs to the wind.

Santos tests his cup rim against his lower lip and blows. "Whose?" he asks.

Barbados aims his finger, Yours.

Santos hands him his cup and squints again at the mound lying motionless in the sand and begins to walk. There is little but the minor squalls of snow in the air, no shout, no murmur. He ducks under the caution tape. The other cops stop what they are saying. Santos looks and they look away. So Barbados has told them. Santos doesn't know what was said or why, and he'd just as soon walk away from here as find out who else in his precinct got found on this day besides the South American who fell from his ride to paradise, the runaway wife killed in a squatter's shack, the Russian paperhanger whose throat was cut from ear to ear then kicked ten flights into space. Tagged and printed and photographed and zipped into plastic sleeves in stairwells and bars and salt marshes and parked cars and subway tunnels, finally in that state they will not need to explain. No longer capable of transgression, free from the forest of perils.

The darkened afternoon is ripped away. Noonlight, handheld, explodes from the boardwalk. A reporter stands clutching her mike with one hand and the collar of her trench coat with the other. Other news vans have pulled up, their antennas telescoping skyward. Here, the silent crowd is scared and excited, craning their necks. There, kids mug for the cameras. In the klieg lights Santos watches his shadow lie down at his feet, stretching toward the waterline. He reaches for the plastic sheeting over the face. All eyes on him, he feels like a character in a play with cast and props but no script. He is a sucker, a dupe. This no job. How does it turn out this time? He is here, he now understands, to see someone he knows.

**7 P.M.** Night, and the lights of New York expose a curdled, festering sky. Snow sifts over the city, filling dents in car tops and windowsill flowerpots, purifying the trash in the street. White lattice collects on the sewers. Snow touches the manhole covers, sits softly and is gone, leaving black circles in the street, screw holes where the city is held together. Somewhere a sanitation truck fitted with a plow recedes block to block, scraping the slush down to rails and old cobbles entombed by skins of asphalt. Though only dinnertime the streets are filled with a midnight vacancy, as though the city lies under curfew.

Claire brushes the grease and crumbs from her palms and holds out her hand. Ruth takes it uncertainly, shifting her briefcase to her other hand, then spreads her coat over her stool.

"Ah, the old drink," Ruth says happily, eyeing Claire's glass. "Martini for me, too," she calls down the bar. "Another?" she asks Claire.

How is the glass empty already? Should she? She hates to drink on Sundays—she's always thought it a bad sign. But as long as Errol is gone she's made up her mind to do what is necessary. Claire lifts her empty glass and gives the Greek a little wave with it.

"Ruth, thank you for coming—" she begins, then stops herself, feeling pathetic that she beeped her, obviously to deliver some well-planned speech. But her strategy and poise have evaporated in the bar light. "Can you tell me what he has done with his—?"

"Life?" Ruth fills in with a snort, picking at her frilly-frumpy white shirt, then shrugs and delivers one of Nathan's own expressions of helpless wonder, like a kid sister who will despise what she's learned but use it anyway. Her mimicry is so obvious, Claire turns away, embarrassed for her. So this is what Nathan's been doing. Though he and Ruth couldn't be sleeping together. First of all, she's stuck around, or he's let her. And then there's the matter of his little habit, his geographical devotions. Ruth, obviously, is disqualified. It is her compact heaviness, her hushed, mannered way—a little shrug, her sudden silences—of punishing with her disapproval.

"I hear you're well," Ruth says. "I always liked Legal Aid myself—"

But Claire politely waves the subject away. She knows well the patronizing compliments that come next. Though by now her work is like any other, unheroic and time-consuming. It all seems a conspiracy to reward her for her inertia. "I took a case from him today."

"Did you," Ruth says, as if she'd already known. And she has, Claire is sure. Ruth and her spy's clubby demeanor, her transparent smile. Homely, so plain, so oppressively plain as to make her invisible. She was built for surveillance.

"Gross negligence." Claire is fuming. "He just abandoned another client. How does he keep it up? How do you keep it up, working for him?"

"Not *for* him," Ruth insists. "Just when he needs some help and I have the time. And Nathan has always treated me well."

"He always did."

"He pays me too much."

"I'm sure." Claire smiles with recognition. Those tips he always left. Waiters and cabbies and the Chinese delivery boys in the dead of night, making a bargain of *their* affection. As at a store's liquidation, buying up whatever was on sale just because he could, treating his merchandise better than he treated his actual human beings.

Claire lifts her fingers, offering the thick air a cigarette. Still, though, Nathan did always foot the whole rent, pay for the movie, and the midnight waiters at Gambone's, the *zuppa di giorno,* the baskets and baskets of bread, the espressos, gaining weight before her very eyes. Even then he sat there, overweight, a mobster-in-training, with the vest and the pocket watch and his stomach swelling through the suspenders. Fat wads of cash, though it was mostly twenties wrapped in a hundred or two, all of it for show, while his lawyering was bringing in nickels and dimes. Always just a baby step ahead of the collection agencies. The details of life, the bills and RSVPs and grocery lists, bored him. It was the grandiose that lured him. He was operatic. He performed when the lights were on. He lived on praise. He lived—brilliantly, she always thought—on credit, on air.

"So why don't you just call him?" Ruth asks.

"Who says I didn't? You can't reach him. And when you do, he won't call back. He never called back."

Ruth tips her head. "That's true."

Claire permits herself a laugh, letting down her guard for Ruth though she never felt it go up. She pats her old law school–mate's pudgy fingers. "Why should that have changed?"

A pained look crosses Ruth's face. "He needs to see people now."

"He needs," Claire repeats, trying it out on her tongue. It tastes like a joke. Nathan needs. "What for?"

But Ruth is into the bar mix, rummaging around for something, a missing ingredient. "His friends—"

"I'm not—don't call me that. His friend. Does he even mention me?"

The hitch in Ruth's voice says no, though Ruth says, "Here and there."

Here and there. Claire watches the speech she prepared shredding, spinning like confetti in her drink. So unthreatening, so respectable, Ruth is the perfect front, the perfect accomplice. A woman who asks nothing. She's always had that mind like a steel trap. No wonder Nathan likes her around.

"We've all been friends a long time," Ruth says.

Claire raises an eyebrow. "Have we?"

"I can't speak for him."

"You mean you won't. You know what he does. You can probably put him away all by yourself." An irresistible thought comes to her: "Maybe that's just what you're doing."

Ruth sighs, weary. "I don't know what you're talking about. Do you?"

"I don't need to. There was always something. I knew when Milton took him in that it was the end. He was all right on his own. He would have made a hell of a lawyer."

"He is."

Claire looks up sharply.

"In his way," Ruth suggests. "But it's true, too, that you don't see everything he does. He has his pro bono cases, like everyone else. You know that in his heart he is a saint."

"We're all saints in our own hearts," Claire replies.

She lifts her head, suddenly, at a sound. Across the river, above the South Street Seaport and the cluster of tall ships the city keeps chained to the docks, balloons of lavender smoke drift like thoughts toward open water. Fireworks, celebrating—she can't imagine what. The overcast a flashing riot, the skyscrapers half disappeared up in the clouds like splintered amputations. The city seems under attack. Downriver, the triple-decker ferry drifts away from its mooring, hunched low and dark like a refugee ship escaping to the safer ground of Staten Island.

They watch a minute in silence.

"Tell me, does he even know he had a son?" Claire asks, realizing, perhaps, the true reason she called Ruth.

Ruth turns her head. "Benny?"

"Benny?"

"But Benny's not his. He couldn't be—"

Across the water, overhead, sail the little gray parachutes of clouds from the fireworks.

"—Nathan's son."

"Of course not." Claire looks at Ruth, unconsciously watching her, the frilly bow at the neck, the brown bob circling her ears, the piercing black eyes. To read her face you'd need a map. "God, you can be beautiful. What a fool Nathan is."

Ruth isn't even blushing. "You have a child? You and—"

"But of course you knew."

Ruth says nothing.

"You knew I was pregnant, Ruth. I know you. You understand everything, you have all the information. You *hoard* information. And you don't give out a thing. That leaves you in charge. You pull the strings. I like that. I respect that in a woman."

Ruth gives no reaction, betraying nothing.

"So you knew," Claire continues on. "Though not many did. I'm not sure anyone did. I didn't even tell my parents."

"Baptists, I remember."

"They don't want to know. And I hid it well, then took that leave. Though anyone who *cared* to know could have seen—"

She looks at Ruth, amazed. "Isn't it extraordinary, how much is right in front of us, how truth is right there, and we don't see it, won't see it, despite ourselves, just because we don't *want* to? We look right *through* it. How powerful we are, Ruth. How utterly, utterly *magical*."

Ruth is saying nothing. Her eyes are casting about for something to grab on to, something safe, something cleaner. Which surprises Claire. This is just the kind of scene Ruth specializes in: barriers breaking, soft spots exposed, vulnerabilities, and Ruth coming in to sweep up, collect information, and clean, clean, clean.

Claire, watching herself in the mirror, is reduced before her own eyes to the status of her own—and only—witness. Her testimony, flawed, raw, sentimental, will have to be revised to do anybody—even herself—any good.

How lonely we are, she thinks.

"You know, I actually once had an idea," she says. "I don't know why. I've always dreamed of having a farm somewhere with

Nathan. A real one, with that blue silo they have now with the American flag painted on the side. A red barn, of course, an old pickup truck."

"Nathan hates the country," Ruth says with a wife's nonchalant bitterness.

"He does have that East Hampton house," Claire points out. "That mansion, that hideous gargantuan thing. That Sheetrock palace, as sturdy as a house of cards."

"It's beautiful in its way."

"Big enough for a family of ten plus servants, if that's beauty."

"He has all those gardens but never weeds it. All that lawn and doesn't mow it. He even has a pool."

Claire's eyes are blurred with tears. She is laughing, she thinks. "But he can't swim."

"Hates the water."

"Does he even own it outright yet? He probably doesn't even know. There are so many things he used to own, or owns, or thinks he owns. Though all he really has are those stashes in his closets and drawers, the rolls of cash and all those Rolexes, in his suit jackets for god's sake." Her martinis are finally beginning to take pleasurable effect. Claire gives a snort. "Sorry, it's just the idea of Nathan knee-deep in the rhubarb, in overalls and boots and a John Deere hat, a shovel in those soft little hands of his, digging into the manure. All his Armani suits sealed in plastic in the closet. It's almost too much to imagine."

Ruth is laughing, too, but embarrassed, her little dark pouched eyes glinting, beaded and distant.

"What is it?" Claire asks her. "What's wrong?"

"I think of him differently. Maybe as he should be."

"Ah." Claire spins back to the bar and eagerly swallows what is left of her martini. "And what way is that?" But there will be no reply. "You love him," she says flatly. "That's why you put up with everything you do. Though I don't see how you can. After a while, I couldn't. He would have liked the farm, though," she says, drying her eyes. "Just to own it, like his record collection. Own it just because he could. And he'd have hired some

Guatemalan to run it for him, the wife of some client doing fifteen-to-life. And her daughters, of course. Can't forget daughters. Especially *Guatemalan* daughters."

Ruth clears her throat. "Nathan never told me you had a child."

"Nathan doesn't know. But you did, didn't you?"

Ruth presses on, as a good lawyer would: "Does Errol?"

But Claire's attention has been tugged back to the TV. "My god, isn't that—?" A stunning face in high-school portrait, a strange hybrid of Hispanic and some blood that gives the girl green, bottomless eyes, virtuous, maddeningly off-line to the right; that gummy blue background behind every adolescent's head; her white shirt buttoned chastely to the neck, a tiny silver crucifix looped through the collar. Prim as a nun the day she marries Christ. The face vanishes, spliced into a long shot of Coney Island and its ferris wheel and its long and vacant boardwalk. Finally a pan across the icy beach, focusing on a shrouded corpse. "Isabel Santos of 147th Street, Manhattan," the anchor says with the swagger of one calling a horse race, "a gruesome discovery made earlier today by chilly members of the Polar Bear Club."

"Oh—" Ruth has clamped her hand to her mouth.

"*Errol's* Isabel? My god—" Claire pictures Errol's sister, Milton's secretary, mastering the phones, making the coffee, collating the depositions, then sashaying into Milton's office for *dictation,* the door locking behind her, to actually do god knows what.

Ruth is on her feet. "The phone?" she asks the bartender.

Claire can only stare. "Call Nathan? But they have already—he must already know. After all, they called Errol."

Against the wall near the johns, Ruth dials one number and says nothing. She dials another and turns her back, cupping the mouthpiece with her hand. She hurries back, her coat already on. "I couldn't get him."

"Then who was that on the phone?" Claire asks, then waves off the answer, for a moment having forgotten whom she is dealing with. "I'm sorry."

"I have to go."

"Of course. Some other time."

Claire looks up at the bang of a door and an icy gust and Ruth's hunched bulk shrinking in the frame of the window, trudging away through the snow.

Santos is on the sidewalk before Barbados has stopped the car. The tenements run like hedges, none the same yet all alike. Gaps among the buildings like punched teeth. Arms full of flowers and eyes crippled by memories, Santos lets himself in the front door and leaves it open for Barbados. The derelict building. Upstairs, in the apartment in which he was a boy, plain rooms, pressed-tin ceilings, rough-hewn floors. A gust of wind moans through the windows, prowling room to room through the puckered-glass transoms, making them chatter. Somewhere a clock ticks. His chest is tight, his throat rattling. He goes to his pocket for his inhaler. The clock tocks. Something more than time passes here. The little spray of medicine tricks him: his eyes clear, his lungs rise, his veins run.

"She was clean," he says, turning at the door. "I still don't get that."

Barbados touches the center of Santos's back. "The examiner will know everything in a few hours."

"They did the core temp? Sometimes they pass on the core temp."

"They never pass on it. They didn't pass on it now."

"They pass on it. Believe me. When they don't give a shit."

"About her, they give a shit," Barbados says.

"You saw her nails. They were clean. Do you get that? You telling me she didn't fight? That girl didn't fight? She fights everything. She fights all the time. There were marks. She was fucked up. You saw the marks—"

"Errol."

They watch him from the couch, gathered there below the X-ray light of the fluorescent ring, as for a family photograph. The sister he has left, his mother's hand on her shoulder. Others, old friends and neighbors, line the walls. Here and there, displayed proudly on old, unworthy furniture, gleam the expensive gifts Milton Stein has given Mrs. Santos, his long-time secretary: vases and wood boxes, a brass lamp; in the corner, a stereo system with all of the doo-dads. A neighbor raises a hand, a solemn gesture.

Santos kneels before his mother, rests the bouquet in her lap and takes her limp and clammy hand. "Momma," he begins.

She blinks some signal. Beside her, on the end table, a lush display of flowers. Wildflowers, carnations, poinsettia, their cards. Blood-red roses, *Milton Stein and Nathan Stein*. Santos fingers the card and snaps it from its string and hands it up to Barbados.

"They're fast," Santos says.

"It is their business to know."

Santos's mother slides a finger along his hairline, contemplating. "What was she doing out there?"

Since he saw Isabel lying on the beach he has tried to see her face in his mind but he cannot. He remembers her hand, like a tiny creature in his. He remembers tugging her through a schoolyard fence in the muffled quiet of a winter's day, deploying her to the outfield on a pond of asphalt as blank and featureless as airport tarmac. A playground strewn with old snow, glittering puddles of broken glass. Her even breaths hanging before her in transfiguring balloons. He remembers that while the boys moved listlessly in grimy parkas, Isabel in her white snowsuit scurried here and there, flailing, giggling, blocking the ball with her shins. Errol hit the ball high into the gloom, Isabel staggered beneath, face to sky, hands outstretched, waiting to cradle anything that might need catching.

"Momma, who did she go out with last night?"

His mother is weeping. "She didn't say."

He looks to his other sister.

"Has she been going out with somebody?"

Nothing. A dull shake of the head.

Santos presses his eye with the back of a hand. "I have to call Claire," he says.

At the kitchen table he rolls a bottle of beer in his hands. Barbados puts down the phone. "Nathan Stein didn't call in, but someone else did."

"You call his home?"

"Yes."

"The office?"

"Yes."

"His service?"

"Someone else returned the call."

"Someone else."

"Oliver Schreck."

"Schreck? I don't want a call from Schreck."

"He says he has an idea about Coney Island."

Santos raises a palm, warding it off. "He's zero. He's always been nothing but zero."

"But he called."

"What is he, Stein's boy now?"

"We're going to pass it on in the morning, Errol."

"Just tell me why he's returning Nathan's business."

Barbados sighs. "He didn't say."

"We'll talk to him tonight."

"They're going to put someone else on it tomorrow."

The specter of his sister behind the reception desk of the venerable law office of Stein & Stein, where his mother had sat for years before her. How close she'd come to working for him, too, had he accepted the place Milton offered. In their hands, she quickly took on that lawyerly quiet and seemed neither happy nor unhappy. To Santos she was vaguely cold, an old teammate traded on. Different manager now, different league. Now she is a rag of meat, a puddle in the sand.

There is a knock on the door. Someone says it is the funeral man and Santos begins to cry. He didn't know he was going to and he is ashamed. Barbados looks away. Muffled weeping from the living room. Santos lets his neck go and closes his eyes, but in the dark, guided only by vague notions of human frailty, he does not know what to look for, little even of why.

———

Nathan is off, trailing vapor, striding downtown, his watch aimed at the light. Snow slithers dry underfoot, dusting the cars, the balconies, casting them as marble statues. A bitter draft starts and stops, rattling the trash in the doorways. He stops midstep, making a sudden move for his belt, drawing his beeper. His cellphone appears in his other palm. He pulls its antenna and pokes. An operation that seems vaguely military, like pulling the pin on a grenade.

"No, Serena, you can't meet me here. Did I see what? . . . What boat? I told you, I've been out all day . . . From Puerto Rico? . . . A brother? I didn't know you had a brother . . . no, it couldn't have been. Listen to me. Puerto Ricans don't have to sneak across the water into the States. They're honorary citizens. They're not Haitians or Cubans in some broken-down wooden bathtub, or some Mexican roasting in the engine of a banana truck in Tijuana. They can come to America in a *plane* like human beings."

At the creaking of tires against the snow, Nathan catches a glimpse of a red sedan passing slowly along the curb. Some uneasy flame relights in his gut. Those faces in the window from this afternoon, and other afternoons. And these faces, hovering in the fogged window, snapping away as the car passes, "—Isabel," he thinks he hears Serena say, then flinches, clicks Serena off, and walks on.

Inside Jackie's, an inch and a half of hundreds in his palm, wrapped like a spring roll in a few twenties—a chunk from his fifty-thousand-dollar day, and he hasn't done a thing. What a country. The bartender comes quickly. The shelves are thinly stocked, the bottles well spaced. Nathan steps up but says nothing. Instead, with his hands pressed against the bar's edge, he loses himself momentarily in the opposing mirrored walls. They yield reflection within reflection of a woman past her prime pitching forward over an imaginary pony. The debris of a great dream, the Joffrey Ballet, Balanchine. Her false eyelashes are coming loose. To her right on the short stage, two other women spin on fireman's poles in a urine-colored haze to a medley of rock songs fifteen years old.

"Scotch rocks," Nathan finally manages to say, his elbows landing on the bar. The drink comes and he drains off half the glass, breathes, then drinks off the rest. He now feels himself in a position to contemplate, for a minute, the possibility that everything is normal. He pulls the legal envelope from his jacket pocket and leaves it on the bar before him, stares at it—and clutches, again, the beeper on his belt. Again it is Errol Santos NYPD with his attendant numbers, home, work, beeper, cell-phone, a play for urgency. Already, he can see the conversation. He can see Coney Island.

With a wave from the bartender the show behind Nathan has stopped, and as if by agreement most of the men avert their eyes. The dancers gather pocketbooks, stockings, hairbrushes, rotating to the right they carry their belongings in their arms like piles of laundry. At the farthest edge the last one steps into her slippers and down out of the lights to the floor, chaffing along the bar, tightening her silk robe around her waist. Off stage she is older, without resources.

Nathan catches the bartender's sleeve. "Mind if I make a call?" reaching for the bar phone while the music starts up again, he dials, lifts his watch, counts the seconds.

But the drinkers are spinning on their stools. Something odd is happening. The silence has brought a new girl out of the back through a curtain of beads. Halter top and pleated plaid skirt. Her adolescent knees. A field hockey captain, a Catholic-school girl, her face heavily painted, a touch of glitter, a screen of black hair across the brow. She steps onto stage left while the other two dancers turn their backs and put on for the men in the next sector the same clothes they had taken off for the men in the one before; as if they are not a mere five or six feet away but in another room. The new girl dances badly, stiff, out of sync with the music. Tall, gangly, her long arms outstretched, her lips pursed in a precocious smooch, she can't be more than seventeen. She's in over her head. It may well have been only hours since she was accosted by Jackie himself at the Port Authority gate, fresh off a bus from Gary or Omaha.

Nathan dials Santos's message service and leaves an address in the East Eighties with an hour that may or may not correspond to the time at hand or any time in the near future.

The girl is nude to the waist. While she moves her hips in her underpants, the other two dancers throw her dirty looks. But the girl's eyes are not unsure, unamused; they work the room with haphazard confidence. Nathan thinks it isn't impossible that her night on stage at Jackie's—her debut—is no more than a lark, a perverse holiday from the tedium of the Dalton School or Spence or her freshman year at NYU, or even her outlay against a lost bet made at her best friend's birthday party.

Nathan sits with his elbows cocked behind him on the bar. He believes he understands. The girl is putting them on. He enjoys a good joke, even at his own expense. Bills fall over her feet like leaves.

A tightness, though, has begun in the back of his neck and slips over his head like a hood. It is the sight in the open door: Oliver Schreck in green blazer and cowboy boots strides in reaching for his belt. He unclips and waves his beeper with one hand while shaking Nathan's with the other. His palm like raw meat coated in pretzel crumbs.

"It's fucking Johnny again, Nathan. It's the fifth time in the last two hours. I thought you were going out there today."

His accent is heavy on the outer boroughs. The Bronx, Brooklyn. Thick-wristed, balding, under his blazer he has the thick, sloped shoulders and long dangling arms of a fighter. He knows the streets. It is easy to see he never left them, P.S. 132, Queens College, New York Law nights while working in his dad's deli.

Nathan shakes his head. "Too busy. I've been crazy all day."

Schreck waves for the bartender, pointing into Nathan's glass for another round. "Because his family really wants to know what happened to the bond money."

"It's in transit."

But Schreck isn't listening. He snatches at a bowl of pretzels. "Well, thanks for inviting me down. Haven't been here in ages."

"I didn't invite you, Oliver. You asked where I was going to be, and here you are."

Schreck smiles, his mouth full of mash. "So Coney Island. How'd that go?"

Nathan turns aside. "Zip."

"Zip? I thought—"

"Small fry. Nothing. I let it go."

"And getting you out there Sunday morning. What's Krivit thinking?"

Nathan looks at him. "You tell me."

"That fat fuck," Schreck says, spraying pretzel. "Fuck him. We don't need him. It's you and me, Nathan. And Milton. We all have better things to be doing now."

Nathan half-heartedly raises his glass. "Okay, Oliver."

"So who are you meeting?" Schreck asks.

"Some bad guy is threatening to pay my retainer."

Schreck turns, elbows cocked on the bar, and surveys the room. "Which one is it?"

"He's still in the Tombs. He's sending someone."

"Last week Johnny tried to get me out to Rikers by promising me a pair of tickets to a samba fest. That or ten pounds of veal from his brother the butcher." He drinks his drink. "But hey, who cares. Screw Johnny and his family. With Milton doing that rape case now—"

Nathan raises his head. "Rape?"

"What do you mean? That Riverside Drive thing."

"What's Milton got to do with—"

"You know, that advertising exec getting snatched jogging along the river, pulled into the trees. They banged the shit out of—"

"I know the—"

"What do they call it? Whupping? Whipping?"

"Wilding."

"Good term. Fits them. Fucking animals." Schreck's masticating jaws pause at their work, and his eyes, studying Nathan's face, betray the rules of a new game. "And where's Isabel by the way? Shitty time to disappear. She's not answering her beeper."

A silence between them. Nathan believes Schreck is examining him out of the corner of his eye. He is sure of it. Or is he? Self-consciously he covers his wrist with his hand. Schreck is waiting. Schreck, he is certain, is calculating.

"Isabel—" Schreck begins.

"But what does Milton—"

"What are you talking about? Don't you talk to your own father? It was two days ago. It's been all over the news for over forty-eight hours. Milton Stein of Stein and Stein and—"

"Forty-eight hours? Where have I been?"

"A good question."

"And what do you mean Stein and Stein and—?"

Schreck throws back his head and drops in a handful of pretzels. "Look, you need to expand your horizons. I'm telling you that store-front office in Washington Heights is a great idea. You need fresh blood."

Nathan, smiling strangely, looks past Oliver into the middle distance.

"You should really listen to me, Nathan."

"I'm listening. Who asked him?"

"Who asked who?"

"My father, Oliver. Riverside Drive. I thought those kids all signed lawyers already."

"Did. They *did* all sign lawyers. But *which* lawyers, Nathan. The question is did they sign the *right* lawyer."

"Which one, Oliver, which one is it?"

Schreck beams with mischief. He throws in another fistful of pretzels and chews slowly, savoring the moment. He swallows, wipes his mouth with the back of his hand and lifts his glass. "Williams," he says, throwing back the shot.

"Williams. Jesus."

Schreck lifts his hand for a high five, but Nathan's arm is stayed by his drink.

"Fucking A," Schreck says, his hand chopping the air. "I mean, wouldn't you know it? The fucking ring-leader. Christ, Nathan, today the answering service had to give a whole operator to our line alone. The *Today* show. Charlie Rose. Ted Koppel himself called to get him for *Nightline*. They all think Milton's some vault of knowledge about the seething rage in Harlem, the war between the races, the continuous pulse of violence and greed undercutting urban America. What did Koppel say? Martin Luther King's true legacy? So this poor advertising chick goes jogging one night to blow off steam, she blew a multi-million-dollar account, whatever, she gets on the walkway in the eighties, not so smart maybe, but hey, it's America, why shouldn't she? And they sweep down on her at 102nd like a pack of wolves and drag her kicking and screaming. Christ, Nathan, one of them jammed a fucking Coke bottle—"

"Oliver." Heads are turning down the bar. Though it is, Nathan realizes, a pot of gold. All this will be, he himself will be, very public.

Schreck lowers his chin but not his voice. "I mean, just think about it for a minute, Nathan. Some fat Jewish lawyer driving around in his Rolls rising to the defense of some poor, abused, fatherless, fifteen-year-old walking time bomb, a vacuum of power venting his rage on some young white advertising-exec prodigy, the symbol of the white marketing establishment. Can't you see it, Nathan? Oprah. Donahue. The Daily News wants your father to write a running column during the whole thing. But of course he can't. It's client-attorney privilege. It's conflict of interest."

Nathan is looking at him. "You have it all figured out."

"Me?" Schreck says, his hands spread on his chest in fake humility. "What's to figure? The animals went down like a line of dominoes. They tripped all over themselves to confess. One of them was still wearing the girl's Harvard sweatshirt, her panties practically hanging out of his belt. I mean, come *on*. Even Milton agrees."

"You talked to Milton?"

"Of course I talked to Milton. Didn't you talk to Milton? Don't you talk to your own father?"

Nathan, lifting his drink, hides behind his glass.

"I've never seen him so excited. Who gives a shit what they *do* to Williams. It's what Milton's going to *say*. It's what he's going to *look* like. It's the exposure, Nathan. It's all about exposure."

The barrage of thoughts incites red patches high on Nathan's cheeks. He sets down his glass and touches, again, the wound on his wrist, as if to connect the worry itself, news of Isabel hitting the streets, the papers, with his base instinct: he is, after all, still Milton's son, territorial and protective. The timing is bad. He knows this rape case will turn out to have been everything. The old life will have ended here, and the new life will have begun. Isabel will be a bad coincidence.

Schreck has rested a hand on Nathan's shoulder. "About that storefront. I was talking to someone today—"

"Give it a rest."

"No pressure or nothing, Nathan, but it's a guaranteed gold mine. Got people working on things already. Especially after they see your dad on the tube, they'll flood that office thinking Stein and Stein and Schreck are direct emissaries from the Vatican wangling truth and justice and green cards for all. I need you. I need your Spanish."

"*You* need."

"I'll give you a cut. A percentage off the top. Right off the top. In or out?"

"A percentage. Stein and Stein and *Schreck,* and you're going to give me a—"

At the faint, almost reluctant bleat from his beeper, Nathan peers into his jacket:

I knew you'd be late. You promised. You

—falls off the edge of the screen just as the beeper vibrates again for the second installment, but Nathan, not bothering, rebuttons his jacket.

Schreck jabs the air. "Was that Johnny?"

"What? Yeah," Nathan says, holding his beeper still.

"I swear to god he's going to kill himself if he stays in. And his family. Jesus, what a bunch of wackos."

"I'm going out to Rikers. Not to see Johnny. I'm going to see the girls."

Schreck shrugs. "It's your head. I mean it's *his* head, but it's on your shoulders. Or whatever. Who you have lined up tonight?"

"Amparo."

Oliver snaps his fingers. "That reminds me. Here's another one." He drops an envelope on the bar, pointing at the torn edge with his knuckle, his eyes averted, tossing back a fistful of pretzels. "I didn't see it was for you, buddy boy. Sorry. You know how it is. A thousand envelopes come in to the office, you rip them all open, don't even look."

The envelope is addressed with sixth-grade precision, the *i*'s dotted with smiley faces, return stamped: *Amparo Guzmán, #934782, Rose M. Singer Penitentiary for Women, Rikers Island.*

Nathan skims the letter. Amparo thanks him for everything he is doing for her. Her family in Bogotá tells everyone they know about the great lawyer from New York. She misses him. All she does is think about him. She has more clients for him. She will suck his cock. She dreams about sucking his cock. When she gets out she will give him the sex of his life. Everything he wants. She loves him. When she gets out he will be with a real woman for the first time.

Nathan raises his eyes. It sounds, to him, like a threat.

Schreck has draped his arm around his neck. "But if you don't want to think about Johnny you might want to think about his family. They're all over me about that hundred grand. What am I going to tell them?"

"That it's being processed," Nathan says, peeling off Schreck's arm.

"I mean, they want to know why it takes three months for the court to process a hundred grand. I got to tell you, I don't know what to do with them. They're not your average spics. When they find out where the money is they're not going to take it lying down."

Nathan shrugs.

"You've spent the money." Schreck looks at him. "Am I right? Tell me, am I right or what—?"

"Their boy has ten kilos of coke under their floor, Oliver. What are they going to do, sue us? Sue the big-shot law firm of Stein and Stein and Schreck? Sue the Pope's epistolary saviors?"

"I don't think—"

"Oliver, when they get to the part where they say they want a lawyer, just give them your card."

Pretzel dust rimming his lips, Schreck laughs and lifts his hand in a gesture of concession to Nathan's parting volley, allowing the matter to be put to bed where it belongs, save a last shot of his own, "I don't think they'd bother, Nathan. Because I'll tell you, between you and me," he says, and pokes Nathan in the ribs, "I think they'd rather just kill you."

Turning and pointing, as though at a passing plane, or a shooting star, Schreck waves down the bartender.

Nathan watches him, sober, suddenly. Suddenly, not even tired. "Oliver, what did you come down here for? Why did you want to see me? What couldn't wait?"

A plastic smile, poured and now cooling, sets on Schreck's face. Eyes open—not missing a thing—teeth bared, he slaps Nathan on the shoulder. "Nothing, buddy boy. No reason at all. Just happy to see you."

Again the dancers cease mid-writhe and kneel for their heap of belongings and rotate, the one farthest over stepping into her slippers and down and zipping across the floor along the bar. A new girl surfaces out of the beaded curtain. The off-duty dancer stops in front of Nathan. Her eyes are red-rimmed. She lifts a knuckle to her nose and sniffs, and staring walleyed at Schreck, withdraws from her purse a packet wrapped in butcher's paper the size of a pound of swiss cheese and slides it into the pocket of Nathan's jacket. She doesn't look, Nathan says nothing, and she turns abruptly for the back as though she's forgotten something there, as though the phone in back has rung.

Schreck slaps the bar. "Stay there, be right back," he says, patting his pocket for keys. "I have something to show you."

He runs out, but his presence lingers, like an offensive smell.

Nathan probes the package in his pocket. He pats his jacket for the shape of the envelope. In the mirror he sees Isabel on the boardwalk turning a sloppy pirouette, much too drunk. Her mouth open, so beautifully, in laughter, or a scream—

Schreck returns, steering before him a young girl wearing day-glo lipstick and a little black dress. "This is what I mean," he says, winking, his voice sliding to a whisper. "Consuela wants a green card. What was I telling you?"

The girl eyes Nathan's scotch. Nathan hands it over and she drinks it down thirstily. "Where the hell were you keeping her, leashed up outside?"

Schreck smiles. "Mr. Philanthropist all of a sudden. She was in the car. Don't worry so much. What am I, an animal? The engine was running. But, look, Nathan, can't you see it now? A line of Dominican peasants around the block with hundred-dollar bills in their hands?"

Nathan looks at the girl with alarm.

"No English," Schreck says. "*No habla inglés,* hey?" He grins an even row of white caps at the girl, and the girl grins broadly back, her teeth ragged and gray. "We hire some law students for eight bucks an hour for the shit work," he says out of the corner of his mouth, "get some of Isabel's cousins to watch the door." He leans forward, squinting with sincerity. "Ten percent of the gross, Nathan"—chopping the air—"clean cut off the top. Overhead's my problem. Fair or what? In or out?"

Behind them the music starts again. Consuela, fingers meshed around the empty glass, steps softly to the beat.

"You feeding her, Oliver?"

"Okay. Fifteen. I'll make it fifteen. Fifteen percent, Nathan. Trouble-free dollars. You and your father's name. My work. I couldn't be more fair."

"Just get her a drink." Nathan slips away.

In the men's room, clutching his side, he reaches out and lands on the condom dispenser. He locks the stall door behind him. He has a fever, he feels it on his face like the sun. His own wavy reflection stares back from the toilet water. Crushing his thumbs in the palms of his hands, he looks about the graffitied stall. Limericks, phone numbers. Ten-inch cocks.

The pain is numbing. Laughter, anonymous, fills his head then is sucked out. He leans his ear against the wall to hear within. A vent overhead hums with cold air. His knees draw up sharply and he goes down, the porcelain sweating cold in his hands. Kicks, kicks him again. He holds himself tightly around the waist while the muscles beneath collide and wrench loose the debris down below, his mouth falling open as though he's been punched in the groin, the air rushing both ends, all of him working to expunge what? Again the dry retches burn the roof of his mouth. Then his reflection shatters, the water darkens, the drool reaches the floor. He pats his pockets and brings out the vials. Two labels made out to him, two to Maria. Shaking, he struggles with the childproof caps, finally bringing the vials up over his shoulder and down one at a time against the toilet bowl rim. Pink blue yellow ricocheting like hailstones over the floor, into the water, twirling like confetti in the loose mud. "Fuck it, fuck it." He sweeps together what he can off the sandy floor. Off the urine-stained rim into his trembling palm, picking out one of each. His eyes blurry with tears and pain he spits at the little mound of pills in his hand, spits again and overturns them into the toilet with the rest. "Fuck—*you*," he says.

Panting against the steel partition, his hair matted to his forehead, the trembling of his lips stills as he digs into his pocket, fingering the paper. The package gives with a squeeze. Cornerless. No money. Fuck. Fucking cold cuts I'll kill him, I'll have him killed. Johnny owes me, I'll just have him bumped off, kill two birds with one stone, clean off both accounts.

Working the corner he inserts his pinky and brings it up frosted, like a vanilla-topped creamsicle.

What am I? What—? He thinks for a split moment, like a flash of a bad dream, an old recollection, of all the people he owes. He thinks, briefly, of the Citibank mail sorter in her bunker in Sioux Falls distributing Visa stubs and checks and hate notes into plastic pneumatic tubes, opening a package containing a half-kilo of cocaine, unfolding the note: *To Whom It May Concern: Please accept enclosed in lieu of my debit of eight thousand fifty-four dollars and seventy-eight cents. Keep the change.*

The outside door opens. The tinny music washes in, then chokes off. Footsteps stop outside his stall. An eye peers through the crack of the door. "You all right in there?"

The footsteps retreat. The door bangs softly.

His cell-phone rings beneath his clothes and a choked bleat of sound escapes his throat. The phone rings, then rings again, then stops. It begins once more but is cut before the first ring is done. Then his belt chirps. He peels aside his jacket, hands trembling, thumbing the illumination button. His chest lights up like a flare:

Cabrón. Bastardo. It is 9 o'clock. I rain dead
roses on your bed.

**9 p.m.** Santos rehangs the pay phone and cinches his coat tight at the waist. His heels pace off the minutes, echoing past the house of detention, a highrise of crosshatched windows ringed by a skirt of razor wire. Past a row of alternating pawn shops, bail shops. Past black and padlocked storefronts. Across the river the Manhattan Municipal Building with its spires and grand arches and engraved cornice naming the old quadrants of the old city when all was wilderness. Years ago, Santos arrived there dressed in white and pinned a two-dollar flower to his young wife-to-be and an old black man with a beaten box camera took their wedding portrait against the scuffed marble.

The sky to the west shivers with lightning. Streaks of frozen rain race the snow. He turns in at a doorway and finds Barbados at a table by a window. "He's coming down," Santos says.

"That's awfully sweet of him."

"He said he's eager to help," Santos says.

"How likely is that?"

Santos edges past a dark pinball machine toward the sound of dull chopping and the beating of eggs. At the counter he grips the menu in both hands and studies it. The waitress appears tapping her pencil against her pad. "After all these years you still need to look at that?"

"No. I'm sorry. Coffee, please. A grilled cheese." He looks back at the booth but Barbados is staring out the window. "That's all."

The waitress tears off the ticket and turns to go, then stops. "You okay?"

He sightlessly watches her through her thin blue uniform: as she heads back to the grill; as she stands on one hip in a cloud of steam; as she comes back with the coffee. She sets down the cup with a click and the liquid tilts and slips over the rim and fills the saucer. She covers her mouth and contemplates the mess. Not a pretty face, but eyes that see and lips that form words and kiss a baby's moist head.

"Thank you," Santos says.

In a minute she comes back with the sandwich. Saturated with sweet butter, the filling orange and gummy, crammed with hope. Santos holds a wedge of it to his nose, closes his eyes and chews slowly, but it goes down like a wad of cotton and fills him with nothing he wants or can even imagine and his body registers nothing of it at all.

From the booth, Barbados looks over blearily. He puts one finger in his ear and jiggles it.

The door opens and lets in a cold gust.

"Sit down," Santos says.

Outside, a car sits at the curb. Pellets of exhaust ride up the back.

"Your car is running," Barbados says.

"I have someone waiting."

"You don't plan on staying long," Santos says.

"This won't take any time at all."

Oliver Schreck slides into the booth and Santos slides in after him.

"Isabel was a beautiful girl. I couldn't be more sorry, Errol."

"You said you're eager to help. How is that, Oliver?"

"Let me come straight to the point."

Barbados nods. "That's a good idea."

Santos stabs a cigarette into his mouth, frowning at the brief orange flame.

"I thought you can't smoke in these places anymore," Schreck says.

"You can't." Barbados leans forward.

"Isabel was with Nathan last night," Schreck says.

"So what," Barbados says. "They were working, on a brief or something."

"They were out."

"So they were working late and then he took her home."

"Did your mother say she came home last night?" Schreck asks Santos.

"Careful," Barbados says.

Santos drapes his arm around the back of the bench. "What are you saying, Oliver?"

"All I'm saying is that they were out."

"That's all you're saying," Barbados says.

"They've *been* out. A lot."

Santos, bent over the table, rolls the salt shaker in his palms. "That would be quite a mouthful."

"Look at Nathan's hands," Schreck says. "Look at his arms."

Santos has made a fist around the salt shaker. "Nathan has known Isabel for years."

Schreck leans back to look at him. "Isabel was a very beautiful girl. A girl with promise. Maybe she would have been a lawyer herself one day. Nathan was at Coney Island. You saw him there."

Santos looks across the table at Barbados, who holds out his hands toward Oliver Schreck. "And how do you know something like that?"

"You saw him, Errol. Did you see his hands?"

"How do you know all this?" Barbados asks.

"Did you see the marks on his arms?"

"It doesn't mean anything," Barbados says.

"But it is interesting."

Santos's eyes are locked unseeing on some spot on the wall.

"Errol?"

Santos tilts his head. "It is interesting."

The waitress brings over the coffeepot and a cup and saucer for Schreck. "You want some more coffee?"

Santos's hand is up, warding her off. "We're good."

"I wouldn't mind," Schreck says, and reaches for the cup.

But Santos intercepts Schreck's wrist and brings it down to the table and pins it there. A glass falls to the floor and is smashed. "We're good," Santos says.

The waitress returns to the counter and withdraws behind the coffee urn.

"Why are you trying to give me Nathan?" Santos says.

Schreck lifts his free hand, as if in surrender. "We've known each other a long time."

"You've known Nathan a long time, too."

"We're just talking here," Schreck says.

"I'm glad you brought that up. Why are we doing that?"

"I'm a lawyer," Schreck says.

"Is that what you are?"

"I'm obligated to give you evidence in my possession."

"You're not, actually," Santos says, "as a point of law."

"But you're telling us the truth," Barbados says. He looks at Santos. "He's a lawyer. It's the truth. He says it is."

"Absolutely," Schreck says. "I'm done here."

Barbados says, "Because you do have the right to remain silent."

"What are you, reading me my rights?"

"Don't look so worried," Barbados says. He is grinning openly. "Did you understand that part?"

"Am I under arrest?"

"Are you with me, Oliver?"

"No, I'm not."

"You have the right to consult an attorney, and to have an attorney present during any questioning now or in the future. Do you understand that?"

"You guys are fucking with me." Schreck smiles at one face then the other. "I haven't done anything wrong."

"Don't count on it," Santos says.

"If you cannot afford an attorney," Barbados says. "One will be provided for you without cost."

Schreck is sputtering. "I *am* an attorney."

"Is that so?" Barbados says.

Schreck begins to smirk. "Though I do *have* a lawyer."

"Who might that be?"

"But it's Nathan."

Silence erupts among the three of them, as if they've all just realized their part in the farce, that they could have gone right to this part, skipped the rest.

Schreck laughs with relief. "You guys are fucking with me."

Santos's eyes are dull with grief. "We could never use this conversation," he says.

Schreck lifts a shoulder. "I see a man in need."

"That's not why you're here," Barbados says.

Santos is shaking his head. "I know Nathan Stein."

"No, Detective Santos, I don't think you do."

But Santos does know Stein. He sees with perfect clarity a picture of Nathan with his arms around him and his new wife, the three leering drunkenly, smiles pasted and eyes gooey. He catches Nathan watching from the East Hampton living room across the patio, observing through two glass doors as they fucked in the yellow bug light of their room. Behind them, writhing on the wall, their silhouettes a pair of underwater swimmers dolphin-kicking in embrace. The shadows of moths flying overhead like a mute flock of birds.

They slept in that house where he lived, the weekend house listing on a hill pale and blind. Nathan had brought Santos shopping for the bed. The matching sheets, the night tables. Pick a pattern for the carpets, he'd said. Ralph Lauren. Givenchy. Nathan and his rubber-banded rolls of C-notes. Nathan was responsible for his own supply of companionship, and he summoned them one by one to his second-floor room. Agency maid. Waitress. A toll collector. Dime-store clerk. And all of them something good to look at, disarming, razor-tongued, schooled in unarticulated sorts of street intelligence. Nathan made his opening moves as in chess, well rehearsed, without hesitation, feigning interest in their mundane and clocked days. And then he offered an invitation to a swim and then dinner and then a drink on the pool deck. And then. Then night became a holiday, a celebration in honor of Nathan's catch. The speakers filled the surrounding woods with music. The four of them laughed and drank in the gurgle of the pool and the hum of its filter and the slish of Santos's new wife as she passed beneath his feet and emerged in the shallow end scaly and slick as a reptile, and Santos looked up, to the window where Nathan Stein passed with his night's reward.

And all this time there had been Claire. The lonely Claire left at home, the serious Claire left studying, loyal Claire in Louisiana to visit family and friends. Or sad Claire, merely left. Santos would have been happier with her, with any of the Claires, happy enough, as Nathan was so obviously willing to let her go.

In the morning Santos woke to find Nathan gone, or going, or just returned.

Stein and antistein.

Not actually Stein but a cardboard construction. A life-size figure of a celebrity, the kind you stand with to have your picture taken; a celebrated figure who once, many years before, when you were a child, might have been your best friend. The kind with a father for whom your mother works, cleans, takes dictation, performs duties and functions shrouded in obscure and pleasurable forms of compensation. Vases and wood boxes. Stereos.

Santos had known him most of his life, and yet in law school Stein became a kind of celebrity to him, and to Santos's sisters and parents. Hours behind schedule, he would drive up to Washington Heights in the famous father's sleek and expensive cars, a different one every month, a Mercedes, a Lincoln, a Cadillac, another Mercedes, but not the Rolls, never the Rolls. He would come straight from court where, dressed like a dandy, he'd assisted the maestro, ready on his tongue—he could hardly get through the door before it fell out of him—an impossible story about Milton's latest client, the drug dealer or thief or rapist whose guilt was beyond question but whose rights were invariably violated by the police. The Santos family rolled their eyes. Even the mother, Milton's secretary of twenty-five years, as though she hadn't been there, hadn't helped prepare the motions, taken them down, collated them, glanced them over, passed them to Nathan herself in the well of the courtroom; as though she hadn't witnessed Milton Stein's angle, Nathan's angle too now, Stein & Stein's best and most successful defense: the irrelevance of guilt in a court of law.

Nathan's lateness was less forgiven than sanctioned, as though they wouldn't have him any other way. And what was to be celebrated, a birthday, a holiday, was instantly forgotten, and the party they had been waiting for to begin, with Nathan's arrival, began. And the time would grow late, it would reach two, sometimes three, with Nathan sitting on the opposite end of the couch from Santos's father, both of them with their eyes closed, listening to selections from their favorite operas, highlights they would have chosen together from Mr. Santos's vast collection. Half drunk with wine and half with the opera, upright on the couch together, they lifted their hands in concert, conducting the same passage in the score.

Nathan seduced them all. The family's love for him, its dismissal of all the questionable things it collectively suspected—the things Mrs. Santos could confirm—was almost sexual in its blindness, in its ability to look past all they did not want to see—the already sordid, the bordering-on-criminal—to see straight through to what they'd known as chaste and pure, all that he was born with. His *soul*. They all looked on him, went to him, with the adoration for a lover returned to them after a long absence. Nathan Stein the celebrity. As though in his presence you felt—as Errol did, always, even at the end of that time—that there were things, so many things, you had yet to do or be.

Still, after Nathan left, Santos's own father would stand, unsteady with exhaustion, and point through the closed door, down the creaky stairs, into the night, between the tail-lights fading down the street. "Beware that," he said, about the boy he'd watched for years. "He sees everything and nothing."

Soon opera became Santos's own need. Not the music, but something else. He listened on his shitty little stereo with the librettos before him, as Nathan instructed. Santos wanted to learn it, to duplicate the cultured and intelligent sides of Stein. The studied knowledge of Stein. Stein. Something redeeming, something tragic. Something Downtown, something Village, something Upper East Side. To do justice to a tenement life. The deficiency being himself. He was envy. He lacked the words to describe the fundamental. He needed Nathan Stein's good looks, even their deadliness, to gain vicarious thrill. Toward Stein, toward his looks, toward the agency maids and waitresses and barrio queens he was blind devotion. Even after he married, toward Nathan's lovely fiancée, toward Claire, he was desperation. The larger reward being forgiveness. The two young men pass silently the spotlit marble of Lincoln Center and the Metropolitan Opera House and its pink and blue illuminated fountain, the rainbow arcs of water; through the pre-opera dinner crowds chaffing in their sweat-soaked evening wear, discouraged by the blundered nighttime promise of cooler temperatures; the happy-hour crush unknotting their ties and letting down their hair. Santos follows a half pace behind Nathan through these crowds and up Columbus Avenue while into Nathan's left ear he calls out his list of inconsequential questions. Blindly he chases Nathan toward a banner and through a door and into an air-conditioned vestibule, beyond which clumps of besuited and coiffed young men and women lean on white linen and a high mahogany bar. The customers are perfect, outrageously alive, monstrously vital. The vastness of their futures. And Santos, like a dog hanging off a backyard gate, panting toward the tall grass across the road. The night is young, is always young, its possibilities limitless. And they, he and Nathan, a couple of greyhounds in pursuit of the unseen and unnamed that lay ahead in the night. A man and his spic apprentice—

Santos has gone to the bathroom. The knocking almost brings the door down. "Errol, you all right in there?"

Santos bends over the little sink and kneads his puffy hands. In the dim glass his face cracks into the geometric shapes of fatigue.

Barbados is standing in the open door, Schreck a few paces

behind him, looking contrite. Santos wipes his mouth. Barbados says, his voice flat, "I think there's someone else we have to talk to."

The doorman is asleep in his greatcoat and epaulets like a Red Army soldier.

"Ivan," Nathan calls.

The doorman rushes the door and Nathan enters the plush, cavernous atrium. "Ivan. Good to see you again." Nathan tugs on the man's epaulets.

Ivan stands back, heavy-lidded, swollen-faced. He smiles a gold-capped smile and presents Nathan with a double thumbs-up. "Señor Nathan, you have grown very thin. Very strong. Like a hard bull." He jabs the air with his fists. "Like when you were a young man. You exchange last year's costume for a better model. It's the señoritas, no? Keeping my boy in fighting condition?"

Nathan shakes his head, smiling. Compadre. "Only bad luck with the señoritas, Ivan."

Ivan scoffs and waves him away. "You? Please, Nathan. Look who you are talking to please."

The two men set their feet and exchange mock blows, ducking and fending off flurries. Like old friends who have made good their bond in rougher places and harder times. Nathan lets out a little laugh, as genuine a discourse as anything he's let pass all night.

Then Ivan connects, a little slap to the side of his head. A small twinge and the lobby tips back. Nathan staggers. Ivan's hands are on his shoulders but still Nathan spins.

"Are you drunk?"

"I'm fine," Nathan says, brushing off his coat.

"Your eyes are yellow."

An edge of cold slips through the cracks of the door into the lobby. Outside, the padded silence of a car passing through the quilted streets.

"How's my father?"

Ivan wags his finger. "We men have to take care of our fathers. In the end there is no one to understand but other men."

Nathan eyes the doorman warily.

"Señor?" Ivan asks.

"No, nothing. Forget it."

"Your father is very fine. Now he is a famous man. Tonight the sexy TV ladies were waiting for him." Ivan extends his arm and sweeps it through the lobby, indicating where they stood waiting. "You are working on the big case with him?"

"Of course," Nathan says.

Ivan smiles broadly. "Then you will be famous."

"Of course."

"Like that other case."

"That was a long time ago."

"The big victory."

"Ten years ago, at least."

"And your face, it was everywhere." He takes Nathan's shoulder in his strong hand. "I used to lift you to my shoulder and take you upstairs like a package of groceries."

Ivan shakes his shoulder once, but still Nathan will not raise his eyes. Ivan opens his fingers and Nathan walks out from under them toward the elevator.

"You need sleep," the doorman calls.

He tries four or five keys from his ring before he finds one that fits his parents' door. But the door is unlocked to begin with, and when he turns the knob he stumbles in, and, stepping through a patch of streetlight to a foyer of herringbone wood, instantly regrets having come. A living room of fluted columns, teakwood newel and finial beginning a balustrade that swirls like the hem of a woman's skirt to a second level. Furniture scattered amidst a garden of low potted trees. Cherubs watch from the high corners. Nathan stands as in a small cluttered room, as though he can turn this way and that and touch the things and the people he knows, dead and alive and in various stages in between, ghosts of themselves, led by himself, the chief ghost, at eight, ten, fifteen, a package of promise and possibility.

In a picture window branches encased in ice beckon him, like the gnarled fingers of old women. He steps into the frame and looks down to the avenue on which he was a boy, on which he did boyish things. The buildings across the park are lost in a cross-hatched blur. Up and down this street, strings of Christmas lights flail like spastic jump ropes.

Through a cut in the skyline he can see a fragment of the East River. A light passes there, police boat, garbage barge, the luminescent ice floes running to the harbor, the water ferrying them a black and silent broth, strangely, he knows, now almost level with the road. Everything is flooded. Things north have melted. But that river has always given him a childish obsession, a thrilling fright, even more than the Hudson, which is four times as wide. The Hudson—five avenues behind him—is all relaxed grandeur, with its Rip van Winkle history and its source supposedly that little mossy Lake Tear of the Clouds up in the Adirondacks. A tour of America, all of it—its sail boats and water-skiers and skim ice—sliding between Westchester's old-money mansions and New Jersey's Palisades. The East River on the other hand is a moat, a razor-wire fence, all rawness and urban fuckup. Running heat, eddies of unnamed spew splitting off into competing currents, rivers within rivers, one with waves and whirlpools while the next is all smooth secrets, all of it accelerating through the Bronx, then Harlem, racing down here between mid-Manhattan and the fallow cranes and dumps of Long Island City and the Brooklyn Navy Yard, the barred dry docks gaping eye-sockets staring unblinking at the sky. Nathan has seen them all up close. More than one client of his has turned up broken like a rag doll at the weedy bottom. The East River is his river; that river he will take, even if it kills him. The soul thrives on its sufferings. Keep the Hudson, its sailboats, its boatdocks.

A long, tympanic roll of thunder. The window pane trembles. In the sky, the clouds are climbing, feeding on themselves. A wind has kicked up, sending waves through the trees of Central Park below, the stripped heads boiling. Something in the jagged strength of the skyline, in the designed wildness of the park, seems to be shouting at him, a voice whose cry is familiar, some youthful passion, some point of pride, the desire to do, he thinks, what is right. The tasks materialize before him one after the other, Isabel, the Russian weasel, Rikers Island, his pills, his diagnosis, his sentence, Isabel—

He quickly turns from all of it, and, sitting back on the windowsill with his legs stretched before him, looks at the room and its gaudy furniture, at the darkened doorways leading right and left into still more familiar regions, and with fascination remembers that occasionally he once knew great happiness here. Happiness: yet it was, he knows, a life lying in wait for annual rituals to give meaning to the dead space between. So it was a sort of life, the roads out of it to this place here where he stands already overgrown. Childhood and what? What is that? And what, he wonders, looking around the shadows of the room, at the streetlight playing through the branches on the wall—of course knowing the answer all along—was *that*?

That one late autumn morning, the last day of his childhood, a clean line between before and after. He was eighteen, home for Thanksgiving from his first semester of college in already frozen Syracuse. His father had once again invited to the apartment the citizens of his own strange country, his specially cultivated blend of Treasury agents, cocaine merchants, soap opera stars, convicted rapists, gold shield detectives, a virtuoso soprano from the Met, a Colombian money launderer, a famous composer; and sprinkled throughout, a small legion of anonymous women in tight wool sheaths who might have been models, who might have been prostitutes, who were probably a little of both, coming and going without introduction. The presentations of names and occupations were carried out in code. "Pedro is in sales," "William is in protection," "Barbra sings," "Leonard writes"—not to conceal or to be cute, but as though to leave what you did at the door with your hat and coat in order for things to settle to a better level, to the spirit of the day. These meetings were an annual suspension of hostilities, during which Milton's guests stood crowded at the bar and picture windows in virtual cease-fire. Sharing paper plates sagging with bagels and nova and whitefish salad, talking about the Giants, kids, the weather, anything. Below, between them and the park, passed the Macy's parade. The solemn marching bands, the human snowflakes, the sanitation department brigades, the goliath balloons, happy heroes and quacky demons inflated to the size of buildings. Milton's guests gazed downward, giddily talkative, as though relieved by their proximity not to the parade but to each other. Broadway's Little Orphan Annie and small-time Harlem dealer, District Attorney and money launderer for a Chinese crime family. As if this, this day and this food and this glass-enclosed apartment, were real life and their occupations were the contrivance, things to engage them until they slept again, those long days and nights until this meeting same time next year. Liquor flowed and the hills of food slowly leveled off, then flattened. The air was alive with sexual tension, the sense of abandon that comes with twiddling the forbidden fruit, punctuated by the rhythms of the passing drum corps below. It was the middle of the day, late morning even, crisp and blustery, but inside this sprawl it was midnight in a moonlit garden in springtime. People overate and drank too much.

Nathan was standing at the window of his parents' bedroom, which had a view downtown, fielding questions about college. Directly behind him, alone in the corner, stood the city's latest hero, champion of law and order, a thin, stooped, bookish man with an unruly beard, a narrow, meatless head, sunken temples, narrow beakish nose. He had the vacant, preoccupied look of a discouraged Jesus. He spoke to no one; he looked on the verge of speaking to himself. The month before, he had killed an aggressive subway beggar with a penknife. The tabloids had dubbed him the Philosopher King of New York, model of decisiveness and integrity and moral action. And Milton Stein had stepped forward as Christ's champion and spokesman, his John the Baptist, a model of generosity himself, having offered his legal and public-relations services free of charge. Standing at the window in his ragged clothes, the parade passing below him, the man spoke to no one. The heaping plate of food had been foisted upon him, and he did not touch it. He looked about the room disapprovingly, more angry, still more discouraged. The experiment—his, presumably—had gone awry. He was a lunatic and everyone knew it, but he had taken on the role of an expensive and exotic pet.

And Nathan was beautiful. His adolescent features had come into focus. He had grown tall and trim, and the frame made by his cleft chin and high forehead converged nicely at the tip of his Grecian nose. He had watery, feminine eyes deep with character that outran his own. His stature as the best-looking man in whatever room was an obligation. And here he stood, before a woman as old as his mother, who, holding him by the elbow, cheerfully drank everyone at the party under the table. Nathan could have said nothing, it would not have mattered. The woman referred to her Kandinskys, her Picassos, to her schedule—her husband's evenings away at poker, her maid's days off—and the silence and loneliness of a Park Avenue triplex. And all those ridiculous paintings staring down at you, accusing you, so why not—the old lyric—give them something to accuse you *of*. Nathan's father was simply divine. Now she had to know, like father like son?

Nathan excused himself, waving his empty plate, he would be back. They exchanged winks, she tweaked his arm. He gave a winning smile and was gone, twisting through the crowd, carefully eyeing everyone he passed, considering the consequences of a bump—the bodyguards, the violinists, the whores—he achieved the living room, where the wall of law journals and case books rose above the heads of the criminals and custodians like a monument to the system of criminal justice, inscribed with the names and numbers of laws deceased and irrelevant.

Suddenly the sun dimmed. It felt like an eclipse. People were turning toward the windows. The first of the gargantuan balloons was passing. Goofy or Daffy or Superman—not the whole figure, just passing elbows, cheeks, feet. The gusts took them against the wires, against the buildings themselves, against the most wealthy of the spectators encased safely above the masses, Milton's guests, who, laughing nervously, held firm to their plates of whitefish salad as the passing monsters ferreted them out, the giant eyes filling the apartment windows like some parody of King Kong. The room giggled and screeched in a brave show of silliness, then quieted with an unsettled strain. The cease-fire was called off, as though, despite the concealed arsenal of small weaponry—ankle holsters, switchblades—nowhere was safe. Hostility settled in. The room began to empty of guests making parting comments about the traffic, missing the rush.

Nathan felt someone beside him. It was the Philosopher King, twitchy, eyes deeply abstracted. There was commotion down on the street, a faint roar from the crowd. A pillow-waisted Santa was rolling down Central Park West on the flatbed of a truck, his recorded ho-ho-hoing blaring tinny and staticky through loudspeakers. Waving at the crowds. The crowds waving back. Lifting his fat, rouged face up toward the buildings. Toward the windows where the children were raised in fathers' arms aloft. As though at some signal previously agreed upon the fathers would send the infants tumbling out the windows up and down Central Park West, some mass move toward infanticide, fathers offering up their young sons and daughters in sacrifice to the Santa god. Upstairs, meanwhile, Milton Stein's guests streamed out, pouring out onto the street. The Philosopher King hurried across the living room and disappeared through a narrow door, the back stairs down.

A lone figure pushed through the congested hallway into the apartment. A tall woman, young, Nathan's age or younger, he couldn't tell. He stopped and stared at her. A client? But what could she have done? There was something vaguely familiar about her; he'd seen her before, he knew her, and he was equally sure they'd never met. Not pretty enough to be a model, not that pretty, not one of the set of anonymous women. She was the color of coffee, with Caucasian features, faintly like an Arab, or a Somali.

He stepped forward, but the girl moved away, heading confidently toward the kitchen, as though the layout of the apartment was not merely familiar but home turf. As though she lived here. Nathan followed her into the kitchen, where his father's secretary, Ellie, was helping herself to another bagel with lox. The girl came up behind Ellie and kissed her on the cheek. Ellie turned, and the two women looked at Nathan, who stood dumbstruck in the doorway. Their bodies were the same height and build, the benign expressions the same, the intelligence and competence of their eyes. But the girl's eyes: though the expression was the same, the shape was not. They were green and almond shaped; they looked roughly like his. Her lips, no—foreign, neither here nor there. But her nose, narrow, almost hooked, flaring out at the end in a knobby bud. Nathan gazed at the nose, and if he squinted, blurring her color and her hair, the nose was the one he looked at in mirrors and window panes across the city. The nose was his, a Stein nose, distinctive in its attempt at a puggish waspiness, its failure coming at the hooked bridge. Before his own mother pushed by him, before she greeted Ellie and this girl with the comfort and familiarity usually saved for family, before she'd introduced the girl—it struck Nathan standing there, as his mother was pushing past, that what he was seeing would have been a mirage had this been a desert. Before him stood a perfect fusion between Ellie, Milton's secretary, and—how else to explain it?—his father. Here, in no need of introduction, stood Nathan's own half sister, his black twin.

Nathan nodded hello. Ellie turned away. The girl did too. Nathan was left with his mother, her face set with determination, as if she knew she was staring straight at her betrayal and knew that the consequences of not enduring it were worse than having to live with it. She had coped and accepted and put it in its place, permitted the betrayal, nurtured it.

"That's Isabel," his mother said.

"Of course," Nathan said.

"Ellie's daughter," his mother said.

"I understand."

Nathan stands now in the light of the open refrigerator. He takes a long hard look inside at each shelf, contemplating the eggs in their little cups, the month-old apples collapsing in the crisper. A half-eaten TV dinner. The same food, the same locations. The whole thing kept carefully and lovingly empty, as though his parents had neither eaten nor shopped nor cleared these shelves since he last left this apartment some number of years ago he would not remember. Since that Thanksgiving morning, when his mother so off-handedly introduced to him his long-lost sister; that face that seems now to have launched his thousand ships.

He pours himself a glass of milk, drinks off half then refills it and drinks another half, then leaves the last half on the shelf next to the container. He goes looking for replies to questions still unknown to him. Through the high rooms with their marbleized plaster and faux wainscoting, past a dry fountain where an old bronzed angel aiming bow and arrow stands lit in ambient street-glow. He finds one answer. He stops in a small study and sits at a desk before a typewriter. His hands awash in the green nimbus of a banker's lamp. On the stationery of Stein & Stein he calmly types, *Maria Rosa, Last Will and Testament,* and recommits to paper as best he can in numbered paragraphs and noted subsections all Maria asked him two years ago, as her attorney, to put down and notarize, including the sole rights of one Nathan Stein to titled property on the priceless paradise, a stretch of as-yet-undeveloped coastline on the Honduran island of Roatán.

Along a narrow hall the door to his old room is locked. At the hall's end another door stands open. In the silence, he can hear his parents snoring together in a duet of practiced confusion. Then only one, his father, goes his own way while his mother gurgles and whimpers through lonely dreams. The sheets shift and Nathan feels someone standing in a doorway behind him. Footsteps? Somewhere a door closes. Nathan turns. The doorway is empty. Clutching the deed to his freedom, he steps in, filling the doorway, and through to the next, and the next, stopping and filling doorways until he stands in his parents', open as it had been. A room sour with sweat and old breath. They lie there like corpses, his mother spreadeagled on the king-size mattress, hands up overhead as though shot in the snow. Milton rising beside her like a sudden hillside, his belly pale and monstrous. Beside a glass of water his toupee askew on an eyeless wig stand.

Nathan leans and touches his elbow to wake him. "Milton," he whispers. "Daddy—"

He steps away, as though he's caught a whiff of something bad. In the bed there is, as there has been, nothing. The room is deserted, the blankets undisturbed. Only a copy of today's *Post*, open to a double-page spread where Milton Stein is pictured striding out of court with Schreck at one arm and Ruth at the other. *Stein to fight for Williams,* the caption reads.

"Hello," Nathan says. A voice that calls from room to room and back again.

In the lobby, Ivan is asleep upright on his bar stool, arms folded, chin in his coat.

Nathan tugs at the doorman's elbow. "Where are they?"

Ivan opens his eyes with a snort. "They are away for the rest of the weekend. But of course you knew?" He looks at Nathan. "Do you need a doctor?"

Nathan thumbs down the door latch and sets himself free.

**11 p.m.** Barbados drapes over the steering wheel, peering up. "This is where he does his fun?"

"In a manner of speaking."

"You ever go in?"

"Just the one time."

Gleaming sports cars and long sedans circle a hunched building with blackened windows and no markings but a line of purple neon above the door. Behind and on either side, chop shops, blocks of buses packed in herringbone patterns, school yellow, Greyhounds; hangars marked with the cyclops seal of the Department of Sanitation. This could be an old diner, or a bus depot, refitted and camouflaged as a garrison to hide atop the pavement on the outer edge of all this industry.

"I always wondered about this place."

"You don't want to know," Santos says.

The door opens on another door within and a tall woman descends the steps flinging a stole around her neck. Despite her great height she has a floral delicacy, the purple light a halo for her teased hair. As she walks toward them Barbados's hands stay gripped to the wheel. His eyes follow her but not his head.

"She's a man."

Santos nods.

Barbados can't help it. He turns in his seat and watches her climb into the back of a limousine. "Chinese, or something."

"They're Filipino. That's part of the thing."

"I don't get that."

"Don't think too hard about it."

They sit a while in silence. Santos watches the door, blinking steadily.

"What if he's already inside."

Santos looks at his watch. "We'll wait until twelve."

A stream of false women comes and goes. The novelty of the parade wears thin, and they are quickly bored. A car pulls up across the street, out of which Krivit steps and looks about, hesitant. He walks quickly toward their car and Santos opens his door and Krivit stops, expressionless. Without a word he opens the back door and slips in. His hair redeployed across his head in countable strands. Eyes watery and half closed. He wipes his forehead with his handkerchief.

"I didn't think this was your style," he says.

"I like talking to you," Santos says.

"Not that much."

"Enough."

"You have fun in there?" Barbados asks.

Krivit holds his stare until Barbados looks away. "Fuck you," he says.

Barbados holds up a palm. "No offense. It's just that I never thought—"

No one says anything.

"It doesn't matter," Santos says.

Krivit nods out the window, into the night. "Look at these fine cars. They say it's going to snow like hell tonight, but the lot's full. Think about that. You'd be surprised."

"I guess I would," Barbados says.

"Enough," Santos says. "I want to hear about Coney Island."

Krivit nods. "My deepest sympathies," he says flatly.

He doesn't mean it, Santos knows. He doesn't mean it and it doesn't matter. "You met Stein today."

"Which one?" Krivit asks lazily.

Santos stills.

"I saw you with Nathan Stein."

"You want to talk *about* Stein or *to* Stein? Because you can join me inside."

Santos looks up at the blank door of the club. Noiseless, hermetically sealed.

"In there?" Barbados asks.

Santos blinks. Nothing this night will surprise him. "Nathan or Milton?"

"Either. Both. Like father like son?"

"I didn't think the South Pacific was their flavor," Barbados says.

Krivit shrugs. "The Steins have generous and shall we say heroic appetites."

Barbados waves. "Give me a break."

"I'm a merchant. I buy what I think I can sell. I sell what I have. I always sell what I have, and what I have is always real."

Santos passes his hand over his face. "I'm listening."

"What do you think I can tell you?" Krivit asks. "All I have is a little news. It may be neither here nor there."

Santos feels Krivit looking at him but he doesn't move. "Okay."

"Someone is a very large player right now. Let's call it a high-profile—yet delicate—place to be. A place where unwanted news would do damage."

"What kind of news?"

"I'm not doing your job."

Santos lifts his eyes to the pilled ceiling of the car. "This is not a game."

"Here's the broadcast: open your eyes, Errol. You don't have to look far. Nothing is a coincidence, nothing is chance. What Milton is doing, what Nathan has done. These are not unrelated things."

"You're talking about Isabel. What is it with you, what are you saying? First Schreck, now you—"

"Schreck? That fuck—"

"He tried to sell me Nathan."

"He'd sell his mother. Listen to me, Errol—" Krivit slides forward. "What he did, what Nathan did—"

"What did he do?"

"And who is who. We don't always know who we are."

"Give me something, give it to me, something real."

"What I have is always real. I sell real."

"Fuck it, Krivit, I'm buying real."

"It's not nice."

"Fuck you."

Krivit sits back, hands folded in his lap. "Secrets own those who never wanted to know—"


Now Claire is alone, has been for some time. Her elbows on the bar, her eyes up toward the murmuring TV but not seeing it. The Frangelico and Ouzo behind the bar green from the TV light and the vodkas blue and the whiskeys the color of thin mud.

Her fingers around an empty martini glass glumly, she steps back with the gin inside her at chest level and stands at the middle window. She can see only the streetlight and where it ends and where nothing begins, and she traces the progress of the liquor downward and outward. A high, optimistic C from a song on the radio lifts behind her and holds for the big finish, then turns tinny and hollow, then only the snap and rain-like rattle of the pool rack breaking, and the liquor bottles and shot glasses flashing like jewels.

She makes a drippy circle in the glass with the heel of her palm and can see now no tracks on the sidewalks. The Witnesses are safe at home with their Bibles, safe here in Brooklyn, witnessing away. Up and down the street she is sure she is the only waking consciousness, despite the little Greek plunging glass after glass into the glass washer and the boys playing pool.

Why hasn't Errol come for her? After all, didn't she know Isabel, too? Doesn't Errol need her now, now that they—the both of them—have to publicly mourn? And she, of course, deserves— she wants—the chance to need him.

Looking out across the street, into the harbor, looking but not finding all the things she and Errol have not yet done, she recalls that as a girl, as Nathan's girl, often up at that earliest hour in an apartment not a mile from where she now stands, she'd been unable to bear the thought of her consciousness being so alone, positive she was the only person in the world alone at night. She'd stay up with her consciousness to give it a companion, until Nathan came home. From night court. Or so she'd thought; such was her logic then. The streetlight falling from the window on the bottom of the stairs, the heat in winter or the fans in summer rattling on, the settling foundation sending creaks through the walls, she'd squat as if by her parents' door as the noises and various lights moved over her. Eventually, whispering to herself, she'd fall asleep, more often than not atop her and Nathan's disheveled bed—on top because to go under signified to her her submission, to the house, to him—always with the light on, not for him to see but for her to see him when he returned home, and so she would have herself for company if she should wake.

Claire senses someone behind her. "Nathan," she says, hopefully, she realizes; she heard the little jump in her voice. She turns, not toward that one but toward the specter of the infant, who, when born, moved the doctor to silence. A nurse had gasped.

The bar stools have emptied. Though a bar never seems to sleep, Claire believes, it should never be so deserted, or so quiet, or the bottles so straight, so ready. A bar empty and quiet seems to her too much the terminal abode.

As if to prove her point, on the other side of the frosted glass a bulky shadow-figure is raising and lowering its arms in the streetlight, and Claire rubs a new circle in the window to find a man and a woman on the sidewalk, kept upright only by their attachment at their hips. The man, stone sober, has descended, Claire sees, into a black mood. The woman, caving a little, bumps her head on the glass at Claire's fingers, as though seeking her blessing or absolution. The man props her and looks up, pleading with Claire for a loyalty that once had to do with the great history of drinking and drunks. But Claire pulls back and is already looking beyond, angrily peering into a circle of spotlit snow beneath a distant streetlamp, as if at particular moments of Nathan's secret life strolling down the street before her.

What it had become with Nathan was primarily an arrangement of recognitions, a series of checkpoints at which Claire had reassured herself that she could, like him, act without loyalty to a thing. Nathan, she'd assumed, would be vastly different. The others she'd known before they introduced themselves. They were always big and thickly muscled and confessional, and she knew them in her father and her three brothers and every one of the men at her small southern college. She knew what car they drove and at what escalatored and potted-planted mall they bought their records, how they would kiss and how they would make love to her and what they would say about it and her and themselves afterward. Initially, about Nathan, she'd thought she'd known nothing. Not his order of things, not the ritual before or after, his foreign but still obviously male conceit. She did not know what to do when he first met her in her small law school dorm room and undressed before her, this Jew, the head of his cock unsheathed. Though he was not, her southern-belle mother had agreed, a jewy Jew, hook nose and all; he almost could have passed for one of their own. Nor did Claire know what to do when she was liking it and the sex was not, after all, very much like what she had had before. Nathan was forceful and investigative. The others had always been effusive, tender before, absent afterward, but ultimately unintelligent.

Still, every morning after a night with him, she woke breathing heavily, with Nathan breathing heavily beside her. She closed her eyes again and found herself trying too hard to sleep; not because she did not want to be tired the next day but because in the morning she felt fear, fear of being awake at dawn, the dust taking flight, the vodka still sharp in her head, the light slowly revealing Nathan encircled in her arms.

Then Claire made her discovery.

Outside of her, it seemed, Nathan had a favorite brand. Marlboros or Camels. Coke or Pepsi. Caucasian, black. Nathan's was

Latina. It was like an aspiration. It had become a joke among Nathan's law school friends, to whom he had always brought his women for their stamp of approval, their clubby endorsement, that until Claire every one of his dates had fit a precise mold. Each of them had been extraordinarily, unusually beautiful, each finely done up, and each a young mother, a mother before twenty, before they left Honduras, Puerto Rico, Guatemala, Colombia. Not merely Latina but a specific Latina subspecies: tall, athletically lean; light skinned, a shade darker than a Spaniard, say, or an Egyptian; and tightly sealed in a thin cotton shift or leather dress that left nothing to the imagination. As though Nathan had laid the outfits out on the bed. As though he had a closet full of little black dresses. And his family, Nathan's family, even his friends, Claire's friends, they'd all been complicit. All of them—even I, Claire thinks, we accepted our role, took it on, as it were—over time we became Nathan's accomplices.

Claire shifts uneasily on her stool. We were his bait. His foreplay.

Of course, Maria was disarming. Claire, actually bringing herself to follow him, saw her once from a distance. She possessed a quick tongue, Claire could tell. And she wore—well, practically nothing. A little black leather something, an afterthought. You looked everywhere. It would have been impolite not to.

After that, Nathan himself became a pattern. Claire discovered that she did after all know his lines ahead of time and found herself moving her mouth with them in the dark: also that she knew by heart his strategy in lovemaking and had found herself lying in wait in certain positions of her own. She became aware of him acting with the usual bravado of a man with all the cards. It crossed her mind that perhaps all that time she had been employed as a pontoon bridge, and that Nathan and his immigrant mistresses had been communicating across her span, exchanging goods, finding little understandings with which to build treaties of further, deeper understandings. This is how cultures self-destruct, she thought to herself, fuck by fuck.

On the other hand, she was free. Gone was any fear she might have secretly harbored that Nathan would show himself to be remarkable. Sometimes, with him, she had forgotten many times through the night that she was even with a man, and after a while had been only thinly conscious of being shaken by some hands, not knowing whose they were until the light came on and she recognized the fingers clawing her belly. She might leave those hands tonight, or next year, it would not matter. She knew she could, and would, go anywhere. The world was now clear, a transparent plain on which she would ride free from turbulence, from geographical seams. What had bound her was her illusion of another, more perfect, world. But now Claire was free from all that. Nathan had seen to it. She was freer than anything. She felt as capable of cutting through lies as walking through air.

Her last night with him, five years ago, Claire waited atop their bedspread with her back against the wall, feet extended. Her red hair was pulled back tight, her throat forward, damp, the creases faintly lined with grease. Their wedding, a myth until the invitations arrived that day in a box from the printer, was taking shape somewhere without them. Claire—her small, elegant features now undone—wore the look of the deeply pious who had jumped ship.

Nathan took off his jacket and sat at the edge of the bed, knees apart, tie loosened. Claire stood. Mosquitoes, having fought their way here through the smog, had been waiting and drew to her face. She ducked slightly, raising her arms, and pulled off her dress, letting it drop at her feet. She rose now out of the faded material, her arms and neck and face bronzed, the rest illuminated pale blue sunlessness. She reached and switched off the bedside lamp. The mattress sank beneath her. Nathan collided with her knees. She lifted her legs. He fell to her side and began to caress her face. "No," she said, and pried at him and slid under. Nathan began to kiss his way downward. "No!" she cried, and pulled him on top of her. She felt his lips against hers. She very nearly softened and opened, but then his sourness—his, the others', Maria's—appalled her and she turned and stiffened. Nathan, having given over to her demand, began the stale, anonymous thrusting. He hardly breathed. They themselves made no sound. The bed jousted beneath them. Their hands did not touch.

In the morning she woke not only fearful but also perspiring. She closed her eyes again and found herself trying hard not to think, and she sat up. Nathan slept beside her, one hand between his chubby thighs. He too was sweating, the dampness had already reached her through the sheets. Carefully, insistently, brown dawn came. The street, the cars outside, the floor and tables and chairs, her hands, everything a shade of brown. The Brooklyn-Queens Expressway began its morning whine. The monstrous boats rusting in the harbor.

Claire cradled her belly. She began to murmur to it. She was pregnant with Nathan's child. About to marry a man already emotionally gone. She'd bring it to term, though. She'd have that. From Nathan now she wanted nothing else. And he was gone, with no more than his usual lukewarm whimper of protest.

He has come by the apartment for the dog. A tree-lined street, the leafless gloom. Pale window light falls across the walks like trap doors in the snow, ways out to sunnier, warmer times. Hugging himself he hesitates at the stoop, looking up to the address in confusion. He has been giving out a street address on scraps of paper, corners of envelopes, the backs of business cards for years, We should get together, hear some jazz, grab a bite to eat, drink a drink, the address in the East Eighties. This is West Ninth. He brings out a ring as big around as a janitor's, sprouting dozens of keys. They all look alike, apartment keys, office keys, security door, doorknob, dead bolt, various other drawers, cabinets and bus terminal lockers what holes they fit he can't remember. But he can't de-ring yet. Something might catch up to him, something, anyway, that might need opening. Trying one key then the other he works expertly, glancing up and down the street, as though he is breaking in, until the lobby door gives and he hesitates in surprise and lifts his head to the sound of forgotten doors opening on the hallways of old addresses and slamming closed one by one. A stack of mail bearing his name has toppled across the lobby table. He eyes it cautiously and picks at it here and there, all of it official, credit bureaus, law firms, department of parking violations, the office of the United States Marshal. Two pieces of overnighted mail signed for by a neighbor he has never met. The postmarks go back weeks, but that doesn't tell him when he was last here. He could have left the mail three weeks ago, two weeks ago, last week, yesterday. As he leaves it now.

Inside his first-floor door, a tropical warmth. The radiators knock and hiss. His entrance has set off a commotion at the far end of the apartment. An English pointer takes a wide corner at full gallop and is upon him, all tongue and breath and claw and raw, impolite power. Nathan kneels and presents his face. The dog braces itself on Nathan's shoulders and Nathan struggles up and past, bowing and twisting away from the blows to the crotch and defending his jacket, dancing his way down the hall. "Baron, stop."

The lights are on, every one, bedside, chandelier, the microwave is ajar, a mug of coffee spotlit on the carousel. The sink blooms with waste, flower-stenciled dishes spilling onto both wings of the counter. In the bedroom there is no bureau. A single sock petrified by the heat seesaws on the radiator.

"Get, Baron—away."

His footsteps echo in the back room where a black leather easy chair is an island on an otherwise bare wooden floor. French doors letting out onto a small patio are flanked by a pair of man-sized speakers. In the corner blinks the readout of multitiered controls, a solar system of green and red stars clustered in this one remote corner of Nathan's universe.

He sits, sighs, aims the remote control once, fires, fires again. A muted horn leaks out of the speakers. The soft lick of a drum. Civilization strides in. The apartment phone rings but Nathan doesn't budge, as though it has been ringing all day—and it has, he knows; the solid red light on the answering machine tells him that the tape is full. The dog sulks by and sits shivering by the doors. How long has he been waiting? Nathan can smell it now, the reek of nervous waterings and clandestine shits. The dog turns his head, pleading out of the corners of his sad cue-ball eyes. Nathan is seated, and tired, but sighing he gets up with a wince and throws open the doors and stands there clutching the doorjamb. The dog circles his own old piles deodorized by frost, sniffing his way one to the other, connecting the dots, holding back his new batch for signs of an imaginary intruder. Looking out into the garden, Nathan remembers having taken this apartment for the exuberance of its growth, the little ordered rows of pachysandra and hyacinth, its brave stand against the perpetual shade between the buildings.

The dog has sulked off against the back wall of the brownstone behind. He squats silent and without reflection in the dark, as though understanding how alone he really is.

Nathan, meanwhile, has been observed. His neighbor, Mr. Somethingorother, shoveling snow at their common fence, peers at him with open disapproval. He is being silently condemned, Nathan sees, and feels hemmed in. Gone—long ago now—is his little vision of floral order. What else his neighbor must have seen—

Barton. The neighbor's name is Barton.

In the back room the now-familiar chirp of his cellular. Nathan recognizes the voice of someone he knows, faint among the other voices. He knows none, he knows them all, he can't decide. It doesn't seem to matter. He raises his own voice. "Isabel—found?"

He must pack. A phone slams, but which? The dog pushes his way through Nathan's legs and Nathan closes the door and sits quickly in the chilled leather. He closes the phone, then his eyes, as another CD, another selection, wheels around. Here comes Chet Baker, singer and trumpeter, discovered not long ago in a puddle of his own bones and gristle at the base of his Amsterdam hotel, a dozen floors beneath his well-appointed room. Nathan feels a certain kinship with him, always has. The voice of an angel, the face of eternal boyhood, quiet and patient to the point of transparency. A living ghost. Those old standards about lost love slipping easily out of that throat. As if he really knew. Nathan had actually believed Baker a young woman the first time he heard him, he had that kind of sensitivity. Maybe that was the problem, Nathan wonders, for it was all a lie. Baker was all surface, his bewildered innocence, his wide-eyed sincerity. His arms pinched to hamburger by needles, his veins coursing with crank. Everything he did—even the music—to get laid and high, and his silky boyhood face cracked like a window into a web of fissures with his little pug nose in the middle like the thrown stone that brought it all down. Inside, he was rotting, contaminated by self-absorption and sloth. Like us all, Nathan thinks, the pressure from within building and building, what we really are pushing its way to daylight and leaking over our pretty faces.

Nathan sags deeper into his chair. The millimeters pass like miles. Lovely Isabel floats by in her long red dress. Hey, sister. He found her competence in denying the obvious sympathetic, extraordinary even, worthy of applause. After all these years he'd taken it upon himself to tell her. So last night, on a whim, he asked her to take his extra seat at the opera, then dinner at Gambone's, then after the wine he took her to the New Haven to hear Eddie Young. Aged in the years since Nathan last saw him, Eddie Young stood in the colored haze flagging his fingers at the keys of his alto sax, working the changes through a competent Charlie Parker. The tight acorns of muscle throbbing in his cheeks and his throat leaping and the octave hammer sputtering like the top of a kettle come to boil, a hint of white froth at the corners of his mouth. In his presence Isabel, like everything else, receded behind an even greater tragedy, a more urgent memory.

Once, years before, when Nathan was in law school, Eddie Young, playing after-hours at a lesser club, invited any in the audience to join him at the mike. Claire was sitting beside him. They were drinking heavily. And it was Claire who whispered in Nathan's ear that night to go on, here it is, what are you waiting for, and nudged him up. Nathan cinched his strap. The band patiently idled. The pianist flitted over the chords in a playful meander. Smoke swirled through the cones of those blinding lights, the dark beyond them in which his constituency stiffened halfway between approval and embarrassment. The gentle rebound of the keys beneath his fingertips, the heat and crescendo of the band. The bell of his saxophone swung out into the dark. Then the unlanguage and uncharted buzzing of the reed on his tongue. Eddie Young cocked his eye, as though he'd heard something small he liked. He stepped to the side and briefly roused the unseen home team with head-fakes, clapping the new phenom on. Then he clapped him quickly off, and there came Nathan's slow promenade around stands of bottles and glasses back to his seat where the vodka had gone tepid, where he heard himself murmur in Claire's ear that he really did love her, he really would marry her. Marry me, be my wife. "Someone to Watch Over Me," Chet Baker croons now, today, a man famous for watching over no one.

Nathan's eyes sting. Sweat runs off his brow. At some point he has risen and—knees cold and weak—sat back down. Through the glass of the french doors, through his own reflection, he sees his neighbor, armed with his shovel, glaring away. Woozily, Nathan gets back on his feet. He digs his hands in his soaked pockets in a heroic attempt to appear nonchalant. But it is all in vain. He lurches forward, shattering the image he hoped to convey, a kind of lawyerly majesty, peering out his windows, taking in the view, plotting his next point of order. Objection, objection! Barton scowls, and Nathan's eyes rendezvous with his neighbor's at Baron's latest deposit, a steamy green log set artfully atop a small mound freshly snowed, like a cairn showing the way. Across the little yard Nathan offers up an expression of profound surprise. Again, he drifts—

"Who's the kid?" Isabel had asked last night.

At the end of the New Haven's bar slouched a tow-headed youth of sixteen or seventeen. His body was a pubescent collection of lines and angles, his white hair as fine and feathery as a child's. Nathan noted the saxophone case between his knees.

Nearing the end of "Cherokee," Eddie Young pulled up short. He twisted off Parker's finish with a riff of his own, then ceased mid-run, his saxophone in a pose, his quivering lips receding off the mouthpiece, teeth bared like a whinnying horse. Then Young nodded at the blond kid, who, without ceremony, took his case across his knees and assembled the saxophone with the trained, passionless calm of a sniper snapping together his weapon. He gave it a neck and a mouthpiece and hung it with its strap and, sucking on a reed, took three strides toward the band. Tedium and indifference had long ago veiled Isabel's cherub face. Really, was all she'd replied, unenthralled, when Nathan told her he used to play the saxophone. After that he ignored her. She, like the others, couldn't understand. Claire was the only one who cared about all that, who understood the perils of an abandoned dream. Why had he given up? Why is the sky blue? Why was it so hard to attempt, so simple to stumble, so terrifying to risk all that polluting ambition? Claire was the only one who urged him to play in the privacy of their apartment. To play, to do, to be anything, to keep playing and playing and playing—

Nathan watches, watched, as Eddie Young brought the microphone up to the boy's saxophone, then bent to talk into it. "Here's a young man I'd like you all to know, ladies and gentlemen. This morning he won a contest at the Conservatory. I had the honor of being the judge of this contest and also the grand prize. The award was to come down here tonight and share this late gig before you-all." He paused, then, extending an arm toward the boy: "Mr. Ernest Filch. Ladies and gentlemen. Ernie Filch."

Sparse applause. The band picked at their shirts. Eddie Young led the way into an old standard. When the bridge came to an end the drummer and keyboardist backed down, settling their pitch. The youth's hands snapped to life like a majorette's. In one fluid motion the mouthpiece neared, the teeth struck. No one was prepared. The entire club was overcome, as though everyone had eaten the same thing at once. The boy was terrifying, working the changes fluidly, as though he'd begun practicing his finger movements on the spindles of his crib. Nathan pictured his own saxophone in dissembled pieces, the neck wrapped in the chamois cloth, the strap rolled away, the reeds tucked in their paper sleeves, all of it entombed beneath clothes and tennis racquets in a back closet at Claire's. He reminded himself that he still burned with the flames that everyone—the great New York lawyers, his instructors at the Manhattan School of Music, the audition jury at Juilliard—once spoke of as a kind of genius. When Claire used to whisper: How fine you were, how wonderfully you played. Together—what a team!—they were wonderful.

They were wonderful. How fine.

And where did it go? Where did the music go? Where did Claire go? Then it was years later and Nathan hadn't picked up the saxophone, and when he did one day on a whim the instrument was a small strange animal stiff and lifeless in his hands, and he put it down, his affections for it like old teenage love, leftovers from the first great meal of his life left too long.

Nathan has changed out of his suit. He stands before the french doors as before, though now in a blue blazer and light gray turtleneck, garnished with a nautical motif. A burgundy leather portmanteau hangs from one hand, his attaché case from the other. After the New Haven he had fully intended to bring Isabel back here for a nightcap and then out to East Hampton. Schreck could have handled the arraignments, Ruth the pleas. Somewhere he changed his mind. Somewhere he wanted to show her where Milton used to take him. Coney Island, capital of night. Somewhere it went wrong. She sobbed loudly. A car door slammed, but whose? Her flight along the boardwalk, her heels catching between the slats—

Outside now Barton has gone. Snow crosses the blue security light in the garden, a single beam of frost drawn through the night, daring Nathan to cross or stay. He is conscious, here and there, of new aches.

"Baron, come."

But outside on the stoop, Nathan and dog both are stopped by the sight of Oliver Schreck standing across the street. Snow has collected on his shoulders, salted the toboggan hat on his head, dusted away his tracks as if he has been there always, like a stanchion pile-driven into the sidewalk. Though Nathan believes he's caught Schreck clapping shut a cellular phone.

He leads Baron toward his car. Schreck, his feet ripping free of the snow, heads him off: "Nathan."

Baron begins to growl.

"Oliver, what are you doing here?"

"Good dog, good."

"How did you know about the apartment?"

"What are you talking about? Nathan, what the hell happened?"
Nathan's arm, as if of its own accord, waves behind him. The
apartment, it seems to say, will explain it all. "This address—"

Schreck eyes Baron warily. "I've been here before what do you
mean? I was—you *invited* me, Nathan. You let me, you know, use
it. Once or twice. You don't remember?"

With a glance toward Schreck, Nathan feels a peculiar embarrassment, that sense, almost, of indecency that he has been
Schreck's partner, his confederate in forgotten adventures. In the
snow, wrapped and hatted like a child, the prick looks so vulnerable and friendly. "Oliver, I'm in a hurry."

"Where to?"

"Rikers Island. We talked about this."

"Don't go."

"Not to see Johnny. It's Amparo—"

"Don't. Nathan, it's Isabel, didn't you hear?"

"Hear?"

"They found her, buddy boy," he says mournfully. "She's dead."

Nathan can't read him. Did Schreck think he was breaking the
news, or just confirming the obvious? His own face a mask,
Nathan considers him as something he might buy, a display of
clothing in a window. But he can't afford it. "I don't know what
you're talking about," he says, letting Baron in the car.

Schreck cocks his head. "Why are you lying?"

A cab pulls up and Ruth emerges and settles in the snow beside
Schreck, her bulk swaddled in red wool. They stand together, a
mismatched pair sending off their child to college, or the prom.
They exchange a glance that registers strangely with Nathan: is it
worry or pride? Ruth and Schreck have exchanged only venom
and vitriol, nothing remotely civil since law school. Not until now.
Or so he thought.

"And then there's this matter of Krivit," Schreck says. His voice
has lowered an octave, matured. As though one of the Oliver

Schrecks is an act. This Schreck, that Schreck. "Are you working on the brief?" he says flatly.

How does he know? Why does he know? Why does he care? Who is Oliver Schreck? These thoughts pass through Nathan's mind like little grace notes. "I told you, I didn't take the job," he says.

"Milton's worried," Schreck says.

"*Milton's* worried. This is nothing. Next to Riverside Drive this isn't peanuts."

"He wants you to take care of Krivit. Krivit's doing a lot for you. Milton just wants you to finish it off, you know, follow through with things. He wanted me to pass that along."

"Krivit's doing a lot for *me?*" Nathan glances at Ruth, but she is looking down at her feet, embarrassed, ashamed, or both. Nathan settles on a different thought altogether: Escape. "It's late," he says, and shuts the door.

Car and dog are one. The silvery hair is everywhere, woven into the seats and carpet. The paneling oozes dogsmell and rainy runs through the East Hampton woods. Beach sand sprinkled under the dash. The damp and sinewy pointer, his legs planted firmly in the back well of the vehicle, drapes himself over the front seat and rests his paws on Nathan's shoulders. His tongue now and again sneaks a swipe around Nathan's cheek into his eye; his hot breath in Nathan's ear; panting jowls resting on the top of Nathan's head. Like a person he demands attention, and when refused, takes it anyway.

It is eleven o'clock. And Nathan doesn't understand, anything, it seems. Quickly, like an addict hurrying the hit, he feeds a CD to the dashboard, then floats away on the streetlight's amber glow, the night before him stretching out like a rolling sea on which one sets sail primarily to be disoriented and lost.

But beeper then phone go off one after the other.

"Dominicans, Serena. It was Dominicans, not Puerto Ricans."

Still, he is relaxed. It is the music, the swell of spontaneous inspirations, emotional tremors. He leaves the silent phone on the dash and digs through a pile of bagel wraps and coffee cups, rescuing a remote control for a stereo six inches away. He points, fires, cocks his head, listening, and his hand lifts off the wheel, as if of its own accord, to conduct the grim opening strains of *Don Carlo*.

"No look, Serena, it's not that I'm just in a car. I'm sitting in traffic look . . . Who? I told you I'm with Oliver . . . No. Really. My *partner*. Yes I have a partner. *Oliver*."

Nathan blithely holds the phone toward the dog. "She doesn't believe me," he says. "Say something."

The dog pricks his ears, cocks his head. Nathan's eyes fall on the empty passenger seat, and for a moment he wonders why someone—he wonders who—isn't actually there.

In the rear-view mirror, the red sedan has pulled out thirty yards behind him. Its headlamps swing wide, then lock on the mirror. Nathan stops along the curb. The sedan stops half a block back, idling in the middle of the street. The two figures smoke steadily in the darkened car, the fringes of their hair and collars glowing behind the glass.

Nathan brings the phone to his ear, in case they might want to talk, but he hears only crackling silence and slips the phone into his pocket. His car creeps from the curb. "Isabel," he whispers. Baron barks at enemy apparitions, ghosts of dogs and figments of dog imagination, at nothing, anyway, that Nathan can or will ever imagine. In this city a thousand million lights come on, a thousand million lights go off. Passengers on the woollen sidewalks tip into the snow, clutching at hats and scarves. But Nathan feels in the air a sense of black conspiracy, as in a cove full of boats slowly turning together before a storm. Turning, as the winds shift, toward him. He accelerates past an office tower, the illuminated news aloft passing around the corner of the building, news of mass slaughter in Burundi, an orphanage bombed in Sarajevo, forty-two Dominican illegals drowned in a boat disaster, the Knicks' afternoon loss to the Celtics in Boston, of, suddenly, nothing, snapping off into muteness, as if something—the world, his own capacity for information—has come to an abrupt end, and there is news of nothing at all.

———————

Santos leans solitary and lamplit against his car, sucking his coated teeth. In the shelter of this block the snowflakes swirl softly. Across the street the address Nathan left for him on his message service stands dark save a single window, on the ground floor, dimly lit behind a thick curtain. A figure passes before it, passes again. Someone small, someone's child. Three stoops down an old man spends this cold night in a doorway in bewildered repose.

Santos is considering giving up as Nathan's car stops and Nathan himself climbs out. "Cold enough for you?" Santos says.

"What—?"

"It's Errol, Nathan."

Nathan takes a step toward him, looking about, hesitant.

"You told me to be here," Santos says.

"Of course."

"I didn't realize you had an uptown place, too."

"I lost track of the time."

"This is a terrible day to do that."

"I know, I'm sorry—about Isabel. It's—" His hands move slightly with the wooden smile he manages. "It's unspeakable. I don't know what to say. I don't see you once in five years, now twice in one day. But over this—"

Santos shifts a little on his feet and watches him. "You know why I called. It wasn't for you to express your grief."

Nathan just looks.

"You sent the flowers," Santos says carefully.

"I did?"

"It was your father."

Nathan shrugs. "He doesn't do anything. Maybe his secretary—"

Santos pinches his eyes. "Jesus christ, Nathan, just do me the fucking courtesy."

Nathan looks away and Santos lights a cigarette, points to Nathan's wrist. "Tell me about the scratches."

"Is this an investigation, Errol? Are you interrogating me?"

"It is what it is. Answer the question."

"Is it your investigation?"

"Answer me."

"Because if it's not, you won't be able to use a thing."

Santos watches the cigarette smoke spiral and unwind in the snow. The rope pulls through his chest, the knot in his lungs tightening. He reaches for the bulge in his coat pocket but looking at Nathan leaves the inhaler alone. "Just tell me about the scratches."

"It was a cat."

Santos looks back at the car. All the windows have fogged. The ghost-shape of the dog hovers in the rear, nosing the glass, his huge pink tongue pulsing. "You hate cats."

Santos doesn't mean to, but he feels it coming—reaching up, he touches his eyes with the balls of his fingers. Then he grabs Nathan. "What the fuck did you do? She was my *sister*."

"You don't know what you're saying," Nathan says.

Santos presses a finger into his own chest. "Who are you talking to here? She was like the others, and the others, and the others. It's not like I've forgotten anything. You think I'd forget all that sick shit? I know, Nathan. I know you were with her last night."

"I was, but we saw Figaro at the Met. We had dinner at Gambone's. We went up to the New Haven."

"Jesus, all your haunts. You were working her over, giving her the business."

"I know what this looks like, but I have nothing to hide."

"Don't"—Santos lets the shout out into the night, but it dies in the snow, falls at their feet—"lie to me." He pulls Nathan down a step. Their breath mingles and coils and Santos can smell it in him, sweet death at the edges. No one's but his. "You don't exactly look like an innocent man."

"We both know it's not how someone looks, Errol."

Santos says, his voice giving way, "This is no time to be playing lawyer. I'm talking about my sister. You never had a secretary you didn't fuck."

A strange smile crosses Nathan's lips. "And she's been my secretary for four years. What finally brings you out tonight?"

Santos breathes. "What—?" His arms drop like a stricken puppet's. "She's dead, Nathan."

"I've known for hours."

The tightness has spread from Santos's chest to his arms now, his hands. "Maybe you've known longer than that."

"You're no saint, Errol," Nathan says. "None of us are. But you've done well. I'm sure Claire would say so."

"Nathan, my god—"

"Of course I see the romantic predicament you two are in. I'm not angry about you and Claire. In a way I was glad it was you."

Santos runs his hands over his face. "How do you do it? How do you make everyone want to kill you, and then want to save you?"

"We're tied together, Errol. We grew up together. You don't kill your friends."

Santos drops a step back. "There's a point when you do. There's a point when you have to, when they're the only ones worth killing."

"And worth dying for," Nathan adds.

Usually, Nathan is slippery, his eyes skipping along the surface of things, skidding, his hands fidgety. But now he seems to still, his eyes focusing, leveling at Santos a steady stare. "There's something you don't know."

His breath thin and thinner. Santos looks at Nathan warily. "Tell me one thing I don't know."

"You don't want it."

"I want it."

"You'll have to talk to Ellie."

"My mother would be happier dead right now. She's in no condition. What does my mother have to do with this?"

"You won't ask her?"

"No."

Leaning, Nathan whispers something in Santos's ear. Santos coughs into his fist, his chest hard as wood. His heart thuds, getting hot.

As Nathan speaks, Santos raises and lowers his arm two or three times, trying to compose the news out of the air. Then a headache, sudden, blinding. Squeezing the bridge of his nose between thumb and forefinger, he feels the weight of the whole of the city behind him, the permanent daylight, the trace lamplight, the lightning beyond the clouds. At night in this city, around every corner, everyone a potential murderer, everyone a potential murder. Santos sees how he used to wake as a boy in the night in terror of the uninvited ghouls that crouched in the dark corners of his room. The imagined gargoyles and demons that dropped from incandescent webs. He sees his parents and their one boy and two girls and the stretches of angry silence that sent them to opposite ends of a small apartment. He sees the last time he and his sister touched: adults outgrown in their childhood home she ripped the phone out of his hands for no reason at all and he pinned her shoulders to the wall. A spat that lovers might have. Fighting the hideous urge to kiss her. Calmly, she threatened to scream, Rape. And then she did scream it. She took a breath, looked at him, her eyes full of mischief, then screamed it again. His glare dimmed and his hatred softened and he considered the line between lust and indifference and the fact of their blood relation, and he released her. She screamed a third time, at first he thought for the hell of it. Though she seemed to mean it. She was shrieking, tearing at her hair, as if she saw someone else in him, someone worth running from. And maybe he was, someone to run from. He sees her coming at him with a pair of scissors and he sees himself fighting her off, flinging her across the bed and turning and running away, and boarding the downtown bus he leaned his head against the plexiglass and closed his eyes. Remorse in his throat like a hot cinder. He hadn't seen her since, until today.

Somehow did he know?

Because of Isabel's green eyes? Because he couldn't bear to see her again, because he wrote them both off—her and Nathan— together, Nathan because of what he'd become, Isabel because of what she'd always been? He'd understood that of course he'd be able to have, possess, love, neither of them. They shone in a secret constellation in which he was some imploded, snuffed star, at the center of which, drawing everyone in, unseen, menacing as a black hole, hovered Milton Stein.

The day he said goodbye to them all he rode the bus and walked the Brooklyn Bridge to Claire's apartment and for the first time, with hardly a word between them, they made love; as though she understood as well as he, as though she had been waiting for him, or half expecting him. It was blind sex fueled by a lusty terror of the truth. They were both Nathan's dupes, patsies, and foolishly Santos believed he was making Claire an offer of reconciliation, to generously fill the void left by Nathan with something better, at least something honorable. He would love her as she deserved to be loved. But he was only filling himself. The spic apprentice. And he knows now that he was thinking he wouldn't miss a sister he had coveted for unnatural reasons but may never have actually had. And he was thinking that those things we go out of our way not to ask we know to be true.

All that we have done, Santos sees now, all that we do, is no longer a question of rehabilitation. It is, like everything, merely a question of outlasting the consequences.

Winded, buried in worlds of his own making, he squats in the snow like an ape, his back to Nathan, crying openly. "God help you," he says.

He hears the heavy door behind him swing open then closed. A lock turns. Nathan's footsteps fade down a hallway. Santos grips the iron banister and hoists himself up and turns and steps down to the sidewalk, and with a drunk's meticulousness crosses the street through a circle of spotlit snow and fades into the dark other side.

Inside, the lamps are off. The dark smells like a sleeping child, warm, pungent. Outside, Santos's car pulls away and fades down the street.

A low light comes on against a far wall. Nathan quickly steps through a doorway. Another, distant lamp comes on: an unmade bed, a nightstand littered with prescription vials; an IV propped in a corner; a black brassiere draped over the back of a chair.

Heading for the bathroom, Nathan stops at the bed. The pillows are dented, the sheets wrinkled, the blankets thrown back. Evidence that he has lain here. Of Maria as she was five years earlier, dancing with her girlfriend in the middle of Limelight's dance floor. The gray cashmere wrap keeping her to small twitchy movements, ginger motions of hips and shoulders, not restraint as much as a suggestion of wider possibilities. Her head tossed back, her hands running up and down her own thighs, she seduced the room with her self-sufficiency.

Nathan had been standing in his suit with his elbows propped up against the bar, his briefcase wedged between his feet. It was a Wednesday night. He was not the only man alone, or wearing a suit, or the only one with his eyes trained on her, but at two o'clock he was the only one to walk over. She looked at his briefcase, then up at him, as if he were breaking some rule. And he was, he was sure. He wasn't dancing. She looked at him again. He asked for her phone number. She didn't hesitate, but she didn't seem to give it much thought. He called one week later. She said no, he'd waited too long. The next night he arrived at her apartment with flowers, and the night following he picked up her things and her boy and by morning she had her name on his mail slot and her mail forwarded to East Eighty-ninth Street and Benny was pulled out of that school and put into this one. The delivery trucks came and went. A new bed. A new TV. A desk and chair for Benny. An Electrolux. A thoroughbred English pointer Maria named Baron. In the morning Nathan opened his eyes to the smell of coffee and Maria standing before the mirror making, again, small movements of hips and shoulders in her new tweed suit, with flowers in her hair.

Nathan opens a dresser drawer and feels along the bottom beneath the underwear. He opens another drawer, then another. He sweeps his hand under the mattress, squeezes the pillows. He flips clothes, tosses shoes. Stacks of paper topple. A bottle of perfume upends and fills the room with sickly sweetness. Under something, behind something else, Maria's jewelry box: inside, a legal-sized envelope. Nathan slips out the contents. Maria Rosa. Last Will and Testament. Revised a month ago, prepared by, dated by, signed and notarized by one Oliver Schreck. Nathan's quivering finger rests on Roatán. On Benny.

A medicine cabinet opening, he prowls through the contents. Full prescription vials fall clattering like maracas to the sink. He counts pills and puts them between his teeth and bites. He picks another vial and overturns it and cups the entire contents in his palm and stares into the mirror, looking at nothing, not even himself.

His eyes open level with the sink. At some point he has fallen and is left now in a low squat. The taste of saltwater on his lips, his eyes burn. He squeezes a vial in his palm but it slips out and rolls to the wall. Miraculously he stands, fills the sink and slips in his rashy wrists. His eyes slide to the side, listening, his face a convergence of rivers of thought, lips twisted, one eye half closed, interrupted—

Maria here in this bed. No needles. No tubes. Just a Washington Heights beauty queen and happiness once, for once real happiness, for one good year, then a second, distinctly less good, then their common verdict and three more years as cell mates imprisoned by their living death. All the while, after leaving Claire, there was his other life as a bachelor in his own downtown garden apartment. Two beds to change, two faces to wash, two sets of delinquent bills and their attendant threats. Two skies to simultaneously breathe.

He pulls the rubber stopper to let it all drain. The water slides slowly and evenly down the wall of the sink, the drain gasps, and the rest of it is sucked away.

She did this. She killed me.

"Daddy?"

A small sleepy voice. Nathan catches his own eyes in the mirror and remembers his first night alone with Benny. Maria had gone out, some place with friends. To leave the men to themselves, she'd said. But the boy fell asleep quickly. His breath pulled in and out between his bunched lips, his fine hair fanned over the pillow, the perfect skin of his pouched cheeks, flushed with heat but drained of vitality. Looking down at the boy, a dead place had opened in Nathan and he felt the terror of a child's sleep so heavy one fraction of an ounce more and slumber might slip through the skin of life and plummet through to infinity and death. He reached to the boy and lifted his arm, pudgy and kinked, to confirm for himself the boy's warmth and the hesitant breath, the steady, steady pulse. Still there. He slid a CD into the stereo, Bill Evans on piano, a blessed jangling, chattering glass, that must sound very like a dreamworld, even to a boy. He thought it might inspire something in the boy's imagination, but what would it be? What did it inspire in his own? He rattled around the apartment. He turned on all the lights, he turned on the television. He drank scotch and leafed through *Vanity Fair*. He moved things from here to there, touching everything he passed as if he could add the furniture and underwear and books and the smashed plastic toys and even the dog to his life's inventory and stuff that emptiness, fill it, fill it up. The music wasn't doing it. Sitting on the edge of his bed he hugged his knees and braced himself to slide across the chasm between the darkness and the time when in the blue flash of morning sun the boy appeared, resurrected, atop the big bed, apprehensively petting his mother's perfect face, just as Nathan had touched the boy's, to confirm sweet life; as Maria, the night before that night, had touched Nathan's, while Nathan faked sleep. Sweet life.

He had awoken to a scatter of black vinyl crumbs in their bed, across the floor, in his hair. The remains of his vast collection of irreplaceable LPs, his purest—maybe only—joy. These discs that ask nothing but only give and give, hurled, obviously, one after the other against the wall, entire epochs of music history, their composers, their virtuosos, annihilated, until the room looked as if it had rained coal. The cardboard jackets and their liner notes and librettos torn to bits. Maria swore it hadn't been her. Why would she have done it? Though, on the other hand, now that the records were gone, she was sorry she hadn't thought of it herself. But if it wasn't her, then who—? After all, the shards were strewn in his hair, not hers. It was his liter of Dewar's lying empty amidst the rubble, not hers—

Maria's last will and testament dangles over the sink. Nathan lights a match.

"Daddy?"

The small voice creeps up on him. He locates in the mirror the boy standing in the reflection of the living room. It takes a moment for Nathan to adjust to his realization that he knows this boy. How easy it is to forget. This child has to be somewhere. Where else would he have been but in his mother's apartment?

The paper flames brightly then quickly shrinks and blackens, run through by worms of red ash.

"What are you doing?"

"Benny, go back to bed."

"Did you see Mommy?"

"I saw her. Your grandma come by after school?"

The boy nods.

"She gave you your supper?"

The boy keeps nodding. "When is Mommy coming home?"

Nathan, fugitive from a half-dozen lives, shuts his eyes, summons the lie. But what to base honesty on? These little alternative versions are superior, happier, cleaner, evidence of a better, more just, world. The kid will sleep, he'll get through another night, another day, week. Maria can hold on another week. "Soon," Nathan says. "Soon."

Retreating, Benny turns in time to see the crack of light melt away as the door closes, leaning against the wall in wait, on the boy's face the same resigned expression—hopeless expectancy—of the expectant dog.

Eventually the boy goes back to bed, and Nathan trades the apartment for the cold. He goes down the stairs to the car, to the empty streets, and to Baron, who does not get left behind.

**MIDNIGHT** She has a shadow, Claire sees. The snow is holding. The neighborhood is quiet, even the boats in the harbor. The moon, making an appearance, moves swiftly against a current of clouds, recasting the frontage street as a blue field, where the sidewalks and the approaches to the brownstones and tenement walk-ups and the jetties across the street end without warning and begin the harbor.

She takes off her coat and hangs it on her arm, half believing half wishing to feel the cold. But she doesn't, she can't, feel a thing. It's there somewhere, but the liquor, thank god, is warding it off, bracing her with a strange disaffection. But she is alive, she has an effect—nearing her street she sends dogs behind some darkened window barking, and the barking follows her up that street and around the corner and the rest of the way home.

Inside she tries to walk the hall quietly, but the floorboards are old and her care only prolongs the creaking. With the sleeve of her coat she loosens the bulb in the hallway fixture so that it will not be the light to wake the baby, should he still need waking. Through the door she hears a loud silence, the silence of someone there but not saying anything, maybe someone asleep. The door is unlocked. Some smell has set in, seeped into the floor, the walls, the drapery, slightly acrid, slightly smoky.

She swears the moonlight bends over him in luminous strips, defining the child—for he would have been a child by now, wouldn't he, not a mere infant?—spread across the mattress, not stillborn, too late for that, but still nonetheless. How odd that at birth he already had Nathan's blocky nose and eyes the color car salesmen call sea foam. The baby's hands tangled in his wispy sprigs of hair, his mouth hung open, those eyes all frozen pupil. She in her gauzy nightie had taken him on her shoulder and walked him around to get the air up, or in, but poor thing he was so floppy and limp, his boneless limbs no help at all, he couldn't hold on.

With her coat still on her arm she watches the corner beside her bed where he used to breathe. On the counter, darker shapes rise out of the darkness, a glass, an arranged plate. The window rattles. It has begun to squall again. The lamplight brings it all in: the various darknesses, the breadth of her bed, the snowshadows raining silently through the blinds, the slow tapping of a water drip, the knocking of the radiator. And here the smallest of the boy's ancient rises and collapses. Claire feels the riot of it all in her head and through her veins; she feels it leap from her heart and she wants to leap after it, bound onto the bed with her little boy in her arms to tell him how glorious it all is—how joyful, how glorious!

The door closes. Claire slumps against it, barring the way. The taste of seawater in her mouth rides her throat where the rage is so thick she needs her palm flat against her chest to catch her breath. Tears sting her blind eyes as she swims her way chair to chair to table to bed. Outside a car door slams, an engine coughs to life, and Nathan, she is certain, is pulling from the curb, untethered now, floating away downriver. She traces the fading hiss of tires until it is a single grain of noise in a night teeming with life, and Nathan is washed away, absorbed by the hordes. And still, after all this time, it is not her fault. The bastard. She didn't hear the baby go upright, or gurgle, or choke for that matter. He was clutching the blankets to his throat for warmth, his little shrunken shoulders bare. Claire had seen in his staring, beaded eyes two windows letting out on their future, the future something irrecoverable, lost along the way, or never found—

The blue snow-light moves across her, across her face in the mirror. She primps at her hair, fixing a smile of courage so she will not cringe, mouthing something while she put the baby's mouth to her breast, still sore and leaking with milk. But he didn't take, poor thing he couldn't grip the nipple, so she opened his mouth and dropped it in, whitening his tongue, the watery milk running sideways and down into the crevices underneath and gooing up the back of his throat, pooling in the little ditch between lip and gum. The throat didn't budge, the windpipe surprisingly tough but infuriatingly still. Drink, baby. She lay with him again on the bed, her nightie rolled to her waist like a life preserver, keeping her afloat while she tried one breast, then the other. The sky that early morning had been a gray, empty radiance, no kind of dawn. She turned the knob on the radio but when she found something she liked she clutched her face with her free hand and immediately began to cry, her tears running between her fingers. She didn't bother staying quiet because she didn't mind waking somebody, the faceless neighbors above her and below, their damn footsteps and the thudding bass of their music, damn Nathan, where was he while she pressed the baby to her lap, between her legs, maybe to get him back up there, start it all over again. Still sore from stitches, the delivery not the easiest, and the baby stone still in the leaching light—drink, baby, drink—already blue, already dead of everything and of nothing in particular. As if there was simply no room in this region for one more life, even this one innocent piece of Nathan in all this world.

Claire looks at her watch. Damn you, Errol, where are you?

All at once the dark gives, and the shadows belong to the false streetlamp dawn. Off the back of a chair hangs a white brassiere, her blue jeans. Claire collapses on her bed and reaches. On the bed stand a light clicks on. A half-gone glass of water. A book that will help her last perhaps until two or three.

As Santos lets himself in the front door of his mother's apartment he thinks he hears his name called somewhere by one of those headless voices that announce his fears. The windows are open. The curtains flutter like flags.

His mother waits at the kitchen table, seated among votive candles. She fingers a pewter picture frame, another gift from the Steins. Though he can see only the felt back, Santos knows whose face it contains.

"I can't help wondering what she was thinking about," she says. "Was she terrified, did she know? Did she feel the animal's claws around her neck? Did she fight?" Her spectacles wink in the light as she lifts her head. "Where have you been?"

Past supplying answers, Santos listens for evidence of others in the apartment but hears nothing and is grateful for their absence. Who knows what he knows? Who would have believed it could be true? He draws a deep breath. A kink has formed in his stomach and now takes the form of nausea. He feels as if he has just this night stumbled upon the misfortune of being a grown man who has in his life understood too little and trusted too much. Breathe, breathe: he feels more than ever as if his lungs are not deep enough. "Where are they?" he asks.

"Sonia is in her old room, the boys in yours. The others I sent away."

"You don't want company."

"There is nothing to talk about, unless you are here now to tell me they know who it was. Do they know?"

Santos sits. The teeth of flame shift and steady in their columns of glass.

"Go to Claire," she says. "You are more her husband than my son."

"We're not married, Momma."

"You should be."

"Did Claire come? Did she call?"

"And to be with her you divorced that poor girl, ruined her, a good Catholic. Claire was Nathan's, Milton's son's girl."

"I wasn't good enough?"

"She was never meant for you."

"She was no one's."

His mother lifts her chin with indignation, her mouth firm. "Isabel will always be more my daughter than your sister."

She says other things, old, bitter things, swinging at the countering claims of enemy apparitions.

"I saw Nathan," he says finally.

"He will miss Isabel," she says. "More than you."

"I'm sure. Maybe he has more reason to."

She turns her face on her son and he returns her stare.

"He told me," he says.

A flickering look of impatience in her face, then her mouth makes a move very like a smile.

Santos can feel the pressure behind his own face, something welling in back of his eyes, words, beliefs, memories. He says, "I want to know, is it true."

His mother rests the picture face down and drapes a hand across it.

He nods at the picture frame. "Did Daddy know?" his voice suddenly sounding to him too small for a man.

"He knew."

Whispering, "How did he stay? How did he stand him, Nathan, and his stories, and me, me and my trying so hard to be him?"

"Life is not clear, Errol," she says. "He of all people understood that."

"He. What do you know about clear? I've seen brothers decapitate brothers, mothers stab daughters, boys run over their fathers. It is not our instinct to avoid misery, but if you survive it's because that's what you've done. Let me tell you what was clear—Isabel's body wrapped in seaweed and shit, naked on a beach in front of bums and whores and strangers."

She looks up, hands trembling on the frame.

"You've dipped us in shit. Tell me after Isabel you stopped."

"How can I explain this to you? We had nothing. He gave us—"

"He gave you!" Santos roars, and here it is, the source of his own envy—what the Santoses had, what the Steins had—what they *gave* them. "Look at the shithole you live in, this crap neighborhood. The trinkets Milton Stein has given you over the years have only made this place more pitiful. It's payoff. What he gave you, Momma? He *gave* it to you in his office, on the floor—"

"Errol—"

"I know him, I know what and I know where and I know how. He's a legend, in case you didn't know. Though of course you had to. You probably set up the rendezvous, his loyal private secretary. I always knew. I just didn't, obviously, always know who."

"My god."

"And I don't care. Just say you stopped," he says. "After she was born. Can you say that?"

She says nothing.

"Then how many years? From when to when?" Santos cries. His fear has chased him down, cornered him. This too.

She is crying.

"What year to what year?" The knot in his stomach flying undone, the little pulse of air rising to his throat, "Please god tell me I'm not his."

She manages to motion no.

He reaches across the table and clutches her wrist. He raises it, her hand flopping like a puppet's. "Swear it," he whispers.

"I swear."

Dropping her hand, he considers her. "Can I believe you?"

She says, "What do you want to believe?"

"How do you know for sure?"

Fearful, her face awash, she raises a quivering finger. "Look at you."

He grabs for the picture frame and slides it out from under his mother's hands and sandwiches it protectively between his palms. "Look at me," he says. He turns the picture. His own face superimposed on his father's, feature for feature. He cannot conclude. Maybe. Christ, maybe. He can't be sure.

He knows now the meaning of his father's last plea. A father warning off his son. To have gone to work for the Steins would have been to be pulled under, dragged into that dark constellation. Whether or not there was a genetic tie wouldn't have mattered. Blood would have passed: Milton's son, Nathan's brother.

"And Sonia?"

Her unfocused eyes watch his hands. They slowly close, then open. "Your father's."

"You don't even know," he says. "What makes you think Isabel didn't take your job completely? Bred for his pleasure. Look where she worked. Look what she was surrounded by day after day. Like you said, more your daughter than my sister—"

She slaps the table. "He was her father."

Santos feels the cruel smile on his mouth. His mother clasps both hands over her face. The past is drowned in the bitterest mistakes, and the future, in one clear moment, is upon him. He can see Isabel's funeral, he can see his mother's, Nathan's, Claire's, Milton's, he can see his own. He sees the whole cast, who will be there and how they will be situated, sitting, then standing and, crying, riding to the cemetery. And he knows who will be buried, will lie wooden, varnished, a blanched powdery sack on a bed of bleached satin cushions. The terror so great it feels already like nostalgia, like something lived and over with, memorized in an old and distant sorrow.

What has begun is already over. And here now is how the dead are beyond death. Death is what the living carry with them. The living ferry the consequences but the dead do not remember, and nothingness, Santos sees, is not a curse. Far from it.

Nathan leans into the cold wind, his arms at his side, his briefcase in one hand. Behind him the Rikers Island waiting room like an airport's, plastic eggcup seats and columns of cigarette sand and dingy light and a large window letting out onto a blank expanse. The shuttle bus's headlights appear across the stretch of empty tarmac, the snow before it coiling and whorling. Beyond shine patches of yellow light. Glinting billows of concertina wire.

The virtues of prison are not lost on him. He's considered the ease of a morning meal, an afternoon meal, an evening meal, an hour of exercise, a menial job. In the last months he's weighed the pleasures he could take in boundaries against the jail of his current boundlessness and found that, quarantine or full exposure, it could go either way. A thousand hours he's spent already inside this prison, nodding at the declarations of virginal innocence, the lies, the crudely fashioned alibis. He mentally calculates his clients' worth, constructing a plea bargain in his head. Then he sells them. He puts them on the block like highboys at an auction, and the young A.D.A.'s, overloaded, begging for pleas, will give what he wants, as long as it's something. But Nathan gets paid either way. In fact, he gets more for a guilty, more for the appeal, still more for the parole hearings, and then a last retainer for the inevitable parole. And then, of course, they'll be back. Out and back in through the revolving door. And then there are the friends his clients make in the clink. The calls Nathan gets in the middle of the night. They need his fluent Spanish, his sharp wit, his way with the lady judges. Always everyone is worth more in jail than out.

When was the last time Nathan threw a curveball at a jury with an actual innocent man? His first two years out of law school, before he joined up with his father, Milton called in a favor and got his now-famous friend Sidney Frankel to take his son on. Frankel let Nathan watch him serve up witnesses through cross-examination and pound them over the net until, flinching, they were something less than their former selves. That booming voice, that six-foot-six-inch frame bearing down on you. He knew everything, he knew when you were lying and when you were telling the truth. And even the truth, Frankel had always said: Truth was just a better lie. You pick one and you dress it up with evidence and motivation and hope. You build a world around it, you found a country, identify it by what it's not: it's not a murderer, it's not a rapist, it's not a dealer. It's bad but not *that* bad. Who among us is as pure as the driven snow? A simple case of wrong place at the wrong time. There but by the grace of God. Otherwise it looks just like you and me. You and me. Judge not lest ye be judged. And hopefully after all that a sun will rise and set and the world you have built will spin. This is how we construct our lives. There's no difference. Life is a trial. We spend our days making our case before a jury of our peers, Frankel always said. Are you innocent,

Nathan? Even you, the lawyer. Are you pure, are you chaste? The juries of our lives never can know. In the end, only you are certain that you're not. But still, I'll let you convince me that you are.

Then that was gone, lost. Frankel sent him away. Now Nathan sells off his clients at market value, usually three-to-life. Who's to say no? After all, as Frankel always said, they're all guilty of something, if not this crime then another. Nathan deposits their money then gives them away. The crestfallen parents, babbling on in their Dominican Spanish, weeping in the corridors.

Headlights stab through the snow, speeding forward, a tail of exhaust, just as he sees again his last act as Frankel's proxy. Frankel had handed him the controls for a sentencing. A mere formality. A three-time loser with legal bills a year overdue. The atmosphere in the courtroom was unexpectant. There was no suspense. Frankel himself couldn't have cared less. Nathan can't remember now what the charge was, attempted murder, aiding and abetting, it didn't matter, there was nothing to discuss. It was going to be life at Greenhaven without parole. They were all waiting for the bailiff to bring him out of the bullpen. Nathan was chatting with the A.D.A., the judge with his clerk, the court officers amongst themselves. The stenographer was filing her nails. The bailiff swung open the door. The stenographer screamed and threw up her hands. The officers dropped to their knees and drew their revolvers. The judge ducked under the bench. Then everyone slowly stood. The officers holstered their guns. Nathan rose off the floor. A pair of sneakers swung in the doorway, halfway up, a pair of limp, blueing hands. A bench lay on its side. Nathan didn't even know the name. He looked down at his notes: there swung one Raúl Gómez, father, husband, son, someone's brother—there's so much to be—formerly residing at 67-54 Fordham Road, the Bronx, twenty-one years old forever.

Frankel said word had gotten around Centre Street. Everyone was talking about the young attorney who couldn't get his client to prison alive. Nathan wasn't doing enough, and there was too much reputation to lose. The next day Milton gave Nathan a set of office keys.

The headlights swing wide then stop. They stab into the dark, run through with large flakes of snow. An old school bus, windows fitted with steel mesh. The doors fold open. The driver, seated in a cage, peers down at him. His eyes wet—is it the snow?—Nathan steps aboard.

In the ward the guard leads him into a space partitioned by glass into three cubicles. A back door swings open. Two women file in. Gray flannel uniforms that look homemade. Both are young, Latina. The first, a teenager, is pregnant. She is blank, anonymous; on the streets she would be invisible. The other enters like a force that strikes him. Carefully groomed, heavily made-up, her long jet-black hair pulled off her wide forehead, her eyes chips of coal. A beauty that is at once an advantage and an impairment. Even in her uniform she seems ready for a party as yet unannounced or unplanned.

She pinches Nathan's arm as she goes by.

"Buenas noches, Amparo." He smiles.

She takes in Nathan's face, apparently with pleasure. "You said six o'clock."

"Buenas noches," Nathan says to the other, trying to summon the salesman's charm he saves for prospective clients.

The girl ducks; her lips attempt a smile but fail.

A guard comes up behind them, shooing them on. The women sit in the far cubicle, Nathan in the middle, the guard nearest the door. Nathan rests a legal pad on his knees. He nods at the guard. She stands and goes out.

When the door closes, Amparo peers over the edge of the partition into the hallway. The guard there has left her desk. The others in the booth have turned their backs. Amparo prods the pregnant girl to her feet and leads her into the next partition with Nathan. The girl's face is cut, he sees, her bottom lip swollen. Amparo and the girl sit.

Amparo takes out cigarettes and lights one. The girl reaches for the pack but Amparo pulls it back and holds it over her head as if away from a small child or dog. She blows smoke in the girl's face.

"Don't you know you can't smoke when you're pregnant?" The girl looks blank-faced and Amparo rolls her eyes at Nathan. "A peasant, my cousin. She's never left America but there she sits unable to speak the language."

"She's your cousin?" Nathan asks.

"Sorry to say." As though struck by a sudden thought, a long-forgotten memory, Amparo whirls on the girl. "Jíbara! Nunca tú irás de este país, y sin embargo nunca aprenderás su lengua."

The girl slouches in her chair, her face fixed in an expression of deep dismay.

Crossing her legs Amparo bounces the top one as though testing the knee. "The peasant needs you. Tell Mr. Stein what happened."

The girl speaks at the level of whisper. Her fingers flutter. "Hoy me acuchillaron por buena, al paracer no les gusta la gente feliz, hay que estar realmente loco. Fue la chica que supuestamente me iba a cuidar, ella fue la que me jodió. Era la chica que estaba supuesta ayudarme, fue la que me contuvo."

Amparo leans forward conspiratorially. "She got cut today for being too nice. They don't like happy people here. You have to be mad, she said. She said it was the girl who was supposed to help her, she was the one who held her down. Her boss in the law library." She smokes thoughtfully, then leans and stubs out the cigarette in an aluminum ashtray and gestures vaguely in the air with one hand. "My cousin is a retarded Snow White. She didn't do nothing wrong. And her baby's coming. When, darling? Cuándo nacerá el bebé?"

The girl, crying, turns away.

Amparo shrugs. "I think next week maybe."

"Of course," Nathan says, and taps the pencil eraser repeatedly on the paper. "Who was your lawyer at the arraignment?"

The girl begins to speak, but Amparo interrupts her: "Herbert Harvey," she says. "Or Harvey Herbert. Siempre me olvido. Idiot. He wants her to plea to save himself the trouble, but I'm telling you she didn't know nothing about what was in that box. She was sitting in that apartment waiting for her man Arelis, who was delivering. So it's smack. So what? So it's none of her business. She's sitting filing her nails like a good girlfriend, keeping her feet up on the whatchucallit, el marco de la ventana."

"Windowsill," Nathan suggests.

"Windowsill. Minding her own business. A beautiful day, you know? She's listening to the radio, doing a little cha-cha out the window, rubbing her belly, talking to her baby, making it feel better about coming out into this piece of shit world. Then there's a knock on the door and it's the mailman with a box. She's expecting a box of baby stuff from the hospital so she signs for it then sits back down to make her nails nice. Then the next thing she knows her door is broken down and six cops are running around the apartment with guns."

Half rising out of her chair, Amparo aims her fingers with thumbs cocked.

"They got dogs. The dogs are tearing everything up. They make her lie down on the bed with her hands over her head while they empty her closets. One of them sits on the bed with her and plays with her tits, for as you see, she has very nice tits. Then they make her open the box in front of them. She thought it was baby stuff."

"From the hospital," Nathan says.

Amparo turns to the girl. "Que había en la caja?"

"Fórmula, pañales y otras cosas."

"Formula and diapers," Amparo explains. "It's a free program they got."

"What was the return address on the box?"

Amparo waves Nathan away. "So it's Bogotá." She shrugs. "The peasant doesn't read."

"Baby supplies from Bogotá," Nathan says aloud, just to hear how it will sound to the judge, maybe jury. He sighs. He puts pencil to paper. "When?"

"Three months ago."

Nathan looks up. "Why not bail?"

"She can't make it," Amparo says.

Nathan taps the pencil tip against the pad. "How much?"

"Five hundred," Amparo says.

"Cinco," the girl spits, thrusting five fingers at the air as if against an invisible wall.

Nathan looks back and forth between the girl and Amparo. "She couldn't make five hundred dollars? You?"

Amparo shrugs, as if to say, Why should I help?

"Is Arelis the father?" Nathan asks. "Arelis es el padre del niño?"

"Sí," the girl says.

But Amparo shrugs. "You think she knows?"

Nathan looks at the girl a long time, as if trying to decide, or deciding whether to decide, or if any of this warrants a decision. He writes, because he thinks he should, on a random line in the middle of the legal pad: *Arelis*.

Amparo leans back and the girl leans back with her. They conference quietly and Nathan drifts down a strain of music floating by in the wake of a ribbon of thought: Johnny Hartman crooning, "My One and Only Love"—

"She don't know anything else about anybody else," Amparo says. "But someone has been here."

The girl hands across a business card. Nathan holds it with both hands and looks at it a long time. It is Claire's. He pockets it and puts down his pencil. "Forget about this," he says. His pad of paper is blank, save *Arelis,* a name that floats in the middle of the yellow pad without context and without identification. The entire case. He'll sell.

"So how is my case progressing, Mr. Stein?" Amparo says coolly.

"I talked with Roberto tonight. He said—"

She slumps forward on her elbows. "Is it safe?"

"I talked with him tonight."

She taps her chin. "Did you."

"That's what I said. It's safe."

"Who says? You or Roberto?" Nathan doesn't answer and she pulls hard on another cigarette and cocks a wary eye across the table at Nathan. "Because Manny thinks Roberto's out of town. So I wonder how you could have called him."

Nathan scratches his arm. The wounds there have begun to itch in the warmth.

"I suppose you'd tell me if this isn't true," she says.

"Of course."

Amparo leans back, fragile and exposed. She seems to hold this news close to her breast. "Because if you are wrong Roberto will kill me as sure as I am sitting here before you. And if I am killed I will leave orders. You will not live five minutes." She smiles broadly.

"I talked to him," Nathan says.

"Why don't I believe you?" Her fingers shakily turn the burning stub of her cigarette on herself. She ignites a fresh one, which leads into her mouth like a fuse, and waves it in exasperation. "You still have the money I gave you?"

"Of course."

Amparo pushes her hands at the air between them. "That I don't believe, but I have no choice. Tomorrow then. You make the payment tomorrow by noon and then it's all safe and you take me to a beautiful lunch. Then we go lie down in East Hampton."

Nathan nods. "Of course. But it's cold. It's winter."

"Winter. Of course. In here one forgets these things." Amparo smiles and leans over the table, playful now. "Now this matter of my payment. My payment to you. For your services. It's good. It's beautiful." She lifts her arms, indicating the space behind him, as though offering a tropical beach, white sand, paradise. "A Land Cruiser," she says. "Forest green. Leather everywhere I am told. It sits in your garage."

Nathan stiffens. "My—?"

"East Hampton. They had to move the motorcycle. Manny says it's a very nice motorcycle. He says it rides real nice. He said you have nice toys inside the house, a very nice kitchen. And the bedrooms, he said, magnífico. That bed of yours he warned me was as big as the lawn, but you need to clean the pool."

Nathan looks at her. He pictures the house, at the end of a cul-de-sac, hidden behind a stand of thick trees and brush. "How did they know the house?"

Amparo laughs pleasantly. "How many times do I have to tell you that I know everything? I know you don't believe me, but I do. All of us, we all know where you live."

Then as if to prove it Nathan's telephone chirps in his jacket pocket and Amparo points and rolls her eyes like a wife who's seen too much, who knows it is too late so who chooses not to see. "Aren't you going to answer your telephone call from your little friend?"

"Friend?"

Amparo taps her temple.

The chirping ceases, the beeper vibrates. The weight of the girl's gaze blankets him, with comfort, or suffocation, with some malignant combination of the two. He unclips his beeper and holding it up to the light fingers the controls and once more brings out of its memory Serena's latest bulletin.

"I know you went home to see her," Amparo says.

Nathan looks up. "See who?"

"Not the one who calls you."

"Then who?"

"The burro perra. Mujerzuela. The cunt." She smiles. "You went to that apartment where you leave her and that poor boy. This child that you have. That you keep in that small, dark place all time alone. How kind of you, Mr. Stein. To me you should be so kind." Amparo's eyes flare with self-congratulation. "So," she says, "how is she?"

Nathan smiles woodenly. His hand comes to rest upturned on the table, releasing what is already gone.

"She is fine."

Amparo shakes her head, smiling meanly. She puffs her lips with spite: "She is dead." She plucks at the cuff of Nathan's sleeve. It is the arm without the cuts but Nathan gets her point. "And this," she says, "was not even your big mistake."

The door swings open and the guard points at Amparo. "Phone call."

"Maybe it is Roberto," she says, and stands. But before she goes out she whispers something to the girl that Nathan cannot make out, then locks eyes with her and nods, something decided or sealed. By the time Amparo is gone the girl's eyes have located the bulge in Nathan's jacket pocket. Tears dried, instantly expert, she sweeps her head back and forth, toward the closed door, over the empty supervisor's seat, the abandoned control booth in the hallway.

"Mañana te saco de la cárcel," Nathan says.

But news of her imminent release does not change her expression for the better. He says, "The five hundred dollars." He has decided to give it to her himself. But she is still looking at him coldly. She is concerned with matters more pressing, more immediate. He withdraws the packet wrapped in butcher's paper and drops it on the table and stands up and away. In one motion, a plastic card appears in the girl's hand, a straw. The lines are drawn, then done, and she sits back. The paper bag lies unpeeled on the table. The girl's eyes, glazed, lock on a point halfway between Nathan's neck and his belt. Her nose runs and she prods it with her knuckle. Nathan leans forward and slips the straw into a nostril. His eyes slowly close. A thin line of blood draws its way from inside his nose to his lip and pools there on the ridge. He reaches for it with his tongue and tries to forget about his body, thinking instead about the atmosphere, the various hums; the low one, like distant traffic, of the prison's air circulation; the high whine of the fluorescent lights. He sits waiting for the plane to land. For Claire to come to him with a key in her hand, maneuvering like a ghost of mercy down the roadless beach—

But a finger, not his, draws along the rim of his lips, spreading the blood, and with one eye open Nathan sees the girl hold up her pinky, red-stained. And what does he do as she kneels before him, as she tugs at the belt and withdraws the spindle and unloops the polished leather, running it out through her fingers as if measuring it for some later purpose? As he is taken out into the air he considers Amparo's letter, a threat being made good, a promise actually kept. He lets this happen. He is always letting it happen. As he is letting it all happen now. Briefly he opens his eyes, like a man asleep who wakes from a dream of misery to an even greater affliction.

The girl stands. She wipes her mouth, where there is a small smile. "Bueno," she says.

Amparo, who has been waiting and watching on the other side of the glass, gives him a little nod.

Across the prison causeway, he sees the red car parked beside the gate. There is a second car parked behind it. Two of the secret agents, or whoever they are—there are three now—are patrolling the shoulder. One is shorter than the other, and thicker, older; they are like father and son. The third is chatting with the guard. They all stop when they see Nathan's beaten 4×4, and when he passes they get in their cars and follow one behind the other.

He retrieves his cell phone and he calls her now. "No, Serena, I'm not being paranoid. No, I don't think everyone is out to get me."

She is cynical. She tells him that the men following him are just out for a drive. She says she is certain of it. She then hangs up. How, Nathan wonders, can she be so certain?

The car rocks side to side, the broadside wind ripping like cloth. Street salt and debris ping the glass. In the well in back Baron snorts and waves through his dreams. In the rear-view mirror, a pair of headlights maintains his pace exactly. He slows, and they gain a little, then drop back. He looks ahead, up, at the same old factory along the expressway stamped BARCLAY BAR- CLITE FURNITURE CO. in erratic red neon, dark, out of business for years now, the sign left on by some mistake. It is crowned now with a sedan import, its caption WHY STRIVE FOR PERFECTION WHEN YOU CAN DRIVE IT? as long as a city block, subtitled by a digital readout, 21°F . . . 12:54 A.M. . . . −6°C . . . 12:55 A.M. The whole thing seems to him a cryptic message that our possessions are really negations of our actual selves that remain more primitive than we think. The numerical readout merely the meter of our lack of control, a high-concept call for religion.

"I don't believe it." He pulls abruptly onto the breakdown lane and peers up through the windshield. Ropes and scaffolding breach the Barclay Barclite walls, partially hiding a half-finished billboard draping across the entire width and height of three floors. The message beneath a remnant of a campaign by the NYPD, splashed across the back of buses all over town:

1-800-COP-SHOT
$10,000 REWARD FOR INFORMATION LEADING TO

now overridden by

BUS ACCIDENT? SLIP AND FALL?
HOSPITAL MALPRACTICE? POLICE ABUSE?
SEXUAL HARASSMENT?
WHY HURT?
YOU ARE ENTITLED TO COMPENSATION
YOU ARE ENTITLED TO MONEY
EARLY RETIREMENT PLANS AVAILABLE
CALL NOW
PAY NOTHING UNLESS SUCCESSFUL
SCHRECK & STEIN ASSOCIATES
1-800-PAY-BACK

Primitive pictographs—stick figure falling, stick figure in head wrap and sling, stick figure fending off stick-figure assailant—bullet the possibilities.

Nathan crosses the Harlem River, he crosses town. A horse-drawn carriage emerges from the park, pausing at a traffic light and moving on past cars pebbled with snow and mud and road grease, its robed and bowler-hatted driver and an old, distinguished couple blanketed to the knees, their heads and shoulders finely powdered, and the stiffly prancing horse smoking from the flanks. So much of another time that Nathan grips harder on the steering wheel and casually clears his throat to convince himself that here he sits and here he breathes. A taxicab sits at an oblique angle to the curb, its nose buried in a snowbank. A white rag hangs from its cracked windows, no signal for help from the cold but a sign of surrender in hope of a general amnesty.

Book open on her chest, unread, water untouched, Claire looks through the window to the simple pity she'd once felt for Nathan's mother. Not daughterly empathy and not sorrow, but pity laced with contempt. To Milton flaunting his women, and she and Nathan actually having drinks with some, dinners with others. All that time wondering at Nathan's mother's blindness. How could she *not* know? Though of course she did. And of course that blindness returned to Claire as a kind of thin strength, the sort that comes with mere survival.

She has seen Milton on the news now. She has seen him in the papers. Battered now, bloated, everything about him coarse and puffed, Milton still has shards of Nathan's old beauty and all of his presence, more than all his charm. Years ago, during family gatherings, when she was more daughter than anything else, Claire sat on Milton's expensive chairs, looked out Milton's expensive views, watched his wife tracking the great man around the room the way she herself tracked Nathan at parties and clubs: she knew where Nathan was, whom he was talking to, the level and quality of his effort. Always measuring the angle at which he leaned toward the women peering up at him, the intent of his smile. And he, running the two middle fingers of his right hand along the rim of his lower lip. And she, not wanting to know, not wanting to be caught watching; unable to stop. As Nathan's mother had not been able to stop.

Then, before she'd made her first discoveries, before spotting then denying evidence of the first woman, the third, the others— the faceless crowds of women—she understood the lie had exhausted itself. And for such ridiculous reasons—for the sight of his wrist, a white shirt cuff folded back, the tan leather of his watch strap against his tawny hairs; the way his back looked as he crossed the floor of her room, naked, and adjusted the blinds; the feel of his hands spreading on her pelvis; his eyes, thighs, smell, taste, his heat—he was always warm, always burning, always she held on to him like she was holding fire. By the streetlight leaking through the blinds she stared at him as he slept. In her office, across the desk from a client, he floated in front of her eyes until, humiliatingly, she blushed. It was all humiliating. That in a crowd he and not she would draw everyone's eyes; that she was just one of the great flock of women wanting him.

Then, toward the end, as her blindness broke down, there was her attraction to Nathan's mother. Pain, fury, longing, desire, Nathan's mother—not more foolish, just stronger—had endured it, as she was enduring it. After it was all over she sent that old woman flowers on her birthday. She still did. In one of the cards a few years ago she told her about Nathan's baby, and that it had died. Even her own mother did not know. Nathan's mother wrote back. It was a small card, and on it small words. It said, beautifully, accurately, that it was horrible and good that it was dead.


Nathan expects, for some reason, St. Luke's to be full to overflowing, the emergency room to be filled with accident and gunshot victims, but the lobby is empty, the wards quiet, and the regulated air everywhere is still but for the low hum of distant floor buffers. He walks the linoleum floors, between walls shimmering in the bluish light. Through open doors here and there the perfume of oxygen and iodine, machines announcing flutters in pulse and heartbeat. He stops before the elevator he's ridden a dozen—two dozen—times and stands staring at the dark line between the doors. A bubble of light floats up and the doors open and hold apart while an orderly inside waits. Get in. Go up. The orderly looks at Nathan, then releases the doors and they close again and the line goes dark. Nathan turns and walks on down the stairs to the basement cafeteria. He expects to hear the woman with the washerwoman's face behind the register say, It's about time, she needs you, where have you been? But she says nothing at all.

Scattered about the long plastic tables are insomniac patients in paper slippers and the relatives of patients already long established in endless stretches of wait and wonder. Paper cups, half-eaten bowls of canned fruit, sandwiches wrapped in plastic. A doctor in her white coat, hunched over her coffee, her eyes closed. A pair of men sit against the back wall, whispering together, one old enough to be the other's father. The younger one kneads his hands together and nods as the other offers counsel.

Nathan chooses a middle-aged man with a coat slung over his shoulders, tapping a plastic spoon.

"You have someone upstairs?" he asks, lowering himself diagonally across from him.

The man looks up. "You?"

Nathan nods. "I've been up there already today. Now I'm just, I don't know, hanging around, I guess."

"I know what you mean."

"To be nearby."

"I understand."

"I tried, but I can't go up."

The man slides a box of Wheat Thins across the table. The little square crackers inside seem somehow wafers of repentance, and Nathan accepts. He is happy just to hold them in his palm. He hasn't eaten them in years; Claire used to keep them around the house.

The man is chewing slowly, and they don't have much to say to each other, and that's going to be fine. Nathan strains his ears now to hear anything in the hushed hospital basement. The click of plastic chairs against the linoleum. Sometimes he thinks he hears a new baby crying, shoving its way out of its mother's bloom; a doctor laughs; a taxi honks in the street outside the high mesh window. These sounds are enough to remind him of life. He would not expect Maria in her death to make a human noise.

Nathan, clearing his throat, relents. "Who's upstairs?"

"My wife."

"She going to be all right?"

"They say so."

"She having a baby?"

The man shakes his head. "No. We're done with all that. We have three at home. My sister's over, taking care."

"Three children. That's wonderful. I'm sure everything will be fine."

"She's going to pull out of it."

Nathan nods. "That's the way to think."

"I'm going to sit here all night," the man says.

Nathan slips off his jacket. "I'll stay with you a while."

The man looks at him. "Maybe you should go up? You look like maybe you want to. It'll make you feel better to, you know, just pop in, say hello." When Nathan doesn't reply the man shrugs. "Whatever makes you comfortable," he says, then stands and heads for the coffee urn at the front of the cafeteria and Nathan watches him as he goes. The man's shoulders are low slung, his gait slow, his hands thick, his knuckles like gnarled knots of wood. He works, this man, he's in a union and he scratches and scrapes and leaves tooth-fairy coins under his kids' pillows. Nathan sees in him signs of old Joe, his grandfather, Milton's father, sweet Joe the plumber. Maybe that is why he chose this man to sit by. Joe's pillowed hands veined with grime— he'd left school at fourteen, he and his encyclopedic mind. His stacks of opera recordings and shelves of Dickens and Proust, gibberish to a household of immigrant brothers, all but him willing to throw away their days calling down through the windows to their friends, taking positions on the street as though awaiting the enemy. He kept vocabulary lists on old napkins, envelopes, telephone books, and finally diaries, scrawling over the day and date, leaving them scattered around the apartment, fingering them with his beefy fingers like an actor rehearsing all day the script of what was to follow. Trying out for a different part. Meanwhile, he sweated pipes and ran iron snakes through waste lines beneath Brooklyn and groped through the shit of countless babies and ingrates and dreamers, squirreling away the stray dollars to send Milton, his only child, to law school. Nathan knows little but enough to understand that from this man he could have learned everything. But he chose the wrong generation to copy, one son too late.

The man returns with two coffees and sits directly across from Nathan. "They save your life and send you on home and then kill you there with the damn bill."

Nathan blows across the top of his cup. "Insurance?"

The man shakes his head. "Nothing at all. I have a pension, but they'll take that and more. What about you? Who do you have?"

Nathan looks at the man. "It's hard to say," he says.

"Parent?"

"No."

"She's not your wife."

"Not my wife, no. My girlfriend."

The man raises his palm. "None of my business, I apologize."

"We live together," Nathan explains.

The man nods. "That's okay. I'm sorry I asked. Didn't mean to be nosy. She'll be fine, I'm sure."

"I don't think she will."

The man blows on his coffee.

There is a distant chirp, another, insistent. "Your phone?" Nathan asks.

"Me? I don't have one of them things."

Nathan warily eyes his jacket then picks through the pocket.

"Yeah, it's me. Where am I? It doesn't matter—" He toes at the floor. He blinks, blinks again. Feeling the man peering at him from across the table, he turns aside and faces the wall. He lifts a finger to one eye and then the other.

"When did it happen?" Looking at his watch, dropping it, wrist and hand, against his thigh. He looks to the door of the cafeteria, through the little square window to the hall outside, through the hall to the elevator and up the shaft to the sixth floor, where in room 614 there is no sound and no breath and the machines have stopped and Maria's mouth has frozen shapeless. "I see. I understand. No, she would have never wanted that. All those tubes and wires, they made her feel like a marionette. . . . They need me to

ID the body tomorrow? . . . Yes, I'll come in. No, he's at the apartment. Don't go over there. I'm going. I'm going home. I'll tell him myself."

When Nathan refolds the phone the man across from him is nodding over and over. "Well, you were right here," he says. "You were right with her."

Nathan is looking at the sugar dispenser in his hand. He blows on it and shakes his head, the distorted image of his face in the dispenser's metal top misting away and returning.

"Can I get you something? I'll get you some water," the man says. He quickly stands and walks off.

Nathan exhales and lifts his jacket off the seat next to him, feels for the envelope of cash in the pocket and fans what must be ten or fifteen thousand and tugs it out and slides the bills between two napkins and leaves it next to the man's coffee. He sips at his cup then sets it down and looks up at the little window leading to the street. There is a small pool of spilled coffee on the plastic tabletop at his elbow and a fly, fellow traveler through this hermetic monastery, is crouched at the edge, wading in. Nathan turns in his seat and sees the man standing next to the woman at the register, both of them staring at him. He gets up and goes out.

Santos stands in the doorway, his hair dark with damp, as though dripping with blood. He has rehearsed on his tongue lines that will be warm and appropriate but it strikes him that there aren't any words to say. Claire reaches up and leads him down to the bed by hand. Santos puts his arm around her shoulders, leaning his wet head against her hair like a child, and for a moment it is as if a cloud of timeless tenderness closes around them, guarding, watching. Even here in this bedroom where nothing has changed since Nathan left it. Wallpaper of eagles and bells. Clothed, shod, Santos sinks into the bed where days after Nathan moved out, he and Claire first made love with teenage shamelessness.

Claire sits up. "I tried to wait, but I was so tired."

"I'm sorry."

"She was beautiful, Errol. I loved her."

But he presses a finger to her lips and paws her hair. Smell of soap and mint. Once he envisioned for them a month of Christmas days blue with permanent twilight, rooftops crusted with moonlit snow, tire chains clinking as cocktail glasses would, the living room windows up and down a safe and neighborly street beacons of warmth and privacy. This hope that has kept them together.

She whispers: "I needed you to call. Where have you been?"

"Claire, it was terrible."

"I'm so sorry."

The long sweeps of hair and squared bangs frame her face. Her pale eyes. Her grim endurance practiced in making irrelevancies of the things they've spent their lives waiting for.

They sit close, hands clasped, and he tells her about the beach, giving all the details—not Krivit, not Nathan, only Isabel. She nods, as if agreeing quickly, and he talks on like a furloughed prisoner whose clock is running down, steadily losing time.

When he is done talking she drags her fingertips across his face, sending him back into the pillows, toward sleep. He drifts through rooms of dreams—barren, unpeopled—he can't see in the light. He smells the rooms smoldering. It feels hours later—probably it is only minutes—when her lips bring him up, the strange cold compresses on his shoulders, on the nape of his neck, unwanted, but he doesn't stop her. She blows lightly on his eyes, as if to open them, and when he does the streetlight has partitioned her, revealing the facts of her, stern, lurid, one who calls bluffs. He obeys wordlessly as she feels for his underwear and slips it off. For months she had seemed completely beyond arousal. Now, tonight, tonight especially, she moves him across the bed like a nurse, with a firmness that excludes options.

Words are pointless. How to explain any of this, where there was purpose but no reason? Her eyes open and glassed, the straight line of her mouth blue. Santos reaches to touch her face. His lips part to speak, but she puts a finger over them. Her rhythm is slow and exact, calm, her eyes turned inward, mute eyes that seem to be looking at him from the bottom of a pool. As though this lovemaking is more an ambition than it is desire, to right a wrong or at least smooth a way. Claire's thighs tighten and her stomach heaves and she gulps air and she shudders, then she caves into a cloud of their mingled breath. He clutches to her as to a life preserver. Maybe saving him, no matter the consequences, is her ambition. Burying his face in her red hair enormous and everywhere.

Hours later his eyes startle open. He turns his head to his reflection in the window and takes Claire's hand—she is asleep—and places it, like a living mask, over his face. But from beyond the bars her fingers make, Isabel returns his stare. Her eyes are flecked with grains of sand, and they are making demands.

**2 A.M.** In an overheated lobby filled with weak and twitchy light, Nathan shoulders open another door and steps into a little apartment where there is no sign of movement, plant life, air. Through the curtains, up in the clouds, lightning, continuous, splits the sky in fiery convulsions, illuminating like signal flares the surrounding apartment towers. A blank grid of wide boulevards named for plants and trees. From behind the walls at the development's edge, trees rise coated in glass, like the hands of drowned giants.

He stands in the opening between living room and kitchen, breathing heavily. Clothes are strewn across the carpet, the door to a highboy unhinged, a shattered bowl, its chocolate-covered candies scattered like birdseed. Against the far wall, the long shelf of opera records that belonged to his grandfather, Joe the plumber, has been rifled through, the old vacuum-tube phonograph below it, long ago burned out, torn from its perch and made off with.

The spotted legs of an old woman surface out of a corner shadow. In a leather easy chair, a gift from Nathan years before, she leans forward, closing her robe at her throat. Her tangled cloud of hair crinkles electrically.

"It's me, Rose," Nathan said.

She reaches, loose and frail, and the hand that clenches at him trembles like a bird.

"What are you doing up?" he asks.

"It's late."

"Surprised I'm here?"

"I didn't say that."

Nathan looks around. "What happened?"

"They were here to fix the pipes."

Nathan looks back at the kitchen table. Her pocketbook has been upended, lipstick, billfold, candies, pennies, three prescription vials spread over the table. A low, continuous murmur of Yiddish pours out the radio.

"Were the pipes broken?" he asks.

"I don't know."

"Did they have tools?"

"I don't know."

"How many of them were there?"

She turns her head toward the kitchen, toward the front door, toward the short hallway to the bedroom, as though sending her memory to rewalk the route. "I don't know."

"Two? Three?"

In the darkness she wrings her hands.

A leak of indignation has sprung in him, but he doesn't know where from, or in what receptacle to catch it. The thieves could well have been his clients. He has fought for and won acquittal for men who have done far worse.

"They take all of Joe's things?"

She says nothing.

"When?" he asks.

She turns her head.

"Two days? Three?"

She nods, little bobbles of her chin.

"You've been sitting here for three days? Why didn't you call Milton?"

She shrugs.

"You sure you're all right?" No reply. "How much did they get?" Nothing still.

"What was in the purse, Rose?"

She holds out her hand. Her lip is quivering now. Her voice like the cry of a cat. "Maybe five dollars."

He walks back toward the bedroom. His name is called behind him. "Are you hungry?"—an old routine: she hasn't cooked in years.

"I already ate."

"I can heat up some eggs."

He stops along a wall and is confronted with his genealogy, everything aslant, a gallery of faces glowing darkly out from behind picture glass dulled with grease. Everyone dead or ceased breathing in that form. Their various guises: ballplayer, graduate, attorney. Milton in his first days as a T-man, turned to display the contents of his shoulder holster. The child he sees beside him, in the Silver Shadow, heading to school, watches the man's massive shoulders and arms jerkily spinning the wheel. Up the boy goes to his knees and, kneeling high, takes measurements with his hand between the man's head and his own, shifting as necessary and craning his neck if need be to make their heights exactly, precisely the same. It is all the boy can be sure of passing off: from the back and at a distance two heads in silhouette are two heads in silhouette, anything the boy desires, a pair of friends, a couple of cops, two grown men and not the father and his little boy that they are. And this man, this boy's mate, pays no attention to the pesky hand hovering around his head.

She clears her throat in the room behind him. "Which one are you looking at?"

"What do you mean?"

"You're looking at the pictures."

"No."

"I can hear you."

A baby in his mother's arms. "Third from the right."

"That's you."

"That's not me."

"Yes that is. That's you."

Watery eyes stare out at him. At seven years old a wisp of

golden hair. He'd forgotten he started out blond. All night he has
tried to raise that child's face in his mind, but all he can remember
is an old summer in which the huge hand clamps to his as he is led
to the Coney Island carnival and the passing image of his own eyes
open to the Wonderwheel toppling, its passengers spinning in
place. The tattooed girls writhing. Invisible rockets shooting aloft
and scattering in colored spiders and dripping, like the caps of gargantuan fools, into the countless eyes, the faceless sea of upturned
heads, heads like his. Upturned to his grandfather, Milton's father,
Joe, sweet man.

One night early that winter at seven, during the first impressive
snow of a winter of impressive snows, Joe and Rose came to stay
the night and were given the master bedroom. This was in Queens,
before Milton's big cases, before Central Park West. Their modest
row-house on a street of row-houses. Nathan's mother moved to
Nathan's room and Milton and Nathan moved downstairs to the
convertible couch. The actual incidents of the visit are gone from
his memory, but Nathan assumes them, as one can: the moments
spent passing a fragile coexistence, a faint hostility; ice clinking in
glasses, a shiny and crowded dinner, a fire.

Then a blundered moment. A little after midnight, Nathan
woke beside his father on the pullout couch and opened his eyes
to a succession of threatening sounds. He checked his body with
the body at his side, unconsciously mimicked it, calculating the
required adjustments. But Milton was sitting bolt upright, yards,
hundreds of feet, above him, as still and as silent as though this
was the position in which he'd fallen asleep.

The boy, Nathan, reached up. Hands clenched in rage, Milton
warded off the touch. There was something deeply wrong. The
room gyrated with snow shadows, rained with the blue streetlight. Tree branches and ice chips slid in sinister silence along the
walls. Table and chairs turned and danced and all the storm was
silent, as though mimed, its fierce howls chained somewhere safely
outside. Camouflaged, wrapped by the arms of light, Nathan
could not escape if he tried. So he turned, as Milton had turned,
toward french doors where beyond there was groaning, whistling,

snorting, and a soliloquy in a strange language. Through the spinning trees and snow in the next room moved the faint image of Joe with an overcoat wrapped perilously around his shoulders. His head bowed, he stuttered, stopped, gestured wildly, then stumbled forward, dragging his feet across the living room floor, and again stopped in a deliberate sort of hesitancy. Milton, no longer immense but merely unwieldy, clumsy, did not scoop and cradle the boy in safety. He did not save him. Instead, the boy watched his father's watching and his grandfather's confused slog into the interpretation of old dreams. In a month the old man was dead.

In the bedroom doorway Nathan finds himself shoulder to a column of pencil markings in the wood, random dates beside each in his grandfather's scrawl, the last just below shoulder level: *Mr. Nathan, nine-years-old.*

His grandmother's bed is made but the cover is askew, the pillows fluffed and misaligned. The bureau drawers lie overturned on the floor, underwire brassieres and stockings and pennies crushed beneath them. A coffee tin, her secret stash for phantom grandchildren and rainy days, lies empty on its side, its top flung away. Nathan stands looking at it.

"Good thing they didn't get to the coffee can," he calls down the hall.

"They'll never find that."

He squats over it. "How much do you have in here?"

"I'll never tell."

Nathan straightens his leg to get at his billfold and what change he has. He peels off a few bills and restuffs the can.

He returns to the living room and when he grabs her her shoulder seems to come apart in his hands. "You mind if I put on a light?" He tries one lamp then the other. He bends to peer under the lampshades. There are no bulbs.

"When was the last time you had bulbs in these lamps?"

"When was the last time you were here?"

Nathan can't remember. "Hasn't Milton been to visit?"

She says nothing.

"He says he comes every few days to see you." Nathan waits

but still no response. "Then he didn't tell you about the new case."

"New case?"

"He's a bastard," Nathan says.

"He's my son."

"He's my father."

"You don't talk that way about a father."

"Well."

Nathan sits across from her and stretches his feet before him. He reaches for the back of his head and holds it steady and yawns.

His grandmother cocks her ear toward the hissing drone in the radio.

"You like that," he says.

"Stories for old women. Can't I get you something to eat?"

"I'm all right."

"Here, let me."

"I will. I'll do it. You sit."

In the kitchen he stands before the refrigerator he has known all his days. It once bloomed with life, leaves and fruits and wrapped candies and bottles of sugary drinks. Bloody meats and eggs with sacs of golden yolk. Tonight, a brown banana sits on a wire shelf, kinked and shriveled like a link of old sausage. Nathan rattles around, makes noises.

"Thank you," he says.

"Good?"

"You sure I can't get you something?"

He eyes the phone, considers the call, the money.

"I couldn't eat a thing, honey," she says.

Ashamed, Nathan leaves the phone, walks on.

He takes from his jacket an envelope. He takes out a half dozen sheets of paper and holds them up to the window. *Maria Rosa, Last Will and Testament.*

His grandmother cocks her head, her eyes blankly attentive.

"What do you have there?"

"Just something I want you to sign for me."

At her side he kneels and sets her fingers around the fountain pen and leads it to the line at the bottom below a signature already there, his. The pen droops, and he sets it upright again and kneads her fingers back into place. Her other hand he takes and straightens, pressing her fingertips to the space she is to fill, guiding her to guide herself.

"What is this?" she asks.

"You're my witness."

"To what?"

Nathan opens his mouth to answer, then shuts it.

"Is it a will?" she asks.

He smooths the papers on his grandmother's knee. "For my corporation."

"Your corporation."

"Yes."

"I can't see it," she says.

"You don't need to see it. Here it is."

"But I don't know what it says."

"It says just what you'd expect."

A pulse of sight surfacing one last time through her dead pupils holds him where he kneels, as though to assess and decide. For months after she insisted she could no longer see she gave directions from the backseat of cars and never failed to distinguish the denominations of her money. But now her eyes, drifting, are off by a degree, as though she is searching for something in the next room, for something, an answer, written on the ceiling, to make itself known.

He bears down on her hand, guiding it toward the page.

Meekly: "Who is in your corporation?"

"Me."

"Just you?"

"Just me."

"Can you have a corporation with just one person?"

"Yes, you can."

"Why would you want that?"

Nathan breathes. "To protect me. They can get to the corporation but they can't get to me."

She reaches out for him and misses. "Who wants to get to you?"

"I wouldn't bother you with it."

They sit for a time in silence. In her presence, an ease of routine gestures and automatic rhythms. The dark and dry heat of this old apartment like a dreamroad in which everything that has gone wrong has not yet begun and everything that will be right is yet to come. The window, he knows, faces east, and beyond the landfill and the harbor lie open water and the horizon. They sit a long time facing that direction. The night, lightning-struck, cracks like glass and is mended back again.

"It will be light soon," Nathan says. He looks nervously at his watch. "Just a few hours."

After she signs she does not pull away, and Nathan does not let her go. Her hand is cool and slack, and they sit holding each other, waiting. He watches the window, she the ceiling, as if they are bracing for the thunder.

Sometime later she pats his knee. "You're a good boy," she says. "It's a good day when you visit. It's going to be a good day."

# MONDAY

# 6 A.M.

He falls in sleep into the windless pocket of a rowboat, squinting one eye then the other, seesawing the pale gray light across the bridge of his nose. It is midday, or seems to be. The sun, what he can see of it, is a high dim peephole into a suspended furnace. The surf slides away against the rocks, pinching white geysers into the air. Strewn about in the seawrack the green faces and the splayed legs of women dragging their toes in the foam, their robes pooling beneath them. Their breasts afloat on the rocks. Ropes of hair fanned as if to dry. A cloud of frenzied gulls darkens the sky. The birds shuttle back and forth from their midair float to the bodies below, gangs of them carrying out coordinated sorties on one and then the other. Amongst them, on no particular rock, a sandwiched pair scuffles, the woman beneath gulping, the man on top arching rhythmically, doughy buttocks and head bucking. The man turns his head toward the sea. It is Nathan himself. Nathan watches himself smile menacingly, turn away, concentrate downward. Jammed in the last of the boulders lining the beach the first of three rows of crosses faces the ocean, the crosspieces like the arms of irritable fathers hoisting their dozing sons, picking at their sagging elbows to keep their eyes on the show. The wind is stiff and wet and when it drops he can hear the cries from the back row of crosses where the blood-oiled wood glistens in the sun. The heads tick-tock like metronomes. Pinned wrists and ankles pry at the iron tacks. He sees himself stand from the rock. The woman below is not moving. He knows that face, he knows her name, and he can see himself clearly, can see himself clearly—

What time is it when he senses someone or something nearby? Nathan opens his eyes to the cloth ceiling of the car, fingering a birthmark on his own neck. His blazer is laid over his chest like a blanket, the steering wheel crowding him, the dashboard clock blinks its odd hour in incandescent green, while outside nothing at all is clear. The growing dawn—if that's what this is—is violent and webby. It is still sleeting, or sleeting again.

He wipes away his stale breath from the glass and looks up to the high parlor windows of 11 Cheever Place. Its sweeps of white curtain, the soft glow of the lamppost. The flower boxes are empty, which he thinks strange until he reminds himself again what month this is. Here and there the stoop lights have been kept on, beacons of happiness, ways home. Furry tinsel rims the windows; plastic reindeer graze the little yard of blue-stone slate a few doors down. A young father in an undershirt leans out a doorway, bending for the morning paper in the snow as though offering the invisible authority of the day his freshly washed head. Nothing seems to have changed. The same beaten trash cans, a few more cracks in the sidewalk. The same neighborhood on the wrong side of the edge of respectability.

Claire must be up. She'll have court, she'll prepare notes at the table letting out on the little garden, pour herself a second cup of coffee then let it grow cold and leave it for the office—

"Honey," she will say. "Look at me—there's nothing keeping us here anymore."

Nathan is sweating, his whole frame trembling.

"What are you afraid of?"

"Everything."

"Let's go. Let's go today."

He puts his arm around her for support, dropping his damp head on her shoulder like a child. A shield of tenderness and guardianship has fallen around them. "Why not," he says. "Let's get away now while we can."

—piercing the wild sky, the roiling clouds, toward the perfect golden yolk of sun, the crisp mountains stretching end to end along the horizon—

"Do you *mean* it?"

"I mean it. I mean this. But, Claire—I've fallen, somehow. I won't be the same."

Sweetly, a hurried whisper: "Never mind."

"I can't do what I used to do."

"Yes."

"But, Claire—"

"I don't expect you to. I know it will be hard."

"But we could be happy, couldn't we?"

"Yes," Claire says. "We could be happy."

—and far across the ocean, the little bungalow, the unseen roar of surf beating the sand, the strong clean onshore wind—all of it waiting—

It is six in the morning. The thunderclaps above, and the thunderclaps just beneath the surface of his skull. And yes, that is Errol Santos's Chevrolet parked out front.

Nathan tries to send back his confusion like a bad meal but he can't. Blinking, he stretches his legs, slowly focusing on the readout display of his beeper, fourteen messages: *New York Times* . . . *Doctor E* . . . *Errol Santos* . . . *New York Post* . . . *Errol Santos* . . . *Errol Santos* . . . it goes on, but he doesn't, he can't, he aims the beeper at Baron, who is sitting upright in the passenger seat beside him. "What do you think? Staying silent, I see. Of course, you're right, as always." Clipping the beeper safely to his belt, Nathan presses thumb and forefinger, his messages flying off to wherever they fly, to message heaven, the graveyard of electronically snubbed pleas and particles of undesired need. His memory now clear, he slips in a CD, Ben Webster and "Soulville," slow and heavy as a dirge, recasting the gray day as a blue idea. Now he knows where this day is going, how it ends. And it will end, it must.

The dog's eyes, meanwhile, are following some distraction outside the window: the red sedan, drifting slowly down the street between the rows of motionless cars. Its windows have fogged, but Nathan can make out the father-and-son shapes of the driver and passenger sipping at paper cups of coffee, struggling with wrapped doughnuts. Blurry-eyed—they must be tired—they pass on, slowing as they drive by Claire's. One seems to be peering into Errol's car and writing something down. Then they drift away, turn the corner, satisfied for the moment, it seems, to have merely taken the temperature of the situation.

Quickly Nathan lifts his head. The living room curtain has fallen. Or has it? Maybe it was a draft? He remembers old number 11, those big windows with their shaky panes and chalky glazing; the breath of the day threading through, hot or cold, even in the stillest weather. But the curtain settles, and now Baron's behavior has begun to interest him. The dog has caught something—maybe a fly, hatched obviously in the warmth of the garaged car—but instead of swallowing, he seems to hold it on his tongue, playing it in his teeth, as if to present it to Nathan alive, fetched for the master to devour himself. Nathan feels a surge of paternal pride, and he is happy for his hunting dog, all that mass of purebred instinct finally coming to use. Utility. How that must feel.

Nathan reaches over and gives the dog a good scratch behind the ears. Baron, his grimace easily mistaken for a smile, clamps his long teeth, jailing the insect, and swallows.

Errol Santos is standing in the doorway, squinting worriedly upward, hugging himself against the cold. Halfway down the stoop he picks up Claire's *Times*, unfolds it, then, obviously seeing something he doesn't like, releases it, dropping it in the snow. Nathan watches him drive away as his own little cube of environment swells with a throaty ballad and the tail-lights on the Chevrolet recede to mere punctuations in the early morning.

Baron, whimpering now, punches at the glass, ripping loose squeals and farts. Nathan opens his door and the dog hurdles him, bolts into the day, snout to its first solid ground in ten hours. Proudly, he lifts his leg and pisses a hard stream across the driver door. "Jesus christ," Nathan moans, then snatches the dog by the collar and drags him to a dead tree stump where he prances reluctantly, as though with something else in mind. Sad and self-conscious, Baron eyes Nathan, who obligingly turns as the dog squats, strains, and finishes up with a little downward dab. Nathan stands peering at the steaming, gleaming pile, obsessing on it like a drunk, then kicks it under the wheel of the next car, dragging the toe of his shoe along the sidewalk. "In," he commands, pointing the way toward the open car door.

A little wobbly but steady on his feet, following the faint blue shadow the light behind him casts down on the walk, Nathan heads for Claire's door. He shakes the paper free of the snow. There on the front page of the Metro section, just beneath the fold, is Isabel, Isabel young and silly, not the Isabel he knows. A three-inch column continues inside deep alongside the seam separating Sports from National Weather where beach volleyball is the new rage and the Yankees are contemplating an off-season deal and a quadriplegic ex-lineman for the Jets preaches legislation against licensed aggression. Then Nathan's eyes flit across his own name, his father's, Errol Santos's. He turns the page where a kidnap victim demands retribution. Meanwhile, in Croatia. Meanwhile, at Columbia-Presbyterian Medical Center where the Riverside Drive jogger. In Mexico City, meanwhile. Meanwhile, Nathan doesn't fold the paper but rolls it into a tube, panicky, he pats himself down for his phone, flipping it open and presses buttons. Messages, messages, where did they go? Tell me I am alive. Tell me I will live.

Halfway to calling his own 900 number he disconnects. How strange that would be, to be billed a hundred dollars by none other than yourself. Whom would you owe? Whom would you pay? And if you didn't? If you ignored the billing, as you always do, driving it to the brink, waiting for the collection agencies to send the registered letter, to serve the subpoena—could you be defendant and plaintiff in the same case, *Stein vs. Stein*, in which the defendant, Nathaniel Stein, rightfully billed $99.99 for the legitimate use of phone number 1-900-945-5343, commonly known as 1-900-W-I-L-L-D-I-E, owes owner of said number, Nathaniel Stein? So fine. He's making, what, twenty grand, forty? He can afford to be merciful just this one time, let himself off the hook, forgive the debt.

A single clap of thunder explodes midair just behind, over the river. The slate beneath Nathan's feet gives a little jolt. Holding out his hand for the rain, he peers up at a sea-green sky. Smears of black smoke descend behind the buildings.

The heavy, well-oiled door still makes no noise as it swings open. Unhurriedly, meticulously, Nathan lifts his face to Claire, who is cinching tight a robe he remembers from winters past. She looks radiant, youthful, even angelic. Though not stunning. Those slightly jumbled teeth, a flaw that always gave her imperious beauty its vulnerability, a way in. The long red hair wispy and electric. Nothing has abandoned her over the years, not her simple hairdo, not the crimp in the corners of a mouth that still seems ready in equal measure to smile or frown.

"Don't look at me like that," she says.

"I'm sorry."

Claire lifts her head with wonder up to the spindly trees. "I don't think I ever heard you say that."

"Yes, you did. I just didn't mean it."

She hesitates but he makes no move. He and his little blast of honesty have confused her.

She holds out her hand: "My paper?"

Nathan tosses it into a trash can. "Everything's terrible. You wouldn't want to know. Surprised to see me?"

But Claire just stares. She's sniffed out danger, poised to leap. That long body, perfectly still—she's all kinetic potential.

Trying to calm her, Nathan replies with that particular smile of his, the one that can agree with you or fight you, depending on the depth of your disbelief.

She sighs wearily, and her free hand, palm upward, involuntarily indicates the air, as if in irritation, or an unconscious plea. "No," she says. "I'm not surprised. Nothing you do would surprise me. You just missed Errol."

"I'm sorry."

"There it is again."

"But I saw him last night," Nathan says.

"Did you. He said afternoon. He didn't mention anything about last night."

Another explosion, double, nearer. Black clouds like swarms of bees crisscross at a low elevation.

"They're saying it's going to be the storm of the century," she says. "You'd better come in."

Claire leans into the trash and picks out the paper, then heads with it into the dark of the hallway, leaving the door open behind her.

Inside, at the sudden change in temperature, the shift in pressure, every nook in the apartment nudges a remembered cranny in his brain; every chink in the wall snags on the irregularities in his mind. But willfully he won't remember, until he sits at the old table and runs a finger along its worn edge. "We used to love these early mornings," he says. His voice, though not his hand, is steady now. But feeling something on his tongue he wouldn't like to actually say, he swallows hard, tamping it back down.

She is staring at the paper. "You never think these things happen to someone you know."

"Which thing?"

Claire's eyes widen with alarm. "But you know, don't you?"

"The Riverside jogger?"

"—dead, Nathan. They found her, Isabel, out on—"

"Yes."

"Have you spoken with Errol? Yes, of course, yesterday afternoon." Claire looks down at him. "What happened to your hand?"

He covers one with the other, though that one is no better. The bites have become infected, damp. "I was fixing a flat."

"You? That's likely. What was her name?"

Nathan focuses on a kitchen window across the little yard, the back of the next block of brownstones. He used to watch the tenant there, a hugely fat man, leaning into the sauces steaming on the stove.

"By the way, Errol was wrong," Claire says. "You look terrible. Did I say that yet?"

She says it not to him but to the window, at his reflection superimposed on the fat man's building. As though the distance the glass grants them provides a vacuum of time, making him—harmless, unthreatening—someone else, out of reach. And she is right, he sees. He looks awful: sallow, his lips bluish, the hollows below his cheek bones, once sculpted, sunk to divots.

"But you look good," he says.

"What do you want, Nathan?"

"I was in the neighborhood."

"At six in the morning?"

"Is that what time it is?"

"You look so tired," she says in a voice near a whisper. Sitting beside him, her hands falling away, into her lap, she is still addressing his reflection: "You look so tired. I was going to fax you, actually. Until this thing with Isabel. I just thought you should know, I took one of your cases."

"Regina Núñez," he says flatly.

"So she's already fired you. Good for her. Maybe she's not as stupid as—"

"I saw her last night."

"Well, don't do that again. She needs help. She doesn't need you. She's about to give birth, Nathan. Or didn't you notice? You've abandoned her. You've missed her court dates."

"Abandoned her?"

"What else would you call it?"

"I'm going to help her," he says.

Laughing, she shakes out her hair. "You and your delusions."

The phone interrupts and Claire, startled, is on her feet before the first ring falls out of the air.

"Why don't you let the machine get it," he says. "That's what they're for."

"That's not what they're for, Nathan," she says, and then before she can stop herself: "You never answered the phone. God forbid you ever did without screening it or making me, running across the room drawing your finger across your throat, whispering, I'm not home, I'm not home, without even knowing who it was." She pauses, blushing. "God forbid you got lassoed into something you couldn't control."

Nathan gazes at her, at the conversation exactly as it was left years ago. Its preservation is a biological condition, he assumes, an instinct to keep us from returning to old used lovers again and again across eternity. Across all the time and the silence Claire has not stopped piling on the complaints and Nathan has not stopped slithering out from under them. "Who is it this early?"

But Claire is having none of it, heading already into the silence that has followed another ring, standing across the room over the phone, waiting. "It's none of your business. You don't live here anymore, remember? Hello—?"

Nathan, his hands together in that same attitude of prayer, remembers.

Her back turned, Claire's hands cup the mouthpiece. She is mumbling, but she does nod her head, once, turning obliquely to the wall, Nathan assumes, to keep him there, in peripheral view.

"Yes," Claire is saying, holding tight to the phone one beat longer than she should. As though afraid of floating off.

"Who was that?"

Again addressing his reflection, his ghost, transparent, half gone. "Nobody. Work."

"Errol."

"No. He's got more important things—"

"Maria is dead," Nathan says. "I thought you should know."

Claire is looking at *him*, finally, Nathan in the flesh. Her pale eyes, bottomless, little circles of reflected sky, examining, rationing attention in measured doses. "You mean Isabel."

"And Maria."

"Jesus. What, am I next?" She gives a little laugh, then touches her mouth as if to rearrange it. "I'm sorry," she says flatly. "No, I'm really sorry. It's terrible. How, how did it happen?"

Nathan has wrung a paper napkin to shreds. "It's complicated."

"It's awful."

He doesn't even believe she thinks that's true. "So where are *you* now?" Nathan knows that the question can be read a dozen ways; whichever road they travel will be her decision.

"Sorry, but don't tell me this is all about *that*. This little visit. You're free now, you have what, some time? That you're here because Errol's left for work, because Maria's—"

"I am going away," he says, startling even himself. "I want—I'd like it if—" The words roll off his tongue before he knows it, slipping out of him from he doesn't know where. Is it really true? He has no idea. As if he is caught in a continuum of possible emotions, from which he plucks the most fascinating without considering the consequences. First he tells a lie, then the lie tells a lie—

"—if you came with me."

"Don't joke."

"This isn't a joke."

"Of course it's not a joke."

"I mean I'm not joking."

They sit a moment in silence, both of them weighing the multitude of possible replies. Claire lifts the backs of her hands to her eyes.

"I'm not talking about a vacation, Claire."

"You want to run. You always wanted to run. Well, too bad."

"Claire—"

"Just hold on, Nathan. Just *please,* all right? Just don't let's start with that curious tidbit."

"Curious—?"

"Because you're a *freak!*" she sputters, clutching at her hair with one hand, pointing back at the silent phone with the other. As if news of his character had just come through it. "You sit here and it's years and years later. So Maria is dead now. And Isabel, God help her. And now here you are. Always after something new. But you forgot, Nathan, I'm not new anymore. Whatever you liked me for is what you ended up hating me for. You don't like me if I'm strong, you don't like me if I'm weak. You don't like me if I'm funny, or if I'm sad. You don't like me if I'm ugly, you don't like me if I'm beautiful. You don't like me if I'm white, you certainly don't like me if I'm Hispanic."

She tilts her head to the side, as if she sees she's hit the mark: "There's something wrong with you, isn't there. You look terrible. Is that what Ruth meant?"

"Ruth?"

But Claire is waving him away. "You haven't changed, Nathan. How can you stand it?"

Mouth open, he can feel his face go numb, her anger like dentist's gas, shutting him down. Outside, trails of snowdust rip away from the roof and pass on the horizontal gusts. Somewhere down there, in the tiny plots of greenery, in some herb garden, wind chimes clang at regular intervals, as at the opening of a Catholic service, announcing—what? He doesn't know. He doesn't know what Catholics actually *do*. Something, he's sure. Something practical. He'd like to know.

Leaning on one hip, Claire has been watching him. "So what are you going to do?"

He looks confused. "Do?"

"She has a son, remember? Doesn't—" She looks fearful. "Didn't Maria have a son? Don't you two have a child?"

The boy's sweet pastiness rises to his eyes like a flash card, both sides—word and meaning—of a vocabulary of some life not his. "Benny," he remembers.

"Benny. What are you going to do about Benny? Your son."

"He's not mine, really."

"How does that feel, Nathan, to be a father?"

"I'm going to keep him," he says, surprising himself again. Is this why he came here, to hear out this strange—maybe better—version of himself?

She stares and stares. "They won't let you do it, Nathan. Not you."

"Of course not." He glances at his watch, half rising out of his chair. "I should go see him before school. I should tell him."

She frowns. "Tell him?"

"About his mother."

"You mean he doesn't know?"

"How could he know? It happened last night, they weren't going to call *him*, after all? The kid's nine, or something."

"Or something. Excellent, Nathan. You haven't even told that boy his mother's dead? What are you, *mad*?" She's in the doorway, wringing her hands, blowing a wisp of hair away from her eyes.

"Who was on the phone?"

She has his coat in her arms. The front door is open. "Get out." She is sobbing. "I have to be in court in an hour. Get away."

He lifts his hand to touch her. "Who was it?"

Leveling at him a fiery gaze, "Don't you dare!" Her face bunching and her eyes bitter, her hand rises in a parody of a karate chop and whip-snaps, knocking away his purpling swollen fingers and swatting him in the tender cushion between jaw and neck. Both of them gasping at the cold. With the tip of his tongue Nathan probes his lip. Claire's hair is scattered, her robe pulled aside revealing the pale slope of her breast. Hands still clawed. She comes down a step, bereaved and grief-stricken. "Don't say anything," she pants.

"I—" he says, beginning yet another thing he can't finish, I, I, I, I—

"Hey, remember me?" he asks the next brownstone down, the next block, the day, the world. "Remember?" A last appeal.

Claire steps up, backward, retreating. "Please go away."

The door crashes shut, the tapping brass knocker punctuating Claire's final words with a fading ellipsis.


She lies for long minutes on her bed, the coffee within reach on her bedstand untouched and cold. She listens to the sidewalk patter of the Jehovah's Witnesses heading off to their little Kingdom, their slice of waterfront heaven beneath the Brooklyn and Manhattan Bridges, the young women in their long coats, their hair stiff and brilliant even in the storm—mothers all of them, she is sure, their apartments crawling with bright, blue-eyed babies—the men combing and buttoning, clasping their Bibles while the dregs they pass—she, her neighbors, friends—seem more disheveled and what children have survived are less defined and more quiet and more ill, everybody more in need than ever.

She looks up, quickly, as if at a sudden sound. There, before her, is the winter Sunday years ago, their last year of law school, when she and Nathan and Errol were strolling arm-in-arm together with a forgotten purpose down this street, that street, alongside the Brooklyn-Queens Expressway stretched out below them in an open pit. Traffic whizzing by and kicking up clouds of road grease and mist. Alongside, finally, a school-yard fence.

In the muffled quiet of that winter day, six boys were playing baseball. Like apparitions, she remembers, one kid with a bat stood in the corner, penned in by the skeleton of a backstop either half built or half gone, the others spread over the asphalt. Basketball stanchions stooped at the perimeter, the rims netless halos.

Like inmates, she, Nathan, and Errol stood with their fingers clawed to the little diamonds of fence, watching as the one with the bat tossed the ball and swung for the school beyond the out-field and missed everything. The kid, seeing them in the corner of his eye, picked the ball out of the snow again and again and eventually reconsidered and tapped a few around the yard, grounders, skippers, getting the others involved.

Then—not a word had passed between them—Nathan and Errol palmed down their hair and ducked through a space where the fence had been pried away. The clop of their footsteps lifted the kids' heads, three Chicano, three black. Nathan and Errol walked like gunslingers, mercenaries. They cinched their coats. Dressed the way they were, Claire knew the kids thought they were cops. The kids' eyes slid and stared.

Errol's voice echoed off the back of the school. "Strange time of year for baseball?"

Nathan headed for the kid with the bat and held out his hand, a gesture vaguely menacing. Warily, the kid handed him the bat and grabbed his glove and took his place atop a small island of snow in center field.

Setting his feet with care, Nathan flipped up the ball and caught it in the palm of his hand. From the fence Claire saw its leather skin was all but gone. Only the mysterious petrified core was left, which was nothing like what she'd expected inside a baseball; it seemed insidious, full of worms. Nathan was rolling it nervously in the fingers of his left hand, jiggling the small wooden bat in his right, searching for minor adjustments he may have thought he'd forgotten to make but hadn't. Errol called out for him to hit the damn thing, to show them what he's still got, and Nathan takes a practice swing, panels of the overcoat straining, the lapels in his face. Claire can see this feels good to him, this twisting, this uncoiling like a human spring again. He looks light, almost heroic. The body machine. Metal and rubber and grease never forget. The body doesn't either, in its way. With a mind of its own, it will reach down through the years to fly again despite you and all your aspirations. The past etches itself on your tendons and bones, even if it's the last thing it does.

She can see Nathan breathing hard already. Errol bends forward, his hands on his knees, pensive, as if there is something more at stake, them and the kids, them against the kids, to prove something, to her, maybe, about time and the body. Just a few years before such a close target as the school wouldn't have inspired in Nathan even a thrill. Now it's the cheap seats, looming high and far as he tosses the ball and the kids disappear from view and Claire looks up into the luminous murk, waiting as Nathan brings the bat around, intending to connect up near his eyes. But he swings through it, and the ball bounces and settles amidst the shards of a broken bottle at his feet. It's his body that lets the bat go. It falls to the ground, pointing somewhere like an hour hand, or the point of a compass. Where it points Claire—watching Nathan's eyes—doesn't know. Nathan steps over the bat looking apprehensively to center field at the kid he's taken the bat from, the hitter. Claire's mouth fills with the metallic taste of unquenched thirst, rage for Nathan, on his behalf, at the kid, at the bat. At herself; for she sees something in Nathan's face that terrifies her, not the disappointment but the apathy, the letting go so easily of what used to be his to keep. He doesn't fight for it. He doesn't take another swing or even seem to care, but walks off with a shrug.

"Fuck you," Errol says at something one of the kids said, covering Nathan's escape.

"Yeah, fuck you," Claire mutters. She is feeling testy, closed in, intensely loyal, intensely afraid, and she doesn't know why. Nathan has been frightening her, letting things go right and left, sloughing off the little things he was, ballplayer, musician, the lives he'd wanted to lead.

Errol follows Nathan through the fence.

Nathan waves. "See you around."

"We will," Claire says fiercely, hooking an arm in each of theirs and pulling them on. "The punks. One day they'll walk into the wrong side of our office. All those kids."

They stride with purpose, it seems, toward Court Street. Church bells peal in the distance. The federal court with its scrubbed and spotlit colonial splendor would make a convincing birthday cake. A Disney set surrounded by the grime of downtown Brooklyn. New York is inside out, Claire knows: the old looks fresh and better preserved, the brand new already tired and out of date. It's the past creeping up on you and the future falling apart. The surrounding office buildings—blank and anonymous as cliffs—are wrapped in an alpen glow. Borough Hall. The board of ed. Labor. Night court. Empty, abandoned weekends and after hours.

And then, at the curb in front of Barney's Cut Rate, there is a throng of people, strange for a Sunday. On weekdays those corners are choked with city bureaucrats and their attendant beggars and hot dog carts. And by Sunday the Friday papers usually have the whole street to themselves to tumble happily around and pile up in the lees of doorways. A strange collection has gathered: Chinese waiters, the help at McDonald's, a smattering of homeless, a few locals in slippers and housecoats. A lone dog wearing boots of grime. They all look to be waiting for a bus.

An ambulance pulls up at an angle against the curb. A police-woman stands in the street waiting to direct traffic that isn't coming. A bank clock has nothing to add, frozen in neither morning nor light.

"Jesus," Errol says, and stops.

Two police cars pull up. In this light everything is fluid, including the time; everything an apparition of itself, full of shadowy possibilities and illusory goodness. Like the man standing on the ledge of the apartment house in the middle of the next block. There are fifteen or twenty stories between him and the street. The balconies are filled up and down with spectators, as if they are lining the route of a vertical race. The jumper is in a parka, arms straight out, measuring his dive.

Claire bites down a chill. "He wouldn't dare," she mutters, still in her feisty mood. As if it would be something to admire.

Nathan seems wrapped in a preternatural calm. It's that apathy again, that waiting as if for a cue. Something is missing.

The police, meanwhile, seem bothered, milling around helplessly with no one to arrest. There are no psychologists or experts and there is no giant trampoline. Just the wide river of street and a few parked cars and the crowd on the corner looking upward expectantly.

In the corner of her eye Claire can see Nathan peering upward.

"Jump," she whispers, half because she wants to prick him, spark him, maybe to impress him with her morbid sense of humor; half because she knows the jumper never will.

But Errol is gripping her elbow. "Don't say that."

And he is right, Claire sees, because she looks up and feels the jumper already dead; he is still up there, but he has nothing left to give. He is no faker, he is not screwing around, just gathering the courage, aligning his powers with gravity's.

"What did he do?" Nathan wonders aloud.

"What *didn't* he, more likely," Errol replies.

"He needs a lawyer."

Something up the block catches Claire's eye. Another police cruiser is making its way over, lights off, in no hurry, trailed by a dark ambulance. Something is already done. They're coming—but who for? By the time Claire turns back someone is already screaming, someone near. The shriek trills off all that glass, the concrete barriers and orange barrier tape of a nearby construction zone, off the parked cars and uplifted faces. Then a loud explosion, a crisp report, like a rifle shot, and for a second Claire thinks the police car hit something, maybe the ambulance. Nervously, she lifts her eyes: the roof ledge is empty. Everyone is peering off the balconies, following the route down. In the street lies a level mound of clothes and shoes. In the middle of it something is heaving. A fist clenches and unclenches then freezes in a claw. There is no blood, a clean harmless bundle too compact and flat to be an actual human being. We're small in death, Claire thinks, but then sees the jumper has sprung a leak. Steaming, it begins to spread beneath, black and thick as oil, as though he is melting into the frozen asphalt.

No one approaches the corpse. The police turn their backs, focusing on crowd control now, on something they can do. Claire's hand crawls into Nathan's and begins to probe. She hears herself crying softly. "Oh God," she says—

And she says it now, again, "Oh God," seeing ten or so years too late, the curious familiar glare in Nathan's eyes, the blank stare that terrified her to the end, a kind of inward-facing dread, that eventually swung outward and swept over everything, denying everything, that swept over, turned on, and denied her.

And there, as Claire lies on her bed, in the pit of her mind is the image of a woman—not a man, not the jumper—a woman very like herself twitching like a marionette, throwing her fists again and again at the ground.

"Why," she says aloud, "did you do it, did you do it, did you do it?"

Quickly, to steady herself with other news, she scans her *Times*. Spotting something absurd she brings it closer. In parts of the Bronx and Spanish Harlem, she reads, South and Central American women with unbaptized children are hurrying in droves to their neighborhood churches and storefront chapels and lining up their babies for emergency baptism. Word has spread that the Antichrist is coming this Christmas and will murder the unanointed. Those women merely pregnant, in a panic, are having their bellies blessed. No one knows where the rumor originated, or why. Outside, the icy rain still falls. The day is silent, but it is not calm. She hears distant foghorns and sees the windows flicker as the lightning flies, and waits, in vain it seems, for the thunder. The storm seems to come and go at will.

She notices the time and runs to her closet. She runs through her apartment, through the door, through the sleet.

**8 A.M.** Will this work, this jangling? Nathan shakes the keys at the door like a shaman with his amulet. Eventually spotting the downtown ring he tries one key from that, then remembers that he is uptown and picks still another. Finally, less with luck than with random interest, he finds a key that fits. But the door is already open, the lock half-cocked. The red sedan comes to mind. He looks behind him and through the window in the lobby door finds only a square of empty street. He lurches in, calling, "Benny?"

In the half-dark of the living room the old woman sits upright on the couch, her hands rooted deep in a heavy, coarse overcoat. Simple black dress beneath the coat's hem. A pair of orthopedic shoes. The room around her is tidied, books reshelved, CDs stacked, his clothes folded and piled on the kitchen table.

"Mrs. Rosa. I'm sorry. Maria—"

The sink is empty, the dishes done and put away. Nathan looks over his shoulder. "Where's Benny?" he asks, and pokes his head into the small side room. The boy there is sprawled across the bed, the blankets bunched and kicked aside, his head twisted violently away from his shoulder, as if fallen from a roof, left randomly on the sidewalk.

Nathan sees his own bed is made. Maria's clothes, once everywhere, are nowhere. Her drawers, her side of the closet, empty. Boxes, suitcases, plastic bags—there is nothing left. The sink has been scrubbed. Also the floor, and that ring in the bathtub. Maria's mother came every day so that Benny did not return from school to an empty house, but she never once cleaned; didn't bother, Nathan always assumed. Now, everything after all these years gleams. As though with Maria's last exhalation all signs of her and her belongings all over town vaporized, accompanying her to the steamy other side.

He squints at the clock. "Benny has to get to school."

She addresses her hands: "He isn't going to school today."

"Did you tell him?"

"Maria's brothers are waiting at my apartment. I will take him there. He will be with his family when he learns."

"Of course, you all want to be there." Nathan glances at his watch. "What time do you want me?"

"No—" Up comes her hand, her face, insistent. "No."

"I thought I'd be the one to break it to him."

She folds her arms across her chest and turns her head to the window.

"We've been living together, I should be the one," he says, trying to keep up with his own logic. After a long pause, he floats the idea, like a trial balloon: "I'd like to keep the boy."

Her eyes widening in fear, she slips forward on the couch, ready to stand, or spring. "I am taking him away from here," she says.

His nod is less an affirmation than a failure to deny the truth of it. Of course it is a ridiculous idea. "I have to go to the hospital now."

"Go look at my girl," she says.

Across town the traffic in the St. Luke's lobby is already heavy. No one asks his name or offers a direction. On the sixth floor an unmanned cart bristling with brooms and mops and clean linens sits stalled outside a room near Maria's. A male nurse at INFORMATION sends Nathan to the basement.

The gurneys are lined up end to end along the stainless-steel cabinets, the mounds blanketed in baby-blue paper. Here and there a manila tag tied to a leached and shriven toe.

Nathan rubs his eyes. "Busy night."

"Busy week, month, whatever," the attendant replies. "They're dying of everything."

When the steel slab slides out on its silent bearings, Nathan is sure there has been some mistake.

"This is her?"

"There's been some swelling, just so you're prepared," the attendant says, and, without delaying—Nathan wishes he'd wait just a minute—lifts the sheet, making a loose tent down which Nathan can see all. He reaches toward her as a blind person might. Darkened leather face senseless as a handbag. Eyes, half-closed, squint dully into the middle distance. She looks to Nathan punched out, bruised. Even the bridge of her nose has spread. Below she is as shapeless and bunched as a baby. The sheet flutters down.

"Sign here."

When all the words are written, the attendant feeds Maria back in with a little shove, the throbbing hum of the hospital boiler just the other side of the wall some suggestion of where she's going. Nathan steps back against the massive cabinet. "You all right?" the attendant lamely asks. Nathan turns to rest the side of his face against the refrigerated metal, choking on a sorrow he has never known, but which, like his death itself, has hunted him these months and years.

"She wanted you to do it, no one else."

Nathan raises his head to find the attendant gone. In his place is a short man in a black pants suit with his throat clutched in a white cleric's collar. His head outsized and closely trimmed, perched on his neck like a golf ball on a tee.

"Cleary," he says, holding out a hand.

The priest seems about Nathan's age, and oddly it's the near-baldness that makes him look that young. Coming down from the rarefied air of fight and recovery into the basement of the damned and defeated, Cleary, robust, energetic, seems to thrive where he can admire his work, the fermenting corpses stretched out like loaves in their individual ovens, rising, getting ready to go. Cleary gives Nathan's hand a special squeeze, and for a second Nathan is sure the priest will never let go. Maybe he's sizing him up, taking Nathan's spiritual pulse while he adds together all Maria has confessed with what he now sees before him. So, here, finally, Nathan Stein.

"Maria," Cleary says, finally dropping his hand and nodding toward Maria's drawer, "spoke of you all the time. Especially toward the end. I heard you were down here. I've been wanting to meet you."

"I bet you have."

Cleary seems almost glad for the opportunity, glad even for the circumstance. Strange how the professionally faithful seem to run right over social nuance, as if their faith has shielded, or freed, them from the necessity.

"She knew just when she was going to die," Cleary plows on.

Nathan pictures their own non-goodbye, Maria preoccupied with her tranquilized neighbor, and he slipping out from under her blank stare. He'd assumed she was staring at him, but now he knows it wasn't him she was seeing at all. How long after he'd left had she actually stopped breathing? He should have gone up last night. He would at least have liked to say something to her, anything at all. Though what it would have been he has no idea. "She knew yesterday afternoon?"

Cleary's nod turns into a continuous, mechanized bob, smug with amazed discovery. "Down to the day. The hour. Yes, she knew." Inclining his head, the priest leans against the enormous cabinet, the fluorescent light glancing off both his shiny forehead and the wall of stainless steel behind him, ankles and arms crossed, as if waiting for the bus in the cold sun. "Yes, Maria spoke about you quite a bit."

But Nathan just stares, bracing himself, unwilling to rise to this bait. He is starting to resent the way Cleary isn't letting him have it, giving him a stern talking-to, like Maria would have. Either he doesn't know his job or it's part of that grand strategy they all seem to have of letting you probe yourself, reprimand yourself, levy your own fine. Nathan can feel the growing annoyance in his gut. When was the last time he ate? He slaps his coat pockets for his pills.

"Looking for a smoke?" Cleary asks hopefully, and brings out a heavy silver lighter.

But Nathan shakes his head. "Not for years."

"Ah, self-improvement. You're a more honorable man than I." Cleary squints and pauses, then raises at Nathan a pair of startled eyebrows. He clears his throat, smiles. "Should I take that back?"

Nathan shrugs. "Go ahead." He searches for signs of wear on Cleary's face—every day here a Sunday, every day requiring hurried, last-minute conversions—but finds nothing. He envies for a moment the priest's ability to fend off all the chaotic lives that end, muddled and humiliated, in his hands. All the weeping families, all the bodily fluids. Until it all lies here, all his little experiments, sent away every one of them. And he'll never know where to—or even if—until he follows them himself.

"So why me?" Nathan asks. "Why not her mother, or any of her brothers? To ID her."

"I guess she wanted you to see," Cleary suggests.

Nathan's reply is automatic: See what? But he holds it in, knowing the confessional game to follow: see what he saw, and what did he see? As though this exchange will bring him to say, "himself," then cry and weep and beg forgiveness.

"She looks terrible," he says instead.

"Yes," Cleary agrees." She does."

"Was anyone else with her?"

"She said goodbye to everyone else, then made them go. She was waiting for you. She was filled with remorse. She wanted to apologize."

An unlit cigarette has appeared in Cleary's fingers. He rolls it in his fingers, then finally puts it to his lips. Nathan is surprised at his own indignation. The cloud of felonies around him pulling apart to reveal this single misdemeanor. "Are you allowed to do that in here?"

Cleary's lighter pops. He inhales, squints, and raises his eyes to the cabinet. "I doubt anyone here would mind." He waves his hand, trailing flags of smoke. "Anyway, you didn't come back."

Nathan lifts a hand in protest, "But I did," then drops it, "in a way."

The priest nods, a disapproving twinkle in his eye. "She

thought you might actually be with her. She thought you'd know to do that. She gave you a lot of credit that way. She believed you were highly intelligent."

Nathan wrinkles his nose at the gauze of smoke. The priest looks pleasantly surprised, as if to say, Does *this* offend you?

"So you were with her when she—"

"Stopped breathing, yes," Cleary says.

"She wanted you to be?"

Cleary's smile turns apologetic. "People do. She requested her own last rites. That's never happened to me before."

"You don't know her," Nathan begins, marveling at the urge to tell him this: "When I met her, guys left and right, drugs."

Cleary frowns. "That wasn't her. There's always someone who wants to be found." He nods toward the steel wall. "Who she was just before she died, that's who she always wanted to be."

"Well, at least she wasn't alone," Nathan says.

"She was looking for answers. When she came in to the hospital this time she was paralyzed with fear. She knew she was going to die, and she didn't know what to believe, or if she should bother trying. She had a lot of questions. She really was a religious woman, she just didn't know it. For instance, one question she had was, What did she do to make you leave? Beside the obvious, of course."

"Me? I didn't leave. I don't know what you mean. I've stuck it out these last three years while she was sick."

"Maybe I'm asking the wrong question."

Nathan eyes him warily. "I have court soon."

"Just tell me this, Nathan," Cleary says in a tone eerily familiar, as if he's known Nathan all his life, or men like Nathan, legions of Nathans marching lockstep into the chapel since the beginning of time. "Why are you here?"

"Maria wanted me to identify her body."

"And why you?"

"I don't know what you're driving at."

"Did you always do what Maria wanted, or only this one last

favor?" Cleary lifts his chin, observing Nathan down the length of his nose.

"Look, Chaplain—" Nathan says.

"Reverend is fine."

"This—" Nathan gestures to Maria's door. "This isn't my fault. I didn't do *this*."

Deftly, Cleary pats Nathan over the heart, summoning his mercy: "We have to take care of what we have left. *I* can't forgive you."

"Forgive me for what? *She* did this to *me*."

Cleary bows his head.

"So everything, then?" Nathan says. "I'm responsible for everything?"

"Only for what you do. We do what we can but then it's ours to keep. You can't keep cutting your losses, Nathan. Eventually, there is nothing left to cut."

Nathan looks to his wrist for the time but the watch face is a blur.

"Isn't the reason you came down here that you really wanted to *see*?" Cleary says. "You know, what it's like, what it'll be like for you in a few months or, God willing, a few years? Don't you think Maria had that in mind, too?"

Nathan is tapping his foot, looking up, away, anywhere.

The priest regards with doubt what's left of his cigarette then stubs it out against the handle of one of the square steel doors.

"Okay, let me ask you this," he says behind his lighter's flame. "Do you believe in God?"

Nathan wants to laugh but can't find the spark. "Should I?"

Cleary's eyes latch on to Nathan's, his curious gaze narrowing to a hostile glare, rounding out to something like horror.

"So what about you?" Nathan asks. "You believe in God?"

Staring at Cleary's pinched collar Nathan is not sure the question is off the mark. Something about the priest is smug to the point of defensiveness, insecurity, self-convincing. Still, Nathan knows he's committed the cardinal sin, drummed over and over by Sid Frankel into his head: don't ask a question in court you don't know the answer to. Don't hunt, don't fish, don't set your-self up for an ambush.

But Cleary turns out to be less savvy than he first gives off. "I do right now," is the meager answer.

At first Nathan is startled by the ease with which Cleary offered that up, this nugget that seems to carry the weight if not of truth, then of honesty. Nathan is impressed. "But not always?"

Cleary toes the floor. "No, not always." His head comes up inhaling, the cords of his neck unwound, nostrils flared. Uncon-sciously, he has moved back a step. "Why do you ask?"

Nathan looks skittishly to Maria's door, as if she could answer for him. Though now he's not sure which address is hers; his eyes skip from one compartment to the other.

Boiler rumble surges beneath Nathan's feet, or the subway, or tectonic wind. The mounds of dead bumper-to-bumper along the walls seem to lurch, inching forward. He grits his teeth against the chill, blinks at the sting in his eyes.

"You're sweating, Nathan."

Nathan clears his throat. "What about Hell?"

Cleary doesn't hesitate: "Hell I believe in."

Up and outside in the day, a veil of thin rain, Nathan circles the block for his car, his overcoat billowing behind him. His slow aim-less orbit. The car is nowhere. Tapping his coat pockets for his pills, he uncaps them, pouring nothing into his palm. He shakes the empty vials, tosses them into the street, under the cars, and follows after them, wading into the twitchy morning traffic. Endless strings of abuse are turned on him from all sides. He cups his hands over his ears and all disappears but the exploding sun. Church bells, samba music, the concussion of fireworks leaping off the Coney Island beach like mortars, their harlequin rainbow umbrellas re-flected in a pair of raven-black eyes narrowing at him out of a gargoyle's head. Hideous pariah. Two men squatting against the hospital's retaining wall, blackened and shredded blankets and feet of gauze, peer over like birds of prey. In the silence someone touches Nathan's shoulder. When he turns no one is there.

———

Errol Santos leans back in his old chair. Barbados is walking quickly toward him. The two are surrounded by empty desks. In the corner a civilian secretary attends to her nails. Faces are everywhere, primitive sketches and Christmas photos and dated school portraits pinned and Scotch-taped to the walls and peering up from the desks atop piles of more faces. The back edge of Santos's desk is layered with stacks of manila folders, unsolved cases, cases nearing solution, and cases, like his sister's, that have just begun. The office has one window, but it looks out on the brick face of the building next door, offering little hint of actual outside, even less of sky.

"Are you going to tell me what Stein said to you last night?" Barbados asks.

Santos looks woodenly at the photo atop the pile on his desk, as though the figure in it will offer some reply: Isabel lying in the wan light of the crime scene photographer's flash, seaweed strewn through her hair like a crown of wildflowers, the shredded cloth of her thin dress clinging across her cold nipples and across her pouched belly and thighs. Her blue lips parted. Then there is nothing for him to look at except the place where the body had lain, a scooped and smooth bed of sand.

"Sign out, Errol. Go home. This is not helping."

"What do they have?"

"You know you're off this case. You should be working something else, probably shouldn't be here at all."

"Tell me what they have."

"It's all in the folder. But it's not much. They think they might have hair. They think they have a time, but that's it."

"Blood?"

Barbados shakes his head. "And the fingernails were clean, like you saw."

"What was the time?"

"Twelve to three the night before."

Santos nods. "She was still with Stein. They have a cause?"

"Errol."

"Just say it."

"Her neck was snapped."

Santos drags his hand over his face. What he can't stop considering is the possibility that it took her a while to die. He can't stop seeing it. He looks around the room.

"She knew something," he says. "She had to. Krivit knows more than he's saying."

"The rat smells bad," Barbados agrees.

"Cleaned up afterward to keep the innocent innocent," Santos mumbles to himself.

"Look at me, Errol. If you know something, now is the time to say it. I don't know what the man said to you, but go home, leave your gun in your desk. Don't go down with this guy."

The pinned and taped faces Santos passes watch through the windowframes their photographs make. As he goes by they turn and follow him with their eyes.

Rocking side to side in a subway car sprinkled sparsely with riders, he watches the subterranean world pass like a filmstrip through the windows. Graffittied darkness then flashes of light, the subway car, empty in Brooklyn, filling as the train heads uptown through lower Manhattan. Old people laboring past the poles with their plastic bags of toys; black families with sleepy children teetering in their eggcup plastic seats. A transit cop going past, pulling himself from pole to pole. A leak sprung in the tunnel showers the car, the beads of street water racing across the windowpanes as if from a sudden rain. Fulton Street, City Hall, like various small towns each stop a station in a life Santos can identify with a day, a night, a face. Three A.M. rides in subway cars like this, giddy-drunk with Nathan and Claire swinging on the poles, the three of them singing, the two of them pawing at each other. Errol the dateless third wheel, the loyal butler, Nathan's man Friday. He has known Nathan, looked on him with adoration, all his life. He has coveted his woman, then divorced his own to take her. Which makes him what?—an agent provocateur, a double agent, assassin. Where do his allegiances lie? He feels himself reaching back for ancient guidance. Looking for answers, he squints upward at the illuminated advertisements overhead. Remedies for hemorrhoids, foot fungus, ripped earlobes, unwanted pregnancy, male pattern baldness, bikini wax, allergies, fecal urgency, diminutive and surplus (mostly female) body parts, the ailments, the plagues, the toll-free numbers to make it all go away. What of emptiness, what of ruin?

At Union Square, the doors open and the cold from outside fills the subway car. He rises and exits, proceeding through other weather. Santos with his miles to go, his immeasurable desires to correct. To still things in motion. Aboveground, hailstones nip at his face, but something in the wild day other than rain and snow is shouting down at him.

Showing his badge he is let through a service gate behind the brownstones along West Ninth. He hops fences and crosses frozen gardens and jungle gyms encased in ice. In the middle of the block he stops at a dog's shit field. His old shoes creak in the dry snow like chalk. He shrugs at his overcoat. Frozen lines of salt rim his nose and upper lip. He has been crying. He taps at the french doors, drawing his gun halfway out of its holster.

"Nathan," he calls.

But his voice is soft, and he half desires no answer. He tries the handle and finds it turns easily in his hand and he stands there looking at it. He pushes on the door an inch or two and waits for the dog's snarl and the avalanche of paws, but he hears nothing. He throws open the door and starts in. When he hears something he doesn't like he stops where he is, pools of snowmelt collecting under his feet. The lights are on. There is nothing to be afraid of that he can see but much that he can't. For instance why he is here: because his sister is dead; because she was Nathan's sister, too, and because Nathan seduced her, or he didn't seduce her, or because he won't say; because the ties to him have become more tight and less clear and are bound to become less clear still; because there are no absolutes in human misery and things will always get worse; and because he has believed that Nathan has done nothing wrong all these years, though now he believes Nathan might do—have done—anything. He has always seen in Nathan what he envies most. Now he sees what he most despises.

For every single thing about him that he once agreed with, or wanted more of, he now has another reason to see him dead. The same Nathan, who once, more than anyone he knows—certainly more than he himself—had more reasons to live.

"Nathan," he calls again. He raises his gun. "Nathan—"

Somewhere, a radiator hisses.

After a while, he returns the gun to his belt, closes the door softly behind him, hops the fence and goes away into the morning.

The clutch of birds streaks across his cracked windshield at the entrance ramp to the FDR, knocking and darkening the glass, sweeping Nathan through a reverse car wash of water sounds and whirring feathers and mechanical squeal, finally peeling away to reveal a dozen lightning strikes of viscous drool. He reaches for the wipers, but he must have sucked the plastic tank dry on the Belt Parkway last night because the glass smears white as noon.

He gets out brandishing a torn square of tissue before he notices that the road he wants has been closed. The East River is running level with it, its testy new edge, white and scummy, has begun to snake across the merge. Ahead, across the river to the east, the darker clouds are steadily climbing. A new round of snow veined with mute lightning.

Nathan backs onto York and heads down Second Avenue. His cell-phone rings as this sector of lights is turning to a string of reds. His hand crawls through the glove box, landing the electric shaver and—ignoring the complaints of cabs and grocery trucks stacking up behind him—tugs at the rear-view mirror and scrubs the shaver across his face. An alarm—is it time? He sees but does not consider the face in the mirror, a face not his own. He swipes at the halo of wispy tangle atop the head, then works the shaver methodically, digging at the cleft in the chin. Finally he draws the phone, mid-ring, and leaves it mouthpiece-down amid the heather of dog hair on the seat. Some voice buzzes its protest. He calibrates the volume knob on the CD against Serena's high-pitched drone and closes his eyes on his first peaceful dark in days, in which Coltrane—the stars, the moon, the morphine sedation—is in full serenade. Depthless float. The peace and slide of a life that should have been. Other numberless and nameless things that should be. Gently, Nathan's fingers touch out a new rhythm on the steering wheel. Flamenco Sketches. The side-step lilt into the Spanish bridge, that call to the good old days, while behind, Bill Evans on his piano all sweetness and light, then like the day itself, like this day itself, turns dark and ominous. Nathan's eyelashes dampen shut. Miles, muted, the call of the lark, heralding— what, a new day or the end of this one? Sad now—not this is where we've been, but this is where we're heading. The tears are real, and adhesive. He will not open his eyes until the music ends, and it does end, badly, with a hitched fade-out. And his eyes do open, on themselves, in the rear-view mirror. He finds there chips of green ice so pale now it is hard even for him to see that there is anything behind them. So pale they look blind.

The cop in the window, an eclipse of the already sunless day, is tapping impatiently with the end of a nightstick. Nathan doesn't look. He can't bear it, or doesn't care to. Dead ahead, ahead, ahead, he blinks and toes the accelerator, the car lurches, the cop staggers back. On through the red, sending the traffic charging at his door into a screeching hook slide. He slaloms downtown around the emissions of the breathing ground, foul clouds rising from the pierced sewerlids.

Against all logic, it has grown even darker, greener. Tornado weather. Thunder explodes just overhead. Before him the vertical world, the craggy skyline, the faceless columns of the World Trade Center, has drawn nearer, towering up over the little ants, little humanity.

Alone on the sidewalk, Nathan peers up at the old building, spitting distance from the courts, a layer cake of bail bondsmen, immigration lawyers, slip-and-fall, import-exporters. All those endless hallways and their frosted doors. Milton had bought for Nathan and himself a share of an office of high-class transients, a traffic lawyer and a man named Chang, who, with his cadre of stunning and stealthy Asian secretaries, hordes secrets and smooths out the indignities caused by various anonymous factions of the

Chinese mob. Milton brought to the mix his own son, Nathan, Isabel, her mother, and, of course, the irrepressible Oliver Schreck.

Two red-and-white NYC sheriff cruisers, country cousins to the more officious police, squat at the curb. Some deadbeat getting snared for child support, no doubt. Or parking tickets. Nathan's got piles of his own for this car, that one, the other.

Nathan winces at the door. Is he going in? Must he go in? It seems he must.

At the sight of Nathan, the lobby man Jorge—a mere allusion to security in his toy soldier's uniform complete with gold shoulder boards—looks stricken. Nathan knows he's not looking his best. Today of all days he must make an impression.

"Qué pasa."

"Qué pasa."

"Un momentito, señor," Jorge suggests, finger raised as if testing the wind. "Con permiso—"

But there is court. The judge won't mind his relaxed attire. East Hampton in the offing—if anyone will understand, it will be a judge. And he is late, he is always late. But the question is, How late? He must hurry.

And that deposition to be taken uptown later—or after later?— Isabel had said so. There must also be preparations for the Riverside Drive case. Milton will be upstairs fielding calls. And now—it strikes him gravely—they have no secretary. Busy, busy, busy—

"Hasta la vista, Jorge," Nathan says, giving a little wave.

The twenty-second-floor hallway, usually bustling at this hour, is deserted, though anything but silent. It echoes with ticking: his watch, his heart, the heels of his shoes, his conscience, impatient fingernails on some desk, the one thousand clocks of this building tracking appointments kept, appointments lost.

He stands. Has he sat? It seems he is always falling and having to get up. Now he slows. Someone, it appears, has left the door to his office open at the end of the hall. The yellow light of the reception area spills into the hallway, splashing up the opposite wall. Behind him the elevator doors clatter open and pause. No one emerges. Then no one still.

Nathan whirls. "Isabel, why is the door—?" He stops himself. The reception desk, cheap plastic veneer, sits unmanned. But the waiting room, as quiet as the hall, crawls with life. Ruth and Schreck, changed since last night into blue-black court attire; the traffic lawyer wearing below his droopy mustache a gray leisure suit and loafers, ready to field his 1-800 calls about fender benders and lawsuits for untimely deaths; and slippery Chang in his double-breasted Armani and wing tips, surrounded like a pop star by his four young secretaries, a small mercenary army. Before them stand four New York County sheriffs, like troopers in their Smokey the Bear hats and striped trousers; as if, having taken the wrong exit off the thruway, here they are to ask directions. The guests hold their breath. A sheriff steps forward, parting the claws of his handcuffs: "Nathan Stein?"

Nathan recognizes the voice from the movies; the formality that authority seems to require of itself. Then he recalls the dozens of scenes from the films of his clients' lives. How many times has he himself stood beside a lone, doomed figure before the bench, always on the right, always the right.

Nathan shuffles to the right. Maddeningly, black dots do-si-do before his eyes. "Isn't it a little early?" he asks. He feels a giddy drunk coming on.

The three other sheriffs step forward.

"Don't say a thing," Ruth instructs from the rear.

Nathan looks at her, slightly amused. Then at Schreck, grimly, and says, as to Judas: "Do what you're here to do." One arm then the other is seized and pinned behind him. "I told Errol Santos everything I know."

Ruth is gripping his arm. "No, Nathan—"

"My father?"

"He's on his way."

Nathan faces the sheriffs: "Don't you know who my lawyer is? Don't you know who my father is?"

One of the sheriffs addresses the silent crowd: "This *is* Stein?"

"That's him," Schreck says quickly.

Nathan nods his appreciation. "Thank you, Oliver."

"He doesn't feel well," Ruth warns them.

Schreck looks at his watch and mumbles, "Milton said he'd be in at ten."

Pimples of sweat pop to the surface of Nathan's face. "Then he's *not* on his way?"

"Hang in there," Schreck says. He makes a consoling fist indicating some vague fraternal bond.

"Oliver, I saw the damned billboard. And Maria's will. Were you going to tell me—?"

"You have the right to remain silent—"

"I know this part. Somebody, Baron is in the car. He'll be hungry."

"We'll take care of the dog," Schreck says, a comment vaguely menacing.

The traffic lawyer, hiding his eyes, walks away shaking his head, his loafers zipping across the gray industrial carpet.

Nathan staggers forward, but the doorway fills, blocking the way. Already with the handkerchief blotting the back of his neck, the crescents of hair around the ears dark with damp. "Well well," Krivit says.

Ruth points at him. "Not a word."

An ironic smirk crosses Krivit's face. "What did he do?"

It is a good question. It hasn't crossed Nathan's mind to ask. Though these are sheriffs, not police officers; that limits the possibilities. This can't be about Isabel. Nathan looks up with genuine interest. "What *did* I—?"

"Nothing," Ruth blurts before Nathan can finish asking. "You pissed on a judge. It was the tax returns."

Nathan wants to laugh. "This is for that? Judge Acevedo actually called my bluff?" He'd like to say, *Good* for her, but thinks it imprudent.

Krivit eyes Nathan. "Contempt of court?" he says archly. "Now that's rich."

Contrite, Nathan shrugs, "Ask my lawyer," and raises his head to the room full of them, of which, suddenly, he is no member.

Krivit lowers a brow. "Did you finish?"

"Did he finish what?" Schreck asks.

"Be quiet," Ruth snaps.

Krivit squints at Schreck. "What do you mean what? You know what. Where the hell is it?"

Nathan nods at the little drama unfolding before him. Schreck knows about the writ; he said so. Of course Ruth knows that Schreck knows. They all know everything. Even the little rat, Krivit.

He hears in his ears again the pledge he'd made to himself early this morning that despite Claire he would have Amparo's cousin released. A slam dunk at redemption if there ever was one: call the A.D.A., finesse the girl's charges, tug lightly on the string or two still left him, pay the $500 himself if he has to. He can still work a deal. Consider the baby, he'd have begun, as with everything, he would have begun so well—

"I hope this won't take long. I have to be in court," he says, then spins, remembering Regina Núñez's file. "I need something in my office."

The sheriffs murmur and look uncertain, then stand aside and follow Nathan toward the back of the suite, past the mahogany-lined rooms, Milton's with the cases of law books and journals and diplomas fixed haphazardly, like fieldstones over the walls, and the glass-topped desk with the view of roiling sky, into which Milton and Nathan separately stared while seeding secretaries and clients' wives and their girlfriends past and present and their sisters and selected members—females, all but one—of the building maintenance crew. And the time when Milton kept an office full of clients waiting for an hour and a half. One impatient client stood and marched toward the door and flung it open, revealing for all to see a woman spread among the depositions and pen sets on Milton's desk, her skirt hiked, her legs splayed, Milton kneeling below and between, his head nodding—

Nathan stands at the threshold to his own office. The sheriffs are behind him and Ruth and Schreck behind them, all wondering, Nathan is sure, what it is he could possibly need.

"What is the charge?" he asks again, trying to narrow his search: himself or Regina Núñez, he's already forgotten who he's supposed to help. But he answers before they can, with a nod, "Contempt," and steps in.

Negotiating the crowded floor, he looks about. No credentials here. His diplomas peek out from behind cracked glass amid towers of paper and newsprint climbing the walls to the ceiling. CDs in staggered columns, collapsed like his mail across the bookless shelves. A clearing in the woods for the gleaming stereo. Nathan's desk is buried beneath the scatter of books and year-old magazines and styrofoam cups. Atop it all a laptop, still on, possibly for days, seems to be in charge. Piled in the office's corners the empty boxes for the stereo, the computer, the new phone, old phone, coffeemaker, other appliances long gone, and just empty boxes whose duty—coming/going, in/out?—remains a mystery. The overwhelmed file cabinet and its three tiers of manila folders hangs open. A room with no chronology. No order. No language. Only the now, the tick of time occupied by this moment's breath, gone already with the exhalation into a container of everything before. A blind distant past housed here in this mausoleum of lives tried and pled, of briefs and writs begun past deadline, set down for the morning paper and forgotten and left unfiled to mulch beneath the compost of new paper, new briefs, obsolete news.

"Mr. Stein—?"

He looks about. As he had, standing last week at the open door to the Church of the Immaculate Conception on Fordham Road. Serena had begged him to come to mass. Purge and be purified. Be cured. Inside, the acrid sweetness of incense hung in the air. Pausing by a plastic seashell filled with foggy water, he peered down the long aisle through the halfdark where a chipped and sallow Christ hung spotlit and suspended from invisible wires over the altar, not unlike a trapeze artist. Oblivious beneath his spiked crown. Pierced palms and extruded ribs drained by the wounds freshly repainted with lipstick. Ankles crossed and riveted, the toes curled in, which Nathan thought a nice touch, feminine. Mater Dolorosa hanging stage left. Serena eased Nathan—it was not one of his best days—into a pew halfway down. Four figures slumped against the dimness of the nave, the light upon their shoulders and heads making of them silhouettes, targets, contestants, saints. Before him a wooden container missing the Bible it once offered up. A long felt bench stretching aisle to aisle, bleached and dimpled in evenly spaced pairs, as if the nexus of the spirit were the connection between knee joint and floor. Feeling the thousand hours he'd spent in his synagogue in Ozone Park, the sin-riven and unrepentant target of Rabbi Jupiter's pearls of wisdom, the virtues of a virgin's pregnancy were not lost on him.

Serena in leather pants and a gauzy blouse entered the confessional. He heard her crying. A dark figure in dark robes slipped through the wooden locker's curtains and the slide shot back and instantly there was a faint murmuring, as if from an old endless ramble never interrupted. Nathan kept his watchful eye on the statuary, expecting the worst. The stained glass of the windows deadened by the day's hazy overcast. Random panels replaced with murky plexiglass. Here and there, a saint was pierced and lit in cobalt blue and a diluted orange among the pews. The distant hiss of traffic on the Grand Concourse. In four or five months, during the quiet of a Sunday mass, Nathan knew the pagan roar from Yankee Stadium would inspire the lines of little Christian boys in white fitted frocks to near riot and the material ghosts slumped in the nave to titters.

In the confessional Serena's admissions became a singsong chant, and Nathan, having seen it before, saw her then: eyes glued with tears, hands twitchy, her pouched lips puckered and waving at the air to let out the stumbling flood, failing to keep up with the list of her transgressions: the lines of coke; the unmade phone calls to a grandmother left in San Juan like an old plant too dusty to clean; her obsessions with the gringo out in the pews, the accelerant to an already aimless life. Meanwhile, in Nathan's ears, the church-building murmured with tales of misdemeanors and fratricide and a shepherd in search of his flock and women sentenced to eternal damnation and a ram slaughtered and disemboweled and offered up to an unrepentant and hungry Lord. No respecter of persons. Nathan's grief at what he had done. These evil-doing and sex-crazed vagabonds. Good men gone to seed, bringing on the great storm. A drowned race of perilous incurables. Six-hundred-year-old Noah captaining his floating zoo. And that was only Genesis.

A hand shook Nathan gently. He had been sleeping. He looked up into a wan and featureless face, very like that of his clients, a man in powder-blue jumpsuit and clerical collar. Serena close behind him, clutching her sequined handbag as though it contained the ashes of her incinerated misdeeds.

The priest, in Puerto Rican accent: "Are you waiting to confess?"

Nathan slowly pushed himself off the bench. A shadow off to the side scuttled for the deeper dark. A string of whoops from a passing fire engine approached, whined by, and bent into the distance. Movement above, in the lightless rafters, the flutter of birds.

"No."

Serena threw the priest a knowing and resigned look.

"I'm tired," Nathan said.

"Nathan," Serena begged.

The priest tilted his head, confused. "Excuse me?"

"I'd just fallen asleep."

Nathan sidestepped into the aisle, his hand raised protectively to his forehead. "Maybe tomorrow," he murmured.

Serena's voice raised to a shriek, a little girl on the run, a tearful drizzle. "Nathan, just say sorry!"

The priest was waiting. Was he? Am I, am I? "Of course," Nathan replied. "I'm sorry."

"Stein?"

"Nathan?"

Ruth stands before him, her face bunched with concern. Nathan feels the brick of cash in his inside blazer pocket and, lifting his head, closes his eyes. Milton will reel him back in. Hours from now he'll be out. Another forty-eight, and, offshore, the sunlight will snake its way through and he will inspect the changeless shapes of the sky and study the thunder of surf. He will drink tequila while standing ankle-deep in white sand.

"Ready to go?" the sheriff asks.

Nathan blinks, afraid of the answer. "Where?"

# 10 A.M.

An hour passes as the hours will pass here. In this concrete room the iron door clanks shut the wrong way. The holding cell murmurs with the hyperintensity of men who are not yet the state's wards, prisoners only of the moment, still with lives to lose. Nathan receives sidelong glances from jailers he's known for years, men he's paid off for a variety of client services, women, food, extra minutes. Now his pockets hang down along his legs like socks. His shoes, stripped of their laces, flop like slippers. He clutches his blazer to his chest like a life preserver. A high naked bulb dangles from the ceiling, directing the light nowhere.

He hangs on the bars and peers out. Someone in an orange jumpsuit is coming backward down the hallway dragging a plastic bucket on wheels by a mop submerged in brown sludge. Across the hall, in another cell, a darker corner sputters in laughter. Nathan catches the eye of the man there, a shawl over his shoulders, his face darkly greased, the eyes and mouth whited out like a miner's. "Don't look at me," he says.

Nathan turns and finds himself admired by a man cradling himself in his reedy arms, a horse whinny leaping from his lips, as if identifying him as either potential prey or long-lost kindred spirit. Nathan rolls his blazer and curls on the only spot left him, a square of concrete slab beside an unflushed porcelain bowl half filled with liquid shit. Pale winter light falls through the welded iron windows. He can see upside down the crown of Yankee Stadium;

the belly of a plane vanishing, crashing the wrong way into the clouds. He shuts his eyes to sleep, but on the back of his lids sees mirrored there his own pale stare.

"What are you?"

Nathan raises his head to a huge black man seated against the wall, his legs stretched before him. His neck spreads like armored wings to the nubs of his shoulders.

"Same as you," Nathan says.

"I don't believe so." He looks at Nathan's shoes. He looks at the bites and scratches on Nathan's arms. They are beginning to stink. "What did you do, yell at your wife?"

"I'm not married."

"I'm not married either. Not after this morning. I just killed her. Her and her boyfriend. Ice pick, man." He brings down his arm once, slowly, to demonstrate. "Daily News said I'm tomorrow's page one."

"Impressive."

The black man shrugs. "But I don't know anymore since that fucker came in." He aims his finger like a rifle across the room. "Dude did the same thing, but he used an ax."

Like a child lost in a parade Nathan peers through the crooks of elbows and crotches at the man who was scrutinizing him. A beacon of peaceful madness in the hubbub. His lips are waving, his head twitching, as if in animated conversation.

Nathan turns back to the double murderer. Hands pillowy and worn like leather mitts, like tools. "Maybe you shouldn't admit things so freely."

"It's what I did."

"The beauty of things," Nathan replies, eyes fluttering closed for an instant, as if awaiting a symphony's fateful moment. "It doesn't matter what you actually do. It's what you say."

A small smile creases the face. "You aren't a lawyer, are you?"

Nathan shrugs.

"Shoot. Legal counsel." He slaps Nathan's shoulder. Others have overheard and squint uncertainly in Nathan's direction. "I'm going to need a lawyer."

"I can't help you."

"You'll get out. What did you do, anyway?"

Nathan sees no reason to hold back. In here, a sort of homecoming. He's with his kind. Anyway, he's with what he knows. "Pissed off a judge."

"Hell. How did you do it?"

"She wanted to see my taxes."

"Why didn't you give the judge your taxes?"

Nathan shrugs. "I never file them."

The man laughs. "My kind of lawyer."

Nathan can't resist. It comes to him as easy as breath. "Then one thing."

"What's that?"

"The best angle, the best and most successful defense."

"Tell me."

"The irrelevance of your guilt in a court of law."

The double murderer, smiling goofily, waves his hands before his eyes. "Shoot."

Nathan blinks through his grin at his new friend, superimposing upon him images of a man and woman lying in a briny pool of blood and vomit on a ragged carpet, the man's leg twitching, an ice pick quivering like a flag planted for God and country in the woman's heaving chest. The black sits, knees up against the wall, humming at the ceiling. As though beneath a tree on a hot summer's day, not a care in the world. Glad to be rid of her, glad to lighten the load. My successes, Nathan knows, are society's failures.

A young kid grasps the bars of the window, hauling himself up, his arms shivering with the strain. All he can see is the same wedge of sky with the same plane as Nathan. Feet anchored against the wall, he heaves himself up higher and he freezes. Nathan can tell he's caught the same slice of Yankee Stadium, maybe a glimpse of tarpaulined field. Beyond that the low rubble of East Harlem, which the kid beams at as if he's spotted a beach, a woman spreading out a towel and stripping off blouse and skirt in the wavy gas of heat. Her arms raised, pinning back her hair—

A man has straddled the bowl overhead, his pants shackling his knees. Nathan rolls away just in time, gathering his blazer and finding himself against the opposite wall squatting beside the ax-wielder. The murderer smells of swamp and unholy death. But then Nathan compares favorably the cuts and scratches on his own arms with his neighbor's and turns aside to dream old dreams of Sid Frankel's face as he led a prosecution witness to stand the truth on end, to look for all the world like confusion and certain acquittal.

The kid hanging from the window bars holds on as long as he can then drops to the floor. "Man, that's beautiful."

His name is sounded and he rises and enters the wrong end of the arraignment hall and sits on a bench, his face hidden from the gallery like a game-show mystery guest. Shoulder to shoulder with wife batterers and car thieves, weekend warriors, others who may have done worse. No one has done nothing. At his back, he knows, is the matinee audience of mothers and sisters. The dignitaries in the front row, the private lawyers and Legal Aid catching cases, nod Nathan's way and whisper among themselves. The court officers are smugly amused at this little soap opera, a ripple in their days of sodomizers and pickpockets.

"Mr. Stein." It is a small voice at the end of the bench. Possibly the voice of conscience, he believes, a voice he had spent his life drowning and refashioning in the guise of Puccini and Coltrane. But Nathan leans, just to be sure: Regina Núñez, Amparo's peasant cousin, sits at the end of the same bench holding her swollen belly in her hands. His face heating with embarrassment, Nathan gives her a little wave.

"Amparo—" the girl begins to explain, her expression dark, full of foreboding.

"I wanted to help you today," he tries to explain.

In through the crack in the door flood commitments and forgotten pledges, but they are too much and so amount to nothing, easily forgotten. Nathan offers no defense. Briefly, he considers a plea. Then he simply leans back, out of the girl's peripheral view, ending his torment.

Claire, though, can't be far away, he knows. He peeks over his shoulder, and there, in the front row, in her nimbus of virtue and decorum, sits his own counsel, Ruth, in black dress and pearls, a manila folder in her lap. But she is too stiff, too indignant, as if she's stonewalling someone's gaze. And as Nathan untwists he catches in the corner of his eye a flash of red hair. A stack of manila folders and yellow legal pads clutched to her chest like a shield, Claire is staring at him, her face blank with disbelief.

Nathan grabs the back of the bench and begins to stand. Two court officers half rise, hands on the stocks of their pistols, and he lowers himself, clutching his own thighs, surprised to find them sinewy, atrophied.

At the bridge officer's call, four of Nathan's neighbors rise. Boys with round faces, hands clasped with contrition and eyes filled with mischief. Four attorneys—friends, colleagues, sworn enemies of Milton—meet them elbow to elbow in the middle of the floor and escort them like groomsmen to the table and face the black-robed judge and the calendar Scotch-taped to the front of her bench. A dozen women in the first rows of the gallery lift their chins to hear. Their hair teased and their faces freshly painted; their church clothes unearthed and pressed for their brothers and sons. Five court officers rise together, hands poised near their guns, covering the angles between the suspects and the gallery.

At his lectern, a rookie assistant district attorney with slick blond hair reads from a manila folder a harrowing tale of a posse of young men roaming the subways, leaving a trail of fear and broken ribs and empty pockets. These four young suspects surrounded a couple and threatened them with box cutters. Removed from said couple's possession: one radio, one watch, one wallet containing thirteen dollars cash. The audience utters not a sound. One attorney after another, feverishly picking over the files—some of them, Nathan knows, for the first time—speaks in reverent tones of his client as a community asset, of his rock-solid family. Two of them work as stock boys in a warehouse. At 2 A.M. they were merely returning from work, your honor. They were imploring the alleged victims for change to make phone calls home, nothing more, they were late, their mothers—all present, your honor, to show their support—were worried. Panhandling at best. The box cutters not weapons but tradesmen's tools, evidence of their willingness to work for their families' survival. The whole thing was a misunderstanding, an overreaction. You honor, everybody is worked up over the case of the Riverside Drive jogger. These men are not animals. We're all a little tense, all a little trigger-happy.

Nathan would like to laugh. He could have done better.

The judge, grim-faced, does not lift her eyes. Bail is requested at $10,000 each by the assistant district attorney. A collective gasp rises from the women relatives. The judge grants the A.D.A.'s wishes without hesitation and the women begin to wail. They reach over the partition. They hug each other. The victimized boys glance back, all innocence and light. The court officers hold their ground as the women exit weeping.

Nathan hears his name and immediately rises. And immediately the floor seems to fall from him. He watches his feet cross the floor. Ruth grabs his elbow smelling of flowers and country nights, of the perfumed nylons that contain her thighs. Nathan, for a moment, shuts his eyes.

"Are you going to be all right?" Ruth asks.

He stands rocking from side to side before a judge he has danced with in court often enough and eviscerated just as often outside of it. He's made fun of her pocked face and heavily painted lips, her floppy jowls and buoyant hairdo. But she's no joke now. She levels at him a scrutinous glare, as though considering all the battles she's lost and all the directions she can now go. Sweat traces the back of his head.

Ruth leans in to whisper: "The disciplinary committee called."

Nathan waves his hand.

"It's not just not filing 1099s."

"They have nothing."

"They have fraud."

"They have nothing."

"They have larceny by false promise."

"It's nothing."

"Trickery by deceit."

"The burden of proof is too high. The disciplinary committee is not reasonable doubt. It's moral certainty."

Ruth shifts on her feet. "They have it, Nathan. They have moral certainty."

Nathan presses his lips together like a prig. "Moral certainty," he says, and lowers a brow at her, as though to say, Don't be dramatic, what is that?

The bridge officer states: "Docket number ending 483. The State of New York vs. Nathan Stein. If the attorney has not yet appeared before the court."

"Ruth Gutman appearing on behalf of Nathan Stein."

Nathan sneaks a peek at the legal pad in her hands. On it is written nothing at all. Nathan manages a rueful smile. Touché. "Where's Milton?"

Ruth squeezes his elbow.

"Counsel, do you waive the reading of the rights and charges?"

"So waived."

"Where is he?"

Ruth subsides into a berated doctor's stony silence.

The judge, leaning forward, glowers. "Step up, counsel."

Ruth and the A.D.A. approach the bench.

"What the hell is Mr. Stein doing before me?" the judge asks.

"Mr. Stein was taken into custody this morning at his office," the A.D.A. states. "Judge Acevedo so ordered because Mr. Stein has failed to produce tax returns she requested."

Ruth turns aside so that Nathan can hear: "Mr. Stein is a respected attorney."

"I know what Mr. Stein is," grumbles the judge. "I understand there is also a disciplinary action filed against him. What is the nature of the proceeding?"

The A.D.A. breaks in. "A pattern of various client abuses, your honor. Theft of bond. Larceny by false promise. Theft by deceit."

Ruth does not flinch. "Mr. Stein is an upstanding member of the community. He's stood before this bench on a number of occasions. His community ties are manifest. He is not a flight risk. I urge you to release my client on his own recognizance while he works this out with Judge Acevedo."

"Step back, counselors. For the record. People?"

Back at the lectern, the A.D.A. duplicates his performance in a slurred monotone: "Charges of contempt against Mr. Stein derive from his failure to produce tax returns requested by Judge Acevedo."

"Mr. Stein is a respected attorney, your honor."

The judge has hunched over, going at her paperwork with a bureaucrat's joyless determination. Scratching out a note, she does not raise her head. "Nature of proceeding?"

"A pattern of client abuse, your honor," the A.D.A. says, the efficiency of his performance bordering on neglect. "Theft of bond. Larceny by false promise. Theft by deceit."

Ruth clasps her hands behind her back, rises up on her toes and down. "Mr. Stein is an upstanding member of the community. He's stood before this bench countless times. His ties to the community and its ties to him are manifest. All his family and friends are here in this city. He will not flee. He doesn't even like to travel. Your honor, you should release Mr. Stein on his own recognizance."

The court clerk is whispering in the judge's ear, handing her a sheet of paper. The judge looks it over, initials it, returns it with a smile.

Ruth sighs. "Mr. Stein is an upstanding—"

"I heard you the first time, counselor. People?" With her eyes the judge cues the A.D.A.

"Your honor, the people request Mr. Stein serve the maximum thirty days unless he produces his tax returns."

Ruth knows, apparently, as Nathan himself knows, that to fight is pointless. Still, there is the show. Nathan nudges her onward.

"Your honor, Mr. Stein will not flee," she says quickly. "He has"—she hesitates, continues—"nowhere to go."

Nathan bobs his head in full agreement.

But the judge has turned to her clerk before Ruth is done. "Mr. Stein shall remain incarcerated while in contempt up to but not beyond the maximum thirty-day period. We'll have a recess here."

"I'll need a couple hours," Ruth tells him.

"I have some money at the property desk. It's fifty thousand, no forty, maybe thirty. It should be enough."

"It's not enough. It's not going to get you out of this."

Thunder shakes the panes of the courtroom. The lights dim, flicker, then surge as before.

"What will?"

Ignoring him, Ruth gives the ceiling a dirty look. "Maria's wake is at three o'clock."

"Today?"

"They want to get her in the ground. New Life Missionary Baptist Church in Bushwick."

"Well, they wouldn't want me there."

Ruth's black eyes darken deeper with a disapproval Nathan knows well. "Benny will be there. And what about her will, Nathan?"

"Will?"

"They want to know where it is."

"She didn't have anything worth leaving, Ruth."

"They want to know what it says."

"Where is *Milton*?" he asks.

She looks at him. "I'll need a couple of hours to arrange everything. Sit tight. Don't get hurt in there."

"Don't worry. I've made friends."

"What about the will, Nathan? You didn't answer my question."

"You didn't answer mine. Where's my father?"

Ruth sighs, squeezes his elbow, hushing him. "It'll be over soon."

"Nathan."

It is Claire, he sees, standing at the gate. In a boyish reflex of embarrassment he blushes and stands to his full height, trying for any advantage. Are her eyes really sweeping over him sympatheti-cally? Then the light goes out and they harden, and as quickly as she opened to him she has sealed shut again.

"I told you I'd make it to Regina Núñez's hearing," he says.

"Look at you, Nathan. Finally in handcuffs."

"Contempt of court has a nice ring to it," Nathan says.

"Tax evasion doesn't. And whatever else. Even when you think you're coming through on your white horse to save Regina Núñez you are incapable of not screwing it up. Eventually you get in the way of everything good you try."

He bends forward, near her ear. "Come with me," he says, believing, for once, at his own risk, his own certainty. Then he sees her expression, and reality, the day, comes crashing down around him. She has begun to walk away. "Claire," he says quickly. "Then do me one favor. Maria's memorial service is at three. Obviously, I can't make it."

"You have got to be kidding."

"She respected you."

"That's not fair."

"It's true. She deserves attendance—" he begins to say, then stops himself. But it is true. She deserves. "Somebody's got to be there."

He cranes his neck, catching the double doors at the back of the courtroom beating like wings then punching closed. In the little square window Claire's hair recedes, flecks of light in the murky hallway, the catch of his life, slipping away.

# 12 noon
He runs toward the sound of her retreat, her clippety-clop across the mosaic floor of the courthouse atrium. "Claire!"

She turns. Her wild red hair, her eyes red-rimmed and damp. "Errol? What are you doing here?"

"Where is he?"

"You mean Nathan." Claire sighs. "News certainly does travel fast. So the celebration has extended to Brooklyn. But isn't there some place you should be? Your family—"

"What about the bail?"

"You think that judge would deprive herself of the pleasure of saying to Nathan, 'Bail denied'? Now that he's in the system she'll put it to him every chance she gets."

Santos peers at her. "I don't understand. This isn't funny."

"You don't think Nathan arrested for contempt of court is funny?"

"Contempt of—?"

"—court. Not that there isn't a soul on earth Nathan isn't contemptuous of." She lifts a hand and presses the back of it cold and clammy to his cheek. "You have bigger fish to fry right now. You didn't sleep at all. I felt you tossing and turning all night. Nathan can take care of himself. It'll be good for him."

Santos's face goes blank. He touches her elbow. "Look, where are you going now?"

"Back inside. I have to clean up that little mess of Nathan's. Poor pregnant kid he's left rotting—what's wrong? Please, Errol, go home. You look terrible." He doesn't seem to be responding. She sighs, looks at her watch. "I have ten minutes."

They stop at the door, beyond the metal detectors, to gaze outside. Sculpted regiments of black cloud march across the sky beneath the overcast. The McDonald's across the street lists like a plastic Ark, its playground drowned. A trail of penny candy stores, five-and-tens, discounters, makes it way upstream against a current of water and its attendant trash.

"My god, if this isn't Hell," Claire says.

He takes her briefcase and puts it on the floor then takes both her hands in his. "I have to ask you something."

She looks at him first in one eye then the other and back, to confirm. "I don't like what I see."

"They were out together," he says. "He and Isabel."

"He's always out. And never alone, let me add."

"They were out that night."

"What night?"

"Saturday night."

"Who told you that? Saturday night Isabel was dead. What are you saying?"

"I can't get into that."

"Oh, no, please do."

He rakes his fingers through his hair. "This is ridiculous."

"Nothing, you should know, if it's about Nathan, is ridiculous," she says, then stops and tilts her head, as if to inspect from another angle. "Christ, Errol, you're investigating him. Now look, listen to me. Nathan is a lot of things but he's no"—she laughs nervously—"murderer. He couldn't have done *that*. He doesn't have it in him. He talks and talks and has all these grand plans, but he never goes anywhere except to the opera, and that ridiculous mansion of his. He's steeped in gooey nostalgia. He's lost in it. He wouldn't harm a fly."

"I want to know one thing. I want to know if you ever in the back of your mind believed that Isabel was—"

She puts a hand to his chest, stop: "Are you asking me if he and your sister could have been sleeping together, because as unpleasant as the thought might be to you, knowing Nathan and that father of his, I'm sure you don't need me to give you the answer. After all those years of you and him running wild. It was inevitable. I don't know why you let her work in that place."

"I know they were sleeping together. That's not what I'm asking you."

Her breathing slows with the realization of someone who has considered all avenues of attack except this one, the one great perilous possibility, unspoken and unaddressed and feared all the same.

He says, "Nathan told me she is—was—*related* to him." Then, looking at her, seeing the change in her face, in the shape of it, the color, he stops talking, bows his head.

"Interesting," Claire says scientifically. "I thought you were about to ask me if your sister was Milton Stein's daughter."

"That is what I'm asking you."

"You're right, this is ridiculous."

"You know what I'm saying."

"You bet I do. Is that what he told you? Because you know how he lies. You know how he creates his life as he walks down the street. It's all that opera he listens to. He thinks he's Rudolfo, he thinks he's Marcello, he thinks sometimes he's Romeo."

"I am not talking about opera. I am not talking about a story. This is real. You know them as well as anyone. Everything you've heard, everything you've seen, could it be possible—?"

Claire leans forward, whispering, "I would like to know what it is you imagine you're saying."

"Just tell me if it's possible and I'll tell you what it says."

She lurches. Her hand appears, as someone else's, an attacker's, from below, clamping over her mouth, choking off a cry.

He studies her there in her cage.

"And do you know what that would make you?" she manages to say, her voice hardly a whisper. "I figured Milton had to have children all over town, but are you his, too? Are you and Nathan *brothers?*"

He reaches. "No— I don't know."

"Don't touch me, Errol, you don't *know?* You mean you *might* be? Jesus christ, Nathan had his little señoritas and now you have me, and you've passed me on like frat brothers, passed me on like a little trophy."

"Claire, this isn't about us."

"It's all about everything. It's all a web, a trap. I've waited and I've waited, hoping all the shit would just *vanish.* And my god, Errol, you want a *baby?*" She throws out her hands. "You wanted to bring a child into this? You carry around that inhaler all the time, but I'm the one who can't breathe. Why don't you just hang my head on your wall—"

She turns away, waving as if at fire. "I'm sorry," she whispers. "I'm sorry I said that. I know you haven't talked to Nathan in years, not until you saw him yesterday. I know you gave him up. And now Isabel—I'm going to be sick."

Her shoulders bobble. He refuses to run and steps around her and wraps her in, stilling her, his chin on the crown of her head.

"Do you think he can kill?" she asks the air. "He's your, what, your brother for god's sake—"

"I don't know that, I don't know—"

"Of course you do. He is. He has to be. It's the only thing that makes sense now. That nothing at all makes sense. What twisted life is this?"

She turns now, faces him head on. "Did he do it, Errol? Did he do it?"

Santos lifts his eyes to the mural painted on the dome above, helmeted Justice atop her horse-drawn chariot, in all her various guises: muse, gatekeeper, executioner.

"Yes."

The prisoners go like dreamers, following a yellow line painted on the floor out the long corridor to a caged school bus with RIKERS ISLAND scrawled on ripped cardboard in the window. Through the beams of klieg lights pass cyclones of paper and hail and rain. The water on his face is warm and granular, smelling not of the sea but faintly of musty loam, as if whole acres of farm have been scraped up in the Midwest and carried here.

A hand grabs Nathan as he is about to step aboard and pulls him out of line. A guard says, "You're gone."

Wrists pinned in plastic cuffs, Nathan follows him in. Another guard approaches with a pair of snips and frees his hands and leads him to the property desk. There in a cage of wire mesh sits an old friend in a cop's uniform, a ham sandwich before him in creased waxed paper.

A clipboard comes through the slot. "Sign here, Mr. Stein."

"Thanks, Harry."

The sandwich comes through. "I expect you haven't had your lunch."

"I'm okay."

"You're welcome to share with me if you like."

"No, no. Thank you, though."

Harry takes back the clipboard and considers Nathan. "I don't know why a guy in your position would put himself in jail."

"It's a living."

Harry considers his sandwich. "How's your father?"

"He didn't come down?"

Harry shakes his head. He slides through the slot a zip-lock pouch. "Well, there you go, then."

Nathan holds it up. His life in a plastic sandwich bag very much like the one they sell goldfish in. One Rolex watch. Four prescription vials. Various coinage and rubber bands, one pair shoelaces. His beeper, his cell-phone. He removes the bundles of hundred-dollar bills and weighs them in his hand.

"Want to count that?"

Nathan purses his lips.

"You ought to count that."

Nathan slips the bundles in his inside pocket. "No one came by for this?"

"Now you know I couldn't do that."

"Of course you couldn't." They exchange a smile.

Harry leans forward over his sandwich. "And I didn't," he adds.

Nathan slips on his watch. "So if my father didn't come down, who sprang me?"

The property man shrugs. "Someone from your office. Very good-looking. You have a new secretary? She said your people called your accountant."

"My accountant?" He has never had a need.

"She brought down your tax returns. Isn't that all they wanted?"

Nathan holds his breath. He hasn't filed a return in three or four years.

"What did she look like?"

"Chinese, or Japanese, or something. Great legs."

Nathan squints at the ceiling. "One of Chang's?" he considers.

"Whose?"

Nathan waves his hand. "No, never mind." He bends and snakes his shoelaces through their eyelets and crosses them and ties them. "Okay," he tells himself. He brings up twelve messages on his beeper, *Serena, Serena, Amparo.* What was Regina Núñez saying about her? *Errol Santos.* And now Chang. He erases them all. "Okay."

Harry says, "No need to hurry away."

Nathan eyes the wire cage. "I'd better go."

As he gets to the door Harry calls out. "You watch yourself, now. You know what I'm saying."

In continuous guerrilla assaults the rain and snow combine forces. The wind juggles it all back in a swirling stew of grit and road grease. Overhead the sky is the color of bruise, a vertical massing of purple and blue eddies. The storm that came all at once yesterday afternoon and just as quickly seemed to pull apart must be traveling in a circle: the real onslaught is upon us.

There is no sign of Ruth. None of Milton. So no one has met him. He squints through the headlight glare at the line of cars idling across the street. Drivers slump in the windows. Passing gypsy cabs beaten and pitted like discarded tins. A riderless city bus kneels by the curb, its wipers swinging at the hail.

His eyes stop on the red sedan at the curb. His two friends are standing a few steps from the car, their collars up against the cold. One gives him an almost friendly nod, as if Nathan's imprisonment—his short brush with safety—had been a little prank they'd all enjoyed together. One actually gives him a wave, and Nathan feels a sudden nervousness at this sign of intimacy, as though it suggests more intimate moments to come. His being in jail was obviously an inconvenience to somebody. Now Nathan is back in play.

He thinks food, to go with the simplicity he sees now in everything, and turns up his collar and pivots left, toward the Stadium, and quickens his pace. Though he knows he is thinning by the minute the rollicking of his body feels heavy. His thighs drag. The flat stretch of sidewalk grows steeper. His wet clothes are plastered to his legs and back, but the cold is still vague and distant, as if he has sunk into a kind of anesthetized drunk. Still, he hugs himself, and, with a vacant pleasure at life's little things, strolls on. The neighborhood around the courthouse a blur of brick and pigeon-stained facade and window holes blinded with sheets of plywood, speechless in asking the question, Why does anyone live here? This underside of a universe that contains grand boulevards, parks, monuments, opera houses, seas. Traffic lights that twirl like toy lanterns. He heads toward the illuminated globes for the C and D lines, watching the speeding clouds through the tracks of the El above. At the subway entrance, an unmanned cargo van sits parked at the curb, its side panels asking ARE YOU SAVED YET? A pair of pink cherubs with wings hover in profile, facing each other across a sliding side door airbrushed with gold leaf to depict pearly gates. The quarterpanel offers to make, free of charge, Nathan's travel arrangements to the beyond, 1-800-FLY-HOME.

He teeters at the top step, peering down into the subway, propped by the dank air blasting up at him and the icy rain at his back, taking measure of his options. He makes a mental note: call Planetarium Travel about ticket to Roatán, one-way. Though for this trip out to the house he needs only his car, his bag, the dog. They will be downtown at his office. If Schreck didn't give them away. Or take them himself; the pictures float by: Schreck sitting behind his desk, Schreck walking Baron, sleeping in his bed, driving his car, eating dinner with Mom and Dad, the son they never had; standing on Claire's step, ringing her bell. A tasty thought: could that have been him calling her this morning? *Would* it have been him? There has been no consistency to his self-deceptions, why should there be a logic to the cast of his deceivers? Why can't they all—all his people, all his lies—know one another? Why don't they? But they must.

All around him crowds are heading for the subway. But there is something peculiar. They are all young women, Dominicans and Hondurans—Nathan overhears them as they pass—either pregnant or cradling fresh babies or with small children in tow. They seem to come mostly from the direction of the storefront Good News Chapel and Prayer Hall behind him. Nathan follows them down.

Before the token booth, the crowd has drawn around a huge black man in a white judo suit cinched with a black belt. Between the women and the martial artist stands a ring of white teenagers, mostly blond, the boys dressed in ironed khakis and argyle sweaters and the girls in the candy-striped dresses of Connecticut WASPs. The tallest boy holds before him a stack of five stubby planks.

The martial artist rolls his sleeves. "This isn't going to get it, no!" he booms. He makes a sweeping gesture back behind them and up the subway stairs and out into the streets above. "No, this just isn't going to do it. Friends, this isn't where it's at. The power of God, friends, the power of baptism, surges through my arms, my legs, my feet. It's here, it's here—"

Leaning back and lifting his right leg, the black-belt preacher uncoils at the stack of planks and halves it with his heel with a sharp crack that matches a peal of thunder overhead. His assistant displays the shattered wood to the audience like a game-show hostess.

"Your children can have this power, they can all be saved this very day," the preacher says. "You will need the strength to flee the clutches of the Antichrist. Because he is among us, friends. You have all heard it. That is why I am here, running from the storm in the bowels of this great city. I pledge to you on my faith he will make himself known on Christmas Day and will mark for doom all those guilty of disbelief and all those unsprinkled with holy waters. Look at the storm over our heads. I'm telling you the born and the unborn and the almost dead—it don't matter to the Antichrist. All those unbaptized will suffer and burn beside him in Hell."

The preacher is grinning. The teenagers, their eyes twinkling with love, are handing out pamphlets. As if in exchange the parents offer up their babies. Those merely pregnant eye with dismay and panic their swollen bellies.

"You. What about you. Are you saved?"

Nathan looks at the preacher, who had picked him out and peers at him over the crowd.

The preacher answers himself: "No."

Nathan rests both hands on his chest in false modesty. "I'm Jewish," he says, and almost chokes on the excuse. It's half a lie, the bigger half. He'd be a fallen Jew if Jews actually fell; but here they remain working the earth, working it hard.

The preacher points. "This one isn't saved," he cries, as if it isn't obvious, Nathan and his soaked clothes and stubbled jaw and filthy hands. "He thinks because he's a Jew that makes him ineligible." He makes a motion and a girl in a blue print dress comes forward with a porcelain bowl of water. "Friend, don't miss the point. The Lord doesn't care what you are."

"I think He would," Nathan replies softly.

The preacher glares and makes it simple: "Come beside me if you want to be saved."

Nathan gives his head a shake.

"If not you, then who?"

It is a good question. Nathan considers Claire but, figuring news of this gift in her honor would get back to her, does not want to add to her resentment. Willfully, he draws a blank.

But the preacher is patient. He'll wait. He has all day, all eternity. And it must be obvious Nathan is trying. Then a solution does actually strike him. "A friend," Nathan finally says.

The preacher's grin widens. "Born or unborn?"

Nathan steps by, twisting through the crowd and the phalanx of purebred angels and stops toe-to-toe with the preacher. He is reminded of his moment in the sun on his bar mitzvah morning, standing beside the rabbi staring out at the tuxedo sea, the gangster faces imported for the day by Milton, drug lords and porn kings, assistant district attorneys and even a pair of judges, as on those Thanksgiving mornings a truce called, battle lines forgotten for a holy importance. Sunbeams crashing down like piano chords from the stained-glass synagogue windows. His mother swaddled in pastel gauze. His father—he still can't see the fat face hidden behind his glasses, behind a carpetbagging smile. Soft-focus rite of man. Entrance into adulthood's blood cult.

The preacher dips a ladle in the water and lifts it high and Nathan raises his hands to ward it off.

"Not *me,*" he insists.

The preacher, not missing a beat, closes his eyes, bends his head at a solemn angle and, genuflecting slowmotion over the empty space beside Nathan, begins, "In the name of the Father, the Son, the Holy Ghost—"

The others mouth the words to themselves, and Nathan is alone amongst them. But not entirely alone. There are the hanging stalactites overhead. Nathan feels more in common with them than the flock gathered around. More even than with the empty space beside him, the empty shell of his potential.

Something hits Nathan all at once. Jealousy. Envy. He glares at the empty spot, as if at an old friend about to leave, and before he can stop himself he ducks under the preacher's ladle and away, catching a drop of water on the back of his neck, which he fingers then smears on his cheeks and his lips, where it might do him some good.

Fruitlessly he shoves through the bulletproof plexiglass toward the subway collector the only kind of bill he has, a hundred, for a single token. But the collector refuses old Ben with an officious shake of his head, so Nathan stands at the turnstile in his wrinkled turtleneck and soiled blazer with nautical insignia and herringbone slacks like a gentleman farmer who has lost his way, without a small denomination to his name, rocking on his feet, asking mothers pushing carriages and even their children in tow for change of a hundred. Crazy stares, wild looks. A new brand of beggar, harbinger of times to come. He fails for long minutes and eventually hangs his head and seems to drift into a restless snooze. Far off, the subway trains rumble through, the horns blowing like trumpet blasts while the preacher one by one works his way through the crowd of children and embryos until the last one standing in the tunnel is Nathan himself. Someone puts in his palm a token then turns the hand over to examine the festering wounds, then quickly drops it. Nathan opens his eyes. It is one of the bible-camp teenagers, a pudgy boy with a cherub's head, staring at him nearsightedly through horn-rimmed glasses. The remains of a sweet grin hangs off his droopy mouth. Something made him frown. Nathan looks at his own hands and finds wounds there he doesn't remember, circles in his palms like bloody blisters.

He loves Hell. And now, finally, he is back there.

Downtown, up on the street, Nathan ducks through an old familiar door. A narrow space with a long, empty floor and empty stools. The barroom deserted, the jukebox with its old 45s dark. The ceiling mottled with the blue light of a mute TV.

"Cy," he says.

An old man rises from a stool at the far end of the bar. He rests on Nathan's shoulder a liver-spotted hand. "Haven't seen you in a while. Hit that door, will you?"

Nathan shuts the door, letting in a distant noise from far below, of surging water, or subterranean ruin. "Business slow?"

"You and your father are neck deep in shit."

"I wouldn't know."

Cy looks at him, then cracks a sly grin. "Just do me the favor, when you get the little fucks off keep them away from my place."

"They're Harlem kids, Cy," Nathan says.

Cy shakes his head. "Here, there, they don't care." He touches Nathan on the shoulder. "You all right, son?"

Nathan pouches his cheeks, unsure. "Maybe a little drink. Scotch rocks."

He leans back, elbows cocked on the bar. Faded jerseys of dead ballplayers hang from the rafters. Maris. The Mick. Posters announcing the fights of boxers long retired. The warning click of an approaching train, then the screech and groan of fatigued metal. Gusts of icy rain drum the windows. Everything in the bar shifts at its joints, loosened like a fighter's teeth by the years of blows. The noise outside grows to a roar but no train appears, then the roar fades, come and gone like a ghost, and Nathan glances nervously at the door, feeling less sheltered than he expected.

"Say," Cy says down the bar, "that girl they're talking about, the one that drowned out at Coney Island. She isn't yours is she?"

Nathan twirls his glass in the yellow barlight.

"I just saw her last week. It's a terrible shame."

Nathan lifts his head.

"She was with your father," Cy says. "Carrying his briefcase. Looking pretty chummy. She was quite a dish. Your father always had taste." Cy nods his head toward the TV. "Well now, how about them apples."

Nathan looks up to the screen to find his own pale eyes peering back at him, his own chin hidden there under all that fat. On the TV on the wall, Milton's face is bearded by a clutch of microphones.

Cy aims the remote and turns up the sound. Milton has lowered his own volume, chosen solemnity for his emotion du jour.

"I have no problem with representing Kevin Williams," he is saying. "Everyone has a right to a fair trial."

Another question. This case so obviously not about just a mugging. The kids used bottles, they used a bat.

Milton looks at his questioner with the intensity of a man actually listening. "The facts are cloudy," he is saying, for the thousandth time, Nathan believes. The five thousandth. Nathan mouths the words along with his father: "What are facts? What do we know about what really happened? What will we ever really know? Kevin Williams is a pathetically abused kid. Everything about this case is still speculation at this point. Representation for the disadvantaged—it's what's made this country great."

Other questions, other words, and Nathan finds himself, head up with the desperation of a little boy, nodding over and over in agreement. The mountainous man is great, impressive, the best, and Nathan, deciding on an emotion as on a stuffed toy on a shelf, would buy pride if only he could afford it.

"He's a good one, your father," Cy says. "Wish he was mine."

"You need a lawyer?"

Cy shrugs. "I figure we all do."

But then something pricks Nathan, some idea, some piece to a puzzle he has not known he is assembling. The Williams case is monstrous, extraordinary, and nothing at all about the rape of a Madison Avenue executive. How good it is for his father. How good it is for his person. And how good, suddenly, for this news of Isabel, to have lost someone so close to him. The Santos family was so loyal; Isabel a second-generation secretary. And to have lost her so viciously, so coincidentally *now*. How human it will make Milton, how big, how vulnerable, how moral, how intensely, intensely real.

Nathan stares and stares, feeling his father's own overblown affections collapsed within him. Arbiter of dead souls.

On the TV, a last microphone is thrust in Milton's face. "I understand the body of the young woman found at Coney Island yesterday was your secretary. What about her murderer, Mr. Stein? Would you be able to defend him?"

Milton's pillowy face fills the screen. He stares hard into the camera. Father and son square off, Milton looking out through the window of bright lights and sunny endings. His eyes, pale and blank, moisten, and Nathan, peering in, doesn't fight off the desolation. Nor does he search his way out of the blackness in which he sits. He can see the calculations in his father's eye, which way to play it: straight and cold and lawyerly or let it go and pull out handkerchief and gut-wrench? Because this is now not just about a rape case. This is the human condition writ large, loss and gain and tragedy and deliverance. Ours. And Milton, maybe now by his own design, has cause to represent us all.

Milton Stein offers his reply slowly and quietly, but Nathan has already heard it. And the TV picture, in a crafty bit of programming, cuts away to file footage of the Coney Island beach. Maybe Isabel is even more of a convenience for his father than he thought. And maybe she's no coincidence. Maybe she was his idea from beginning to her end.

Without looking up, Nathan leaves a hundred-dollar bill on the bar and leaves.

He sags with relief, briefly, against a plate-glass window on the safe side of the revolving door at his Broadway office building. Jorge is nowhere in sight. In his place behind the little booth sits a sullen stranger. His suit is too big and he wears Jorge's name tag and looks vaguely like the Mexican delivery boy from the deli down the street.

"Where's Jorge?"

The imposter shrugs.

Nathan nods at the name tag. "You're a Jorge, too?"

The boy, apparently not hearing, looks up at Nathan with adolescent gloom.

"Where is everyone? Is everyone in the building gone?"

This elicits a second, even less committal, shrug.

"Is this a fire drill? No? Is it the storm? Hello?"

Nathan heads for the elevators. The doors about to close, a pudgy hand wedges them open and Krivit enters. His overcoat is dry.

They watch the floor numbers pass. Krivit's breath whistles through his nose.

The elevator car passes ten. "It feels like everyone's left town," Nathan says.

"It's every man for himself."

"Well, I hope you weren't waiting long."

"I heard you got out."

"You had nothing to do with that, of course."

"You worry about you."

Nathan nods. "Words to live by."

"Don't fuck with me," Krivit says sharply. "Not after last night." Out comes his hanky. His forehead has beaded with sweat. "Where is the writ?"

"It's all upstairs," Nathan assures him, listening to himself almost in surprise. As if it really were done and by his own efforts the little Russian weasel, the little Pushkin, will only hours from now be free to roam Brighton Beach, eat a knish then whack the kids who sold him out then fly home and be king.

The elevator car passes twenty.

Nathan says, quietly, as if not to offend, "You know of course what you've done."

Krivit hits the button for twenty-one and the elevator halts, the doors open. Nathan expects something dramatic in the hall-way, as in the movies, a crowd, a gun, a clue. But nothing at all is there.

Krivit braces the doors as if shoring up the world, no mere middleman now but something much more dangerous, someone much farther toward one end, someone in general command. Nathan remembers what Santos said yesterday morning, that he didn't trust Krivit. But it's not that simple. Trust, what is that? He knows his father doesn't trust the fat middleman but he sees now that that doesn't much matter. Krivit is a beautiful thing. Nathan hasn't, over the years, given Krivit enough credit. Not enough credit at all.

"You have one hour to get to court," Krivit says. "They've already postponed twice."

Nathan is sweating again. The air breathes hot, as nightmares will. And the buzz in his ears, the roar lingering from the subway, he'd thought, is instead steadily approaching, getting closer. "You know of course they'll want to talk to you about Isabel."

Krivit's upper lip begins to quiver, as a dog's does at the first evidence of something to defend against, or devour.

But Nathan goes on. "I saw you there Saturday night. I saw your car. I haven't told anyone."

The bag man is holding it in, tolerating him as he would a child.

"Just tell me why," Nathan says, "and who? You wouldn't have done it without orders. Or would you?"

"Just get to court," Krivit snaps, and, as if at the climax of a magic trick, abruptly claps his hands and holds up his quilted palms, scrubbed and empty, setting free the birds. "That, my friend, is you."

Nathan looks upward, away; nothing there, tricked. "That's me."

"I've delivered the message. You're on your own now, buddy boy."

Nathan shrugs. "Like you said. Every man for himself."

Krivit steps back and the doors shut and Nathan, alone, proceeds one flight up, where, whistling, he strolls down the empty and half-lit hallway. The writ in his throat like a wedged lozenge. Swallowing, working it down, he can feel it actually drop, in with the other refuse, the false assurances, the vows disregarded as they were made, dissolving in their juices, adding to his blood the nutrients of his efforts: the money, the blow jobs, the occasional hug of deep thanks, once a declaration of love, one with possibilities—from Claire, who only wanted groceries to whip up her modest recipe for happiness: occasional affection, loyalty, new small life fluttering in their hands, the curbing of his unacceptable pleasures. Was it so much to ask?

The office door of Stein & Stein is locked.

"Hello?" he calls to the presswood veneer, but the door doesn't reply. "Anyone here?" he meekly asks the floor. He pokes at the lock one key after another, achieving, he thinks, success, then leans in with his shoulder, once again breaking into a place he knows and to which he presumably belongs.

The lights are off. Except one. His, he believes, down the hall, the empty fluorescent white splashing out of the open doorway across the floor and up the opposite wall. Two o'clock Monday afternoon, the biggest week in the short, happyish life of Stein & Stein and the twenty-second-floor office is vacant, abandoned, it seems—as does the entire building—for even higher ground.

Nathan pauses inside his office. Etched into his windows he finds himself, and he is alone, an outline scribbled in with patches of blazer but otherwise blank. Beyond him, despite the hour, hovers inky night. Sheets of rain coat the glass. Three fingers of lightning split the sky into a map of white rivers, and for a long moment the sky and office and he himself vanish in white flame.

Reluctantly, he opens his eyes. At his feet Baron is draped like a sphinx over his $500 portmanteau, icicles of drool melting on the burgundy leather, his long leash wound twice around the desk. A parking stub for the lot around the block is wedged into the collar, along with a note saying only: *He has been fed.* A message spike blooming like a flower with little pink slips has fallen to the floor. In the air, the rancid odor of fresh piss. Baron's goopy, sad-sack eyes stare back at Nathan, as if to say, What did you expect?

Nathan drops to his knees to praise and pat the dog, who cocks his massive, purebred head in confusion. Nathan slips him some Cheez-Its bought downstairs then turns to his stereo and calmly, as if he has all the time in the world, contemplates his office music collection, his mood inversely proportional to the chaos outside. He has chosen for this moment Monteverdi. Angelic lamentations bridged by long silences. Bending to address his messages, he peels the papers one sheet at a time, peeking at the names. The paper shivers in his grip, which means his hands must be shaking, too. He's now been two days without sleep, or is it three?

There must be thirty messages, dutifully scribed in impeccable, acquiescent penmanship, obviously by one of Chang's cadre. The usual suspects: Clarido twice, Schreck once, as if he could have forgotten where Nathan was—unless, of course, he knew he'd be back. Amparo called three times; her last message reads: *Left me here to rot. Called brother. Look over your shoulder. Look again. Look forever.*

Despite himself, Nathan does look, and sees: empty hallway. A spectacular refrain of conflicted violins and cellos reaches his ears.

Another message: *Errol Santos.* Friend, foe. Curious, Nathan fishes out his beeper: There is *Errol Santos,* in fact, three more times.

He considers all his messages, voice mail, beeper, answering service: who takes them down? Nathan wonders. Someone on the other end, someone alive. The innocuous, neutral answering service has the power to concoct one's entire life, a life out of reach, telling you who your friends are, who your enemies are. Who called? Who cared? Who didn't? Who won't? It's up to those operators, his message-makers. They are his window out, conspiring with someone or by themselves to paint the view.

He snatches the phone and punches in Serena's number in the Bronx. The phone is picked up instantly. A man barks, "Yeah."

Nathan scrolls through the men in Serena's life, brothers, father—mad, stupid, and dead, he knows them all. Briefly, he attempts to conjure Serena herself but can come up only with general island features, raven-black hair, eyes as black as undreamt night. He seems to recall pink panties. Lately she's been nothing but a miniature readout. Giddily—another joke at his expense—he wonders if this man, this gruff voice, could be Serena, if Serena exists at all.

Nathan hangs up, dials again, this time his 900 number. "This is Nathan Stein and you have fifteen seconds to terminate this call before being charged $99.99." He will pay this bill. He will owe himself. All of him collecting in this one container.

Seated, Nathan dials a new number altogether and hears on the other end a calm, cheerful voice, a man, his proxy: "Nathan Stein's answering service. Message please?"

In the background, the murmur of other operators, keyboards clacking. The world may be falling to pieces, but there will always be messages to leave.

Officiously, Nathan declares, "This is Nathan Stein."

He commiserates with the confusion in the operator's silence. Then he listens for and detects the disapproval. Imagine all that this clerk has heard. All the piss of Nathan's life that has run through the tips of his fingers, collecting as through a catheter in the electronic pouch at Nathan's waist. Despite the doctors and the tests and the retests and the diagnoses and the pills, it is of this that he is dying.

"Message please?" the operator says with tight obedience.

Nathan's eyes widen at the opportunity. His mouth opens. Outside, another round of twitchy lightning. There is a pause in the thunder. Listening for it, he hears instead soft cries and lamentations, wandering, carried by the wind.

"None," Nathan says, and hangs up.

**3 p.m.** Hunched low to the ground, the walls patched with corrugated aluminum, the New Life Missionary Baptist Church sits like a converted outlet for discount beverages, a cross fastened like a hood ornament to the front peak over the open door. The inside is a single cavernous room carpeted with mauve industrial wall–to–cinder-block–wall, exploding up front, as if someone has thrown a grenade of violent color: hothouse flowers surround a casket with handles of painted gold. At first Nathan's body will not respond to an order of WALK. The fatigue is one reason. But there is another, and it is naked fear. He has been spotted. Strange eyes aim his way. He does not know their owners, but willing his clay feet to move one then the other he crosses the room smiling soberly and shaking hands, mumbling thank-you's to offers of sympathy and turning from inquiries after his own health. Maria's mother, older sister, and young female cousin have arranged themselves before the open casket, the mother's hand on the shoulder of the one daughter left her. Inspecting him as he comes up the aisle with his hands empty. Nathan's abandoned family.

It is the sister, Carmen, who steps forward slowly, numb with grief, the room hushing in the presence of this gravity, the soulless dance between those with competing claims. The derelict that they had all taken for the son of light himself stands before them chalky pale, withered seduction artist, thief of sweet Maria's soul.

The bloated corpse levitates behind them, the open coffin

resting on a platform in a ring of flowers. Why is it open? Maria looks worse. They've greased shut her eyelids and lips; and she looks waxy, like a figurine, as if they've melted and reconstituted her in the black dress he bought for her five years ago on their first spree. Her speckled hands, crossed over her chest, clutch to her heart her thumb-worn Bible. Though after all that they couldn't carve an expression into her: her brow clear, she lies poker-faced before eternity.

Nathan bends to kiss Carmen, but she reaches up to his face as a blind person might and holds him steady, peering into his eyes as if inspecting what—if anything—lives behind them, then quickly snatches away her hands.

"Please go," Carmen whispers.

"Where is the burial?"

"We didn't think you'd be able to come."

Nathan says, half appalled, "I wouldn't have missed it." Then it strikes him that he was let out especially for this purpose. He looks over his shoulder. Two men in cheap suits stand at the doorway like bookends, full of menace rather than comfort, like prison guards, happy to let people in but blocking their escape.

"It's at Evergreens," she says, "in Queens. But you wouldn't come."

"Of course."

She exhales through her teeth a derisive laugh. "Please."

"Where's Benny?"

"No. Say nothing to him."

Nathan spots the boy sitting against the wall in a sharp double-breasted suit, his feet dangling above the floor, staring at his mother's remains. Then, lifting his head as if he's heard a whistle, he quickly bounds over, wrapping his arms around Nathan's leg and burying his face in his crotch. Nathan's hand hovers trembling over the boy's head, repulsed as if by an electric field. He lets it drop, crowning the boy with it, bestowing Benny with— what?—but crowning him nevertheless. He reaches around the boy's head and strokes the soft patch under the cranium, button of innocence, feeling in his fingertips a pulse, sign of beating life.

He is despising this, this little melodrama. Still, his eyes have begun to sting and he wraps his other arm around Benny's shoulders in full embrace, leaning into the boy's hair, sniffing his earthy, vegetable sweetness of sleep.

"Come, Benny."

It is Maria's mother who has taken the boy by the shoulders and for a moment Benny is tugged in both directions, disputed over, actually wanted. Her nostrils flaring wet and red with grief, Carmen protests, not on behalf of one side or the other, just the contest itself. A hand lands softly on Nathan's shoulder and he quickly turns his head and again, as before, finds no one there. Thus warned. He snatches back his hands as from a trap and lets Benny go. Maria's mother steers the boy to safety, handing him off to her daughter.

His face burns. His embarrassment is fierce. The entire room is looking at him. Why is he here? Why did he bother to come at all? Didn't he say his good-byes to Maria this morning with no witnesses but the dead and maybe that priest to clear the way? But here Nathan feels close to the truth, just the simple factual truth. Just as Maria last night watched, spellbound and terrified, her neighbor in her death throes, now Nathan has come to observe Maria, out of the hospital, on her way. His own dress rehearsal. And there lies her outer crust, her pod.

He wipes his hand across his sweaty forehead. "You shouldn't let Benny see his mother like that," he says.

But someone insists, "No, he should see." It is Cleary standing before him, taller somehow than this morning. The priest looks nervous, his face with that blushed, babyish swollenness of someone just woken, or sick with worry.

"Isn't all this a little fast, the funeral, the burial?" Nathan protests. "Don't you have to wait a while or something?"

Cleary's expression darkens. He glances nervously toward the door.

"Who are your friends?" Nathan asks.

"I don't know who they are," Cleary assures him. "I half believed they came with you."

"They may have," Nathan murmurs. Nearby, the heads of those talking quietly wheel around. Nathan looks at his watch. "It's getting late."

Cleary nods. "Yes, it is."

"I'm tired."

"I understand."

"I don't think you do," Nathan replies, wondering if the pain in his stomach comes from eating nothing but his pills. He looks longingly to the back table where food is piled high.

"This tragedy will unite you and Christ in a sacred way," Cleary says.

His mind shut down behind that delicious hermetic seal, Nathan sidesteps the priest and heads for the back and picks a shortbread cookie of no identifiable shape. He slips it past his teeth. His eyes close. He can taste nothing; there is no feeling on his tongue or the roof of his mouth. The tips of his fingers, for that matter, feel like brass thimbles. It's been climbing him these last two days, this slow paralysis, giving him the strange sensation that he is turning to stone. Bites of cookie thud like pebbles at the bottom of the pail inside. This last pleasure gone.

"Nathan."

Blindly, Nathan extends his hand. But it is Cleary again.

"Do you hear me?" he asks.

"Sure."

"You should make amends."

"What for?"

"Because a man lives his life and he has to make that important. Whether he's a priest or a lawyer. Or a bum."

"Did Maria?" Nathan demands.

Cleary squints, his expression bitter, as if Nathan has insulted his kid sister. "That woman looked death straight in the eye."

"She was Catholic," Nathan insists, as if that matters somehow, an emotional stand grounded on nothing.

"That doesn't have anything to do with it," Cleary says. "However she did it, she took death in and made it her own. She was in charge. She stopped breathing when she knew exactly who and what she was, what she accomplished."

"No one finishes all of his tasks," Nathan says, hateful, then gives Cleary a sharp nod, hoping he'll go away, or burn himself out.

Instead, a small inconclusive smile plays on the priest's lips. "You are, of course, talking about yourself."

But before Nathan can protest, Cleary's hand comes up. The priest isn't through: "You didn't know her, Nathan," he says. "You don't know what you had."

"I think I do."

"No, you knew her body. Understand me—she was stunning. I don't fault you for wanting her. But your women are piled high, one on top of the other. You know something about the way they look but what do you know of their souls? You've kept yourself busy like a rat in his little cage, running his treadmill, faster faster, wanting more and getting it, but in the end only standing still. You treat them all indifferently and only care where the next one is coming from."

Nathan holds fiercely to the cookie, sniffs it, and smells—now he expects it—nothing. She gave it to *me,* he wants to say, but Cleary has backed away and receded, just one tree in the forest now, and like the others—*all* the others—is blank with shock and horror. The crowd has hushed. The priest heads up the aisle toward Maria.

Where the hell is everyone? Nathan wonders, looking around. Where are my parents? Ruth? Even Schreck, the fuck? Where's their respect?

He sits amidst strangers, his face bunched and spotted like a baby's, poised to come undone. The long pews keep filling. Blacks, whites, Hispanics. Nathan is astonished Maria knew so many people, people of different stripes and heights and weights and ages, until he realizes she didn't, that these are merely church members, Cleary's recruits, commanded by some inner voice to show up to the unveiling of every coffin that comes through these smoked-glass doors, to fill out the audience, to loan their respect, so that no one, especially paying customers, should go out so alone. Women in pillbox hats, boys in powder-blue tuxedos, old men like storks in their black summer-weight suits, the blacks of this ruined neighborhood who drop their tithe into the mahogany box at the head of the aisle, below the church scoreboard, the letters and numbers replaceable from the back like an old baseball scoreboard, the church's 537 paying customers in attendance last Sunday, the scales tipping, last week's eighty-seven dollars and fifty-nine cents against Lucifer's untold millions, bottom of the ninth and the church needs one hundred and forty-five dollars to fix the pews, to fix the men's toilet, to replace the broken window-panes, the colored cellophane—

The choir stands, its adolescent singers, jogging up the aisles to the front like the faithful rushing to the man laying hands and healing them of their limp gawkiness and their very youth. Here and there the cellophane sucks in and out in time to night's heavy breathing. The windows flash. The choir raises its voice over the volleys of thunder. All of it to Nathan like a final prayer meeting on a ship hit and sinking in battle. He wants out. He wants out of it, this, everything, and looks once to the casket, as if for permission. He is crying. He is, in fact, crying hysterically. And Maria, lying there in her plasticine stillness, willfully says nothing.

Claire watches from the door as Nathan pushes himself up from the front bench and slides awkwardly along the wall, to the exit, not surprised to see him running. Though she is taken aback by his tears.

She touches his arm as he passes. "I want to talk to you."

"What are you doing here?" he asks, quickly trying to compose himself. He glances over his shoulder, toward Maria in her casket. A reflex, Claire knows, by now as quick and natural to him as drawing breath. He will always try to keep his women apart, keep them from knowing about each other, even when they already do, and even in death when it wouldn't matter.

Claire smiles. Maria's death, somehow, is registering with her unexpectedly. Maria is taking with her a piece of Claire as well.

"You asked me to come, remember?" she says. "As your representative. Then I heard you got your little gift, your get-out-of-jail-free card, but I decided to come anyway. Out of respect, as you said yourself. That was a nice little trick, by the way, coming up with those tax returns. I thought the judge could have made the condition a moonwalk and you'd be as likely to fulfill it. I underestimated you."

"They weren't my returns, Claire. I'm being set up."

"*You're* being set up? Please, Nathan."

He nervously scans the room. "Someone sprang me. Someone wants me in the game."

"Don't flatter yourself," she says.

Nathan looks at her, uncomposed. "Thanks, anyway, for coming."

Now he is peering through her fearfully, toward the door, the weather out there.

"And too bad Errol missed you at your office. He has something he wants to say."

"My office, what? Errol?"

"Someone told him you'd gone to the office to pick up some brief. That awful little man, I think, that Krivit—"

Not a muscle on Nathan's face moves but the ones that work his mouth. "Krivit told Errol where I was?"

"But I beeped him when I saw you here. He's on his way, if you want to wait. Then again, you never wait."

"Krivit," Nathan says again.

Lightly, she touches his wrist. "But I have something important to tell you before you go."

"This sounds like a farewell speech," he says.

"You are the one who said you're going away."

"There's always the phone."

She takes his elbow and draws him down. "This seems a good time to tell you. I know about Isabel, Nathan. We all do."

She can feel him twist to get away, but she tightens her grip, shocked to feel her fingertips hit bone. He is too weak to resist. This man who once lay atop her so heavily. She could hardly hold him with her arms, her knees, his wide hips bruised the inside of her thighs. "Errol's on his way. I really think he'd appreciate it if you waited. It'll be just a few minutes."

"I don't know what you're talking about—what *about* Isabel do you know?"

"I don't hate you, Nathan. I half pity you. I'd try to save you if I thought there was anything left. Errol agrees. But I will not spend another minute of my life trying to get over you." Squeezing him she draws him closer. "You should be doing more here than you know. There's something I want to say, Nathan. Benny's a beautiful kid. He'll be fine."

Nathan tries to look back. "Yes, he's—"

Her lips against his ear. "I hope he's young enough to forget you."

From his left ear she crosses his face, her lips brushing his, to his right, telling both sides now: "I want you to know that there's a funeral you missed. I never told you. We should have been there together."

Nathan again tries to pull free. She can smell it now: he has begun to scare, to sweat. A gurgle rises in his throat.

"We had a son, Nathan. It was your goodbye gift. You were so oblivious you didn't notice me at three months pregnant, at four. You should have. I was radiant. You didn't notice when I'd taken time off. You didn't see I was gone."

Again, she switches sides. Cruel, petulant. "I won't tell you what his name was. He didn't keep it long. He died in my hands. But he was beautiful, a beautiful baby boy. He had green eyes. He looked just like you."

Claire reaches up and cups Nathan's face. Her fingers, her palms, have him memorized still. She presses on the new divots, the crevasses. His skin, once robust, thick, florid, is now thin and brittle as carbon paper.

She rises up on her toes. "I loved you once. You would have loved our boy. He would have been brave, like you were once. You don't want to wait for Errol? I can see you're anxious to go. Okay, Nathan, then just do what you do so well. Say good-bye."

She faces the congregation. The door opens behind her. The rain and snow, she hears, is falling more heavily. A gust of wind pushes at her and she turns to look: across the street, a little playground is empty. Nathan is gone. But something, she senses, is menacingly wrong.

"Where is he?"

Santos stands before her in the doorway, panting for breath. His car idles at the curb.

"But he just left," she says.

He grimaces, scrapes his fingers through his hair. "And you just let him go?"

"What do you mean *just?* You know where he's going, Errol. Where he always runs. But why do you need to see him so badly?" Then she looks at him. Her hands come up. "Don't—I don't want to know."

"It's him, Claire. Nathan killed Isabel! His prints are everywhere. The time of death, the place, someone can put them there together."

"There?"

"Coney Island."

"I will not—I refuse— Who is it, Errol, who is the someone?"

"He and Nathan were supposed to meet but Nathan called to cancel. Nathan and Isabel were there. He saw them in the car. He saw them fighting. It was Nathan, Claire."

"Who was it, Errol? Who saw them?"

"I can't tell you that."

"Was it that Krivit? Just give me that. Tell me, was it him?"

Santos says nothing and outside in the horizontal rain, across the street, but only for an instant, Nathan stands in the playground amidst the plastic chutes and tunnels. But only Claire has seen him.

**6 P.M.** Like hour hands gone awry, the windshield wipers sweep at the deluge, accelerating the twilight to midnight darkness. Strands of ground fog move with menace along the Long Island Expressway. Across the median the opposing traffic comes steadily down the lanes like a parade of motorboats, passing in clouds of vapor and vanishing in explosions of red-mist.

In the mirror a pair of headlights holds at fifty yards, as for the last hour, no closer, then no closer.

But in here, in this hairy and coffee-stained car, the CD changer shifts around and it is the Philharmonic doing the *Saint Matthew Passion*. It was Maria's favorite piece of music. He remembers her just months ago as she stood in the living room in East Hampton surrounded by night-blackened glass doors, still beautiful in a seamless black sheath, her lips curled in an impish grin, sweeping her withering arms—the crooks IV-punctured, as bruised as rotting pears—conducting, it seemed, her own march down the Via Dolorosa, her demise; and Nathan sitting immobile in the white leather chair, the music deafening, the floorboards vibrating, pinning him there—

He lifts the remote control and fires, and the brooding ends. Maria slips away. Now Paul Desmond's schmaltzy breeze, big band and all, a clarion call to some greater, unpeopled civility. Safety in here, to do as he likes, this place that he loves, his little space capsule on the go. He has his dog, his music, this sanctuary, his little womb-box of paradise, his past vanishing in the mirror and the objects of his desire pulling into view. And he sees his house perched high on a bluff, dry and safe and innocent with its angelic wind chimes and vaulted ceilings and sunken pool, silent now; a fridge stocked with a family's worth of food; in the morning the hummingbirds will approach the sliding glass doors and, wings ablur, peck pleasantly at their reflections. Another day beside his azure square of water, an evening before his large-screen TV, watching the Philharmonic on laser disc, wrapped in the graces of someone else's genius. The glory, the music, the paradise of his loneliness, the paradise of his despair—

East Hampton is abandoned. A squad car sits against the curb, its wheels splayed, the roadside trees bound with darkened Christmas lights. The antique salons, the boutiques, the Realtors with their posted yearbook photos of dreamhomes, the white flowerboxes—everything lovely and elegant is now encased in ice. In giant display windows, drifts of virtuous cotton, spotlit scenes of nutcracker soldiers and cherubs and iceskating angels. Electric trains orbit toy towns very like this one. The glass before everything taped with giant X's to withstand the storm, though to Nathan they read CANCELLED, and seem to offer as targets what glitters behind them.

He threads the car through the debris in the streets and is drawn like a moth to the lit windows of a diner. The snow sweetly sifts on a car or two parked in front. But headlights swing into the parking lot, holding him steady. And between the beams, in the diner window, sits Krivit reading the newspaper—the beefy head, the pudgy fingers, half his meal down the front of his shirt. Nathan flicks on his high beams and Krivit turns, squinting outside, shielding his eyes. Baron collapses against the door as Nathan pulls out and the car fishtails across the vast lot. The dog understands the urgency: he hangs his head alongside Nathan's, eyes quivering, hypnotizing himself with the frantic wipers.

Nathan's beeper, like everything else, is quiet now. Even

Serena. He snaps open his cell-phone and tries for a dial tone and hears only the dead plastic of the earpiece rustle against his ear. The circuitry, the lifeline, is quiet. Everything is quiet.

Letting his head drop against the headrest, he sees now the Coney Island pier where he and Isabel began to fight. He had wanted to bring her there. He had wanted to show her, tell her about the old times with Milton: This is us, he wanted to say. This is the you you don't know. But he can still hear his bitter accusations, his voice louder than the rest—there seemed to be more people in the car than just the two of them; there seemed three people, five, ten people in the car—he thought he spoke for them all. But one of the voices was Isabel's. Another was Claire's. They were both pleading. But it was Isabel who was kissing him beautifully. Her hand was on his thigh. Why couldn't they be married, have a baby, live like human beings?

He hears his pathetic somethingorother reply.

She went on, her reasons accelerating, making perfect sense: It would be a fairy tale. Like a movie, like one of those operas you always go to see. My mother worked for your father for years. Errol would be so happy, it would bring you two together like the brothers you once were . . . grew up together . . . practically family anyway . . . no one knows you better . . . husband and wife . . .

What, again, did he say?

She began to cry.

There are no tracks where he goes now. Slow and solitary, the road out of town is cracked into geometric sections like melting ice floes. In the mirror the streetlights fade behind columns of standing mist. The tires rip through the steady sleet—

After his brilliant arguments in his own defense, he had opened the door and strolled to the boardwalk. She didn't move in the passenger seat. Then she did. She came after him. He stood at the rail, the water below so black, so cold, so still it seemed a sheer drop down to the bottom of a ravine. The heights were terrifying. He held on to the rail. She held on to him. He closed his eyes. How long ago, how strange, how sad, distant as his memory of first love, Claire stood by the window of the printer's shop picking out their wedding invitations; then Claire left his mind and the hands he held to his face were Isabel's and the eyes that met his were Isabel's, were his, really, his father's, actually. Maybe Errol's, too, for all he knew. He saw only faces. Enclosed and surrounded by faces. And the faces seemed to be mirrors in which he saw and watched himself. And he knew them all better than he knew himself, the fear and puzzlement and the fatigue. He was so tired.

In the rear-view mirror headlights dart in and out of the trees, patient, staying back. Blades of light in the corner of his eye, pinlights twirling before him. Closer, they hold steady in ordered pairs. Elfish eyes. The headlights illuminate snouts, racks of antler, breastplates of white fur; a doe's nose no bigger than a rubber doorstop.

We are finished, he said, waving his hand. Tell her, he said. She asked, Tell me what?

Their father authored their humiliation but the orders Nathan followed were no one's but his. There had to be, Nathan knew, some things for which fathers cannot be accused and held responsible.

But I love you, Nathan, she said.

How many times had they slept together? He was going to be sick. His thinking began to slow. It slowed like a wheel turning through the sand and finally hitting the water, slowing and grinding down and stopping. And then he *was* sick—

He hears the explosion before he sees it. The steering wheel raps him squarely on the forehead. Baron spills into the front seat, kicking in all directions with panic, clipping Nathan across the cheek. A squealing spiral of brown and white fur in the glass. Nathan throws up his hands when the car is already stopped and a small doe is splayed across the hood, its loose head, cleaved above the eyes, slapped back and forth by the wipers. Bloody snow rinses across the glass. The doe's round eyes stare in, then blink slowly. Still alive. Howling, Baron jumps the seats, back and forth, wanting at it. Nathan puts the car into reverse and spins the wheels, but the car jolts hard; the back fender has crumpled; a tree spotlit red in the brake lights. The doe doesn't slide. Wheels spinning, Nathan pulls forward and skids to a stop and reverses again but the doe won't move. Baron is turning circles in the back, looking to unload.

Cursing, Nathan is out in the sleet, shielding his eyes, instantly soaked, his shoes full of slush. In the ambient glow of the one headlight left he can see the doe's chest fluttering. He staggers forward waving his hands, and, grabbing above the hooves, pulls hard. Corded mouth snapping, the doe pours off the hood and flips to its back. Nathan stands over it, blinking in the driven snow. Tiny convulsions beneath its fur. It kicks once, twice, then stills, head back, legs upright, like the legs of a table. The eyes glass over, their sight gone. Nathan exchanges the stare, dead with dead, and again finds himself low to the ground, on his knees, filled with a disquietude and unhappiness that is like a deep, twisting visceral pain. The snow showers the back of his neck with a child's kisses; like those of some angel, some mother's desire to treat him gently, like those perhaps of his and Claire's nameless boy's, to announce himself: I am. "I didn't—" Nathan cries, and, blinking, opens his mouth and on his knees he releases the doe and opens his hands before him to find nothing, and the night filled with no reply. I am. He grabs up at the falling snow, grabbing at her, at the doe—it was dead—at Isabel, but she was already gone. She was clip-clopping down the boardwalk, pausing finally to unstrap her high heels and throw them into the surf, barefoot on the ice, quickly fading out of his view. He started after her but he couldn't breathe, his knees wouldn't hold, and he ran until he couldn't, and he stopped. Then she stopped. They stared down the boardwalk at each other, panting, expectant, terrified, like gunfighters. Behind her the dark Wonderwheel and serpent-backed roller coaster like the ruins of a great city. Against his heels he felt the edge of that steep ravine, at his back the interminable drop to the bottom. He stepped away, toward her, and she stepped back and he stepped back against the edge again and she stepped forward. She would not move. Then his cell-phone rang. "Krivit," he said. "I'm glad you called. I'm having a little trouble here. I can't meet tonight. We'll do it tomorrow. Don't worry, yes, I'll be there." Then he was sick again and hanging over the rail and she came at him and he lifted his head and she slapped him hard. His glasses flew off his head. And she was crying. He closed his eyes from that and when he opened them she was in his arms and he first hugged her then took her around the neck, aware of the murderous power pulling him on, forcing him while he remained dispassionately aware of the consequences. He could almost hear his father: Do me the favor. Her teeth were up and down his arms. Pleading up at him with his own eyes. He released her. Coughing, she clutched her throat. He thought for a minute, with a detached, almost amused calm, of the infinite night that waited for him no matter what he did. Leave her, love her, marry her, kill her, they would both burn. And he would drop, into that ravine. But if he could release her, he knew, at least she would live. Then he left her.

In his rear-view mirror he saw her standing against the rail. She was alive. And down Surf Avenue, she was alive still.

At Famous's, as he turned for the Belt Parkway, a car along the curb turned off its headlights. Nathan slowed and saw it was Krivit's car. Krivit was sitting with his hands on the wheel, staring ahead and through Nathan to the boardwalk. Of course he'd have to be somewhere nearby. They were to meet, after all. Krivit had probably watched Nathan while he made his call, his excuses. Nathan drove on.

But at the last minute he glanced again in the mirror and Krivit's car was moving, turning the corner, passing Famous's, heading up Surf. Nathan stopped, turned and followed. Krivit's car stood at the spot of boardwalk where he'd left Isabel. Krivit was not in the car. Isabel was not on the boardwalk. He thought, Get out of the car. He thought, Save her.

Then, he put it together again, for the hundredth time: He'd been fucking her. He was dead. She wouldn't live. She was already dead.

The big house perches high on a hill, its windows punched dark like the portholes of a ship stripped and looted and set adrift. All the windows but one—Nathan can see light in the trees in the back. Even beneath the snow, a yard in ruins. The stripped shrubbery, once manicured, grows beyond any pattern, gnashing at the downspouts, tugging at the gutters, slithering across front steps gnawed by dryrot.

He opens the back door of the car and the dog explodes into the night, slaloming through the trees, kicking up sprays of snow. He slides to a halt and, shivering, trickles on a treetrunk, then is off toward the back. Nathan, as is his habit, follows. The concrete patio is shot through with weedy flourishes gone to seed. A lavish pool half drained and rancid, a frozen shallow brown syrup dropped further beneath an incremental set of scum lines marking other longer periods of neglect and the comings and goings of ice. Old leaves and twigs and snow. A deflated Yankee cap Nathan remembers on his own head now encased in ice. The diving board has been torn out and made off with.

Nathan feels for the back steps under the snow and stops before the open kitchen door. The small window beside the knob has been shattered, the wind whistling through the shards. Inside, a drift of snow has begun to climb the stove. He hears a voice echoing down the hall, and steps in. "Hello," he calls.

Baron shoves by him and skates clicking and clawing along the floors.

Nathan follows a dim path of light toward the living room. The rooms he passes are tossed, the mattresses overturned, the pillows disemboweled, drawers flung into the corners, the mug shots of his life's suspects crossing before him with each clop of his shoes, Maria, Serena, Amparo, his mother, Ruth, room after room where the pickled floors climb blank walls that spire high to a cathedral ceiling. In the dimness above, fans hang like dead and dried flowers.

"We're doing the best we can," the voice says, then abruptly stops. "I'll have to call you back." A phone is replaced on its cradle. "I saw the new Land Cruiser in the carport, Nathan." Beside a floor lamp, a figure the size of a stubby child on a couch, clutching her knees. "Nice. It's just what you need. Whose is—I mean, was—it?"

"You like it? It's yours." Nathan sits on the chair opposite, unsurprised—in fact he realizes he's expected her.

Ruth's face shifts and reshapes in the dark hood of her coat. She is sullen. She wears mittens. "But you're soaked," she says. "You'll catch pneumonia."

Nathan lifts his palms, as if to say, Look, no hands. "Bring it on," he says.

Ruth points. "And your hands are bleeding."

"So they are. Take off your coat, stay awhile. The pool is ruined. It'll have to be relined."

"Why bother? You never swam."

"But you did."

"And never liked the sun for that matter. You were always covering up."

"Skin cancer," Nathan points out. "You can't be too careful."

Ruth begins to say one thing then stops herself. She blows a stream of vapor like cigarette smoke. "I tried the thermostat. When is the last time you paid your gas bill?"

Uninterested in these details, Nathan squints out the glass door, listening for the tinkling of his precious windchime, and notices that the circle of porcelain doves has been shorn off, whoever or whatever leaving just the nubs, like a necklace of broken teeth.

"I thought so," Ruth says. She bends forward and holds out an upturned hand. "Give me five thousand dollars."

Ruth says nothing more and without hesitation Nathan raises one hip and reaches into his pocket. He brings out a handful of bills and deals what is there into Ruth's palm. "Just a minute," he says, and reaches into his jacket pocket for the envelope of cash and tugs out more bills and places them atop the pile.

Ruth takes the money and shapes it into a brick and it disappears somewhere about her person. "For services rendered."

"Any in particular?"

"All," she says flatly.

"Sounds like you're settling your tab."

"Nathan," she begins, and looks at him as if she means to get up and capture him in a hug and lift him back up to the heights from which they have fallen.

But he is already on his feet, heading for the stereo. "I'd like to dance," he announces.

"But you don't dance."

"How about the Duke, for old times' sake, as a warm-up?"

"Nathan."

"Ruth."

"You're impossible."

"Thank you."

"It won't work now."

"The Duke? He always works, always cheers me, always cheered *you,* just try and deny it."

"The stereo, Nathan, it won't go on."

"Why not? How do you know?"

"Because I do. The music's over. It's screwed."

"The music is perfect," Nathan insists, feeling a gust of indignation. "It's the only thing that is."

"Maybe a wire's been cut," Ruth suggests.

"Why would they cut a stereo for chrissake? It's not a car."

Ruth turns to look at him: "They?"

But Nathan doesn't miss the catch in her throat, the little hop of fear, like the cap of a kettle about to come to boil. Ruth is very afraid.

Baron, spent, sidles up beside his master and noses his crotch. Overwhelmed with love—or some emotion—Nathan kneels and embraces the dog's head with his hands. Their foreheads meet. Creatures who ask from each other nothing. Baron's tongue passes across Nathan's mouth.

"Is he coming back?" Nathan asks the dog, though calmly, as if inquiring after the weather. "And I'm not talking about Krivit. I know all about him now. I saw him, can you believe it, in town."

Softly, imperceptibly, in the corner of Nathan's eye, Ruth nods.

"And Schreck, the asshole?"

Ruth doesn't deny it.

Outside, in the lamplight falling across the patio, Nathan can see that the snow has turned to rain. The drops beat down the crust, chunking the skim ice in the pool.

He straightens, surprising even himself with his resolve. In fact, he is full of energy, as if he's just been given a transfusion. He lifts his hand, as if to issue forth a pronouncement. "A walk," he says to no one in particular.

"But *now?*" Ruth asks, gripping her seat. "It's raining, or snowing, or whatever."

Just then thunder explodes like a bomb outside the glass doors. The single functioning lamp dims, wavers, strengthens again. "Nathan!"

"We always go to the beach," he addresses the dog. "Don't we, boy?"

Baron, sensing nothing but his most simple pleasure, cranks his tail.

"Don't," Ruth pleads.

Something is wrong, is very wrong. Her mouth moves, it wants to make sound. Ruth's talent for keeping things to herself seems to be failing her. Nathan lifts a hand, gesturing to the dark house, to the greater dark beyond it. Ruth's got it wrong. Obviously, she doesn't see his freedom.

"I should go," he says calmly. "He's coming."

And he sees he's already been. The tire tracks beat him to his favorite trailhead to the beach. But there is no car. Baron is already down the path, at the rail of the stairway down.

"Here, boy!" Nathan calls, but the wind smothers his cry. He begins to jog after him, clutching the dog's leash, though despite the surge of energy his bones feel ready to splinter. He slows to a walk, to baby steps, and alone, doubled over at the rail, he finds it hard to believe he is really going. The boxy, contemporary mansions teetering on the edge of the bluff, looking out over the bay, like abstract fortresses guarding against invasion from the less acceptable North Fork of Long Island. The abandoned lighthouse and its red punctuation at the end of the finger of land. On Roatán he will have this sight for breakfast, lunch, and dinner; this beach, only more so. Clear water. Azure sky.

Nathan can hardly keep upright in the sea spray. The rain and snow, crosshatched, come from three directions at once. One after the other, huge waves commit suicide on the beach. Baron snaps at the foam, plunging in, scurrying back, then stops stone still, wrinkling his nose, dormant birding instincts surfacing, sensing. Something's coming.

Behind Nathan, a snap, a twig, a slab of driftwood, and the dog, belly-deep, is barking up at the trees to Nathan's right. Just as a forked tongue of lightning touches down far offshore, a current passes along the horizon and a momentary spit of flame leaps from the woods. A yelp from the beach, and Nathan turns to find the dog rolling like a barrel in the surf.

Clenching his fists, Nathan watches the woods and waits for the next shot.

"If you're coming, come!" he cries.

The stubby trees are kneeling.

He looks up full of questions but the wind nudges him, drives him on.


"We can't be here," Claire insists.

"But we are."

The road from East Hampton to Nathan's house is empty ahead and behind, the ground turning at the last minute, rising beneath them like sea-swells. Claire grips the dashboard tightly, barely conscious of the landmarks Nathan used to point out with a wave of his hand, the little family cemetery with its white picket fence, the little lane on the right, the roadside stand and its outrageously expensive pies.

"Nobody's on the road. Why do you think no one is out? We shouldn't be out."

"It's too late."

She feels her heart melting even as the peace that comes with returning to old, familiar ground falls around her. For a moment it is almost as though she and Nathan are returning home from the market, the dog panting in the back seat, standing guard over the groceries—

"My god—" As they pull up the crescent drive, Claire braces herself. This is the address she remembers but hardly the house. From the hill, the windows, gaping like potholes, breathe down at her old memories and new desolations. Everything she planted, the pines along the base of the house, is gone. Tired of nightmares, she asks the air, "What am I doing here?"

But Santos is already out and knee-deep in snow, his gun drawn. Claire trudges after him, turning her head with the wind to breathe as they walk a lap around the ruined yard.

"Errol—" she calls. "Why do you have your gun out? Your gun—put it away, you're not going to shoot him. Nothing is confirmed. Tests would have to be done. If you're going to arrest him you need samples, hair, skin, blood."

"I don't know if I'm arresting him." He walks on.

"You would kill him?" she calls, trailing him. "Is that why you became a cop, you could decide whether to arrest someone or kill him? Jesus, Errol, it's Nathan. I mean, what if he is your brother?"

Santos stops at a Hertz van backed against the front door. The driveway is rutted with tire tracks.

"You still love him," he says.

"No— I don't know, I did. Yes, maybe I do. Don't you?" She turns into the snow now, blinking. "Didn't we grow up together?"

"I don't know if that's good enough."

At the open kitchen door there is broken glass and Santos motions for her to stay back. Inside, shadows criss-cross the hall, muffled voices, none of them Nathan's. She follows as Santos keeps to the walls, hugging corners. Debris and bags of frozen garbage are piled everywhere. The pristine doors she remembers from years before are scabby and gritty with soot, the room in which she and Nathan once made love charred from disuse.

Sounds of grunts and footsteps in the living room. She follows Santos toward a man cradling a stack of stereo components. Boxes of CD's sit by the front door.

Santos lifts his gun. "Who are you?"

Schreck turns, smiling thinly at the gun. "Errol. And Claire. I didn't expect you. It's been years and years—"

At the sight of Schreck Claire can feel a tic, a reflex, jerk the corner of her mouth. "Oliver," she says, with dread. An ancient memory about him awakes, and she looks up, anywhere, toward the ceiling, out the glass doors where the trees are tossing their bare heads in the wind. Once, when Nathan was in another room, Oliver grabbed her from behind. Another time he'd whispered revolting things in her ear. The dirt returns, those pathetic times of believing bad lies and despising the look of her own reflection. He may not have expected her, but she should have expected him. Hadn't he always chased the ambulance to the scene of some crime?

Ruth emerges from the dark dining room, the hood of her overcoat pitched high like a monk's. "Claire—"

Finally, Santos puts away the gun. "Where is Nathan?" he asks.

Schreck heads out the door with pieces of stereo. Ruth picks the shredded remains of a cushion off the floor, drops it on the empty frame of the couch and sits.

"He's gone," she says.

"Where did he go, town?"

Ruth, imperious still, says nothing.

Claire takes in the desolation. "What the hell happened here?"

"Do you want to sit down?"

Schreck returns slapping his hands on his thighs.

"Someone's been searching the house," Santos says.

"Yes," Schreck replies, without hesitation.

"Is all this you?"

"Errol," Ruth interrupts, "as a cop, you're out of your jurisdiction. This isn't Brooklyn."

"But he's not here as a cop," Schreck says, "is he? Are you?"

Santos looks from Schreck to Ruth.

"Does Nathan know you're taking these things?" Claire asks.

"Why?" Schreck asks. "Do you want something?"

She shakes her head. "Where are you taking it?"

"Where Milton can watch his son's TV, listen to music on his son's speakers—"

Stupidly, she knows, Claire points at a porcelain vase propping open the door. "But I got him that."

"Milton would never know if something small walked out on its own."

"Take it," Ruth suggests.

"You're taking everything," Claire says. "Why is everybody doing this, acting like he's already dead?"

Schreck reaches into his coat and brings out an envelope and offers it to Santos. "I've been holding this for you. This is yours—"

"What is it?" Santos asks, taking the envelope.

"That's your share."

Santos lifts out a sheaf of bills. "You neglected to mention this part last night."

An odd smile crosses Schreck's face. "I never lied to you, Errol. Not last night. And not now. You're here to do a job. A man in your position, a job should be well paid, or else why do it. Do what you've come to do."

Claire is shaking her head, looking from one to the other, but Santos seems to come to an understanding, as if from an old arrangement. He hands back the envelope. "I don't want it," he says.

"We don't have more than a few minutes," Schreck says. "There's no time to argue. Take it."

Claire looks at the money. A wave of nausea washes through her. She lies: "I don't understand."

Santos has backed against the wall. "I'm supposed to finish it."

Schreck nods. "Eye for an eye."

"No one ever accused you of being a sophisticated thinker, Schreck," Santos says.

"Am I wrong?"

"I don't know what you are."

"Let me ask you something," Schreck says, "what would you do with Nathan if you found him?" Santos doesn't answer. "You know, we're a lot alike, Errol. You don't want to admit it, but then again, that always was your problem."

"I don't think so. I'm not like you."

"We are, more than you know."

Santos turns to Claire. "They've set us up. They've set us all up."

Claire, hesitating, stands terrified of moving, as though having reached the edge of an unexpected clearing. She was meant to be here; all these years, all the thousands of days, have led her here. And pointing to the open door of the house, like a road sign, is the feeling, *Escape*. But another feeling points the other way, back to Nathan, and to Errol and Schreck and Ruth and Milton Stein and a too clean end to something she hadn't known had been begun. She sees clearly where she stands, the two options, the two paths diverging—strange how brilliantly the image comes to her—like the arms of a man being pinned to a cross.

Ruth has withdrawn into the shadows of the adjoining room. Schreck, squatting behind the stereo cabinet to gather wires, calls off-handedly, "Try the beach. Nathan always liked to take Baron to the beach."

Santos is gone before Claire can reach him. At the doorway she catches sight of him zig-zagging down the hill, arms flailing. Running out, calling to him, she feels her footing give way, and slipping, she tries to regain her balance but pitches forward into the snow. Trembling, trying to rise, to turn for the beach, in a brilliant flash of lightning she spots a shadow streaking through the surrounding forest. "Nathan!" she cries, but she can hear it, and it is not Nathan. Something is approaching with a noise that is not the snow or the wind. It is an animal of some sort. She cups her hands over her ears, but her hands, like conch shells, only amplify the half-human panicked whinny of the thunder. The rhythmic thrumping, galloping, it has to have hooves. She scrambles on all fours to get to her feet. Get back. Get away.

"I knew you'd be back. I kept your card."

Breathing hard, Nathan looks back over his shoulder. The drive from East Hampton was fast, an hour and a quarter, the roads mysteriously clear. In spite of the miles out there and back, though, the red sedan ferrying his little friends has pulled up calmly behind him. Generously, though, they stay seated as he slips out and jogs across the street through the flimsy door.

"What a shitty night," the girl says after a volley of thunder. She fingers his damp lapel.

But behind him, miraculously, the black night has turned to a fall day, that crisp molten football sky. He glances over his shoulder at a family strolling past: the mother laughing, opening an umbrella above her head, mocking the bright sunshine, the father off to the side smiling proudly, offering his hands to the two pretty little children who circle his legs, grabbing at their fingers as they skip past on a carousel. One child, a beautiful little girl with a bow in her hair, turns a series of cartwheels over the pavement. All of them are laughing. Nathan hates the sight of them and they obediently go away, thank god, whisked away and the daylight too—

"I bet you live nice. Manhattan, right?" the girl says.

Nathan can see only her thin legs as she leads him up the creaking stairs, dangling his own pathetic and empty lust up through the narrow stairwell and past the flooded bathroom, the corridor that seems to grow smaller and smaller, darker and darker, past a closed door out of which leaks a sinister cackle.

"Why don't we go back to your place? You can have it all night for a hundred— Hey, you don't look so good."

He can stop it. He won't stop it. They're all down there whoever they are, his people, their people, they all want him—so it is once again him up here in the armpit damp where he knows he belongs. The girl turns her head, moving not in fluid motion but in a broken chain of flinches, as though everything has hit her, and everything will hit her again. He runs his hands over her arms, right over the bruises, stopping on her girlish breasts, her sour pungency, some lingering soap scent drenched with perspiration.

"Why don't you take off your coat." She steps back and sits on the bed, clutching her knees. The bed creaks. She hasn't bothered to remake it, though she did yesterday. The blankets are clawed aside, the sheet ground thin and covered with footmarks, salt rings of old scum, pale bloodstains.

But listening for footfalls in the hall he is afraid. Down to the safety of the bed he goes. The girl draws stiff obedient circles on his belly, three, four, five, then flinging her arms around his neck slides over, arching, she offers her throat, which for the moment is enough like Claire's: faintly blue, a redhead's undercooked translucence, the veins and stringy tendons and serrated windpipe nudging up at him in full view: beating life.

He leans in, touching his teeth to her neck, and the girl's faked moan is so much like the groan of the dying, her cheap imitation thrill like one's last breath, signaling him to bite, penetrating her with panic and self-disgust and the calamity of his own life, god the penetrating pleasurepain suffering giving birth to his own death in this crummy little cubicle.

"Wait a minute, Esquire." Squirming out from under him the girl floats her hand before his face, writhing it like a genie. She opens the drawer of the nightstand and gestures toward an assortment of multicolored condoms scattered like candies across the bottom.

Nathan stares blankly and the girl comes upright, her face hard. She stares straight and fearless into Nathan's eyes, then, determining what is there, pushes off the bed to her feet. She leans on one hip, one arm dangling, petulant. "What's with you guys tonight? Something's got you all wacked out. Maybe it's the weather."

Nathan sits up.

She sighs, takes a pull on her cigarette and drags a metal bridge chair from across the room and props it directly in front of him and drops into it. "Okay, look, it's normally five dollars for the first five minutes, but that's already gone doing all this talking, or whatever, and you owe me ten bucks anyway. So that's already fifteen and nothing's happened yet. It's twenty for ten more minutes." She sits back. "And you can masturbate for another ten." She stabs her cigarette in his direction. "Do you want to masturbate?"

It sounds like a challenge, if not a threat.

"Nobody's looking, Stein Esquire," she says, a comradely nudge. "Just you and me. You don't have to touch it."

Nathan looks confused.

"The cum. I'll clean it up."

He focuses again on the calendar on the wall behind the bed, the same one from yesterday, the band of white beach, this time the numbers blurring and dissembling. Again, the picture comes to life—he hears the sax playing in the distance—and the girl from Ipanema rises like Venus from the water, passes him up the beach, coming into view. I love you, he says—but the calendar, he sees, is flipped now to the future, to January, next month, next year: where will he be then?

Outside, the small eruptions of car doors closing. He traces the sweat behind his ears and down the back of his neck.

The girl glances at a clock that partially covers a hole in the wall. She taps her foot. "Eight minutes left."

He probes the roof of his mouth with his tongue, searching for water.

"You feel all right?"

He pats his blazer pocket, touching Maria's will, his deed to Roatán. "Fine, I'm fine."

"Come on, Esquire, you going to do it or not?"

Nathan can feel himself straining. His tool has begun to swell but by now it is the last thing in the world he wants. His eyes follow the riversystems of cracks up a wall and across the ceiling. "Qué mes?" he asks.

"What? I don't speak that, Spanish, what's that?" She thrusts out her hand. "Thirty-five. Make it an even forty I'll give you something special."

Distractedly: "I have hundreds. I'll need change."

Leaning down she lifts her bag and retrieves a small beaded change purse striped the colors of the rainbow, the sort given by younger brothers as a misguided sign of affection. She sifts through subway tokens and doughnut shop receipts and a stray pink latex condom with nodules and scented cherry for that special pleasure and pulls out five-dollar bills and singles and looks up. "Let's just wait and see honey." Smiling a gapped and rotten smile, shimmying down her pantyhose, shackling her ankles, she tips back the chair, balancing on the two back legs. She parts her knees, her thighs thin and blue, a schoolgirl sitting on a toilet. With one last glance at the clock she transforms, arching backward, her eyes rolling. Her lips part to emit a single moan. That pain again, that cramp or pang of anguish, or something has come to her, a thought, an idea. Nathan hopes. Again she writhes her hand in the air, snaring his attention, and guides it downward where with one set of fingers she pries herself apart and with the other begins expertly to knead.

Nathan's face hardens into a plastic smile.

"Baby, why don't you masturbate?"

Thunder blows open a door down the hall and Nathan whirls on the bed, eyeing the fogged window, the icy radiator.

"Scared?" the girl asks, her eyes filled with maternal certainty that it is the good things that will come to stay. But she's back to work, "Baby baby baby," filling the clammy room with her hasty crescendo, stopping before the climax with a deep-throated *"Yes!"* drops the chair to all fours and looks up, fully recovered and breathing normally. The idea, as usual, has been no idea at all.

His eyes fall on a dead roach in the corner. "Qué hora?"

"I told you, no Spanish. Speak English, hey? Hey, what do you want?"

"Do you have a phone—a phone? I just need—a quick call?"

"A phone? Here?" Eyeing him, the girl quickly covers herself with a dingy robe. "Are you going to throw up?" she says, without sympathy. "You look like you're going to throw up."


Twigs whipping his face, Santos sprints through the corridor of woods. "Nathan!" He has been wandering over an hour. Around him, the snap of splintering branches. His feet numbed by the snow, he braces against the rail. "Nathan!" There is no waterline. Waves explode up and down the beach in random detonations. One rears up and collapses and drops the body of an animal in a boil of driftwood and foam.

Santos takes the stairs two at a time. Nathan's dog is spinning in an eddy. He takes it by the collar and drags it up. One of its eyes has been gouged, or shot through. The other stares emptily, a glass bead, the tongue pooling.

Santos runs, then stops, worried that the exercise will trip the switch that turns on the asthma and shuts down his lungs. He walks the steps slowly, deliberately, then begins a slow jog through the path and along the street toward the house. But, spotting the flickers of light through the trees he is running again, pumping, forgetting himself. Claire is standing at the foot of the driveway, staring emptily upward toward the house. Her hair and clothes are sodden. Her face drenched. "I saw it," she says. "I never believed—"

The door is flung open. The van is gone. Every window is alight. The trees overhead are shrouded in red haze. Yellow flames climbing the back of the house, columns of sparks riding the updraft. Ash pools atop the snow in the front yard. He hears the crackling and everything is burning, the house is burning, his lungs are burning, the dream is burning, but here they stand, he and Claire, inside the house, where everything once seemed fine and the slippery poolwater bathed them in all their incarnations and the air conditioning silently washed them in luxury and the various roads to the future and the law and their affections were secure and they would live forever. There was nothing there. And now the curtains Claire made are crawling with fire, the flames spreading faster and faster, crackling, minor explosions in the kitchen, a large one in the basement, an eruption from below, the world around him now collapsing. The snow around the house is melting. The trees are burning. His chest is burning.

He hears Claire's voice, sobbing now: "Nathan! No! No! Oh god—"

A figure crosses the front doorway, silhouetted by the orange flames behind. Short, pear-shaped, it is Krivit, he sees, dangling from his hand some sort of container, the kind gasoline is carried in.

Leaning into the wind, gasping for his breath, Santos pats his coat for his inhaler. He finds nothing and runs to the car. He empties the glovebox, flinging its contents behind him. He sweeps his hands inside. Nothing. His lungs are hardening, his air coming in thin. He slips behind the wheel and turns over the engine and begins to back away. Claire is beside him. The wheels grind to a stop in the snow and they look together as flames pour out the upper windows of the house. The wipers flail. The car rocks. The fresh tire tracks before him are all but gone. Where can he go to breathe? Where can they go? Where can they go?

Hugging himself in his blazer, Nathan staggers down an alley toward the boardwalk. Behind him, a pair of headlights flash on, wink off. Above the thunderous surf, the gale winds moan through the spokes of the Wonderwheel, back toward the Luna Park Houses continuous and monotone, as if some collective remembrance of the pillared hotels, the old-monied homes, the lights whose aura could once be seen at night thirty miles from shore when Coney Island was the center of the aristocratic world. The larger, permanent suffering of the freakshow freaks and the whores who worked the hotel lobbies. Those living and dead now passing through the outlying slums.

He picks his way along vacant streets, shutting his eyes often, feeling his way. He knows this place. And he knows of another that waits and sees in his mind's eye his sliver of white beach and understands now that that's not the one; that though it rightly, if not completely legally, belongs to him he'll never get there. He goes through the addresses of his mind to find a door ajar and he pokes his head in to find himself in his bed; he tip-toes to the sleeper but finds no sign of life. Drenched in sea-spray and sweat, Nathan comes on Famous's food, eternal with its marquee lights whirling like birthday sparklers every day of every night, but not now, the lights are off, everything is off, shuttered to the storm. Debris and ice ride the current through the streets.

He wades through to the boardwalk. To face the sea he must put his weight forward, hung by the air. The line between the sea and the sky has been rubbed out, all of it a shade of dark past night. The wave-breaks are overwhelmed, the beach nearly submerged, the water running up to the boardwalk, which is buried in spray ice. Up and down, stretches of rail and walk are gone altogether. The thunder, continuous, no longer distinct from the rumble of the sea. It says, Get out of the car. It says, Save her.

The two shots are spaced, deliberate. At first, on one knee, Nathan feels numb relief, then, with a sigh, feels himself stumble backward and turn on his stomach. Nonthoughts drift through his mind accompanied by music he can hear only because now he is finally listening: as if it has been there all along. Wagner? No, something funereal, something quiet, like a lullaby, Chopin, maybe, which in the bedlam of the storm is just like a tiny boy's cries of sorrow. That is it. With a groan he begins to claw at the icy slats of the boardwalk, pulling himself along one then the next as up a ladder. Shapes hover around him, holding his hand, tugging on his fingers, trying to help, pulling him on, or still just trying to pick his pockets—the fold of his jacket is pulled back and what is left of his brick of cash jiggled out. Footfalls fade behind him. His life is slithering away, mingling with seawater, and he feels some mild pleasure in the possibility that those things for which he has traveled a long and undesirable way, things he may not necessarily be able to name but which construct his life-long dreams, he will no longer require. With his last effort Nathan Stein laps at the boardwalk and tastes his own metallic and salty warmth, and raises his eyes to look ahead and up and finds himself alone, absolutely alone, wrapped in numbing silence. Where is the Chopin? Where has everyone gone? His face burns. He decides, because he thinks he should, to think of people to forgive—forgiveness is big in his heart—and begins with himself. But he cannot remember his own name. He has begun to scream. But the gale smothers what he says, and choking now, he cannot hear.

Then he rises. Off the boardwalk, his arms lift, then his legs, floppy in dangled flight like a marionette. Nathan can't wait. Here he goes, found by some good samaritan, rushing along, to a hospital, he hopes. He cannot believe in his arms or legs and he cannot move, but he is aloft, heading for shelter, and awaits the soothing voice, the assurances of safety, the needleprick, the saline solution. So the world is good after all. The world is good.

"Are you all right?" he hears, again, a gentle voice this time. And this time, "No," he finally answers, "No," thankful to be permitted to be so honest. "I need help. Please help me."

Rushing, stumbling, the air whistles through his gut. Nathan gasps. Someone closes the door. Another door closes, and another door closes. Some line, some very important line, has been cut.

In Memoriam

J.A.D.

# ACKNOWLEDGMENTS

Assistant U.S. Attorney Daniel R. Alonso. Paul Cody. Brian Hall. Lamar Herrin. McKay Jenkins. Dan McCall. Tim Melley. NYPD Sergeant Mitch Zykofsky. Friends and teachers all.

Andrea Barrett. Philip Gwyn Jones. Doris Janhsen. Marcy Posner. Christian Strasser. And especially Matthew Bialer and Jane von Mehren. For their loyalty, diligence, and good counsel.

And Liana Cassel, for her work with this book, as with all things, her gracious love.